Praise for
CHRISTINA DODD

"DODD KICKS OFF HER NEW
DARKNESS CHOSEN SERIES WITH A BANG."
—*Booklist*

"Dodd writes with power and passion—
and always leaves me satisfied!"
—*New York Times* Bestselling Author J. R. Ward

"Sexy and witty,
daring and delightful."
—*New York Times* Bestselling Author
Teresa Medeiros

"A master."
—*New York Times* Bestselling Author
Kristin Hannah

Raves for Christina Dodd

Touch of Darkness

"A sweeping saga of good and evil, the series chronicles the adventures of four siblings who try to redeem their family from a pact an ancestor made with the devil a thousand years earlier. This latest promises to be one of her best to date." —*Library Journal*

"Enthralling, intense." —*The State* (Columbia, SC)

"Filled with action and adventure . . . a must read." —*Midwest Book Review*

"Christina Dodd demonstrates why she is such a popular writer in any genre. The characters are boldly drawn, with action on all sides. Readers will be riveted until the final page." —*A Romance Review*

Scent of Darkness

"The first in a devilishly clever, scintillatingly sexy new paranormal series by Christina Dodd." —*Chicago Tribune*

"[A] satisfying series kickoff . . . [a] fast-paced, well-written paranormal with a full, engaging mythology and a handful of memorable characters." —*Publishers Weekly*

"Dodd kicks off her new *Darkness Chosen* series with a bang. A multilayered heroine and a sizzling-hot hero give readers plenty of emotional—and physical—action, and the relentless game of hunter and prey adds an adrenaline ride for good measure." —*Booklist*

"Multigenre genius Dodd dives headfirst into the paranormal realm with . . . a scintillating and superb novel!" —*Romantic Times* (4½ stars, Top Pick)

continued . . .

Tongue in Chic

"Christina Dodd is my go-to author when I want outrageously entertaining romantic suspense. I count on her for stories that deliver hot romance, fast action, and that magic ingredient—heart."
—*New York Times* bestselling author
Jayne Ann Krentz

"RITA Award–winning Dodd's latest sparkling romantic suspense novel is another of her superbly sexy literary confections, expertly spiced with sassy wit and featuring a beguiling cast of wonderfully entertaining characters."
—*Booklist*

Trouble in High Heels

"A book by Christina Dodd is like a glass of champagne . . . sparkling and sinfully delicious. *Trouble in High Heels* is one exciting ride and an experience not to be missed. With her electric style, vibrant characters, and sly wit, Christina Dodd gives readers everything they want in a romantic suspense novel."
—Lisa Kleypas

"Dodd will dazzle readers with this fabulously fun tale of danger, desire, and diamonds, which features yet another winning combination of the author's trademark smart and snappy writing, delightfully original characters, and deliciously sensual romance."
—*Booklist* (starred review)

"Nonstop action, sparkling dialogue, and two characters who burn up the pages. . . . A story that is not only unique, but has pizzazz and leaves readers wondering who the bad and good guys are until the end."
—Romance Reviews Today

. . . and her other novels

"Dodd delivers a high-octane blowout finale. . . . This romantic suspense novel is a delicious concoction that readers will be hard-pressed not to consume in one gulp."
—*Publishers Weekly*

CHRISTINA DODD

INTO the FLAME

DARKNESS CHOSEN

A SIGNET BOOK

SIGNET
Published by New American Library, a division of
Penguin Group (USA) Inc., 375 Hudson Street,
New York, New York 10014, USA
Penguin Group (Canada), 90 Eglinton Avenue East, Suite 700, Toronto,
Ontario M4P 2Y3, Canada (a division of Pearson Penguin Canada Inc.)
Penguin Books Ltd., 80 Strand, London WC2R 0RL, England
Penguin Ireland, 25 St. Stephen's Green, Dublin 2,
Ireland (a division of Penguin Books Ltd.)
Penguin Group (Australia), 250 Camberwell Road, Camberwell, Victoria 3124,
Australia (a division of Pearson Australia Group Pty. Ltd.)
Penguin Books India Pvt. Ltd., 11 Community Centre, Panchsheel Park,
New Delhi - 110 017, India
Penguin Group (NZ), 67 Apollo Drive, Rosedale, North Shore 0632,
New Zealand (a division of Pearson New Zealand Ltd.)
Penguin Books (South Africa) (Pty.) Ltd., 24 Sturdee Avenue,
Rosebank, Johannesburg 2196, South Africa

Penguin Books Ltd., Registered Offices:
80 Strand, London WC2R 0RL, England

First published by Signet, an imprint of New American Library,
a division of Penguin Group (USA) Inc.

First Printing, August 2008
10 9 8 7 6 5 4 3 2 1

For Shannon and Rex.
Best wishes for a long life together,
thank you for the wonderful gift your love
has created,
and congratulations!

ACKNOWLEDGMENTS

Darkness Chosen has been dark, complex, and fascinating to write, and to bring the series to fruition has required the support of so many amazing professionals at NAL: the editorial department, especially the wonderfully creative Kara Cesare; the art department, led by Anthony Ramondo; Craig Burke and my own Michele Langley in publicity; and the whole wonderful Penguin sales department. Thank you all. A huge, special thanks to Rachel Granfield and production. You're the best!

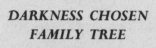

DARKNESS CHOSEN
FAMILY TREE

THE VARINSKIS

1000 AD—In the Ukraine
Konstantine Varinski
makes a deal with the devil.

A Thousand +
Years Later

Zorana **M** Konstantine   Oleg—Many Partners

Emigrate   Change   Many Partners—Boris   Other Sons
to   Surname
U.S.   to Wilder   Gavrie Vadim   Other Sons

Jasha Rurik Adrik   Firebird

Prologue

The Legend Continues . . .

In the snowy winter on the flat, frozen, empty steppes of the Ukraine, when the blizzard rages and night lingers like an unwelcome guest, my grandmother sits close to the oil stove, heating her old bones, and hugs me close. When I beg her, she tells me the old Russian legends: of the beautiful seamstress Maryushka and how Kaschei the Immortal changed her into a firebird, or of the musician Sadko and how he wed the sea king's daughter. When it grows very late and the wind rattles the windows with its icy fingers, I beg for a different story—one that frightens and haunts me.

Most of the time, she turns her head away and refuses. But sometimes, reluctantly, she relates the legend of the Darkness, of Konstantine Varinski and his pact with the devil . . . and her voice trembles.

It happened over a thousand years ago, and sometimes she tells the story one way, sometimes another, but always the main facts remain the same. . . .

Konstantine Varinski stood tall, with wide shoulders and legs like long tree trunks, and skillful hands that could use a knife to gut a man even while he brutally crushed his woman's windpipe. Through hot summers and frigid winters, he wandered alone, preying on the helpless, stealing, raping, and murdering, until at last his fame reached the ears of the devil himself.

Now my grandmother huddles with a blanket pulled high around the back of her neck. She drinks hot tea from a glass, but nothing can contain her dread as she tells about the devil who, displeased with the competition, rose from the depths of hell itself to seek out the upstart Konstantine Varinski and make him sorry he dared challenge the Evil One.

But Konstantine was not only as savage as a wolf, he was also sly as a fox. He offered the devil a pact: He and his descendants would become Satan's dedicated servants, and in return, the devil would grant them the ability to change at will into hunting animals.

Konstantine's daring captured Satan's interest, and so he looked deep into Konstantine's soul. What he saw there pleased and amazed him: Konstantine was evil through and through, a foul and useful tool.

But Konstantine was not finished with his demands.

He and all his descendants would be invincible, never to be killed in battle except by another demon. Each Varinski would be long-lived, and most important—they would breed only sons. They would hail the birth of each new demon, and raise the boy to be a ruthless warrior worthy of the name Varinski. Everywhere they went, they would bring the darkness. They would *be* the Darkness.

To seal the pact, Konstantine promised to deliver the family's holy icon, a single painting divided into four images of the Madonna.

Yet like my grandmother, Konstantine's mother was a good woman. She refused to give in to Konstantine's demands. She protected the icon, the heart of her home, with her life . . . so Konstantine used his knife and his brutal hands to murder her.

As her red blood spilled onto the white snow, she pulled him close and spoke in his ear.

Konstantine, you wish to reign at Satan's right hand, and so you shall—until the day my greatest grandson is born. The babushka lady's eyes glowed with pain and sorrow. *He will be as steeped in evil as you could ever desire, a fitting heir to your legacy . . . yet I foresee his downfall. His downfall is a woman, and on the day he falls in love, the foundation of the devil's pact will crack.*

For she will love my greatest grandson, and their love will be strong, strong with the power of the Madonna herself, and on the day their fourth son is born, your master will face defeat.

Cocky with triumph, Konstantine laughed.

His mother held the icon against her chest and looked deeply into the next world, seeing what he could not. *When the sons are grown, your own descendants will unite against the devil. Against all odds, they will fight, and when they win the ultimate battle of good against evil, Satan will banish you from his good graces.*

Konstantine answered, *Then I will have to make sure they do not win.* He plunged the knife deeper into her chest.

With her dying breath, she said, *I curse you, my son. You will burn in hell's hottest fire.*

He paid no heed to her prophecy or her curse. She was, after all, only a woman. He didn't believe her dying words had the power to change the future—and more important, he would do nothing to jeopardize his pact with the Evil One.

But although Konstantine did not confess the prophecy his mother had made, Satan knew that Konstantine was a liar and a trickster. He suspected Konstantine of deception, and he comprehended the power of blood and kin and a mother's dying words. So to ensure that he forever retained the Varinskis and their services, he secretly cut a small piece from the center of the icon, and gave it to a poor tribe of wanderers, promising it would bring them luck.

Then, while Konstantine drank to celebrate the deal, in a flash of fire the devil divided the Madonnas and hurled them to the four corners of the earth.

It happened a thousand years ago . . . but my grandmother remembers.

She wishes she could forget.

Yet that's impossible, for in the middle of the steppes, on the exact spot where Konstantine Varinski murdered his mother, is a sprawling house filled with men with wide shoulders and legs like tree trunks, and skillful hands that could use a knife to gut a man even while they brutally crushed his woman's windpipe.

They are Konstantine's descendants . . . and sometimes I wonder if my grandmother was raped by one
of those evil men, and bore a son, and gave him
up to them, as so many innocent women have done
throughout the years.

The pact with the devil cost Konstantine Varinski
almost nothing, only his soul, and the souls of his
children, and his children's children, forever and
ever.

My grandmother thinks that's the way it is and
will always be.

But forever isn't in the devil's power to promise,
and a single moment can change the balance between
good and evil. . . .

That moment came thirty-seven years ago, on the
steppes of modern Russia, where a new Konstantine
Varinski roamed and fought.

He was a worthy successor to the first Konstantine,
a warrior, a leader . . . a wolf. Under his direction, the
Darkness worked for dictators, industrialists, anyone
with the gold to pay them. Because of their battle
prowess, their endurance and decisiveness, they became rich, respected, and feared in Asia, in Europe,
and beyond. They hunted down the innocent, fought
in cruel wars, went where they were paid to go, and,
with flawless ferocity, crushed uprisings and demanded obedience. They grew in wealth and power,
until one day the new Konstantine met a Gypsy
girl . . . and fell in love.

Such a small thing, love, and so easy for so many.
But this was a love for all eternity, fierce, passionate,
lasting. For Konstantine and Zorana, love consumed

them. Nothing could keep them apart. Against all wishes and traditions, they wed.

The Varinskis shook their ham-sized fists and swore to kill the girl and rescue their leader from his insanity and her witchcraft.

The Gypsies chased the lovers, furious that a Varinski had stolen the girl who was their seer and good-luck charm.

In secret, Konstantine and Zorana fled to the United States. They changed their name to Wilder, and settled in the Cascade Mountains of Washington State. There they raised grapes, fruits, vegetables, and three sons, Jasha, Rurik, and Adrik, all handsome, all incorrigible, and all bound by the devil's pact.

Like his father, Jasha had the ability to transform himself into a wolf.

Rurik changed into a hawk and flew on night's wings.

Adrik grew up to be a man tortured by the clashing demands of duty and desire, and his dark soul showed itself in the form of a black panther.

Then, for the first time in a thousand years, a child was born to them. Not a son, as the babushka's ancient prophecy had foretold, but a daughter.

Konstantine believed the birth was a miracle, and a sign the pact was failing.

And perhaps it was . . . but when the devil gambles with a man's soul, he plays to win.

Chapter One

Spring, Almost Three Years Ago
Brown University, Providence, Rhode Island

In her dorm room, Firebird Wilder sat with a pen in her hand, ignoring the stampede of jubilant students outside her open door, and stared at the Father's Day card on her desk.

Guess what we've done?

Too coy.

Surprise!

Too flip.

We're in this together.

Too chummy.

In the end, she took the plastic stick with the blue-toned results, placed it in the card, slipped it in the envelope, and sealed it without writing a single word. There were no words to explain . . . this.

"Hey, Firebird!" Jacob Pilcher stuck his head in her open door. "What are you doing sitting there? It's over. Let's party!"

She laughed at him, the honors student wearing his baseball cap sideways, a T-shirt that proclaimed, *Warning, Contents under Pressure*, and a silly grin. "I'm waiting for Douglas."

"Ohh. The wonderful campus cop." Jacob wiggled his fingers like a magician and barely kept the edge of sarcasm out of his voice. "Is he taking you to Bruno's?"

She slipped the envelope into her purse. "That's the plan."

"Okay. That's okay. He's cool." Jacob gave her the thumbs-up. "But I guess that means you're not drinking, huh?"

"I wasn't drinking anyway. I'm twenty."

"I know, I know, but there are ways of getting around—"

Masculine shouts echoed down the corridor. "Come on, man!" "We're leaving without you, man!"

"Gotta go!" Jacob saluted her. "See you there!" Still he lingered, looking at her. "You look great." Without waiting for her to thank him, he turned and ran down the hall. "Wait. Wait, you jerks!"

Jacob was a nice kid. A kid, even though he was a year older than she was, and he'd been in love with her ever since she moved into the dorm as the student resident assistant. He'd been crushed when she met Douglas, but he'd kept on smiling, and now he was cutting loose.

They were all cutting loose. It was the end of finals.

She went to the mirror and smiled.

Her blush was a peachy gold, her mascara was black, her blond hair was twisted into a clip at the back of her head, but Jacob was right—she did look great. Not even the dusting of loose powder could subdue the glow that lit her from within.

"You're beautiful, as always," said a voice from the door.

She turned with a smile. "Douglas. You're early!"

"I couldn't stay away." He walked in, blond hair rumpled from the breeze outside, holding a bouquet of red and yellow flowers in one hand and a big gold stuffed dog under the other.

She ran to him.

He dropped the dog and wrapped her in his embrace.

Leaning her head against his shoulder, she closed her eyes. He was warm and strong, firm and muscled. For her, everything about him spelled security and love—the everlasting kind, like her parents had. Unexpected tears filled her eyes, and she clutched him harder, hoping he didn't notice.

Of course he did. Douglas noticed everything. He pushed her a little. "Hey, what's wrong? Did something go wrong with your finals?"

She sighed. He noticed everything, but he wasn't always insightful. "Everything went great, and best of all, they're over."

He glanced at the door. "Did that guy Jacob upset you?"

"No, honest! I'm just happy."

Douglas caught one of her tears with his thumb. "You've got a funny way of showing it."

Douglas didn't talk about himself or his past, and so far, Firebird had let him get away with evading her questions, because something had put far too much cynicism into his dark eyes.

Something else—her—had brought him joy, and when she caught him looking at her, that stunned expression of happiness on his face, she didn't want to rock the boat.

Someday she'd coax him into telling his life story. Right now, they could just be in love.

"I brought you flowers." He let her go and handed her the bouquet of red carnations and yellow roses. Leaning over, he picked up the dog and offered it. "And a cuddly buddy. And congratulations, my darling—in five weeks, you'll march across the stage and get your diploma."

"Thank you." She grinned, delighted and relieved to be through with finals, with the pressure of finishing a four-year degree in three years, and finishing at the top of her class. "Thank you." She smelled the flowers—there weren't many, only a handful, but for a campus cop the pay wasn't great.

"They're lovely. You remembered the kind of flowers I like!"

"I remember everything about you." His gaze intent, he watched her fill a glass with water and arrange the flowers on her desk. "I could pick you out of a crowd in a full Las Vegas casino."

She laughed, not believing a word. "Now let me see this guy." She lifted the stuffed animal out of his arms and stared in surprise. "I thought it was a dog, but it's a cat!"

"A dog? I wouldn't give you a dog." Douglas sounded grossly insulted. "It's a cougar."

"That's right. It is." A big, fuzzy, floppy cougar with a white belly and dark glass eyes that stared right into her soul.

Wrapping her arms around the animal, she hugged him and buried her face in the plush fur. He smelled like Douglas: like shampoo and spray starch, like the flowers he had carried, and like the rich, intoxicating scent of her first and only lover. "This sweetheart will sleep on my bed with me."

"That is exactly where he wants to be." Douglas watched her with that expression that told her he considered her a miracle.

That was why she'd succumbed to his seduction. To the Wilders, she had always been a miracle, the first female born into the family in a thousand years. But she was a smart girl.

Her father and mother had immigrated to the United States, fleeing his family, the ones known as the Varinskis. Her father had been their leader, and she didn't know what he'd done to win that honor, but whatever crimes he'd planned, approved, and committed, he repented of them now. Yet no matter where he was, in the old Varinski home in the Ukraine or in his vineyard in Washington, he still had the ability to change, to transform himself into a wolf.

That was a miracle.

He'd passed his abilities onto his sons.

Like his father, her oldest brother, Jasha, ran the forest as a wolf. Her second brother, Rurik, soared through the air as a hawk. Her third brother, Adrik, had disappeared when he was seventeen, but he had been wild and rebellious, a black panther who hunted his prey without remorse.

Those were also all miracles.

She was intelligent, she worked hard, yet she hadn't inherited one little drop of supernatural abilities. The rest of the world considered her pretty normal, and so did she.

But Douglas Black, a campus cop, a guy she'd met four months ago . . . he made her feel special.

She dropped the cougar and went back into Douglas's arms. She put all her heart, all her love, into the kiss she gave him, and turned him toward the bed.

He braced himself against the pressure. "No. This is your night to celebrate."

She rubbed against him. "I want to celebrate my way."

"You want to celebrate with your friends, with the people you saw every day in class." He never seemed to mind that he wasn't one of the crowd. He stood apart, friendly, but watching, always watching. "Your friends are up at Bruno's."

"I can't drink. I'm not old enough. And I'm dating a campus cop, so it's not like I can fake an ID."

"I promise not to toss you out as long as you stick with soft drinks." He put his forehead to hers. "I'll let you in on a secret."

"Yeah?"

"I'm the same age you are."

She pulled back. "You're kidding. How did you get the job?"

"I have a fake ID." He didn't smile, but his eyes twinkled.

"You're pulling my lariat." Was he serious?

"Nope. But don't tell anyone; I will lose my job." He released her and went to the closet. "Come on. Let's go."

He held her jacket as she shrugged into it. "You said you'd been a cop for four years."

"That's right."

"Since you were sixteen? That's impossible." Had he even graduated from high school?

"I'm good at what I do, so the police departments ignore discrepancies in my job history."

"What do you do that's so special?"

"I track people. I find criminals. I find missing persons."

She stared at him, uneasy for the first time since she'd met him. "How?"

He shrugged. "It's a gift. Are you ready?"

"Let me get my purse." With the card inside.

They headed outside into the May evening.

The campus was old and lovely, mellowed by age and hard use. Massive trees lined the walks, their leaves still a new, bright green. Springtime had brought a burst of flowers along the paths, and lured lovers out to walk hand in hand. No one noticed when Douglas took her hand in his and kissed her fingers.

"Tracking seems like such an odd talent," she said. It was the talent that had started the Varinskis on their path to infamy and riches.

"I grew up in pretty rough circumstances. I spent a lot of time on the streets." His mouth twisted bitterly. "I can make contacts most cops can't even imagine."

Firebird caught her breath.

At last, a glimpse into his past.

"I guess your parents were poor?" she asked.

" 'Poor' doesn't begin to describe them." He led her around four students lined up on the walk and singing a jaunty opera in Italian. He nodded at them. "That's just not something you see on most college campuses."

But he wasn't going to distract her. "Why don't you like to talk about your parents?"

"My parents were not pleasant people. I'd rather talk about your family. When you talk about them, your face lights up." He hugged her shoulders. "You like them. Do you know how rare that is?"

"No, it's not. Lots of people like their families."

"Lots of people don't." He headed them toward Bruno's Bar and Grill. "I'll buy you a steak."

He had given her a hint of his past, then offered a steak as a distraction.

It wouldn't work. She wouldn't let him succeed. She stopped in the middle of the sidewalk. She faced him and took his hands. "You're only twenty. Is your past so disgraceful you can't talk about it?"

"Not disgraceful. But not the subject for this place and this time." He gestured around at the laughing, shouting students headed for Bruno's.

"Then we'll talk about it later."

He looked down at their joined hands, then up at her face. "Tonight, I'll tell you everything. I just hope that you—" He stopped, his face twisted with remembered pain.

"That I what?"

"Sometimes I wish I'd never started this."

Alarmed, she glanced at the approaching circle of shouting students, then back at Douglas. "What *are* you talking about?"

The students surrounded them. Her friends, jubilant, exhausted, celebrating.

"Hey, Firebird, we did it!"

"Hey, Doug, let's party!"

They jostled Douglas and Firebird, pulling them along the path, separating them. Firebird laughed and talked with them, but she kept Douglas in sight—and he watched her. Watched her as if she really were a miracle.

He caught her as they walked into Bruno's. "Tonight we'll talk. Okay?"

"Okay." She remembered the card in her purse. "Definitely okay."

The place was packed, a distillation of the elation that held the campus in thrall. Douglas kept her at his side, tried to order her a steak—she insisted on a hamburger—and kept her in as many bottles of water as she wanted. Half the guys in the bar tried to sneak her a beer, and she was glad she could use Douglas as an excuse to say no.

She was posing for a picture with three of her best friends when two guys, too drunk to walk, started swinging at each other. The fight spread like wildfire, and Douglas waded in, shouting for quiet, separating the combatants, making arrests. By the time the police and EMTs arrived, he'd impressed Firebird with his patience and his strength.

He worked his way over to her. "I need to stay here and help mop up. Wait for me."

"I can't. I'm pooped." These days, she tired out very quickly. "I'll walk home with the girls."

He looked around at the mess in the bar. "You'll stay with your friends? You'll be careful?"

"Very careful. You'll come by later?"

"I don't know if I can. It's going to be a wild night."

"Then I'll see you in the morning. And we'll talk."

"Yes. In the morning, we'll talk."

The other girls lived in an apartment five minutes from Firebird's dorm. Meghan had Blue Bell ice cream her mother had sent her from Texas. So of course Firebird had to stop by for a bowl of Homemade Vanilla with chocolate sauce and some quick gossip, and by the time they'd gone from high spirits to quiet reflection as they realized their years together were finally over, it was one a.m., and Firebird figured she'd better get back to the dorm or she'd fall asleep in their chair.

The main walk of the campus was still hopping with celebrating students, but the crowds were thinning fast, and when she turned off toward her dorm, it got darker, quieter.

She didn't mind. Douglas had told her the campus wasn't safe, but her father had taught her to protect herself, to be careful, to be aware. She was all of those things, and right now, she was bummed to be alone.

The evening hadn't turned out as she had hoped. Not at all. Douglas had hinted at his past, had promised to fill her in, and work had interfered. And she'd made him promise that they'd talk in the morning, but she'd seen the look on his face—he didn't want to.

What secrets did he hide? He was only twenty. He was a policeman. How bad could his past possibly be?

As she strolled along the tree-lined walk, she at first didn't notice the sounds behind her. She was listening for footsteps, not the rustle of leaves and the creak of branches. But once she heard them, she knew what they boded.

Someone was stalking her, creeping along through the trees, and that someone wasn't all human.

A Varinski.

Somehow, a Varinski had found her.

She didn't look around, didn't indicate that she knew she was being followed. Her heart pounded, her skin flushed, yet she walked at a steady pace.

Don't run, little Firebird, she heard Konstantine's voice rumble in her head. *Running brings out a hunter's urge to chase, and you can't outrun a wolf or a panther. You can't outfly a hawk. But you can outsmart them, and you can outfight them.*

As the Varinski moved from tree to tree, she listened to the sounds, trying to figure out what kind of creature was tracking her. A bird of prey, perhaps, or a great cat leaping between the branches.

Her dorm loomed ahead. Lights illuminated about half the windows. People were awake and nearby. She could scream for help.

But then someone would get hurt.

She opened her purse, pulled out her cell phone,

and debated about calling Douglas. He would want her to—but then, he wouldn't be happy to discover she was walking alone, and if she put her phone up to her ear, that might force the stalker to attack.

How had he located her? What did he want?

As she got closer to the dorm, the sound behind her grew more pronounced. She dug out her keys and threaded them between her fingers so a key stuck out between each knuckle. She opened her phone and dialed nine-one— And before she could hit the last button, the door to the dorm burst open. Eight guys came dashing out, Jacob in their midst, wearing nothing but baseball caps, body paint, and running shoes. They hooted as they passed her. She pumped her fist to indicate her approval, and slipped inside before the door could close.

Then she ran. Ran down the hall and up the stairs to her bedroom. She didn't turn on the light, but crept to the window. Staying well back in the shadows, she looked out.

There it was, crouched in a giant oak, a great golden cat stretched along the branch. The moonlight seeped through the leaves and picked up the smooth glory of its coat, and even from here she could see its dark eyes watching her window, and its tail twitched slowly, as if the loss of its prey had irritated it.

What did it intend to do to her? Was this a rogue Varinski, entertaining himself by stalking and killing the daughter of Konstantine Wilder? Or did the Varinskis have plans to kidnap and hold her as a pawn in their plot to destroy her family?

She had to go. She had to leave. She couldn't wait

until graduation; she needed to go at once—and she couldn't tell Douglas why.

He would never believe this.

"Oh, my love." What had she been thinking, getting involved with a normal guy? He wouldn't understand about the pact with the devil and her family's special talents. How could he? It was absolutely insane.

Worse, as her mate, he'd be in danger, the same kind of danger that shadowed her.

But . . . she stroked the infinitesimal bulge of her belly. She didn't have a choice. She would have to try. This baby deserved a father, and Douglas deserved his child.

Outside the window, the great cat moved at last. It stood and stretched, then lightly jumped down out of the tree.

She got her first good look at it.

A cougar. It was a cougar.

She frowned. Her heart stopped. She looked toward the bed where the large, soft stuffed animal lay sprawled.

A cougar?

As the cat began to change, her heartbeat leaped.

The claws retracted. The bones warped into new shapes: The paws became hands, the back legs lengthened and straightened, the shoulders got broader, the hair retreated onto the head and chest and genitals.

The face changed, too, becoming a man's face, a familiar man's face . . . the face of the man she loved.

She stared. Stared so hard her eyes hurt.

Douglas. Douglas was a Varinski.

He'd come to Brown, sought her out, courted her, seduced her, made her trust him, got her to confide in him. . . . In a brief spasm of shame, she hid her eyes with her hands.

She'd told him she was from Washington. She'd told him she had three brothers, that one was a wine-maker, that her father grew grapes and her mother ruled the family.

Had she told him the name of her town?

No.

Had she given him anything that would enable him to pinpoint her location?

No.

No. Please, no.

He stood out there, naked in the moonlight, a tattoo that looked like great claw marks ripping the skin on his left side.

She hadn't seen that before. He'd taken great care not to take off his shirt in the light.

Smart guy, because that would have tipped her off for sure. Her brothers had tattoos that were just as vivid, just as distinctive, and they had come naturally the first time they became beasts.

Completely unself-conscious with his nudity— well, why should he be self-conscious? Apparently, half the guys on campus were streaking—Douglas turned and loped away.

Virulently, she hoped he was happy with himself. Because he'd managed to get laid, but he hadn't caught her. He hadn't killed her.

And he wasn't going to get another chance to try.

Going to the bed, she picked up the soft, plush stuffed cougar by the scruff of the neck. Its dark, intense eyes mocked her as she walked out into the hall and to the trash chute. But she got the final laugh—she dropped the damned thing down the hole and into the Dumpster outside.

Back to her room, she called an airline and reserved the first flight out of town toward the West Coast. It went to LA, but that was good enough. She could hang out there, try to figure out how much to tell the folks, then catch a ride to Napa to Jasha's winery, and from there on to Washington.

She packed her clothes, leaving most of the stuff— she'd worn it all down to the threads, anyway.

She left the dorm, walking toward the bus stop, and as she walked, she dug into her purse, pulled out the envelope with the Father's Day card and the plastic stick with the telltale blue stripes, and threw it into the garbage.

No matter how hard she would try, she could never forget Douglas Black.

He'd given her a souvenir that would last forever.

Chapter Two

Washington State
Present Day

The Varinski stood in the dark forest and watched the young woman drive up to the small two-story house, park, and get out. She leaned against the late-model Mercury Milan—a sensible car for such a pretty woman—looked up at the starry sky, and anguish twisted her face.

For one moment, he felt almost sorry for her. Almost.

But pity fought with lust, and lust fought with resentment.

Because what did *she* have to be anguished about? Mountains covered with deep, green, primeval forest enclosed this long valley. Vines covered most of the flat ground, but the old-fashioned house, filled with light and warmth and family, occupied one end. A picket fence enclosed the carefully tended yard. Most people would call this setting idyllic, yet if she was restless for the bright lights, it was less than a half hour drive to the nearest small town, also idyllic, and two hours to Seattle.

More important, she had family inside, waiting for her.

Firebird Wilder might be feeling sorry for herself, but she had it made.

With a deep breath, she headed up the steps. Placing her hand on the doorknob, she stopped. She straightened her shoulders.

The door opened under her hand. A man greeted her. A man holding a little boy of two.

The Varinski flinched.

Then he thought . . . no. The man looked like a Varinski. So that was her brother, and the kid must be her nephew.

He didn't like to be relieved . . . but he was.

She stepped inside and the door closed behind her.

Drawn by anger, need, and the pact he had made, the Varinski walked out of the trees. He scrutinized the house, with its wide, welcoming porch that spanned the front of the house, and its windows undraped and spilling light into the frozen lawn. He walked to the back, where he found more lawn, a winter-nipped garden surrounded by a tall deer fence, and a small orchard of fruit trees arranged in straight rows.

This place was soft. One man could attack the house and do damage—significant damage. A hundred men could raze the entire valley and destroy every living thing in it, every creature and every blade of grass.

Konstantine Varinski had forgotten his past, and his heedlessness had put him and everyone in his family at risk.

The Varinski's quiet tread was as much a part of him as his tawny hair and his dark brown eyes. He returned to the front, mounted the stairs, and walked silently from one end of the porch to the other. He looked in the windows, into the living room crowded with life, with warmth, with love.

Although Konstantine had changed, had grown prematurely old and desperately ill, the Varinski recognized him. He sat in a recliner, a tank of oxygen beside him, an IV drip in his arm. He must be almost seventy, and painfully gaunt, yet he had the same strong frame and vigorous head of hair he had sported in photos taken forty years ago.

His wife sat nearby. The Varinski recognized her from the old photos, too; she had barely changed. She was in her early fifties, petite, pretty, a hundred pounds soaking wet. Her dark hair shone and her dark eyes sparked with life.

As he moved from window to window, he saw them all. Three sons who closely resembled their father. Three women whom their sons obviously adored. One lone older man, who tried to make himself small in the crowded room.

Everyone stared at Firebird, watched Firebird. She sat on the floor by the door, her back pressed against the wall. The toddler sat in her lap.

Her face was hard and accusing, and she spoke rapidly, like a woman in the grip of fury, yet all the while, she hugged the little boy as if he brought her comfort.

As the Varinski watched with cruel intention, he deliberately began the change. His bones melted and mutated. His hands developed into paws, paws with long, sharp claws that could rend a man to shreds. His face lengthened and squared; his teeth shaped themselves into fangs; his jaw grew large and strong enough to snap a man's neck. His blond hair spread down his body, becoming a golden pelt that invited the touch of any simpleton who was fool enough to dare caress the swift, intelligent, deadly beast that he had become.

With a single spring, he silently leaped off the porch and raced across the valley, seeking the shelter of the surrounding forest.

Firebird had been in the hospital in Seattle. From the information the Varinski had been able to collect—and he was good at collecting information—Konstantine's children were coming in one at a time to give blood and have tests as the doctors pursued the cause and cure of his unique and life-threatening illness.

The Varinski leaped up a tree and found a broad branch, one that allowed him to observe the house and the narrow road that wound its way into the valley, and mull over all the vulnerabilities that could be utilized in an attack.

And all the while, he wondered, What had she discovered?

What had left her so distraught?

How could he turn the situation to his advantage . . . and destroy the family?

Because he wasn't really a Varinski.

He was the thing not even the Varinskis wanted to claim.

Firebird would never forget this day.

The day she discovered her family had lied to her.

The day she'd discovered the truth.

Now, finding herself in the safe, familiar setting of the place she had always called home, she hugged her baby, her Aleksandr, and in a steady voice that surely belonged to a stranger, she asked, "Why didn't you tell me that I'm adopted? That I'm not related to you? To any of you?" She looked right at the woman she had always believed to be her mother. At Zorana. "Why didn't you tell me I'm not your child?"

Her father had the guts to look bewildered.

Her brothers exchanged glances, the kind she'd seen so many times before, the one that said, *She must have cramps.*

The other people in the tiny living room—her brothers' women, the strange man she had yet to meet—looked the way people did when they'd fallen into an emotional episode they would just as soon avoid.

But her mother . . . oh, yes. Her mother sat pale, frozen, wide-eyed . . . guilty.

Jasha spoke first, in that excessively reasonable, older-brother tone of voice that made her want to scream. "Firebird, are you thinking you were switched in the nursery? Because you were born at home. Remember the story? We all remember that night, and we've told you the story at least a dozen times."

His wife, Ann, touched his arm and, when he looked at her, shook her head.

"What?" His voice rose a little. "I'm just pointing out the facts."

Firebird's voice rose, too. "And I'm telling you what the doctor told me. I am not related to any of you. He made that plain enough."

Everyone at Seattle's Swedish Hospital had told the family that Dr. Mitchell was the best in the field of genetic illnesses. She herself had seen that he was first in the field of arrogance, and last in the field of tact.

"Why the hell are your parents having me waste my time testing you? You're adopted. I'm looking for a genetic mutation that is causing your father's disease. You're no good to us." He turned away.

"Someone screwed up, and it's not my parents." Furious with him, Firebird stood and lunged, catching his arm. "I'm not adopted."

He looked down at her as if she were a worm. "Oh, for God's sake. I don't have time to screw with this. I don't have time to counsel you through your shock and anger. The lab redid the blood test three different times. You're no more related to Konstantine and Zorana Wilder and their sons than you are to me." He flung the chart at her. "Look for yourself."

She had. She'd gone through the chart so many times the results were burned on her eyeballs. It never changed.

Konstantine pushed himself upright in his recliner

and robustly said, "That jackass of a doctor made a mistake."

"No. He didn't. Papa, you are type A. Mama, you are type AB. That means all of your children must be blood type A, B, or AB. The hospital lab typed me as O negative."

"Well, they're wrong." Rurik was the second son, a former Air Force pilot with an officer's forceful way of expressing himself. "Jasha's right. I remember that night, and it was raining so hard—no way anyone was switching babies around."

Adrik was the youngest son. He had been gone, vanished for seventeen years doing heaven knew what. He'd come back changed from a laughing teenager into a stern-faced man. Now he knelt beside Firebird and spoke gently, convinced he was right. "I remember seeing you the next morning. I thought you were the ugliest thing I'd ever seen, all wrinkled, red, and ugly. You were certainly a new baby. The hospital has to have messed this up."

"I checked my card from the Red Cross blood center. I *am* O negative. It doesn't take an advanced degree in genetics to see that someone with my blood type can't be the child of two people who are their blood type."

The men exchanged glances.

"Isn't it possible there's some kind of genetic mutation?" Ann asked.

Firebird looked right at Zorana. "I don't know. Mama, what do you think?"

"God." Zorana stared back, stricken with horror. "God."

Adrik got to his feet. "Mama?"

"Zorana?" Konstantine leaned forward. "What's wrong?"

Big tears welled in Zorana's eyes. She pressed her fingers to her lips and shook her head in violent shudders.

The sight of her mother's conscience-stricken face calmed Firebird's agitation.

The worst was over. She had her confirmation.

It was true. Zorana knew it was true.

Firebird was not her daughter.

In a low tone, Firebird said, "Mama, why don't you tell us everything you can remember about that night when you gave birth to . . . your baby."

Zorana nodded in wretched assent, and began the story Firebird had heard a dozen times. But this time, Zorana told them the details she'd kept hidden for so many years . . .

Chapter Three

Twenty-three years ago . . .

*L*ightning flashed.

Thunder roared.

"Push, Zorana, push!"

Wind slashed through the night.

Rain sluiced down in buckets, in inches an hour, pounding the windows of the Wilders' small house.

In the haze created by pain, Zorana Wilder had lost control of the weather.

"Push, Zorana, push!"

Zorana bared her teeth at the doctor. "Get away from me."

"Get away from you?" Dr. Lewis swayed on his feet, and if smell were any indication, he had swum through a river of whisky to get here through the storm. "If I don't deliver this baby, who will? This old-maid schoolteacher?" He brayed with laughter.

Miss Joyce, the aforementioned old-maid schoolteacher, paced back and forth in the Wilders' small master bedroom,

agitation, fear, or perhaps a bad application of blush plac-
ing a red spot of color on each cheek. She'd arrived with
the doctor, dressed in her usual uniform of orthopedic
shoes, a long-sleeved blue cotton dress buttoned up to her
throat, and a pleated plastic rain bonnet. With thorough
circumspection, she had explained that she'd been with
him when he received the call and thought she should
come and be of assistance.

Zorana barely refrained from snapping that the best as-
sistance Miss Joyce could have given was to keep him
sober.

Some things were beyond even Miss Joyce's authority.

If only Konstantine were here. Always before, when
Zorana gave birth, he had held her hand and encouraged
her with his rumbling voice and his strength. And it had
been ten years since Zorana had given birth. This labor
was grueling. This son was bigger. He'd come quickly, too
quickly for her to get to the hospital, and now she strained
and sweated in her own bed, by the light of two bedside
lamps, attended by a drunkard and a sixty-year-old virgin.

Konstantine Wilder had a lot to answer for.

"Where is he?" Zorana gasped. "Where is the bastard
who got me into this condition?"

Miss Joyce swam into view, the edges of her form waver-
ing, her face distorted, her smile stretched and flat.

"Damn you, Doctor," Zorana gritted between her teeth.
"What kind of drugs did you give me?"

Dr. Lewis adjusted his glasses and peered at her in
astonishment. "You asked for them. Remember? You told
the schoolteacher—"

"No, I didn't!" Zorana shouted. "No drugs. I told
you . . . no drugs!"

Miss Joyce wiped Zorana's forehead with a damp cloth. "She doesn't remember," Zorana heard her say to the doctor.

If Zorana had had a single ounce of energy to spare, she would have leaped off the bed and slapped them both.

"Push, Zorana, push!" Miss Joyce said.

Zorana grasped her knees, took a breath, leaned up, and pushed.

The bed shook with the roll of the thunder.

The pressure inside was deep and strong. The baby was almost here.

"Where is Konstantine?" she cried in a panic.

"The dam on the creek, the one he uses for irrigation, is giving way. It's about to flood the vines." The red spots in Miss Joyce's cheeks grew mottled, and she fanned herself with her hand.

"I don't care about the vines. Let them wash away." Zorana could feel another pain building. "Bring Konstantine. His son is coming."

Dr. Lewis laughed. "You think it's another son?"

Of course it was a son. For a thousand years, the Varinskis, and now the Wilders, had had only sons. She had three sons, strong sons, mischievous sons, beautiful sons. . . . "Get Konstantine here now!" Zorana demanded.

Miss Joyce pushed a pillow under her shoulders, and in a brisk schoolteacher tone, she said, "If he doesn't get the flood under control, the house is going to wash away, and all of us with it."

Zorana looked out the window. The black night pressed against the glass. Then a spear of lightning so bright it seared her eyeballs blasted the darkness.

She moaned. Tears of pain and fear slipped from the

corners of her eyes, and worry splintered her mind. Her other boys—Jasha, Rurik, and Adrik—should be in bed asleep, but no one could have slept through this violent tempest. And Konstantine was out there somewhere, in the rain and the lightning and the shrieking wind, risking his life . . . because the pain and the drugs had eroded her power . . . and the storm battered them with the force of all the storms she'd vanquished. "Konstantine . . ." she moaned softly.

The doctor took a pull from his bottle, rolled up his sleeves, and swiped at his sweaty face with his bare hand. "Not much longer now."

Repulsed, again Zorana shrieked, "Get away from me!"

"Don't be silly, woman. I'm a doctor. You need me." Dr. Lewis grinned idiotically and bent toward her.

"No!" She kicked him.

He staggered backward, arms flailing, and hit the dresser so hard the mirror rattled in its frame. "What do you think you're doing?" He sounded as if he were struggling to get to his feet.

Miss Joyce leaned over him.

Zorana heard a thump, like the sound a ripe melon made when dropped.

Miss Joyce rose, blue eyes bright with excitement. "He passed out."

"That fool." Zorana's voice shook with ferocity.

"You didn't want him anyway."

"I expected him to stay conscious!"

"Don't worry." Miss Joyce rolled up her sleeves and took his place. "I can deliver this baby."

There wasn't a doubt in Zorana's mind that she could. The rumors said Miss Joyce was from Houston, that she'd *taught at a tough school on the Ship Channel, that she'd been brutally attacked by knife-wielding students and had spent six months recovering in the hospital. Yet if she ever suffered residual pain or angst, none of it showed. Miss Joyce had moved to this small town in the Washington mountains not long after Zorana's boys were born, and had taught at the local school ever since, earning a reputation for unshakable resolve. No student ever got the better of her. Neither would a simple thing like childbirth.*

Miss Joyce leaned over. "Push, Zorana. Push!"

Zorana pushed, grunting with the effort of delivering her son. He was almost here. He was almost here. . . .

The lightning flashed so brightly, Zorana was blinded. The thunder snarled.

The lights went out.

She gasped, released.

"Here. I was ready for this." Miss Joyce turned on a flashlight, resting it on the night table. "It's okay." She smiled at Zorana, but in the weird light, her teeth were too white, her nose a wrinkled blob, her eyes dark caverns.

And from somewhere, a tiny wail pierced the air.

That sound. Zorana would know it anywhere. In a panic, she rose onto her elbows. "I can already hear my baby crying."

"It's the doctor," Miss Joyce corrected her. "He's pathetic."

"No, that's a newborn."

"It's the drugs. You're hallucinating. Now pay attention!" Miss Joyce bent over Zorana.

Zorana pushed. Pushed as hard as she could, and felt the infant slip from her body.

She collapsed against the pillows, drained from the effort, soaked with sweat.

The baby screamed, his lungs strong.

Zorana smiled as she listened.

Then her smile faded.

Two cries . . . ? Two babies?

She was going insane.

She lifted her head and saw Miss Joyce holding the bloody infant under her arm as she cut the cord.

Zorana blinked, fighting the effects of the drugs, the ones that urged her to collapse. She needed to see her son before she slept, to assure herself he was all right.

Miss Joyce reached toward the flashlight—and somehow, it flickered out.

In a panic, Zorana struggled to sit up. "Can you clean him? Can you wrap him up? Don't let him get cold!"

"I'll take care of it."

A single flash of lightning illuminated every corner of the world, and for a second, Zorana clearly saw her son, his wrinkled face, his long body.

He was beautiful. Healthy. Perfect. A boy child. Her son. Another son for Konstantine.

"All right," she muttered. "All right." Her formidable will gave way beneath the twin assaults of drugs and exhaustion.

She slept.

"Let me see. Let me see!"

Adrik's high, young voice woke Zorana, but she kept her eyes closed and smiled as she heard the other boys, and Konstantine, vigorously shush him.

Adrik was the youngest, and perhaps a little spoiled. Certainly he paid no heed to the demands for quiet. "I want to hold it!" he insisted.

"It's not an it, stupid. It's a baby." Rurik's voice was scornful, the experienced middle child.

"A very special baby." Konstantine's deep rumble warmed Zorana right down to her soul.

She peeked under her eyelashes.

It was morning. The sun shone through the windows. She was clean. She'd been changed, as had the sheets. All the evidence of childbirth was gone.

Most important, her three boys were gathered around the bassinet, staring at their little miracle.

But Konstantine was staring at her. Staring at her with such love and pleasure, her heart wanted to burst from joy.

Quietly he leaned over her. He brushed her hair back off her forehead, away from her cheeks. And in the soft voice he saved only for her, he said, "Thank you, liubov maya, for this great gift you have given me."

He had tears in his eyes, this big barbarian she called her own, and her ready tears sprang up and ran down her cheeks. "Thank you, my love, for all the gifts you have given me."

He wiped her tears, then turned to his sons. "My boys, your mama is awake at last. Shall we let her hold the baby?"

"Mama!" Adrik jumped onto the bed, bouncing until she winced.

Konstantine lifted him off the mattress and stood him on the floor. "Gently, my boy." He went to the bassinet.

Jasha slung his arm around his younger brother's shoul-

ders. "You're the big kid now. Like me and Rurik." He shot a meaningful look at Rurik.

Rurik slung his arm around them both.

Adrik wasn't stupid. He knew he was being played, but the lure of being one of the big boys was too much. He smirked and wiggled.

Konstantine exchanged a smile with Zorana; then he brought her her brand-new son.

Carefully she embraced her baby, looked at the red, wrinkled face, wondered how this tiny being could have caused her so much agony. "So much smaller than the other boys."

"Well, of course. I have been thinking of a name." Konstantine puffed up his chest. "It has to be the right name, one with meaning. I believe it should be Firebird."

"Like a car, Dad? Like the Pontiac?" Jasha looked as if his father had gone crazy.

Konstantine laughed, a big rumble in his chest. "Like the Russian legend. Firebird Maryushka. It is perfect."

Zorana blinked. "But . . . that's a girl's name."

"Exactly. The firebird symbolizes change, and its plumage symbolizes light. Maryushka is the name of the seamstress who was transformed into a firebird, so it is a good name for this child. Yes?"

He was babbling. He must be babbling. "Why would we want to name our son for a bird and a woman?"

"Our son?" Konstantine gave a bellow of laughter. "Did no one tell you? This is not a son. This is a daughter!" He slid his arm under her, embracing both her and the newborn child. "This is our daughter!"

"That's impossible."

"When the doctor told me, I said the same thing. No girl born for a thousand years. But this is a girl. Our daughter." He hugged Zorana tighter. "We have made a miracle!"

"No." She pulled away and stared into Konstantine's eyes. "I saw him. I saw our son."

"The drugs they gave you . . . You were seeing things. Dreaming." Konstantine fetched a diaper and changed the infant with the brisk efficiency of a man familiar with a baby's waterworks. "When I came in last night, you were so hard asleep, I couldn't wake you to feed the child. I had to give her a bottle."

"Yes, they drugged me, but I saw him. We have a son."

Konstantine frowned with concern. "She is a daughter."

Zorana shoved Konstantine away. Sitting up, she unwrapped the baby from the blanket that swaddled her, unzipped the sack, peeled off the diaper.

The boys peered from one side of the mattress. Konstantine peered from the other.

Adrik spoke first, and he sounded glum. "That's for sure a girl, Mama."

"This is the only baby we have, Mama." Jasha tried to sound reassuring, but it was obvious his mother had him worried. "Look. She's pretty."

"No, she's not!" Adrik said.

Rurik stood shoulder-to-shoulder with Jasha. "And we love her."

"No, we don't!" Adrik said.

"Where's Miss Joyce?" Zorana asked. "She'll tell you it was a boy!"

"As soon as the flood subsided, she left," Konstantine said. "But she congratulated me on a daughter."

Panic rose in Zorana's throat. "What about the doctor?"

"Miss Joyce took him with her," Jasha said. "He hit his head. He had a big bruise on his forehead."

"I gave birth to a son." She had. But her certainty was fading.

Konstantine looked scared. "You had a lot of drugs," he insisted.

Zorana looked down at the baby.

The little one opened her eyes. Babies didn't focus. They couldn't see anything but blurred images. But this baby looked at Zorana—and saw her.

She was so tiny. So perfect. Her toes . . . and her fingers . . . her soft, sweet-smelling skin . . . the baby fuzz on the top of her head . . .

Zorana had had a lot of drugs. Maybe she had been hallucinating.

The baby made a mewling noise; then, opening her mouth, she bellowed. Bellowed as loudly as any of Zorana's boys had ever bellowed.

"Wow." Her sons stared, wide-eyed, at the infant, and backed away.

"We've been giving her formula." Konstantine was seldom unsure of himself, but he was unsure now. He fumbled with the words and shuffled his feet. "I can feed her . . . if you don't want to."

As the baby's screams blistered their ears, Zorana's breasts grew full and hard and ached with tension.

"Mama." Adrik's face twisted with horror as the baby shrieked. "Do something! Do something now!"

Konstantine looked miserable.

Most of all, the baby glared right into Zorana's eyes.

"All right!" Zorana unbuttoned her nightgown. "All right, I'll feed you." She put the baby to her breast.

The infant needed no coaxing. She clamped onto the nipple and suckled hard.

Zorana jumped; then, as her milk let down, she relaxed.

Adrik stared, wide-eyed and horrified. "What're you doing?"

"She's feeding her." Jasha stared stoically at the wall over Zorana's head.

"Euw. That's gross!" Adrik said.

"Yeah." Rurik shoved his little brother toward the hall. "But that's how it's done, so get used to it."

In their rush to leave, the two boys got stuck in the doorway; then Jasha caught up with them and shoved them out.

Zorana laughed softly.

Konstantine shut the door behind them and came back to her. "So it is a fine thing that we have a daughter?"

Zorana looked down at the baby.

She didn't remember giving birth to this tiny creature.

But there was no other baby, and this one held her tiny fist against Zorana's breast and sucked with such strength, love rose in her like a tide. Zorana cupped the soft head nestled against her arm. "Firebird Maryushka, did you say?"

"Do you like the name?" Konstantine sat on the mattress beside her.

"I like it very much."

Chapter Four

Hostility, pain, and bitterness mixed like poison in Firebird's soul. "Is that *really* what happened?"

Zorana's remembering smile faded, and she turned her gaze away.

"Firebird! Don't talk to Mama that way," Jasha rebuked in that familiar big-brother tone.

But he *wasn't* her big brother, and she didn't have to put up with his patronizing ways. "Why not?" She looked right at him. "She lied to me before. She always told me this dramatic story of the storm and the drunk doctor and how he fell over and how Miss Joyce saved the day and delivered me. . . . Now it sounds as if Miss Joyce didn't deliver *me* at all."

"Excuse me." Zorana stood, fled toward the bathroom, and locked the door.

The silence that followed would have oppressed Firebird . . . if she were a part of this family. Which she wasn't.

"If you want to abuse someone, daughter of mine, abuse me. Your mother told me the truth. I did not believe her. I believed it was the drugs." Konstantine's voice was low and steady, quite unlike his usual bellowing.

More than anything, that informed Firebird how truly angry he was. That and his clenched fists. But also he was concerned about his wife, and hurt that Firebird had been so cruel. He looked between the corridor where Zorana had disappeared, and Firebird, sitting on the floor clutching her little boy, and his lids sagged over his troubled brown eyes.

"All right," she mumbled. "I'm a jerk."

"That's for sure," Rurik said.

Maybe these people weren't her family, but she loved them. She loved Zorana.

A big, hot tear spilled onto her cheek.

Konstantine, Jasha, Adrik, and the strange guy all glared at Rurik.

"Nice job," Adrik snapped.

"Like you all weren't thinking the same thing." Rurik looked beleaguered.

"Yeah, but we're smart enough not to say it," Jasha said.

"I didn't know she'd cry," Rurik said.

"She always cries," Adrik said.

"How would you know? You haven't been around for seventeen years. And I do not!" Firebird tried to suck back the tears, which had the unfortunate side effect of making her sob and hiccup at the same time.

Aleksandr patted her cheek and glared around the room. "Stop. Mean boys!"

"Enough." Konstantine snapped his fingers at his sons, then gestured at Ann and Tasya.

Her sisters-in-law swooped in, kneeling beside Firebird.

"Don't pay any attention to that idiot man of mine." Tasya had electric blue eyes, a dark head of curly hair, and a sharp brain that matched Rurik's. Passing Firebird a tissue, she said, "Here, blow your nose."

Firebird blew. "I yelled at Mama."

"The drugs . . . and those people . . . Zorana didn't know or she would never have . . ." Ann hesitated.

"Accepted me as hers? Ever stopped searching for her real baby?" Now that Firebird's tears had started, she couldn't stop. She hugged Aleksandr.

He squirmed and protested, "Mama, don't squish!"

"Mama's sorry." Firebird had yelled at Zorana, had hurt her son, all because she had learned the truth and hated it.

"Aleksandr." The lady on the couch patted the seat beside her. "Bring your book and come and sit with me."

Aleksandr looked at his mother. "Can I go sit with Karen?"

Ann answered her question before she could ask. "That's Adrik's wife. They got married last week."

Tasya indicated the gruff-looking older man who stood by the kitchen door, looking panicked by the overflowing emotions. "That's Karen's father. There was a battle with the Varinskis, and he helped."

"I was only gone one day." Firebird gazed at her long-lost brother, at his new wife. If things were normal, she would have spent the evening asking about his life, listening to his stories, meeting the people he'd brought home with him—his new wife and new father-in-law.

Distantly, she was ashamed for ruining Adrik's homecoming. But today . . . today she thought that things would never again be normal.

"Mama!" Aleksandr tugged at her shirt. "I want to go see Karen."

"Go on." She gave him a boost and watched him as he ran across the room. "He crawled at six months," she murmured. "He walked at nine months. He talked early. He puts together puzzles. He builds with blocks. He's so smart. . . ."

"We all love him." Tasya fumbled for the right thing to say. "He's still the only baby in the family."

Firebird laughed, a brief, slightly hysterical laugh.

The bathroom door opened and Zorana came out, her eyes red and damp.

Firebird scrambled to her feet and stood awkwardly. "Mama, I'm sorry."

Zorana hurried toward her.

They met in the middle of the living room.

"I know. I'm sorry, too." With all her strength, Zorana hugged Firebird.

Firebird hugged her back, and realized how great was the difference between them.

Zorana was exotic, five-one, and wiry, with black hair, and eyes so dark they looked black. Her skin was a beautiful, clear brown, tolerant of the sun and proof of her Romany heritage.

Firebird was five-four, blond and blue-eyed, with

fair skin that required the constant application of sunscreen. Her heritage was probably Irish or English or German. Not Russian, and not Romany.

Zorana said fiercely, "When you first looked at me, you captured my heart, and I don't care what that stupid Seattle doctor said. You are mine. My child. Forever."

All around the Wilders' cramped living room, Firebird's family sat or stood, sniffed or tried to smile or glared in impotent fury as they realized how they'd been betrayed by people they trusted. Firebird's three brothers, Jasha, Rurik and Adrik. Her three sisters-in-law, Ann, Tasya, and Karen. Karen's father. And Firebird's parents. Oh, God, her parents. She loved them all so much—and she was nothing to them.

Only her son was of her blood. Only Aleksandr, who sat tucked beside Karen, trusting because he'd never met anyone who wished him ill.

"You are the best mother anyone could ever have," Firebird told Zorana, and in a world full of sudden uncertainties, that, at least, was true.

"Too bad she named you for a car." Adrik had been gone far too long, yet he hadn't forgotten the family joke.

"No, you impudent boy. We named her after the legend of the bird with such brilliant plumage a single feather would light up the room. We knew our daughter would be like that." Konstantine, bound to his recliner by the terrible weakness generated by his illness, held out his arms to Firebrand and Zorana. "And so she is."

Zorana took Firebird's hand and went to him. Taking care not to disturb the IV line that ran into his arm, Zorana snuggled beside him.

Right now, Firebird didn't feel much like a hundred-watt lightbulb. She felt like a woman who had spent the day in Seattle giving blood and skin samples in the hopes of helping the doctors discover some link to her father's mysterious disease, and had instead discovered she was not the person she'd always thought she was. But her father—or rather, the man she'd always believed was her father—would soon struggle to his feet if she didn't respond, so she knelt by the recliner.

He cupped her face.

Zorana took her hand.

"You're our little girl," he said. "The pride of my heart, and now more special to me than ever."

Firebird knew he meant it, and—oh, God!—how she treasured that sentiment now!

Bending her head, she put it against his shoulder and closed her eyes, for one moment allowing herself to sink into the familiar safety of her parents' affection.

Then she sat back and smiled, and pretended nothing had changed, when in fact her whole world had tilted on its axis. "Enough excitement and angst for one evening. It's past Aleksandr's bedtime."

"No!" Aleksandr protested.

No matter how tired he was, he always protested. He wanted to be with his family, part of the action, playing, singing, stacking blocks. Some people probably thought he was spoiled; the Wilder family called him well loved.

Firebird scooped him up and carried him around so he could kiss everyone. Every aunt, every uncle, took extra care with him, showing their affection to the child, and thus to her. Konstantine reached up his arms for Aleksandr and held him close, rubbing his stubbled cheek against Aleksandr's hair and breathing in his essence. "I would have sworn he was going to be a wolf," he murmured.

The sentiment stabbed Firebird through the heart.

Zorana kissed Aleksandr, and hugged him as if she couldn't bear to let him go. Firebird knew it was more than mere sentiment; Zorana was thinking of the son who'd been stolen from her.

Firebird carried him upstairs to the bedroom she shared with her son.

The house was small and old, with acoustics that let everything echo through the corridors.

So Firebird paused in the doorway, waited and listened—and heard Zorana's low, broken voice say, "Where is my baby? What did they do with my baby?"

Chapter Five

Zorana's plaintive question haunted Firebird, but as she tucked her son into his pajamas, wrapped him in his blanket, and nestled Bernie, the soft yellow duck with the bright orange bill, in beside him, she understood.

How could she not? When Aleksandr was born, she had looked him over. She had thought he was skinny, with long toes and broad shoulders that had given her trouble during the birth, but he was hers, her son, and a fierce tide of protectiveness had risen in her. At that moment, she knew without a qualm that she would kill to protect him.

Now Zorana had discovered her baby, the one she'd given birth to twenty-three years and eight months ago, had been stolen, and she needed to know where he was.

As Firebird looked at her son, sleeping with his hand under his cheek, she knew she would feel exactly the same way.

The trouble was, knowing didn't make the sting of rejection any less painful.

She should wonder about her birth parents, she supposed, but right now, she didn't care about people she'd never met. She cared only about the family she knew, the battle they faced against evil, and whether she could help them . . . or whether she was nothing, superfluous, a burden.

She couldn't go back downstairs. She was tired, feeling sorry for herself, and embarrassed for feeling sorry for herself, because she wasn't the only one hurting here. She ought to go to bed, but worry buzzed in her mind like a swarm of bees. So she changed into a tough, warm outfit—jeans, sweatshirt, jacket, boots. Going to the window, she raised it, leaned out, and grabbed the branch of the huge tree that grew so conveniently close.

In her life, she'd been up and down it dozens of times—to run through the forest, or go to the movies, or kiss a boyfriend. But not recently. Single motherhood had had the effect of keeping her close to home. Her family thought it was because she took her responsibilities to her son seriously, and that was true.

But she also feared that if she wandered very far, Aleksandr's father would find her. Find them. And the consequences of that were too dreadful to contemplate.

Yet now . . . she was contemplating those consequences.

The tree was hard, frozen in the grip of a Washington mountain winter. The bark was icy beneath her bare hands. The broad branches supported her as she slid toward the ground, and above her, the black night sky glinted with glittering star chips. She landed on her feet and took a long, deep breath of air, her first since the doctor had broken the news.

Someone had traded the Wilder boy for her. For a changeling, an infant who had come from God knew where.

Firebird walked around the house, crunching the frozen grass beneath her boots. Quietly, she opened the front gate and strolled down the path toward the vines. Wrapping her arms around herself, she stood looking across the shadowed valley deep in the Cascades.

It stretched long and narrow between two mountains, a fertile plain her father and mother had found and bought for almost nothing, because a series of owners had tried to grow apples and tulips and vegetables—and failed. The soil was rich, but the weather was constantly overcast and wet, with too little sunshine for anything but stunted plants and mildewed fruit.

The people in the nearby soggy hamlet of Blythe had sniggered about the foolish Russian immigrants.

They didn't snigger now.

Konstantine had planted wine grapes. Zorana had planted a vegetable garden and a small orchard. And as if they'd brought the sunshine, the weather patterns changed. The valley—and Blythe—seemed protected by a clear bubble that let in the sunshine and just the right amount of rain.

By the time Firebird was born, the Wilders had established themselves in the community. All her life, this valley had been her home, and when she got pregnant, it had become her refuge.

Now the clear air, the cold temperatures, the relentless familiarity made her face the fact she had avoided all day long.

She had to leave.

As the realization struck her, as she imagined the repercussions, her whole body clenched. She stopped—stopped thinking, stopped breathing, stopped moving. For the first time in two and a half years, she let herself remember the first time she'd seen Douglas Black.

The weather had just turned to spring, and the entire student body responded by falling in love. All of them except Firebird. She was on the fast track, as always, finishing up her degree, and she didn't have time for love.

But when the hot new campus policeman strolled by, she discovered she had time to look. There was just something about a guy in uniform—or at least that guy in uniform—that worked for her. He stood tall and straight, with powerful shoulders tapering to a small waist, and he moved smoothly, his boots never making a sound. He had a hard, sculpted face, at odds with his obvious youth. His golden blond hair contrasted with his tanned skin, yet it was his eyes that captured her attention, eyes intent on her . . . eyes a dark, Gypsy brown.

After she walked past him, she turned to look at his butt and caught him doing the same thing to her. She was so embarrassed, she turned around and walked faster, her head buried in her books while she giggled.

It was painful to remember how gauche she had been, but she had been twenty, the protected daughter of a Russian immigrant family with strict morals and a protective streak. She'd lived with her father and brothers, so she knew a lot about men, but not so much what to do when men were interested in her. The few boys in Blythe who had shown an interest had a tendency to scamper away, never to return, after her father or brothers spoke to them. Nothing she could say ever changed that; her family saw no reason for her to date. If it were up to her father, Firebird had bitterly complained to Zorana, Firebird would live and die a virgin. Zorana had serenely agreed.

Firebird thought she would never see the hunk of a police officer again, but she had not yet realized who, and what, he was. That insight had come later, after she'd found herself swept off her feet, romanced and seduced. . . .

She covered her eyes with her fists, trying to fend off the memories that still had such power to hurt and humiliate.

What a fool she'd been.

She lifted her head.

What a fool she was now, standing out here alone.

From the time she was an infant, Konstantine had walked with her through the forest, teaching her how to listen, what to watch for, when to take flight, and when to stand and fight. He taught her the world was full of dangers, and only a fool was unprepared. He taught her exactly as he had his sons.

No, not exactly—more sternly, for she was a girl, and vulnerable.

Now, here she was leaving the safety of the house, wandering in the night, brooding and paying no attention to her surroundings, all because she imagined her home was safe.

But the forest was too silent.

Something was watching her.

Something hostile.

Something dangerous.

Papa would shout at her for carelessness, but first he would say, *Get back to safety, Firebird. Get back now.*

How to get to the house without alerting that thing out there that she was onto it?

She made a big deal of shivering and adjusting the band around her ears. Turning back toward the front porch, she walked briskly.

She slipped her hands in her coat pockets; in one, she carried a small switchblade, and she palmed it, then brought it out and held it to her chest. The other hand she brought out and swung as she walked, ready to use it as a weapon or a defense.

If she screamed, her family would come spilling out of the house, but it would be better if they could catch this thing unaware and question it. For she assumed it was human. Human . . . and something else.

Worse, if she screamed they would know she'd come out alone and attracted this thing, and been unable to handle it herself.

She *hated* when her brothers had to take care of things for her. They never let her forget it.

Behind her, she sensed movement—something coming out of the woods, daring the open ground to move toward her. The footfalls were almost imperceptible and still cautious, yet the hair rose on the back of Firebird's neck. Whoever or whatever it was, it was a predator, and it was angry.

She moved more quickly, her gaze fixed on the house where the lighted front room windows beckoned.

Behind her the pursuit intensified.

Her heart jumped in her chest. Her brothers and their teasing be damned.

She opened her mouth to scream.

Chapter Six

A drik opened the door. "Hey, Firebird, you out here?"

The predator behind her veered off.

She gave a gasp of relief. "I'm here." Giving in to her instincts, she ran the rest of the way to the porch. She leaped up the stairs and up to Adrik. Putting her face close to his, she whispered, "There's something out there."

Adrik glanced at the switchblade in her shaking hand. Sticking his head back inside, he spoke softly to his brothers, then stepped out onto the porch. Taking the blade, he shut it, handed it back to her, and casually scanned the area. "I smell him," he whispered. "He was on the porch."

Another proof that Firebird was not one of this family. Konstantine, Jasha, and Adrik had heightened senses of smell. Rurik saw with the vision of a hawk. They could track anything or anybody.

Firebird slid the knife back into her pocket.

From the time she had understood about her family and their special gifts, she had envied them, wanted to be like them.

Instead, she had always been completely normal, so normal she bored even herself.

So she'd driven herself to succeed: in school, in sports, especially in gymnastics. When she leaped between the parallel bars, it was the closest she could come to flying.

In the end, she'd reached too high and tried too hard to fly. She'd crashed to earth and shattered her leg. Even now, the cold made her ankle ache where the pins held the bones together.

"Is it . . . is it a Varinski?" she asked in a low voice.

"No. Or at least, not one like I've ever smelled." Reaching inside, Adrik grabbed a coat. He stepped out and shut the door behind him. "If it's a Varinski, it's a Varinski who's had a bath, and that's almost unheard-of."

She laughed, as he hoped, yet worried still. "Whoever it was wanted to hurt me. I could feel it."

He sobered. "They all want to hurt us. Make no mistake about that. They plan to kill us. You must be very careful, little sister. Very careful, indeed."

"I will. I am." But whether it was wise or not, this situation required a little daring.

"I feel like a little fresh air," Adrik said. "Do you want to stay out a few more minutes?"

To keep an eye on operations, he meant. "I'd like that," she answered.

They both knew that inside the house, Jasha and Rurik were changing as they ran to an exit. Jasha leaped out into the night transformed into a muscled

black wolf. Rurik took wing as a sleek hawk. Whatever was out there, they would find at least a trace
of it.

In a parody of casualness, Adrik and Firebird
walked to the edge of the porch, leaned their hands
against the railing, and stared out at the valley.

The hawk soared high into the air. The wolf loped
past, his nose to the ground.

Adrik watched them enviously, then allowed his
gaze to linger, as hers had done, on the length and
breadth of the valley. "I have missed this place. All
the long years that I've been gone, I dreamed of it,
longed for it, and hated myself for being unworthy
to return."

Firebird hadn't yet had the chance to speak with
her long-lost brother, and in the light beaming out
from the living room windows, she examined him.

Like Jasha and Rurik, he was tall and big boned,
but thinner, with the whipcord strength of a great
cat. A panther. "Now that you're back?"

"Karen loves me, and I saved her life. So she points
out, rather sarcastically, that if she's worth something, then I must be, too." Adrik watched the perimeter of the forest, vigilant, ready to fight and kill, if
needed. "She's who gave me the guts to return and
face Papa. I always thought he would throw me out,
and instead he . . . he welcomed me."

"Of course he did." Firebird tucked her hands
through Adrik's arm and hugged it. "How silly of
you to think he would do anything else. He's nothing
but a big marshmallow."

"To *you*. You're his daughter."

Not anymore.

"I was always the rebel son, and he came down hard on me. He used to nag me." Adrik imitated Papa's rumble, and the Russian accent that gave his voice its Old World flavor. " *'Don't drink, Adrik. Don't smoke. Don't change into a panther; the temptation brings you close to evil and you'll fall into the pit of hell.'* "

"Was he right?"

"Of course he was. I did fall into the pit of hell."

Firebird wanted to ask what he meant, how he'd lived, what had happened . . . but not now. Not when her own hell yawned before her. Not when she suspected that, in her fear and anger, she'd left the man she loved to burn in his own hell.

He could have confided in me. He could have told me who he was.

Yes, and you could have hung around long enough for him to explain. It's not like he didn't have a lot of chances to rip your throat out. And it's a pretty good bet that a man who brings a big, cuddly stuffed cougar as a graduation gift and gives you his first hints about his past is winding up for a big confession.

Unaware of her inner argument, Adrik continued, "Yet when I came back, Papa didn't yell at me or say, 'I told you so'; he simply opened his arms and hugged me as if I were his favorite—" His voice stopped, as if choked off by emotion.

She couldn't let her big strong brother humiliate himself and cry, so she smirked and said, "You remind me of Papa. You've done horrible things, but you've paid a great price. So now inside you're nothing but a big marshmallow, too."

Adrik looked sideways at her and cleared his throat. "You're too smart for your own good."

Her amusement slipped away, and with brutal honesty, she said, "If that were true, I wouldn't be in this damn shitting mess I'm in."

He went on alert. "What mess?"

She'd almost said too much, and this so-perceptive brother noticed. "What? It's not enough for me to discover I'm not related to the family? There has to be more?"

"I suppose not—but somehow, I thought your trouble was bigger than that."

"Climbing out the window and attracting something in the woods that wanted to stalk me is fairly awful, too." She felt as if she were dodging through a field of truth land mines. "I have never felt unsafe here. What's happening? How can everything change in an instant, in a breath?"

Adrik covered her hand with his. "It happens more often than you think—but it's not always bad. Sometimes the change is good, although you don't realize it at the time." He glanced inside, where Karen rested on the couch, recovering from her injuries.

"When you look at her, you look as slobbery as Jasha and Rurik do about their wives." Right then, Firebird's pang of envy felt more like a pain.

"You haven't had a chance to talk to Karen, but when you do, you'll see how wonderful she is." Adrik put his hand over his heart. "She saved me from the Darkness."

In this family, when they talked about the Darkness, they didn't mean a lack of light. They were talking about evil, and hell, and the devil, all concepts far too real in their lives.

"Then I love Karen as much as you do." Firebird hugged him.

"She found the third icon." He breathed each word with the quietness and delicacy of a man delivering a precious secret.

Firebird forgot about Jasha and Rurik seeking the predator. She forgot about the cold. She forgot that she wasn't a part of this family. She remembered only that she cared. "The third icon." Her voice was as hushed as his had been. "Of course. How stupid of me. I forgot about the icon."

"How could you? You were here when Mama had her vision."

"Yes. I was here." Firebird almost wished she'd been elsewhere. But then she'd be like Adrik, desperate to hear every detail.

"Tell me everything. I need to know." His eyes glowed in the dark.

"It was too . . . It was awful. I mean, I know that Papa always said Mama was the oracle of her tribe, but she never 'saw' the future." Firebird made air quotes with her fingers. "Not that I could tell, anyway. I figured she was a Gypsy fortune-teller; the tribe dressed her up in scarves, and she read your palm for a ruble. Two and a half years ago, on the Fourth of July, she changed my opinion. We had our usual bash with all the neighbors here." She remembered the heat of the day, the food, the drink, the fireworks . . . the secret she had hid in her belly. "It was a great party, except for one thing. Remember the Szarvases?"

"The hippie artists down the road?" He grinned. "Yeah, I do. Sharon and River. They've got a daughter, right? You were best friends? Her name is Dewdrop?"

"Her name is Meadow," Firebird said with crushing finality. "Are you going to listen, or are you going to tease?"

He sobered. "I'm listening."

"The Szarvases run an art colony, and they teach whoever shows up glassblowing and sculpture and whatever. I work for them in Internet sales, and it is a very profitable . . ." She caught herself, and turned to face Adrik, allowing her voice to reach no farther than his ears. "That day, they brought their usual contingent of apprentice artists, including this college kid who . . . He was quiet."

"Serial-killer quiet?" Adrik caught on fast.

"Exactly. He made a statue of me in clay, and it was the most uncanny thing I've ever seen. It looked *exactly* like me, and it really upset Mama. After all the guests left, the family was standing around the bonfire. Mama saw the statue on the table and smashed it with her fists. When she touched it, it was the clay that triggered something in her. When she turned back to the fire, she wasn't Mama." Firebird felt sick as she remembered. "Her voice didn't even sound human."

"What did it sound like?"

"Deep. Smooth. Flat. As if she were speaking from a long distance away, or from the bottom of a well."

"Do you remember what she said?"

"I wish I could forget." Firebird massaged her forehead. "She said, '*Each of my four sons must find one of the Varinski icons.*' Right away, that was impossible. We hadn't heard from you for years, and we thought I was . . . we thought I was the fourth child."

Adrik hugged her, but obviously he didn't know how to comfort her. And since she'd had experience with her brothers when they fumbled around, trying to be considerate and failing utterly, Firebird was just as glad.

"Mama said, 'Only their loves can bring the holy pieces home. A child will perform the impossible. And the beloved of the family will be broken by treachery . . . and leap into the fire.' "

"I get the part about our loves bringing the holy pieces home. But what does the rest of it mean?"

"Do I look like an oracle?" Firebird demanded.

"Does *she* know what it means?"

"Nope. Apparently it doesn't work that way."

Adrik pondered. "How did she look?"

"Like someone in a trance. I don't know how else to describe it. Believe me, you would recognize it if you saw it." Firebird shivered. "She said, 'The blind can see, and the sons of Oleg Varinski have found us.' "

"For sure they have." Oleg and Konstantine had been brothers, and when Konstantine had wed Zorana, Oleg had hunted them down, swearing to kill her and take Konstantine back.

Instead, Konstantine had killed Oleg, and his sons had vowed revenge—a revenge almost forty years in the making.

"Mama said, 'You can never be safe, for they will do anything to destroy you and keep the pact intact.' Then she pointed at Papa and said, 'If the Wilders do not break the devil's pact before your death, you will go to hell and be forever separated from your beloved Zorana, and you, my love, you are not long for this earth. You are dying.'" The mere memory made Firebird's palms grow sweaty. "Then Papa crashed to the ground. Ever since, he's been failing by inches."

Adrik tapped the railing with his fingers, then lowered his voice even more and told her, "Last year, when I was trying to figure out what was going on with the Varinskis and the Wilders, I went to the Ukraine and into the Varinski house—"

The Varinski homestead was famous in the Wilder family. They'd found pictures on the Internet; it was rambling, ramshackle and dirty, a frat house set in the middle of the steppes, stuffed with hard-drinking predators with no morals or discernible sanitary habits. "How did you sneak in?" she asked.

"Believe it or not, I walked in." At her disbelief, he shrugged. "There're so many of them, and they all look alike—"

"And you look like them." *More important, you're competent, smart, and frightening in your own way.*

Sometimes she forgot that her father and brothers were Varinskis—Varinskis with a name change, but Varinskis nonetheless.

Adrik continued, "There was this old guy, Uncle Ivan, and he's as sinister as anything I've ever seen. He drinks like a fish, he's feeble, and he's blind, with a film of white over his eyes. From what the Varinski boys were saying, Uncle Ivan occasionally has his own trances. Or something. One of the boys said, 'He speaks with the devil's tongue.' "

"What does *that* mean?"

"I couldn't ask. I was trying to be inconspicuous. But I know he told the Varinskis that they needed to get their hands on the women the Wilder men loved, because the women were the key to preserving the pact."

"Oh, no." Firebird was cold, and getting colder. This whole conversation sent fear crawling up her spine.

"He knew about Mama's vision, too. That's where I first heard about it." Adrik scanned the forest again. "May I say, we do have something in common with most of those Varinskis."

"Yeah, what?"

"They're creeped out by Uncle Ivan's visions, too. Make no mistake—they intend to wipe us from the face of the earth rather than let us destroy the pact."

The hawk winged toward them, dipped close to the porch, then flew over the roof.

"There's Rurik," Adrik said. "Jasha can't be far behind."

Firebird watched enviously.

"It's a good thing this is almost over," Adrik said in a low tone.

"If we live through the battle!"

Adrik grinned. "The doctor may have proved you're not related to us by blood, but you *sound* just like Mama."

"Sensible?" Firebird asked tartly.

"I suppose. But isn't it better to get this battle over with so we can be normal, like other men?"

Firebird laughed, genuinely amused on the worst evening—or was it the second-worst?—of her life. "You, my dear brother, will never be a normal man. Nor will Papa. Nor will Jasha. Nor will Rurik. You are and always will be creatures to be treated with respect."

The wolf who was Jasha ran across the lawn, gave them a nod in passing, and continued to the back of the house.

"Shall we go in and see what they have to say?" Adrik offered his arm. "Any bets?"

"Something was out there, but it got away before they found it—because if they'd found it, they would have taken it to the horse barn in back and interrogated it until it squealed."

"You're pretty smart for a little sister."

"Smarts run in the family." The irony of their discussion didn't escape Firebird, for she was about to do one of the two dumbest things she'd ever done in her life—and this time, she'd be lucky to get away unscathed.

The sun was a hint in the eastern sky when Firebird bent over the crib where her son slept, and brushed his hair off his forehead.

He was handsome and smart, a miniature of his father in face and form—except that Aleksandr's hair was dark and straight.

A tear dropped from her cheek onto Aleksandr's, and Firebird wiped it away, then wiped her damp face.

For more than two and a half years, she hadn't allowed herself to think about Douglas and their affair. Now she could think of nothing else.

Aleksandr popped his eyes open, awake as only a toddler could be—totally aware and without a hint of sleepiness. "Mama!" He reached out his arms.

She picked him up and held him close. "Aleksandr, Mama has to leave."

His lips stuck out. "No!"

"Yes. But listen." She put her hand over his little mouth. "Listen! While Mama's gone, she's going to get you something."

"What?" Rebellion still flashed in his brown eyes.

"Something you'll like very much."

Aleksandr considered her suspiciously. "What?"

"Something very special."

"What?" His arms flew into the air in an excess of toddler exasperation.

She laid him down, tucked his blanket around him, and handed him Bernie. "If you want this very special, very wonderful thing, you be good for Grandpa and Grandma. Brush your teeth. Take your naps. Take care of Bernie." Her hand lingered on the worn fuzz of his constant sleeping companion. "Can you do all that?"

"Yes!"

"Then I will go and get your daddy and bring him back to you."

Because Douglas Black was the Wilders' true offspring, their fourth son, their only hope . . . and only Firebird, his runaway lover, could convince him to help.

Chapter Seven

"**G**ramma?"

Zorana half woke at the sound of a little voice beside the bed. "Hm?"

"Aleksandr and Bernie get in with you and Grampa."

Zorana used her rear to urge Konstantine over. With a deep grumble, he moved.

Lifting the covers, she gestured Aleksandr and Bernie in. She hugged Aleksandr close, this grandson of hers, and felt another piece of her heart break.

Damn that doctor. Damn Miss Joyce. Most of all—for Zorana knew whom to blame—damn the devil and his machinations.

"Gramma, guess?" Aleksandr wiggled like a fish.

Never mind that it was barely dawn. He was awake, and he wasn't going back to sleep until he took his nap after lunch. "What?"

"Mama's going get Aleksandr a present."

"She is?" Zorana smiled. "What is she getting you?"

"My daddy!"

Zorana sat up, dislodging Konstantine on one side and Aleksandr on the other. "What?"

"My daddy. My daddy! Mama get Aleksandr my daddy!" His voice got louder with each repetition.

Zorana sat very still, her mind buzzing as she tried to put the pieces of this puzzle together. "Where is she getting your daddy?"

"Costco," Aleksandr said with impeccable childish logic.

Konstantine didn't sound at all sleepy as he rumbled, "Do you buy daddies at Costco?"

"Yes. And a new puzzle for Bernie." Aleksandr chuckled as he imagined the delights to come.

"Aleksandr, stay here. Grandma's going to go talk to your mama." Zorana started to climb over the little boy.

Konstantine stopped her with a hand on her arm. "Firebird left half an hour ago."

Zorana turned on him. "You heard her leave? And you didn't do anything?"

In the breaking dawn, he was a broad lump under the covers. Light glinted off the chrome of his oxygen tank and his IV pole, and she could dimly see the plastic tubes that ran up his nose and into his arm. Yet for all that the disease ate at his body, his eyes were still sharp and bright. "Zorana. *Liubov maya.* We have all had a horrible shock. But none of us has suffered as Firebird is suffering. If she felt she had to leave without telling anyone—"

"Aleksandr!" Aleksandr said helpfully.

"—without telling anyone except Aleksandr," Konstantine agreed, "then I know better than to stand in her way."

"But where is she going?" Zorana demanded.

"Costco," Aleksandr said. "For Aleksandr's daddy."

"That sounds reasonable to me." Konstantine tugged Zorana back down on the bed and put his arms around her and Aleksandr.

Zorana had never felt less sleepy. "All this time, she never would tell us who Aleksandr's father is. Why would she go find him now?"

"Last night, for Firebird, everything changed." Konstantine tapped his forehead.

Yes, and now Zorana's heart was torn. She loved the child she had cherished as a daughter, and she longed for the baby she had lost.

Tears sprang to her eyes. Tears for her, tears for Firebird, and, most of all, tears for her son.

Where was her baby? Happily adopted by another family? Abused and beaten? Or dead, an infant not allowed his chance at life?

She struggled to sit up. "I'm going to call Firebird. Tell her to be safe."

"No. You are not." Konstantine held her in place. "If she wanted to tell you where she was and how long she'd be gone, she would have woken you before she left. As for being safe . . . we have raised her to be smart, and be safe. But we also have raised her to do the right thing, the responsible thing, and we have to trust her to know what that is. She is a grown woman. Leave her alone to do what must be done."

Zorana relaxed and leaned her head into Konstantine's shoulder. "If I knew then what I know now, I would have never had children."

His laughter thundered through him. "Yes, you would."

"No, I wouldn't."

"Yes, you would. You had no choice. In those days, all the time, we were humping like bunnies."

"Konstantine!" Zorana covered Aleksandr's ears.

"Humping like bunnies," Aleksandr repeated in a clear, thoughtful tone.

"Aleksandr!" Zorana glared at her husband.

Konstantine stretched and grinned at her, looking young and carefree for the first time in months. "Those were the good old days."

Delighted, Aleksandr repeated, "The good old days. Humping like bunnies."

"Zorana, we have lived here for almost forty years. Your tribe swore to take you back from me. The Varinskis swore I was mad to love you, and that they would take me back. None of them ever found us—and they should have." Konstantine sounded less like Zorana's kindly husband and more like a general preparing for battle. "I never asked you why."

Her whirling thoughts stilled.

"But last night, a stranger came into our valley. Our very talented sons sought him, but despite their best efforts, they couldn't find him, and when we were alone, they told me he carried the scent of a great cat."

"A great cat," Aleksandr repeated thoughtfully.

"Yes, my boy." Konstantine stroked Aleksandr's

hair. "A panther, like *Dyadya* Adrik, or a tiger, a lion, a cougar. So the stranger was a Varinski, an enemy. I think perhaps for almost forty years you have been protecting us from prying eyes, and I think perhaps something has changed. Heh?"

How could Zorana have imagined she could fool Konstantine? Konstantine, who was so intimately familiar with the supernatural . . . and with her? "I don't talk about it. I don't understand how it works. But I am a seer. I foretell the future . . . but I have no control over when and where. I wish I did. Two and a half years ago, I burp forth a prophecy and our whole world goes to hell. If I could just tap into that power again . . ."

Again Konstantine hugged her, silencing her self-recriminations. "We are grateful for any knowledge sent to us by the good God."

"Yes. Of course we are." She hadn't meant to complain about what she did know, only what she didn't. Sitting up, she wrapped her arms around her knees. "I have another talent. It's a little thing. With my mind, I can make a bubble, like Teflon, over the place where I am. It wards off the bad things. Storms that would ruin the grapes or split the cherries. People who wish us ill."

"Yes." Konstantine understood. Of course he did. "So how did one of *them* get here last night?"

"Maybe he followed Firebird in. I think that might be it. Or maybe I . . . Lately I've wondered . . ."

"Wondered?" he encouraged.

"When we married, the line between good and evil blurred. There are still men, women, beasts who have given themselves totally to the devil. And there are men, women, and beasts who are completely God's creatures. But most people are struggling to do the right thing, and succeeding or failing. You and I and our kids . . . we fit into that group. And maybe whoever it was last night—maybe he fits into the group, too. Wanting to do evil, but not easy with his decision, or evil and struggling toward a change." Zorana turned her head to Konstantine. "He was one of us."

"Yes. You're right. The old rules don't count anymore. The whole world is changing. The time is approaching when we fight the devil's own. And we need to plan our attack."

"We don't know when or where the battle will take place."

"We don't wait for them to make that decision." Konstantine sounded stronger than he had for months. "We decide where—"

"Here?"

"Definitely here. And when. We must plan our strategy, and the first thing we have to do . . . is talk to our known enemies."

"Enemies," Aleksandr said cheerfully.

"Yes, my boy." Again Konstantine caressed Aleksandr's head. "We have enemies."

Zorana didn't even have to think. "I know exactly who to start with."

Chapter Eight

Zorana watched as her sons, the Wilder demons, walked toward the van, their arms swinging confidently, their grins flashing. At the last second, they all made a dash toward the driver's seat. Adrik won by the simple strategy of slamming open the back door and leaping over the seats.

Stupid kids. They hadn't changed a bit.

As Jasha and Rurik stood outside and stared in disgust, Adrik said, "Just like old times."

"Yeah, you're the same pain in the ass you always were," Jasha said.

"Shotgun," Rurik called.

Zorana walked up behind them. "I'll ride shotgun." Taking advantage of their horror, she hopped into the front beside Adrik. "You boys get in the back." When none of them moved, she mocked, "You didn't think I would let you go by yourselves, did you?"

Jasha, always her responsible son, said, "Mama, I don't know if this is a good idea. This probably won't be pretty."

"I don't care about pretty. I want to *know*." Out of the corner of her eye, she saw Rurik nod.

"It's your right, Mama." Adrik turned the key. "You guys getting in, or are you going to chase us all the way to Miss Joyce's?"

As the two climbed in, Adrik asked, "Has anybody ever suspected Miss Joyce before?"

"Not one bit," Jasha answered. "But we should have. She's always been around, watching us, poking her nose into our business."

"In all fairness, she pokes her nose into everyone's business." Rurik tapped his mother's shoulder. "Better buckle yourself in, Mama. Adrik drives like a maniac."

Zorana buckled her seat belt. "What's new? You all always did that."

"Adrik's practiced," Rurik said.

Miss Joyce lived in a little house built in the twenties, suitable for a schoolteacher with no family: one bedroom, one bath, a living room, a tiny kitchen, and a minuscule lawn surrounded by a white picket fence. The place was not far from the edge of town, yet isolated by a stretch of meadow, and the people of the town respected Miss Joyce's privacy.

Zorana pulled open the screen door and knocked.

Privacy. Yes. Miss Joyce would want privacy to hide the truth about herself from her students, her neighbors . . . from the rest of humanity. For she was a monster. A monster.

The silence was profound. The winter sun shone

in the bright blue sky, casting sharp shadows but shedding no warmth.

Zorana waited for an uncomfortably long time, then glanced back at her sons, lined up against the van parked on the side of the road.

Jasha looked solid and businesslike, and nothing about his appearance hinted at the passionate soul Ann had fought for and captured.

Rurik retained the dash of an Air Force pilot and the pragmatism of one of the world's leading archeologists.

Adrik . . . Adrik still nursed a bone shattered in the fight that had almost taken his Karen's life. He had plunged into the depths of evil and barely escaped. He was harder than the other two, broken and rebuilt into a different man, and Zorana had not been there for any of his trials.

"For all that she has done, I will make her sorry," Zorana vowed quietly.

She raised her hand to knock again. Then she heard it: the shuffle of feet across wood floors. The curtain at the front tweaked aside enough for one eye to peer out of the dusty glass.

Slowly, the locks unlatched, the door creaked open a few inches, and Miss Joyce examined her.

Miss Joyce looked surprisingly short. Almost . . . shrunken.

"Zorana, how nice to see you. I wish you'd called . . . I'm in the middle of something right now. . . ." She waved a vague hand into the house.

"I've got a surprise for you." Zorana placed the

flat of her hand on the door to keep it open. "News about one of your students. You always love to hear news about your students."

"So, tell me," Miss Joyce said querulously.

"Let me show you."

"That's nice, dear." Her voice quavered like an old woman's. Which she was, but always before she'd shown few signs of age. "But I haven't been feeling well. . . ."

"I won't take no for an answer." Zorana smiled, but she was implacable.

Miss Joyce looked from side to side, seeking an escape.

Did she realize that the time of reckoning had arrived?

"Let me get my coat and hat."

"I'll wait inside." Zorana pushed the door open.

The stench struck her like a blow.

Miss Joyce, who had always kept an impeccable house, now lived in filth, with newspapers piled on the floor, dust on all the surfaces, and . . . somewhere, something was rotting in here.

"Pardon the mess. I haven't had a chance to straighten up." Miss Joyce struggled into her coat, pulled on her gloves, and grabbed her large straw hat off the rack by the door. Shoving Zorana outside, she followed her out. Carefully she locked the door— no one locked their doors in Blythe—then turned and smiled with false brightness.

Zorana was shocked. The sunlight showed the changes the winter had wrought on the school-teacher.

Always before she'd been proud of the way she

shed the years. She'd been tall, erect, with a full head of wavy gray hair and strong features. Now everything was withered: Her prominent nose was a blob, her stubborn chin had receded, her bones had bent and curved—she was now no more than Zorana's height. And she smelled. Smelled like her house.

What was rotting in there was *her*.

"You aren't well," Zorana said softly.

Miss Joyce stopped smiling, tucked her shriveled lips over her twisted teeth, and mumbled, "It's been a long winter." She donned her hat and looked around. "Now, what about a student?"

Zorana gestured her toward the yard.

Miss Joyce clung to the rail and took each step on shaking legs.

Zorana didn't touch her. Didn't help her. A deep-seated revulsion kept her back. When Miss Joyce had reached the walk and Zorana knew she could not easily regain the house, she called, "Boys!"

Jasha, Rurik, and Adrik straightened up from the van and strode toward them.

Miss Joyce adjusted her glasses on her nose and stared at them. "Yes, yes, it's your three boys. I can see that. The family resemblance—" She stopped, gasped. "The Wilder demons. All three of you."

Adrik stopped before her. "Yes. It's true, Miss Joyce. I'm alive."

"That's good." Miss Joyce took a step back. "Nice."

"Nice?" With the speed of a hawk, Rurik moved behind her and cut off any escape. "Is that all you can say about Adrik's return from the dead?"

Jasha moved to the other side. "You're the one who brought us the news that he'd been killed. Remember? You came to our door with an envelope and told us the post office had delivered it to you by mistake."

"How convenient that it was delivered to *you*, of all people," Zorana said.

"You knew us." Rurik silently glided between Miss Joyce and her house. "You knew just where to deliver the news."

"Lucky," Miss Joyce croaked.

"And the envelope was open." Jasha joined Rurik, pacing with the stealth of a wolf.

"Did you laugh when you read the news?" Zorana asked.

"No. No! How awful! No, of course not. I wouldn't laugh about the death of one of my favorite . . . um, one of my students." Miss Joyce looked around at the circle of unfriendly eyes. "I need to sit down."

"Of course. How rude of us not to consider your sickness." Jasha leaped up on her porch, grabbed the wooden chair, and brought it back, placing it behind her. "Sit."

"I'd rather sit inside. Or on the porch." Miss Joyce glanced uneasily at the bright blue sky. "I have a skin condition."

Zorana didn't believe that for a minute. "Is that why we've never seen you expose yourself to the sun?"

Adrik leaned in and snatched her wide-brimmed hat away.

Miss Joyce covered her eyes, staggered backward,

and, when the chair struck the backs of her legs, she collapsed onto it. Gradually, she took her shaking hands away.

The sunlight revealed what the hat's shadows had concealed. Her skin was covered with a tracery of pale scars that instantly reddened in the sun.

"So the rumors are true," Zorana said. "You were attacked by your students."

"The little bastards—they cut me with their knives. Broke my bones with a tire iron. Laughed . . ." Miss Joyce glared at Zorana's sons. "They got away with it, too. They were tried as juveniles, given the minimum sentence because of their deprived backgrounds. I hate . . . I hate . . ."

"It wasn't my boys who hurt you," Zorana pointed out.

"They're all the same. Men . . . vermin . . ." Miss Joyce caught herself. She shrank into herself and mewled, "I mean, I know, but the sunlight hurts my skin and I can't see very well."

A patch of her hair fell out, revealing a shiny pink scalp.

"Is that why you made a deal with *him*?" Adrik asked.

"I don't know who you mean, dear." Miss Joyce's voice got a little higher, a little thinner.

"With the devil. Is that why you made a deal with him?" Adrik's green-and-gold eyes rested on Miss Joyce without sympathy. "For revenge?"

"No!" Miss Joyce jerked as if surprised by her own admission.

"Then why?" Rurik asked.

She looked around at the trap they had set for her. Looked around and saw their implacability, and she wailed like a child. "Because of the *pain*. You don't know what it's like to have all your joints broken, to be burned and cut. I was a good-looking woman, strong and dedicated. I turned them in because their gang was evil, pure evil, stealing, raping, killing, and what did I get as a reward? I was almost killed. Mutilated. The doctors told me I would never walk again. Told me I'd be on medication for the rest of my life. And when I wanted to die, they told me no, I would live a long life. Would you want that? Would you?"

"So when the devil came to you, you agreed to his deal. He would take the pain away, and you would move here and do his bidding." Adrik seemed to understand all too well how the devil worked.

"Yes," Miss Joyce hissed. She was visibly shriveling.

"Why didn't the devil destroy us himself?" Jasha asked.

Miss Joyce wrung her hands over and over, and each time she did, the bones inside the gloves seemed to warp a little more. "It doesn't work that way. *He* can't interfere directly. He can only give a little push and prod and hire people to work for him. He's not in charge, you know. Please. Rurik. You've said very little. Obviously you don't approve of persecuting your favorite old schoolteacher. Give me my hat."

"You misunderstand, Miss Joyce," Rurik said smoothly. "We're not persecuting you. We're asking for the truth. Is that too much to expect?"

All three boys circled her now, while Zorana stood still in front of her, arms crossed.

"Zorana . . ." Miss Joyce faltered. "I've always been your friend. . . ."

"You delivered my baby."

"Yes. When that stupid doctor passed out and couldn't do it." But Miss Joyce couldn't look Zorana in the eyes.

"I think back and I remember—he was drunk when he got there. He gave me drugs I didn't want. And after he fell over, I heard a thump. Did you knock him out?"

"Why would I do that?"

"So you could trade my son for a girl."

Miss Joyce's ample, sagging bosom heaved up and down, up and down. "Why would you think such a thing?"

"We don't think. We know." Zorana stepped forward, through the circle her sons had formed, and knelt before Miss Joyce. She stared into her eyes. "Can you imagine what I felt when I realized my son had been stolen from me? No, of course you can't. You never think of someone else. You think only of yourself."

Miss Joyce laughed, long and loud, and before their eyes, she discarded her pretense of caring and kindness. "Poor Zorana! Poor little immigrant with her handsome husband and her strong sons and her special gifts, always surrounded by love and support. I'm supposed to feel sorry because I took one of your kids? So what? I left you one in its place. And you were so proud of her. Acted like she was the second coming, when all she was was one of the abandoned ones. He found her and brought her to me and told me what to do. Maybe I wasn't happy about doing it, but he reminded me what I owed him. You didn't lose anything by what I did." She smirked, transfixed by her own confession. "Except you can never break the pact, because you don't have four sons."

"You know about the pact? *He* knows about the prophecy?"

"*He* knows everything. *He* watches everything."

Adrik snorted derisively. "Is that what he told you?"

"He's the devil. He wouldn't—"

"Lie to you?" Zorana finished softly.

Miss Joyce realized how stupid she sounded. How stupid she'd been. At once her shoulders slumped with an audible crack. She flinched, caught her breath, and struggled to speak. "You're right. He did lie to me. He told me he would take my pain away and let me live as long as I did his bidding. But when your children were grown and you spouted your damned prophecy, he didn't need me anymore." She gave a sudden wail. "I'm in pain. All the time in pain, and no matter what I do, he won't come back to me. I sacrifice to him, but my body's rotting. Rotting while I live."

"It looks as if the sun is accelerating the process." Rurik watched as the scar on her cheek opened to the bone.

Miss Joyce cast him a glance of such venom, he stepped back.

"What did you do with my baby?" Zorana stood up over her. "What did you do with my son?"

Miss Joyce turned coy. "What will you do for me if I tell you?"

"How desperate are you to stay alive?" Zorana asked softly.

Miss Joyce lifted her misshapen hand to shade her eyes, and stared at Zorana. "You'd have your sons kill me?"

"I'd kill you myself."

Miss Joyce stared into Zorana's eyes and saw the truth. Zorana not only *could* kill her—she *would*.

"I put it in the car and drove it to Nevada. It screamed the whole last eight hours." In a tone of pride, she said, "I put it out in the night, in the desert, and drove away. But I didn't murder it. That would have made me like the boys who attacked me." Spittle foamed at the corners of her mouth. The old woman had succumbed to madness.

Zorana slowly backed away from her. "My baby wasn't an *it*. He was a *boy*."

"All the better reason to kill it before it could grow up like *them*." Miss Joyce waved her deformed hand at Zorana's sons.

Zorana clenched her fists and took a step forward. Miss Joyce cowered, her arms above her head.

Rurik caught Zorana's arm. "No, Mama," he whispered.

"I'm a pathetic old woman who has been abandoned by her master and left to die in anguish," Miss Joyce whispered hoarsely. "Surely that's punishment enough."

The boys glanced at one another, revulsion writ plain on their faces.

Rurik handed Miss Joyce her hat.

As she put it on her head, Zorana caught the glint of triumph sparkling in her eyes.

Snatching the hat away, Zorana glared at her sons. "No. No, no, no!"

"Mama, are you sure?" Adrik put his arm around her. "Don't do something you'll later regret."

"She took the job of a schoolteacher, a protector and teacher of young children, and taught us to trust her while she did everything in her power to destroy us. Adrik, she told us you were dead. Firebird ran away because of this woman's treachery." Taking a sobbing breath, Zorana whispered, "Most of all, she tore my son from my arms. She deprived you of your brother. Because of her, we can never break the pact, and your father will burn in hell for all eternity. She left my baby to die of starvation and dehydration, or freeze to death under the indifferent stars, or be eaten alive by animals." She crushed the straw brim between her fists. "She can't stand the sun because she made a deal with the devil. If she can make it back to the house, she'll live."

"That's not fair!" Miss Joyce said.

Zorana glanced one last time at the evil, leprous hulk that was Miss Joyce. "It will be as God wills. That's a better chance than you gave my baby."

"You're right, Mama." Taking the hat, Adrik tossed it into the high branches of a tall pine.

Zorana walked toward the van. "Come on, my sons. Let's go home."

Chapter Nine

Doug Black was the first responder on the scene, and all he knew was that a mother and her two kids had missed the curve passing Shoalwater State Park and rolled their SUV.

As he drove up, he caught a glimpse of the late-model GMC Denali half-hidden a good two hundred feet down a slope and in the woods. Branches and moss were tossed everywhere, the rhododendrons had been ripped to shreds, and the forest floor was plowed down past the needles to the dirt.

Yeah, they'd rolled it, all right.

The witness on the scene, a middle-aged white female, ran up to his car as soon as he parked in the lot. He opened the door and caught the scent of blood on the cold air.

Someone was badly hurt.

The witness started talking, and talking fast. "I bought a doughnut and coffee in Rocky Cliffs and stopped in the parking lot for breakfast. It's empty this time of year. Quiet. I like that. I watched her come up the road. Speeding. She was speeding. Driving too fast."

As Doug pulled his emergency kit from his trunk, he appraised his witness. She looked shocky herself, pale and sweaty, kept upright only by her need to report what she'd seen.

"I know her. Ashley Applebaum. Poor thing. I saw her look back. She missed the curve, rolled three times. My God, it was awful. I've never seen anything like that. Not in real life, I mean." The witness stood shaking in cold and fear.

"You're Mrs. Shaw? You called it in?" He strode out of the parking lot and into the woods, toward the wisp of steam and smoke that rose through the trees like a campfire.

Mrs. Shaw followed him, still talking fast. "Yes, yes, I called at once, then I went over to help. Ashley's hurt . . . really badly."

Suddenly Mrs. Shaw wasn't behind him.

He glanced back.

She leaned one hand against a tree and vomited.

He jumped over some rocks, got his first clear glimpse of the wrecked vehicle, and appraised it with a practiced eye. Bark and needles from the shaken tree still sifted out of the sky, trying to cover the accident. All the windows were broken. The metal had crumpled like aluminum foil.

Yeah. They'd be lucky if no one was killed.

Then Mrs. Shaw was behind him again. "Ashley told me to get the kids out. I tried to, but I can't figure out how to work the child restraints. I'm sorry. So sorry!" She gave a sob that would have made him feel sorry for her if he hadn't been so focused on his job.

"It's okay, Mrs. Shaw. I'll do it." Thank God the children had been restrained, or they would never have survived in that crumpled mess of a vehicle.

"Will it blow up? Do you think it will blow up?"

"It might." For sure, they were headed for a car fire.

"I couldn't stand it if—"

He interrupted her self-recriminations. "Are the kids okay?"

"In pretty good shape."

"How old?"

"The boy's seven, I think. The baby's three months. She won't stop crying, but except for some glass cuts, she looks okay. The little boy is in worse shape. I think maybe his hand is broken, but—" Mrs. Shaw broke off and started the whole story again. "She was driving too fast. I saw her look back. She missed the curve. She looked back. Why did she look back?"

"She must have been talking to the kids." He stopped Mrs. Shaw in a sheltered spot in the trees. "Stay here. I'll bring them to you."

Mrs. Shaw kept talking as he walked away. "I don't think she was talking to the kids. That's not what it looked like. It looked like she was scared, like she was watching the road behind her."

He opened the back door. The scent of blood grew stronger. He leaned in.

"I didn't even know she could drive," Mrs. Shaw called.

The baby was strapped into her car seat and crying, a low, despairing, weary wail.

The black-haired boy was silent, cradling his arm and watching everything with wide, dark eyes.

Mrs. Shaw was right. They weren't badly hurt.

In the front seat, the mother stared straight in front of her, her head tilted at an odd angle, her shoulders drawn up in pain. "It's okay, sweetheart. It's okay, baby. Don't cry. Don't cry." She spoke softly, saying the same thing over and over again.

She was the source of the blood. Blood spattered across the dash, across the ceiling, and into her dark hair.

"Mrs. Applebaum, this is State Patrolman Doug Black," he said.

She stopped speaking.

"I'm going to get your children out now."

"Hurry," she said.

"I will." As he pulled the baby seat free of the restraints, he nodded to the boy. "Hi, there." He turned to place the seat on the ground, and Mrs. Shaw was there, taking the baby from him and heading back up the hill.

Frightened to death and still doing what she thought was right. Thank God for people like her.

He leaned back into the car and across the seat, and smiled at the boy. "I'm Officer Doug. I'm here to help you." He frowned at the seat belt. The impact had smashed the door against the boy's cushion, and the cushion now covered the connection. No wonder Mrs. Shaw couldn't get him out. "What's your name?" Doug asked.

"Andrew."

"Andrew, I'm going to have to cut you free." Doug opened his emergency kit and pulled out his knife.

Andrew flinched back, turning so pale that his dark eyes looked like two black holes in white snow, watching the shiny blade. "I didn't cry. I didn't cry at all. I'm sorry about my wrist. Please don't—"

"Don't you hurt him!" Ashley Applebaum's voice rose, and she looked as if she were trying to wrench herself around. "You bastard, don't you hurt him!"

Doug slid the knife under the belt and cut Andrew free. "I didn't hurt him, Mrs. Applebaum." He dropped the blade onto the ground, and he offered his hand. "Come out, Andrew. I need you to help Mrs. Shaw with the baby."

Andrew looked at Doug's broad palm and long fingers, then eased from the seat and inched across to the open door.

Doug stepped back and let him maneuver his way out. Better that than trying to wrestle the frightened child free.

When Andrew stood beside the car, Doug pointed to Mrs. Shaw, up the hill and kneeling beside the baby seat. "That's Mrs. Shaw. Can you go help her take care of your sister?"

The boy looked at him. Just looked at him.

"I'm going in after your mother next." Doug told him.

"Is she going to live?" Andrew was far too solemn, far too knowledgeable.

"I'll let you know as soon as I've looked at her. Go on, quickly. Ask Mrs. Shaw to make you a splint for your wrist."

Andrew went at once, as if the one question was all he dared ask.

Doug tried the front passenger-side door, but it wouldn't open, so he crawled in the back, dragged his emergency kit behind him, placed it on the seat, and crawled over the bloody front seat to Ashley Applebaum.

The smell of death rolled off her in waves.

The steering column had pierced her below the ribs and impaled her liver and intestines. Glass had ripped a face already gaunt and worried. She was dying. Inexorably, she was dying.

"I got the kids out. They're going to be fine." He took his handkerchief from his pocket. "I'm just going to tie this on your forehead to keep the blood out of your eyes." He did, and asked, "Is that better?"

"It doesn't hurt so bad." She took long, deep breaths impeded by internal bleeding. "Listen. No matter what happens, you won't let their father have my babies?"

He knew why she begged so pathetically. He'd heard Mrs. Shaw call her "Poor Ashley," seen Andrew cringe at the sight of his knife, heard the boy beg as if he feared for his life.

Their father abused them. Hurt them.

"Where is their father?" he asked.

"At the house. I hit him. With the fireplace poker. He's unconscious. . . ." Ashley Applebaum gasped, a dying animal. Then she gripped Doug's wrist. "Don't go after him. He sells bombs."

"Shit." Doug pulled his phone out of his pocket

and dialed his chief, Yamashita, and gave him the information.

Ashley continued, "Bill sells the bombs to the white men, the ones who hate the Jews and the blacks and the Mexicans. And I . . . I fixed it so that when he got up from the floor, all the bombs would go off."

"Where do you live?" He waited with his phone in his hand, ready to pass the information to Yamashita.

"Off Highway Six." She sagged as consciousness slipped away from her.

He gave Yamashita his report, and when he was done, Ashley was back, awake, but barely.

"He branded her. Just like he branded me."

"Branded you?"

"With his ring. He heats it up and . . . it hurts so bad." She jerked and shuddered in anguished memory.

Doug felt the familiar, helpless horror tighten his muscles, but he pulled out a wet towelette and gently wiped her face. "It's okay," he said in the same soothing tone she'd used for her children

"He could do that to me. I was worthless . . . but not her. She's just a baby. . . ." Ashley Applebaum's breath came irregularly. "Don't let him get her. She's such a sweet thing . . . and Andrew . . . he doesn't know what real life is like. . . ." As if she could see him, she turned her face toward Doug. "Don't let him have them."

He wanted to promise her he would accede to her dying wish.

Yet the courts didn't care. They would keep the

nuclear family intact. They would give the children to their father.

She knew what the reality was. Painfully, she turned her head toward him, her eyes almost blind with oncoming death. "If God is just, Bill will blow himself to kingdom come before anyone has the chance to rescue him."

Yet Doug knew justice wasn't so clean. "If he doesn't get the kids, they'll go to an orphanage, to a foster home."

"Anything will be better than staying with him." Tears slipped from beneath the handkerchief over her eyes.

"You don't know what you're talking about." He had never meant anything so much in his life.

"*You* don't know what *you're* talking about." Each breath was irregular, a pain in her chest. "Pray that I killed him. Pray . . ."

A muffled explosion blasted the air. The ground shook, rattling the SUV.

She smiled, a bare, ghastly grimace of justified pleasure. "There it is. There it is. I've only done one thing right in my life, and that's it. He's gone."

Ashley Applebaum died right before Doug's eyes.

The Denali was smoking, and he needed to be out of here. Yet he cupped her eyes with the palm of his hand and closed them, cherishing her lost life for one last moment.

Then he leaned over the seat, slipped into the back, grabbed his kit, and was out the door. He ran up the hill, away from the impending car fire and toward

the small group—the baby, the boy, Mrs. Shaw—
huddled on the hill.

He heard the sirens in the distance. The sheriff, the
state police, the EMTs—they were all on their way.
Kneeling beside Andrew, Doug hugged his shoulders.

"My mother . . . ?" Andrew saw the answer in
Doug's face. He gave a convulsive sob. "My
mother . . ."

Doug held the boy as he cried.

Mrs. Shaw looked up grimly. "Look what Andrew
showed me." She peeled back the baby's onesie and
displayed the little girl's shoulder. A brutal red burn
had ripped a mark like a lion's face into the smooth,
clear pale skin. "That bastard Applebaum branded
the baby, the same as he did to Ashley on their wedding night."

"That explosion?" Doug looked meaningfully at
Mrs. Shaw. "She finished him."

"It couldn't have happened to a nicer guy," Mrs.
Shaw said sarcastically.

The ambulance and the county sheriff ripped into
the parking lot, sirens blaring.

Andrew grabbed Doug's arm and dug his fingers
into the flesh. "The baby girl doesn't matter, right?
Girls are possessions. Just possessions. We have to
show them who owns them." The boy repeated his
father's credo as if it were gospel, but still he cried,
big, childish tears at odds with his cruel sentiments.

Doug looked into his eyes. "Girls are people. They
should be cherished. They should never be hurt.
That's not right. That's never right."

"Really?" Andrew looked into Doug's eyes and sagged with relief. "You mean it?"

"No man has the right to hurt a woman. Never. Never." Doug had never meant anything so much in his life.

Looking up at the branches waving in the early-morning light, he remembered his first glimpse of Firebird after more than two and a half years. He'd used tax records to track her to Szarvas Artist Studio, where she worked. Sitting outside the big compound, he'd waited and told himself that it wouldn't matter, that she wouldn't be as pretty as he remembered.

And she wasn't.

She was beautiful, and she had taken his breath away.

Maturity had given her a depth and a glow that no cosmetics could produce. Then he'd tried to follow her home and couldn't, stopped by a capricious mountain fog that enclosed her like a prison.

So he'd come back the next day, intending to confront her, but one of her big hulking brothers drove her, delivering her right to the door and following her in as if she couldn't be trusted to go by herself. After that, Doug had watched, and he recognized the signs—the domineering men, the mother he never saw, the sister who went nowhere except to work and back, and half the time her brother drove her. . . .

The bright, outgoing girl he'd remembered was now held prisoner by the family she had been so careful not to discuss.

That explained so much—why she hadn't trusted him, why she had abandoned and hurt him.

The EMTs and the sheriff surrounded him, wanting a report, needing him to help calm Andrew so they could take the baby for examination. He did his job, all the while steeled in resolve.

No matter that he'd suffered from Firebird's rejection, by her lack of confidence in him, he had to save Firebird from the family that abused her.

Someday she would thank him.

Someday.

Chapter Ten

A t nine in the morning, Firebird drove along the Pacific Coast Highway, winding through dense groves of Sitka spruce, past Shoalwater State Park, where she caught a glimpse of police and ambulance lights in the parking lot, and at last pulled into the scenic overlook above the town.

Cliffs framed either side of the half-moon bay. The old town nestled down by the water, while, in search of the view, old and new homes spread up the surrounding hills. The Internet said Rocky Cliffs boasted a thousand permanent residents, and that the town swelled to five times that during the summer tourist season.

She drove slowly down the terminally quaint Main Street, with a clothing store that featured bathing suits and coverups, a diner that featured hot coffee and world-famous napoleons, and a remodeled, early-twentieth-century hotel. Down on the pier, the windows of a souvenir shop proudly displayed sea-shell treasure chests and Japanese fans. A sign for the restaurant at the top of the cliff boasted fresh Dungeness crab and smoked salmon.

Rocky Cliffs didn't seem like Douglas's kind of place at all.

Her car surprised her by turning into the When You Are Wicked Diner. Even as she walked in and sat at one of the tables, she scolded herself. She knew what Douglas did here, and where he lived. She had decided on the way she wanted to handle the confrontation. So why was she stalling now?

Because he was going to be angry, and rightfully so. If she'd realized . . . Well, it was far too late for recriminations.

"What can I get you?" The middle-aged waitress stood beside her, a name tag that said she was Gloria on the downward slope of her right breast.

"Bacon, crisp, a Denver omelet, wheat toast, a large orange juice, a large coffee, black, and one of your world-famous napoleons."

The waitress grinned as she scribbled down the order. "I pegged you as one of those women who eat nothing but plain yogurt and herb tea. That'll teach me to make assumptions."

"I like to eat," Firebird assured her. "And I've been on the road for four hours."

Gloria disappeared to put the order in, and returned with the coffeepot. "Where'd you come from?"

"North of Seattle." Before Gloria could press for more information, Firebird dug the address out of her purse. "I'm looking for Three Twenty-three Seaview Road."

Gloria's eyes sharpened as she poured. "That's the old Quackenbush place."

"Quackenbush? Really?" Firebird smiled. "I don't know about that. I'm looking for Douglas Black. He and I are friends." That was an understatement.

"Doug Black? He's only been here a couple of months." Gloria viewed Firebird sharply. "We were starting to wonder if he had any friends."

"It takes him a while to warm up, but once he does, he's really a lot of fun." An unexpected flush warmed Firebird's cheeks.

"First time I saw him, I thought that myself," Gloria said with bawdy good humor.

"I didn't mean it like that."

"Built like a brick outhouse, that boy is. Not that I've ever seen him with a single button undone. He's young, but he's everything you expect from a state trooper. For sure not what I'd call the life of the party." Gloria whisked off, then returned with Firebird's order. "Is he expecting you?"

Firebird inspected her plate, piled high with a cholesterol-rich feast. "Looks great! No, I don't think Douglas knows I live in the neighborhood." Although perhaps he did. Discovering he lived so close had caused Firebird a pang of alarm. He was, after all, a hunter, and one unlikely to forget prey that had escaped him.

Gloria nodded. In the west, with its vast spaces and towering mountains, its brutal ocean and winding roads, "the neighborhood" encompassed anywhere within a day's drive. "The Quackenbush place seemed like an odd choice for him. It's in a little need of repair."

"Douglas is good with his hands." Firebird blushed

again, harder this time. Had she been hiding at home so long she couldn't even make normal conversation?

"I suspected that about him, too," Gloria agreed, and her eyes twinkled. "It's the quiet ones, or so I've always heard."

"He doesn't talk much." Because he was so busy hiding secrets.

"He's done a lot of the big jobs already—had all the wiring and plumbing replaced, and the whole place reinsulated. He's started on the interior—Sheetrock and paint, flooring and cabinets. It's a gigantic effort, not worth it, in my opinion—but he's not interested in my opinion."

"I don't know that he ever listens to anyone."

"Not to mention the fact that he has to be independently wealthy to afford to buy the place—the location is prime real estate—and renovate it." Gloria's face warmed with curiosity, and she leaned forward, ready to hear any confidences Firebird might share.

"I don't know about his finances. We're not that kind of friends."

Gloria's face fell. The bell tinkled at the door, and she wandered off to take care of a party of four—travelers, by the look of them—then two guys dressed like construction workers who sat at the bar.

Gloria came back when Firebird had demolished most of the food on the plate, and warmed up her cup of coffee. "Looks like you're slowing down."

"I'm going to have to admit defeat, but you guys aren't kidding. This *is* the world's best napoleon." Firebird sighed with pleasure.

"I'm living testimony." Gloria patted her ample waist. "Listen, I don't think he's home."

"Douglas?"

"Early this morning, I saw him heading out toward one-oh-one. Probably out there picking up folks for speeding. Picked me up once. Gave me a lecture on how important I was to the community, and how speeding was going get me killed, and all the while he watched me with those dark brown eyes, like he was reading my future." Gloria shivered. "He scared the hell out of me, I'll tell you."

"You don't speed anymore?"

"I do, but I watch my mirrors a lot more closely." Gloria handed over the receipt.

Firebird laughed and dug out her wallet. Gloria peered at her driver's license, but Firebird kept the name turned away. She did not need Gloria, who obviously knew all the comings and goings of Rocky Cliffs, talking about the young woman with the odd name who'd come looking for their local state cop. Not that Firebird expected to sneak up on Douglas; that wasn't possible. But not everybody in town needed to know her business.

"Need directions to the old Quackenbush place?" Gloria asked.

"I MapQuested it." Firebird caught Gloria's wrist. "I'm hoping to surprise him."

Gloria looked at Firebird's hand, then searched her face. "You don't look like a former wife with a grudge or an international terrorist. Darn it. So I guess I can keep my mouth shut until you find him."

"Thank you." Firebird left a generous tip. She put

a stick of gum in her mouth and headed back to her car.

The two guys at the bar thoroughly and obviously checked her out.

Jerks.

Not that she didn't look good. She'd dressed carefully for this encounter, wanting to look casual and carefree, professional and responsible, youthful yet mature. She'd finally settled on comfortable and warm—a pair of dark jeans, a green cashmere turtleneck, and black, low-heeled ankle boots. Her coat was a bulky, calf-length, rain-repellent hooded beast, but Firebird remembered exactly how cold it could be near the Pacific this time of year—or any time of year.

She stopped in the doorway and donned the coat.

The guys at the counter whistled.

Douglas could teach them a thing or two about showing subtle appreciation for a good-looking woman. He had a way about him that had made her abandon the rigid morals her parents had taught her and fall into bed without a thought to the future.

She headed outside.

As she followed the directions to the old Quackenbush house, she knew that was the problem. He had so easily seduced her before. He had made her love him. And after she left him, no matter how angry and betrayed she had felt, she still wanted him. Loved him.

Now, perhaps . . . perhaps all the pain and worry had been for nothing.

Now she had something entirely different to worry about.

She turned off Main Street and onto Sutterman Drive, a narrow, winding road that climbed the cliff at the far end of the town. Just before she reached the top, she knew she'd found it; Seaview Road turned right, toward the Pacific Ocean, and a thirty-second drive got her to the lone house on the street, perched at the very top of the cliff. Douglas's house. She took it in with one encompassing glance. "This is the Quackenbush place?" she muttered. "Looks more like the Addams family lives here."

The house was Victorian, tall and narrow, with a lot of porches, balconies, and bric-a-brac, and a weather vane perched on the top cupola that spun in the ocean breeze. To say it needed paint was putting it politely. In some spots, the salt water rotted the boards, leaving no place to paint. The steps leading to the wraparound porch had been replaced, and a cable was strung between there and the front door, creating a *walk here* path.

Douglas had never seemed the homebody type. So what was he thinking by purchasing this behemoth?

She followed the driveway around to the side of the house. There was a tumbledown single-car garage with a BMW X5 parked inside. A BMW X5 had been Douglas's dream car. That couldn't be a coincidence.

She parked on the gravel parking area and got out. As she scurried around to the stairs, the wind and salt scoured the tender skin of her cheeks, and far below, at the bottom of the cliff, she could hear the waves pounding at the rocks. She walked carefully on the wobbly boards on the porch and to the door.

She rang the bell and knocked at the same time, but no one answered.

Hadn't Gloria warned her he was off in his patrol car?

Firebird didn't want to go away and wait. She was afraid that if she did, she would lose her nerve.

She tried the knob. The door was locked, but the whole lock mechanism rattled as if ill seated in the frame.

She could get in here if she cared to try—and trying beat running away.

It took one efficient slip of her credit card, and she was inside. She shut the door behind her and relaxed, basking in the warmth.

To the left were the sad, faded remnants of a large study. To the right the sad, faded remnants of a large living room. Straight ahead the sad, faded remnants of a magnificent stairway. As Firebird moved through the house, she saw nothing but sad, faded remnants—until she reached the massive kitchen.

The kitchen had been completely refinished, with a black slate floor, cabinets stained a pure, glorious red, a black basalt countertop, and Tuscan gold walls. The long table in the center looked antique, a substantial plank of oak resting on sturdy legs with a single master's chair set at one end.

The colors should have been outrageous. Instead the room was warm. Welcoming.

Absentmindedly, she hung her coat on the chair, wandered over, and looked out the wide windows . . . and at last understood why Douglas had bought this house.

Behind the house, a garden of ocean-hardy plants grew in untended profusion. The edge of the cliff was fifty feet from the back of the house, and lining it, like ragged teeth, a row of boulders protected any idiot who might try to drive into the ocean.

Beyond that, the dark green sea rippled and breathed. Patches of seaweed rocked back and forth in the tides. Sea lions basked on a warm, flat, stony outcropping, and gulls soared through the gray clouds and into the bright blue sky. Far out in the sea, white waves foamed and broke against the giant, towering rock stacks. And beyond all that . . . the view stretched to the far horizon and thence into eternity.

On the surface, this place looked like the epitome of civilization, but in fact it owed its whole existence to the wildness and glory of nature.

The house was just like Douglas.

She needed to remember that.

She ditched her gum in a stainless-steel trash can, poked around the ground floor a little more, then headed up the stairs to the second floor. The finish was worn, the detail battered, but the wooden treads and handrail remained sturdy. On the landing, she turned and looked back. Yes, the house was dusty. Yes, it was faded. But while the outside had been battered by the elements, the bones of the inside remained intact, and for a brief second, she saw the former glory of the house, and what it could be again.

Yet . . . Gloria had a point. How could Douglas, on a state trooper's salary, pay for this renovation?

The upstairs was a match for the ground floor, faded and shabby, with bedroom after bedroom in shambles, and the one bathroom she saw filled with white chipped tile and antique fixtures. Two doors were closed: one at the end of the hall, and the wide double door at the end to the left.

She reached them, and, feeling like Bluebeard's wife, she opened the door on the left.

The room was small, partially remodeled, and held a desk, an office chair, a file cabinet, and a laptop connected to a keyboard and printer.

His office.

Moving swiftly, she went in and touched the keyboard. The monitor sprang to life.

She felt as if she were invading Douglas's privacy, but this had to be done. She got into the browser, went to her e-mail provider, and typed a quick message to her mother.

Arrived okay. Have found Aleksandr's father. Will update you when possible. Love to everyone. Kiss Aleksandr.

Then quickly, without looking at anything, she put the computer back to sleep and backed out.

Going to the double doors at the end of the corridor, she opened them and found the master bedroom, completely renovated and updated, an oasis of calm and welcome, with a warm gray carpet and matching walls. On one wall, the gray slate fireplace rose to a high white ceiling raised higher with decorative cove molding, and two overstuffed navy blue

chairs waited with a small round table for someone—
Douglas and a friend—to sit with glasses of wine.
On either side of the low bed were wide windows
facing out to the ocean, and above the bed . . . Firebird's breath caught. Above the bed was an original
oil painting, a glorious splash of orange and red, a
single exotic flower opening to the world.

She walked toward the painting, put her knee on
the mattress, leaned forward, and read the scrawl of
a signature: *f. wilder.*

In college, she had been willing to slap paint on a
canvas in wild exuberance, to show the world in the
most vivid manner possible that she was in love. Not
just in love—stupid in love. Stupid, because look
what the results had been.

She lifted her fingers and gently stroked the lifted
ridges of the yellow stamen—and behind her, *he*
asked, "What are you doing in my house? What are
you doing in my bedroom?"

Chapter Eleven

※⊰✦⊱※

She didn't jump; he'd give her that. But Firebird Wilder had always had balls of steel, and now as she turned coolly to face him, she proved those balls were stainless.

"Hello, Douglas. How are you?"

Douglas. He'd tried to forget her, to tell himself that she had never been worth his spit, that she'd changed from the spirited girl whom he'd captured and who in turn had captured him, that he wouldn't care for her anymore. Then she called him Douglas—not Doug, like everyone else—and the old memories came rushing back. The old vulnerabilities.

"What are you doing here?" he repeated. "Why did you break into my house?"

"It was cold on the porch."

"Then you should have left."

"I drove a long way to see you." She glanced back at the painting she'd left behind when she fled Brown University. "You still have it."

"Why would I not?" He'd tried, but he couldn't bear to get rid of it.

"I thought you might have thrown it out when I left without telling you where I was going." She sat on the bed, smoothing the spread with the flat of her hand.

She looked the same, and yet . . . she used to wear her long blond hair down, or caught at the back of her head in a clip. Now it was cut into a retro twenties style straight across her forehead, then straight back from her chin.

He didn't like it.

She still looked taller than she was, but she was no longer gymnast skinny. She'd filled out: Her waist was tiny, curving seductively outward to her hips and breasts.

Before, she'd been a girl.

Now she was a woman.

But then, he knew that. He'd been watching her.

He walked toward her, unsmiling. "Breaking and entering is a crime."

As he loomed above her, she stopped smiling, stopped pretending that everything was normal. "I found you on the Internet."

"I'm not hard to find."

"No." Her razor-sharp blue eyes flicked up at him. "I was surprised at how easy it was."

"You, on the other hand, are extremely difficult to find. After you ran away . . ." He paused, waiting to see if she would deny it.

She didn't.

"After you ran away, I did everything in my power to find you. I couldn't. And I'm good at research."

"Because you're a cop."

"A cop who uses all the resources available." He'd learned for a very good reason. "But you disappeared into thin air."

"I did tell you I lived in Washington."

She had. She'd been chary with information about herself, but once she'd decided to trust him, she gave him information. As it turned out, she hadn't given him *enough* information, because he had searched, and the mountains had swallowed her without a trace.

"My oldest brother has a thing about privacy." She managed to sound completely open and frank, when he knew the opposite was true. "He makes sure that my family isn't bothered by—"

"Undesirables like me?" His temper crackled.

It would have been better for Firebird if she hadn't come right now, while he was still shaken by Ashley Applebaum's death. Right now he was angry about the waste of a life, about the cruelty in which Applebaum delighted, and at Ashley for succumbing to the terror in which she lived. He knew, he understood, how men like Applebaum used their superior strength and craftiness to victimize their wives and families.

But that baby would forever wear that brand burned into her skin. He recognized the signs of abuse on both children. And he wanted to know why, *why* Ashley hadn't left sooner.

And he hated that Firebird had run from him, who would have always defended and cared for her, and back into the arms of her controlling family.

"I was going to say, Jasha makes sure that my family isn't bothered by a ton of catalogs in the mail and salesmen calling during dinner." Again, Firebird showed him what a very cool customer she was. "But you found me finally."

He could be as composed as she was. "What do you mean?"

"You were at my house last night."

He looked her right in the eye. "If that's why you're here, you've made a mistake."

She stared right back, searching his face for the truth. "Are you claiming you were not at my house last night? Not on the Wilder property at all?"

"I was not."

She set her mouth in disgust.

"Do you have a stalker?" he asked. "Is that why you came here? Because I'm a state patrolman and can look into the matter?"

"No. My father and brothers will handle this."

"Your father and brothers could get in trouble if they challenge an intruder. They might get hurt." He scrutinized her, wanting to see how she felt. Were his suspicions correct? Was she afraid of her father and brothers? Was that why she'd sought him out at last?

She looked a little amused and slightly quizzical. "That's unlikely. They're very capable men. The intruder is more likely to regret his decision to, um, intrude."

"That could end in a lawsuit. They could end up in prison."

"The men in my family take care of themselves."

Yes, but who takes care of you?

"Don't worry, Douglas. It's not your problem. Not yet." Reaching up, she caught his hand.

Her grip hadn't changed. She held a man strongly, as if she would never let him go.

"Sit down. I have to tell you something. Something important."

"Then perhaps I should stand."

"Sit." She tugged hard.

He sat. And waited, his gaze cold and level.

She was nervous. If he weren't a law officer, he might never have known, but he'd been trained to spot the telltale signs: the carefully controlled breathing, the cold fingers, the flush on her neck and chest.

For the first time since the alarm had alerted him of an intruder in his house, he wondered if she'd come here not because she knew about him, but because of another reason, one he had not foreseen. "If you didn't come for my assistance . . . ?" He lifted his eyebrows, once more wanting assurance.

She shook her head.

"Then what momentous event has brought Firebird Wilder, my former lover, from her home to mine?"

"Don't be an ass. You're not one of my brothers." She took a short, hard breath. "But you are the father of my son."

He looked good. Older, more mature than the last time she'd seen him, but strong, muscled, wearing the uniform of a Washington State Patrol officer— French blue shirt with royal blue pocket flaps and French blue pants striped with royal blue.

Yet right before her eyes, she watched him grow remote, icy.

"Your . . . son?" The two words dropped from his lips like twin ice cubes.

"Your son. Douglas, I . . ." All the way down here, she'd been practicing what to say, and now, in the face of that implacable stillness, the words fled and she was left waiting, knowing that soon his rage would rise like molten lava around her and burn her to a cinder. "I'm not asking you for anything. You don't have to do anything. I simply thought you ought to know."

"How old is . . . ?"

"Aleksandr."

"How old is Aleksandr?"

"He was two on November first."

He frowned as he calculated the months. "So you knew you were pregnant when you left me."

Remembering the plastic stick with the blue line in the result window, and the discarded Father's Day card, she could only nod.

"He's the reason you left me without a word, without any explanation?"

She toyed with lying to him. It might be easy to claim panic on discovering she was pregnant, easier than telling the truth.

But he caught on too quickly. "That can't be it. If your baby was born in November, you knew you were pregnant for months before you left."

"Not months. We were careful. I didn't think it was possible. I wasn't looking for the symptoms." She stopped babbling. "In fact, I didn't have symptoms."

"What do you mean, you didn't have symptoms?" He sounded scornful, as only an ignorant man could sound.

She leaned toward him and, in a level tone that did not conceal her irritation, she spelled out the facts, and didn't spare his finer feelings. "I mean, I had a period the first month, I never had morning sickness, and I felt great. Why should I think I was pregnant? We used a condom every time."

He leaned back into her face. "Then why should I believe you?"

"That we have a son?"

"That I'm the father of your son. As you just reminded us both, we always used a condom."

Douglas hurt her. Coldly. Deliberately. He knew Aleksandr was his; the first time they'd made love, she'd been a virgin, and so much in love she cried for joy.

"Condoms are not one hundred percent effective." *Especially if the guy bears a resemblance to Superman.* She shoved her hand into her pocket, and in a steady voice, she said, "It occurred to me you might have . . . suspicions."

It had *never* occurred to her.

He caught her hand, held it still. "What are you doing?" His eyes were dark brown and flinty as stone.

"I've got a DNA test." Which she'd brought to obtain the material needed for the test to prove to herself he was the son of Konstantine and Zorana. But if he thought it was to prove to him he was the father of her child, so much the easier. "If you'll let me take a sample of some of the cells from your cheek . . ."

Slowly he pulled her hand out of her pocket and turned it upward.

Opening her fingers, she showed him the plastic package. "It's sealed. It's sterile. Inside is a tube with a cotton swab inside. All we have to do is swipe it across your cheek, seal it in the tube, and send it to Seattle. The lab will run the DNA and let you know if it's a match to Aleksandr's."

Doug let her hand go.

"If you don't trust me, if you'd rather go to a lab *with* Aleksandr—"

"Go ahead." He opened his mouth.

He was so distrustful. He ought to be sitting in her seat, floundering on an ocean of uncertainty, no longer sure where she'd come from, and in doubt of her destination.

He shut his mouth. Taking her chin in his hand, he turned her face toward the light. "Why do you look like that?"

"Like what?" She heard the truculence in her own voice.

"Like someone has hurt you."

"That's life, isn't it? Even when you're in the safest place you can think of, you can still get hurt." That was the irony. Ever since she'd discovered the truth about Douglas, ever since she'd seen him turn from a cougar into a man, she'd stayed close to home, leaving only when she had to. She had lived in fear that he would find her and take their son to be raised as a Varinski. She had believed that at home, trouble would never find her.

It had. Trouble would not be denied.

"I *am* a police officer. I *can* help you." Douglas still held her chin, still examined her face, and for the first time, he sounded almost nice.

In fact, he sounded like he felt sorry for her.

She jerked herself free. "There's nothing you can do to help me with this problem." *In a way, you are the problem.* But she couldn't say that. She wasn't ready to tell him that he'd usurped her place in her family. Not until she had the results of this DNA test.

Not until the last damned minute.

Chapter Twelve

Firebird opened the packet and pulled out the swab. "Open."

Doug caught her wrist and held it. "These results are going to prove I'm Aleksandr's father, aren't they?"

"What other reason would I have to carry a DNA test around in my pocket?" Her eyes were hot and angry.

He had a son. A boy he'd never met, never seen, never hugged, never held.

And now, this woman sat here, angry because she had to come to him and tell him he had a son.

She had guts.

"You haven't yet told me why." His voice grated in his throat.

"Why what?" She tried to wrestle her wrist free.

He tightened his grip—on her, and on his temper. "Why you didn't tell me three years ago. Why you're telling me now."

Her gaze dropped. "It's a long story. It's complicated. Let's just get this test and then—"

"Do you realize what you've done? What you've

denied me?" Did she realize what he had thought? That she'd come to him because she needed him? What a laugh. He flung her wrist away before he hurt her. "I've got a son. A son, and I knew nothing about him. I didn't see his birth. I didn't see his first smile. I didn't hear him babble, see his first step. I've never rocked him or carried him or played patty-cake or held his hand while he tried to walk or clapped while he blew out his first birthday candle— or second birthday candle, either. I missed those things, and I can't get them back."

She made a move toward her purse. "I've got pictures—"

"*Pictures*. What am I, a toddler like Aleksandr, to be distracted by a shiny toy? Pictures are flat. They don't laugh. They don't cry. They don't cuddle. They don't . . ." He came to his feet and strode to the door, on the verge of leaving.

But he couldn't leave now and give Firebird another chance to run away. He paced back. "All my life, I have sworn that when I had a child, I would be there for him. You made me break my vow. *You* did."

"I'm sorry."

"You denied me my time with my baby, but worse than that, you denied Aleksandr a father." This was his nightmare. He was living his nightmare.

"I will never forgive myself for that."

Her low voice made him look at her, look at her hard.

She sounded like she meant it. She looked like she meant it.

"How can you act like this? Like you care that I have missed . . . Oh, wait." Good sense stopped him cold. "It's not about me, is it?"

"No." She admitted the truth unashamedly. "It's about Aleksandr. You said it, and you're right. I denied him his father, and he'll never be the same because of it."

Okay. Doug could deal with that. Firebird put her son first, and that was the way it should be. She believed the boy had missed something by not having Doug in his life.

But he still didn't understand *why*. "Why did you run away from me? Did you think I would hurt you?"

She didn't answer right away. *She didn't answer right away.*

She had actually thought he would have hurt her. "My God, what did I do that you would think that of me? That I'd be mad because you were going to have my baby?"

"It's not what you think."

"What do I think?"

"Just let me do this thing my way. Would you? Would you just let me . . ." Her voice rose, and she bit her lip as if trying to rein in her frustration. "I know you're mad. I don't blame you. I'd be mad, too. Livid. But there's more to it than you realize. This isn't easy, Douglas. I'm not some bitch who took your son away out of spite. There were reasons, and quite frankly, I may have made a mistake about you, but I had a good reason."

"What reason could be good enough?"

"Sit down."

He remained standing and stared forbiddingly down at her. "Answer the question, damn it."

"I'll explain when I'm sure about you. Now." She stood, popped his mouth open, and swiped the swab across his cheek. She sealed it in the little tube, inserted it in the envelope to go to the lab, and offered it to him. "Do you want to mail it to make sure this is the package that goes directly to them without tampering?"

She was challenging him, reproaching him for his skepticism, and as she did, the air between them grew dry and hot, hurting his lungs. "What if *I* switched it?"

"Then I don't want you to have anything to do with Aleksandr anyway." She looked him right in the eyes, unsmiling and fierce when it came to Aleksandr.

And he realized how glad he was that *she* had borne his son. She was strong. She was intelligent. She did . . . she did what she thought was right. He simply didn't understand how she could have thought that cutting him out of Aleksandr's life was right.

But she'd promised to explain it.

Without looking at the envelope, he took it, leaned forward . . . and slid it into her pocket.

Their faces were almost touching.

Her eyes dilated as she watched him.

When he kissed her . . . she didn't lean back. She didn't participate, either—her lips were cool and unmoving, but she closed her eyes and let him taste her.

She tasted the same as the Firebird of his memories, of Doublemint gum and sweet, warm woman and curiosity.

And he echoed that curiosity.

Why had she come . . . now? She had a son. His son. But she'd known about the child every minute since she'd left him. So . . . why today?

Then she slipped her tongue into his mouth, and all his questions were ripped away by a blast of pure, hot lust.

He slid one hand behind her head, into her hair—soft hair—and one arm under her sweater—soft sweater—and around her waist—soft skin. He pulled her against him, chest to belly, and lost himself in the heady lavender scent of her. He wanted to lick her, suck her, take her in every way possible, until she yielded, until she recognized him by his voice, by his flavor, by his scent, until he saturated her through her pores and her nerves, until she missed him when he wasn't inside her.

It was what he'd always wanted. It was what he'd thought he'd done in all those seductions on the Brown campus.

With an instinct long refined by many seductions, he slid his hand up her spine until he reached her bra, and smoothly opened the clasp. Pressing her against the pillows, he slid his other hand under her sweater and to her breasts, pushing the cups aside to reach the treasure beneath. Taking a pinch of the soft cashmere, he rubbed the material over her nipple, around and around, and watched her eyes grow wide.

He saw the moment she realized how far and how

deftly he'd pushed her—and how easily he could push her all the way. Her hands flew to his shoulders; she shoved him.

He didn't sway.

She didn't have a chance against him. Not now. He'd been waiting almost three years for this moment. He'd imagined it, planned for it, laughed at how he would make her come over and over . . . and in the deep, secret hours of the night, he had *longed* to make her come over and over.

His longing was his weakness.

But she didn't have to know that.

Catching another pinch of the rich, warm, soft cashmere, he moved to the other nipple and rubbed again.

With each circle, he felt her yield.

"Douglas. No. We haven't talked. We need to discuss . . . discuss . . ."

He lifted her farther onto the bed. Her legs dangled, but she was prone on the mattress, stretched out like a pagan offering. He straddled her, shoved her sweater up to her rib cage, and unzipped her jeans.

She'd always had the best stomach, flat and strong, with a mole beside her belly button that drove him crazy. Her belly was still flat, still strong, but now he traced the pale white lines that proved she'd carried their child . . . and an unwilling smile crooked his mouth. He could imagine her pregnant, swelling every day as their son grew. . . . He looked up.

She gazed at him, the lines of her wide, soft mouth shattered by anxiety.

"Beautiful," he whispered.

She closed her eyes with relief.

Had she worried he would be so shallow as to condemn her for a body changed by childbirth? By the birth of his son? Foolish woman. She knew him not at all.

He had made sure of that.

When he met her on campus, he had already known who she was. That was why he'd taken the job. That was why he'd sought her out. He had intended to use her for his own purposes.

Instead, she'd made a fool of him.

What a mistake she'd made returning to him now.

As he slid the jeans off her hips, her eyes flew open again. "Please, Douglas. There's so much to say, and we can't take up where we left off—in bed."

"We're not going to take up where we left off. This time, it's going to be more. Much more."

She wore a pair of plain white hipster panties.

Did she think that would subdue him? She could wear granny panties, and his cock would still do an imitation of one of the rock stacks offshore.

Using the banding around the edge of her sweater, he rubbed it across her abdomen, making her stretch and sigh. Then, as if to deny her weakness, she sat up on her elbows and said sternly, "That's enough, Douglas."

"Did you learn that tone while talking to your son?"

Her face softened at the mention of Aleksandr. "It's effective."

"No. Not with me." He moved swiftly to take advantage of her tenderness. Taking her shoulders, he lowered her back to the bed and kissed her. Kissed her with all the repressed passion that raged within him.

When her hands had crept around his neck and her breathing matched his, he spanned her belly with his long fingers.

Her skin felt like velvet, and as he stroked her, her legs moved restlessly.

She'd always been like this, wanting him with a desperation that drove him beyond his black-and-white sphere of wisdom and prudence and into a world splashed with vivid color. And all her passion had been for him. He'd never doubted that.

Now once again he would sink into her body, hear her cries in his ears, know that in this one time and with this one woman, he belonged—

A vibration on his belt froze him in place.

His pager. His pager had gone off.

Like a splash of icy water, the call of duty brought him out of his passion-induced coma and back into the real world, where everything was black and white, and he was just where he belonged.

Chapter Thirteen

Douglas stood up. Looked at the pager on his belt. Said, "I have to go." Straightened his tie and walked out the door.

Just like that.

Firebird lay there, sprawled on his bed, her jeans around her ankles, her bra around her neck, her sweater above her belly—and *he straightened his tie*?

She came to her feet so fast she stumbled on her jeans.

He straightened his tie. That was all he needed to look exactly as he had looked before he had kissed her, run his hands over her, removed her bra and used her sweater to . . . She shivered as she remembered the sensation of cashmere against her nipples.

Then his pager beeped, he stood up, granite faced, *straightened his tie*, and he left her here looking like a slut.

She pulled up her pants. She fastened her bra. She pulled down her sweater.

That bastard.

She had to get out of here. She had to get out of here now.

She marched downstairs and plucked her coat off the kitchen chair.

She would drive straight through to Blythe, to her family, to her son. They'd be disappointed when she came back without solutions. Aleksandr would be upset when she didn't bring his daddy. But they'd still be happy to see her. She might not belong to them, not really, but they loved her. They *did*.

She walked out the door. The wind struck her like a slap to the face. She ran to her car, got in, and slammed the door as hard as she could—and wished she could do it again. She turned out of Douglas's driveway; her tires squealed.

As she drove into Rocky Cliffs in search of a post office, her cell phone rang. She didn't answer. Because she was driving, she told herself, but the truth was, she didn't want to talk to her mother or her brothers or her sisters-in-law. She didn't want to explain what she was doing and why, or assure them that she was well and they didn't have to worry. She wanted to do what she had to do and enlighten them later.

And it was petty, but she wanted them to worry a little.

The ring that alerted her to a message sounded, and with a sigh she pulled into the post office parking lot and called her voice mail.

"Hi, Firebird, it's Ann. Jasha wanted to talk, but I knew he'd nag you to come home, so I wouldn't let him. But we thought you should know the boys and your mom went to visit Miss Joyce this morning. She confessed to switching babies. She, um, didn't exactly say where she got you. She only said that you were one of 'the abandoned ones.' I'm sorry I can't tell you more." Ann cleared her throat uncomfortably.

One of the abandoned ones . . . What exactly did that mean?

But Ann continued, "But she also said she took the newborn boy and drove to Nevada and left him in the desert. Very biblical."

There was more. Some fond comments, a report on what Aleksandr ate for breakfast, a few discreet questions about Aleksandr's daddy, and Ann signed off.

Crap.

Firebird beat on her steering wheel.

She didn't want this. She didn't need this. She was an independent woman. If there was one advantage to discovering she was not a Wilder, it was that she wasn't bound to the pact.

Yet here she was, having second—or was it third?—thoughts.

Because what had really changed? Douglas had been furious at her. She had been defensive. Her pride had taken a knock. Her faith in her own willpower had been justifiably shaken.

Yet he was still the father of her child.

She pulled the DNA test out of her pocket and looked at the prepaid envelope. The lab techs at the Seattle Swedish Hospital knew the Wilder family, and they'd promised to expedite the proceedings.

She deposited it into the drive-up mailbox and headed back to the street.

Her personal feelings didn't count. Not now. She couldn't allow herself to be driven away by a few harsh words, by Douglas's doubts in her, by the tantrum she wanted to throw because fate had done her wrong. The destiny of her family, the only family she'd ever known, rested in Douglas's hands.

More important, Ann had reminded Firebird of a very important fact—the house was small, the family loving, and a person who lived with them had no privacy. Firebird missed her baby, but she didn't want to go home yet.

She turned her car toward Douglas's house. She took a deep, calming breath.

She hadn't slept for over thirty-six hours, and in those thirty-six hours, she'd faced more trauma than any one person should have to face. She was pooped. Maybe she had been overreacting. Certainly, as her anger faded, she knew she was walking back into the lion's den. But she would return to the old Quackenbush place. She was going to climb in Douglas's bed and take a nap, because he might be a cold, heartless bastard who made love to a woman, then stood, *straightened his tie*, and walked out, but at least he never asked questions about her feelings. As far as she could tell, he didn't care about her feelings, and right now, that was okay with her.

She pulled into the driveway, around the side of the house, parked, and got out.

Douglas Black cared about one thing—himself.

* * *

As Doug pulled up to the front of his house and parked his patrol car—the town still called it the Quackenbush place, but it was *his*—he told himself it would be a hell of a lot easier if Firebird had left. And she had. She'd laid rubber getting out of his driveway. Guess she didn't want him for her son's father as badly as she thought she did.

He slammed the car door and strode into the house.

Too bad. She couldn't call him off now. He knew about the kid, and damned if he was going to let his son grow up like he did, always wondering who his parents were, what he'd done to make them hate him so much.

He glanced around the kitchen. It was empty.

And damned if he was going to let those brothers she adored so much be substitutes for him. She could just get used to the idea that Doug Black was in her life for good.

He climbed the stairs, his boots thumping hard on each tread.

She didn't realize it yet, but she was going to need him when—

From down the hall, he caught her scent, lingering persistently.

She was going to need him when his plans came to fruition. It wouldn't be too long now before . . .

He stood in the doorway of the bedroom and stared.

There was a woman-shaped lump under his comforter.

He walked with belated caution to the side of the bed and stared down.

Her blond hair was mussed on the blue linens. One side of her face was rosy and impressed with wrinkles from the pillow. Her eyes were open, and she stared up at him in disgust. "Could you *be* a little louder?"

"I thought you'd run away."

"Run away?" She sat up and stretched. "From what?"

Okay. She did a good job of putting him in his place.

Whatever place that was. Casual lover? Aleksandr's father?

What would she think when he became her savior?

"What are we doing for dinner?" She swung her legs out of bed.

She was completely dressed.

Damn it. "We could eat here."

"Your refrigerator is empty." She sounded so like the girl he'd known, the one who loved to cook and eat, the one he'd built his kitchen for. . . .

If he'd been thinking, he would have bought groceries. But he hadn't. He had expected her to leave. Instead, here she was, acting airy and down-to-earth—in fact, acting as if they hadn't fought, as if nothing had happened.

"So what are we doing for dinner?" she repeated.

"There's a fancy place up on the cliff, serves seafood. It's good."

Impatiently, she asked, "What's the *best*?"

"Mario's Pizza and Italian, in an old house about three blocks over." He tilted toward her. He didn't *lean*. Leaning would be too revealing. But he tilted.

She didn't notice. Instead she stood right up. "Then that's where we're going. I could ride in your patrol car. I've never been in a patrol car." She smiled as if the idea appealed to her.

Whether he liked it or not—and he didn't—her anticipation made his heart lift. But he didn't smile back.

Sometimes, he thought he'd forgotten how. "It's for official business only."

Her face fell.

"We'll take the Beamer," he said. "It's nicer."

"You want to show off your Beemer," she teased. Going to the mirror, she ran her fingers through her hair, pinched her cheeks, and shook her head. "I've got to freshen up." She sashayed into his bathroom with such assurance she might as well own this place.

He stared at the closed door, feeling pleased and disgruntled at the same time, and vaguely interested that he felt anything at all. The last time he'd allowed himself hope, he'd ended up alone, angry, and shattered, and he'd sworn no one would ever break through his barriers again.

Now, here she was playing every chord in his soul like some master pianist on an inferior instrument.

No. She wasn't going to break him again. This time, she was going to cooperate. She had no choice. He knew where she lived. He knew about his son— and whether she liked it or not, he would share the boy's custody—share Aleksandr's custody . . . until other arrangements could be made.

His gaze shifted to her purse, sitting on the bed table.

Without compunction, he opened it and rifled through the contents. He found her wallet with about a hundred dollars in bills, cheap sunglasses, a small organizer crisscrossed with notes, an envelope full of photos, lipstick, powder, and her cell phone.

Flipping the latter open, he noted that the last call had come this afternoon from a Washington number. He looked through the menu at her stored numbers and found it was from her home. He found other numbers, too, family numbers for J Wilder, R Wilder, A Wilder, and T Wilder, the number for Seattle Swedish Hospital, and business numbers listed under the Szarvas Art Studio.

He copied her home number, the Szarvases' number, and her brothers' numbers into his notebook.

She was not getting away from him again.

As he put everything back, she said from the doorway, "What are you doing?"

Casually, he glanced her way.

She looked the same—a little damp around the hairline, but still beautiful. Yet now her blue eyes were icy, her generous lips compressed, and she tapped her foot.

He returned her purse to its place. "It fell over."

"I thought you might be checking to see if I was carrying a concealed weapon."

"No." He returned to the spot in the middle of the floor.

She walked into the room, examining him from every angle.

Had Firebird somehow found out what he was up to?

And if she had, what would she do for him to keep those phone numbers private?

Chapter Fourteen

"Nice car." Firebird punched buttons. She heated her seat, lowered the temperature on his side of the car, changed from recorded music to a radio station, opened the sunroof, then with a shiver, closed it. "How can a cop on a salary afford a BMW X5? This is a sixty-thousand-dollar SUV."

The tone was casual. The question was not.

She accessed the GPS history.

He reached out, caught her hand, and removed it from the controls. "I saved."

"You bought a house, too. That's a lot of savings."

"I gamble."

"Really?" She sat back in her seat and considered him by the glow of the instrument panel. "You *gambled* this into existence?"

He pulled into the parking lot at Mario's, killed the motor, and turned to her, his arm stretched across the back of the seats. "Do you doubt it?"

She examined him, considering what she knew of him, examining what she could now see. "No. I think you've got a great poker face, and when you gamble, you win."

"Exactly." He got out, came around, and helped her out of the vehicle. "All of life is a gamble, so play to win."

As they approached the door, Mario himself flung it open. "Wel-a-come! Wel-a-come! It is-a chilly to-night, yes? Big-a storm coming in! Come in before you freeze-a!" His Italian accent was as phony as his extravagant mustache and his red-checkered table-cloths, but his pizzeria was warm, with a fire in the hearth and the scent of stone-oven-roasted pizza. Al-though it was late, after nine, and almost no tourists were in town, the restaurant was more than half-full—Mario really did make the best meal in town.

As Mario escorted them to a table, Doug nodded to the people he knew. A single nod, acknowledging them, but not inviting affection.

He found it easier to remain aloof than to make friends. Friends expected him to talk, to be convivial, to remember their names, their kids' names, their dogs' names. They'd want him to share his experi-ences, talk about where he came from and who he was. For a man like him, friends were way too much trouble.

"Here you are. The corner table! My best table!" Mario held Firebird's chair. "You, my dear patrol-man, you can put-a your back against the wall. I know the cops, they like to put-a their backs against the wall. Yet your pretty lady can sit by the window and look out over the valley and ocean. Perfect, yes?"

"It really is." Firebird patted Mario's hand. "Thank you. You're the ultimate host."

Doug watched Firebird visibly relax as she looked out over the raging ocean, the dark clouds split by slivers of setting sun, and the lights that came on below, one by one, like constant fireflies.

And he smiled. Briefly, painfully, but he did smile.

"Such a pretty lady!" Mario used his hands to frame her face for Doug. "But you know that, heh? For you, tonight, I give you my best waiter, Quentin. And you-a will have the meal of your life, prepared by these very fingers!" He wiggled them over the table, then waltzed off toward the kitchen.

Firebird watched him with an incredulous smile. "What a nice man he is."

"That accent . . . he's no more Italian than you are."

She flinched as if Doug had stuck a knife in her. "You never know. I could be." Before he could blink, she went on the attack. "And you're the last person to quibble about whether a person is who he says he is."

"What do you mean?"

"There's a lot you haven't told me about yourself."

Yes. And a lot more he didn't intend to tell her.

"We're not here to talk about me. We're here to talk about our son, to decide how we're going to handle introducing me to him."

"Don't worry about that. He's expecting you. I told him I was going to get his daddy."

Doug stiffened. He'd been so pissed about missing Aleksandr's first years, he hadn't considered actually meeting the kid. What did Aleksandr expect? Would he be disappointed? Doug knew his way around children; when he was growing up, he'd had to take care of the others, and as a peace officer, he'd had to deal with frightened or hurt children.

But this . . . this was different. This was his son.

"What did he say?"

"He wants a daddy. He's always wanted one." She smiled as she watched him struggle with stage fright. "You are his dearest fantasy."

"I've never been anyone's dearest fantasy before."

"I wouldn't say that," she whispered.

The peach-soft curve of her cheek, her tender smile, reminded him of those early days of their courtship, when she looked at him as if he were her knight in shining armor.

Yet here they were, almost three years later, with a bitterness between them that would not easily heal. "You ran away."

As she stared at him, the warmth slipped away, leaving a woman who had recognized trouble when she saw it. "Sometimes fantasy is just another word for nightmare."

"What did I do that made you decide I was a nightmare?"

"You changed."

He recoiled. What did she mean?

Her lids drooped, hiding her thoughts. She drew an envelope out of her purse, took the first photo out, and placed it on the table. "That's Aleksandr reading a book."

That was changing the subject with a vengeance.

He should pursue the truth, but she said he had changed. For the first time, he put his anger and his grudge aside and wondered, *Was this separation somehow his fault?*

Then he saw a sturdy toddler sitting in a huge recliner, frowning intently at some kind of women's romance paperback. The child held the book upside down, and, unable to resist, Doug reached for the photo, picked it up, and let emotion swamp him. He cleared his throat and studied the picture, cleared his throat again, and asked, "Isn't he a little young for that kind of material?"

"You're never too young for romance." She placed another on the table. "That's Aleksandr playing in the snow. Last week we got eight inches in one night." She realized what she'd said and blinked, then hurried on as if she hoped he hadn't caught on. "Here's Aleksandr doing a puzzle."

The boy had the brown eyes Doug saw every morning in the mirror.

"Here's Aleksandr with his uncles," she said.

Two tall, strong men bearing an obvious family resemblance stood in a crowded kitchen. They held their hands out, palms up, and Aleksandr stood balanced with one foot in each hand. Three identical mischievous grins lit up the photo.

"I wasn't there when they took that, or they wouldn't have taken it." Firebird shook her head. "My brothers think Aleksandr is their own personal plaything, and if it were up to them, he'd spend all his time running laps, climbing trees, and learning to shoot."

"Shoot?" Doug raised his eyebrows. "At two and almost a half?"

"Baskets. My brothers are nuts about basketball."

"Um-hm." Doug didn't believe that was what she meant at all.

"Here's my mom carrying Aleksandr around while he's asleep." Firebird's face softened as she smiled at the picture. "He's almost bigger than she is, but she won't put him down. She says he sleeps better when she carries him."

The woman was petite. The boy was sturdy. The affection with which she held the child was obvious. "She's stubborn," Doug said.

"She's Rom. Gypsy. The most loving woman in the whole world, but don't get on her bad side. She'll cut your heart out with a sharp spoon." Firebird took the last photo out of the envelope and placed it before him. "Here's Aleksandr with his grandpa."

Doug inspected the photo of the boy sitting proudly in the old man's lap. "Your father's ill."

"Yes."

"What's wrong?"

She tried to smile. "He's suffering from a condition brought on by a combination of old sins, a good marriage, and a pact with—"

The waiter appeared and presented their wine with a flourish. "Sir?"

The worst Goddamn timing in the world. Doug could have kicked him across the restaurant.

Quentin knew it, too. "I can come back," he said hastily.

Doug glanced at Firebird. She kept her head down-turned as she scraped the pictures into a pile.

"No." The moment was gone.

He glanced at the label on the bottle. "Let the lady taste it." Her family was in wine—her dad grew grapes, and her brother owned a vineyard, and Doug had always been amazed at her knowledge.

While Quentin poured a small amount in the wide-bottomed glass, Firebird put the photos back in the envelope and pushed them toward Doug. "I brought them for you. I thought you'd want to have them to look at while you . . . think." She tasted the wine and nodded. "Very good. Douglas, would you order for us?"

She hadn't been so trusting before. Or maybe she hadn't been so willing to let him take charge. "We'll have the house salads and a medium chicken garlic pizza." He waved the waiter away. "As long as we both eat the garlic, we'll still be able to kiss later."

She ignored that. "Garlic and chicken? The pizza sounds healthy."

"No. Too much cheese." He tucked the envelope into his shirt pocket.

The door opened, and he watched two big, rough-looking guys step in. He hadn't seen them around town before, and in one glance, he cataloged every-thing about them. Brown hair, blond hair. Square chins. Slanted, almost Asian eyes. Bulky shoulders and chests. Probably brothers. Definitely trouble.

"What?" She twisted around in her seat, then im-mediately turned back to him. "Oh."

"What does *that* mean?" Doug asked.

Mario seated them by the bathrooms.

"It's the two construction guys from the diner this morning."

Doug focused on Firebird, on the nasty twist of her mouth. "What did they do?"

"Whistled and looked me over."

"I can't fault their taste." He sipped the wine and tasted notes of pepper and black cherry, of spice and sweetness, and thought how much the wine was like Firebird, complex and rich . . . and addictive.

"Thank you, but there's looking over and there's *looking over*, if you know what I mean. These guys could learn a few things about being suave from, oh, King Kong."

Doug nodded. "I'll ask around about them. The town's not big. Someone's sure to know something, especially if they're a problem."

"I'm not trying to make trouble for them." Firebird's voice was low and firm. "I didn't say there was anything wrong with them. I just said they were obnoxious."

"I trust your instincts."

"Do you? Why?"

Because you knew there was something wrong about me and ran away. But now wasn't the time to admit that. Not when she was here, sharing his meal and his wine, showing him her pictures . . . giving him his son.

His son. Of all the things he had imagined when she left, he had never imagined she left because they had created a baby. The idea of being a father . . . it choked him with pride, and with fear. What did a man like him know about responsibility, about raising a child? Going right to the heart of his doubts, he asked, "Why did you run away from me? Did you think I would be a bad father?"

"I didn't think that at all. I didn't know. How could I?"

"What do you mean?"

"I didn't know anything about you. I told you about my father and my mother and my brothers. I told you about my best friend. I told you about falling in gymnastics and all the surgeries it took to make my bad leg viable again." She leaned back, the red-wine glass balanced in her fingers, her eyes as stern as a nun's. "And you told me precisely . . . nothing."

"There's nothing to tell."

"That's helpful," she mocked. "You must have some experiences you can share. After all, you weren't born the day I met you."

He sat in the hard, straight-backed chair and stared at her.

She wanted to know about him? All about him? He doubted that. He doubted that highly.

But by God, she had asked. So let her know whom she had let into her life.

"No. I was born twenty-three years ago. Sometime around the Fourth of July. They're not sure exactly which day I was born, because my parents dumped me, naked, out of their car in the middle of the Nevada desert and drove away without ever looking back."

Chapter Fifteen

~~~~~~~

Firebird looked odd. Puckered around the lips, like she'd bitten into a lemon. And she actually put her hand on her heart, as if it hurt. "I was born on the Fourth of July, too. H-how did you survive?" Her eyes looked big and blue and sorrowful.

"Some rancher was having problems with coyotes attacking his sheep, and he spotted a pack and started shooting. They all ran away except one."

"A female." Carefully, Firebird lifted her wine and took a sip.

"Yeah. How did you know?"

"I understand pack dynamics better than most people."

"I'll bet you do." He met her gaze, and for a long moment, they fell into silence as he willed her to trust him, to tell him—

"What did the female do?" Firebird asked.

Doug needed to remember—Firebird didn't trust him. That was all too obvious. "She was lying on something. She wouldn't budge. The rancher was ready to shoot—the news report said he figured she had to be rabid to face him down. But he heard something cry, thought it sounded like a baby, and went over to check. God bless the beast." Most of the time Doug meant it, but sometimes . . . sometimes he thought it would have been better if he'd died.

"There you were. The mama coyote was keeping you warm." Firebird laughed a stuttering laugh. Then, as if she were answering herself, she said, "Well, of course she was. Doesn't that figure?"

"That's what the rancher said, too. He wrapped me up in his coat and took me to his truck, got out a sheep nipple, and fed me sheep's milk." Doug watched her, thinking he had expected shock that he'd been abandoned, maybe sympathy, maybe a badly hidden worry that her son's father came from a less-than-savory family. He hadn't expected her to act as if he were confirming her worst suspicions. "He called Child Protective Services. They picked me up and put out a call for my parents."

"Was it a big news story?" She looked as if she were memorizing his every word.

"No. A few notices in the local county rag, that's all. Why?"

"It seems the kind of heartwarming story the news agencies would love."

"It would have been heartwarming if my parents came forward. As it was, they didn't, and I was almost dead—second-degree burns from the sun, malnourished, and pretty pissed at the world. Apparently I screamed my whole first year."

"Not a likely candidate for adoption."

"Nope. My first-grade teacher told me I was born

with a chip on my shoulder, and that if I didn't straighten up, and fast, I was going to go to hell." Funny. He hadn't remembered that until now.

Firebird's mouth thinned. "That's not something to tell a first grader."

"My first memory was of squaring off with a bully." He set his teeth in what he called a pleasant smile. "But don't worry. I kicked her ass."

He caught Firebird by surprise, and she laughed. "You beat up a *girl*?"

"I was four. She was sixteen, one of those do-gooders who volunteered to take care of the poor orphans so she could get community-service points with her church. She wanted to take care of the babies, not a bunch of snotty four-year-olds, so she picked on this one little girl who wore ashtray glasses and stuttered."

Firebird's smile faded.

He could see that sixteen-year-old's self-righteous, smug face even now, and hear her screams when he head-butted her right in her soft, flabby belly. "God, I hate a bully."

"Is that why you went into law enforcement?" As always, Firebird saw more than most people.

"No, I did it because I thought that was the easiest way to track my family without coming up on stalking charges." Let her make of that what she would.

"And because you don't like bullies." She smiled at him.

He started to correct her again, then figured, if she wanted to think the best of him, who was he to stop her? "Sure. So anyway, nobody adopted me, and I

lived in an orphanage and in foster homes until . . .
I ran away."

Firebird took the hand he had clenched into a fist
on the table. "Was it all awful?" she asked.

"Not all."

"I thought not." She sat back and let the waiter
place her salad before her.

"What do you mean?"

She picked up her fork. "Someone taught you to
be a good man."

Yeah, honey, you go ahead and think that.

But that was always the trouble with Firebird. She
liked people. She wasn't stupid about it; she was
careful with strangers and knew how to protect herself. But on first impression, she believed the best
about everybody, and when Doug had approached
her at the campus library, she'd immediately put him
on her list of good guys.

The thing was, when he was with her, he tried to
live up to her image of him. What the hell he'd been
thinking, he would never know. . . . Well, yes, he did.
He'd been thinking he'd act any way, do anything, to
get between her legs.

Simple. Direct.

The trouble was, he was sitting here thinking the
same thing now.

"Good salad!" she said. "I was starved."

"You're always starved." Yet built like a model.

"Yes," she agreed cheerfully. "I can't wait for the
pizza."

When he thought how close he'd come this afternoon to making it with her, he wanted to yell at

the driver who'd rolled it on the curve going into King Junction and sent him back to work for the Washington State Police. But the sight of the injured woman changed his mind. Instead he'd helped the paramedics load her into the ambulance, directed the cleanup, and hotfooted it back to his house like a puppy on a leash—and Firebird held the lead end.

Worse, he had done so while thinking she was gone.

He ate his salad quickly—a cop ate when he could, because he never knew when he would land the next meal—and pushed it away. "When I was eight, I got in trouble in Carson City. Something about organizing a shoplifting ring."

Firebird froze, her fork halfway to her mouth.

"In the state's infinite wisdom, they decided to send me to Las Vegas."

"Las Vegas? That's brilliant," she muttered, and put down her silverware.

"To give the devil his due—"

She winced.

"—the idea *was* brilliant. Because there was this lady there. Mrs. Fuller. She took the tough cases like me and reformed us."

Firebird's eyes flashed. "How?"

"She didn't *do* anything. She just lived a good life and let us kids live it with her." He hadn't spoken of Mrs. Fuller since the day he ran away, but he remembered her warm, round, wrinkled face with the clarity of a hope long cherished and never forgotten. "She was a Christian. A real Christian, not one of the ones who are religious on Sunday and the rest of the week you can't find a spit of kindness or charity in their souls or their actions."

"Okay." Firebird relaxed. "How many kids did she have?"

"She always kept three, and for emergencies like me, she'd put up a cot."

The waiter brought the pizza and, with a flourish, placed it on the table. The smell of garlic rose in waves from the perfectly browned, bubbly crust. The chicken nestled in the white, soft cheese.

As Doug watched, Firebird took a long breath and closed her eyes in appreciation. Later, he was going to put the same look of ecstasy on her face. . . .

Glancing up, he saw Quentin watching her with the same fascination and longing he felt.

The bastard.

Doug slapped his hand over Quentin's and squeezed. Hard.

Quentin jumped. His guilty gaze flashed to Doug's.

Doug glared.

Quentin blanched, poured more wine, asked if he could get them anything else, and hightailed it out of there.

Firebird watched, puzzled. "What got into him?"

"He probably had another order up." Doug picked up the server and slid a slice of pizza onto her plate. "Enjoy."

She took a bite. Her strong, white teeth sank into the cheese, through the crust, and she sighed as she chewed. "That's fabulous. In Blythe, we've got a café that serves breakfast and lunch, and that's all."

"You live in Blythe?" he asked smoothly. "Isn't that a little town in the Cascades?"

She looked at him, looked hard, then relaxed, as if she'd made a decision about him. "Blythe is so small, the mice are round-shouldered."

His mouth crooked up at one corner.

"My family lives outside of town on six hundred and forty acres."

"That's . . . big." He ate a bite of pizza, made sure she had another piece before she finished the first one, and kept her wineglass topped off.

"We've got a valley planted mostly in grapes, and a lot of woods around us. My dad and mom got the land cheap because no one else wanted it. Now it's prime property." She smiled proudly. "They've done well for immigrants who came to this country with nothing."

"When I meet them, I know I'll like them."

"Yes. They'll like you, too." Firebird's eyes got almost teary.

He couldn't imagine why, but the idea of Firebird crying terrified him. What would he do? Sit there like a log? Pat her on the back? Kiss her and . . . ?

"This Mrs. Fuller—how long did she work on you before you reformed?"

Man. Firebird recovered fast, and when she wanted information, she was like a heat-seeking missile.

Luckily for him, he was the heat. "The first year was rocky."

"What turned things around?"

"By the time I got to Mrs. Fuller, I was not about to be tamed. I was out there on the streets, picking pockets and running errands for the guys who owned the casinos. She kept telling me she could see the potential in me. She would tell me about great men who had risen above their tough beginnings. She told me to use my head, think things through, go to college and make something of myself. Be the boss, not the gofer. She said if I kept going like I was, I was going to get myself killed before I was twenty." He finished off the last slice of pizza and settled back in his chair. "Most important, she told me I could talk to her about anything and she'd understand."

"She sounds great."

"She was, but I wasn't listening. I would have sworn I wasn't listening. I was such a smart-ass little shit. I thought I knew better than an old lady in a house crowded with those stupid little Hummels. God, I hated those smug, round Swiss faces, so sweet and innocent. I didn't have a damned thing in common with them. Then . . . I landed in the wrong place, doing an errand for the wrong guy, and just about got myself raped."

"Oh, Douglas." Firebird reached across the table and took his hand.

Not that he needed the comfort. That had been years ago, and over time, the horror and the helplessness had faded. But he let her hold him anyway, turning his hand to fit under hers. "Lucky for me I was a big kid, and I was mean and a fighter. I got away, no one was any the wiser, and I was not about to tell anybody."

"Especially not Mrs. Fuller."

Firebird was one smart woman. "Especially not her, because I knew she'd say, 'I told you so.' "

Quentin appeared, carefully did not look at Firebird, and asked, "Dessert? Our tiramisu is world-famous."

"There's a lot of world-famous food here in Rocky Cliffs. But I couldn't eat another thing," Firebird said regretfully.

"Coffee, then?" the waiter asked.

"Decaf, please," Firebird said.

"Full octane." Doug had had one glass of wine, yet the bottle was empty. He wondered if Firebird realized she was buzzed, whether she knew her gestures were freer, her eyes warmer, her voice slightly slurred. He wondered if he would feel guilty for taking advantage of a woman under the influence. He suspected not. He didn't care how or why as long as she would fall into his arms.

Quentin placed the coffees, one caf, one decaf, on the table, with cream and sweetener, and faded away again.

Doug watched Firebird pour half the cream into her cup, add three yellow packets, and stir vigorously. She offered him the cream pitcher, but he shook his head. "I take it black."

"Of course you do," she said. "So how'd Mrs. Fuller find out?"

"I curtailed my street activities—man, I was scared the molester would find me and off me in some horrible way. I hit the books. Behaved like a model citizen." The coffee was hot and full-flavored, exactly what he needed after a day like today. "Thought I was being discreet about the whole incident."

"I'll bet."

He lifted his eyebrows at her skeptical tone.

"I know exactly how discreet a dumb boy can be," she explained. "Remember, I have three brothers. You probably might as well have sent up fireworks."

"Yeah. Well. Mrs. Fuller sat me down, gave me a cup of tea, some cookies, softened me up. . . ." He'd never thought about it before, but Mrs. Fuller would have made a great police interrogator. "Then, bam! She asked me what had happened, and I cracked. Made a total fool of myself. Sobbed on her lap. Told her everything, just like she said I could. I was so embarrassed."

"Did she straighten you out?"

"She didn't have to. After that, I pretty much straightened myself out."

"You went to school, got smart, and gave up a life of petty crime?"

"Mostly."

"What about the guy who tried to rape you? Did you still have to dodge him?"

"Interesting thing about him." Doug's eyes narrowed as he remembered. "Mrs. Fuller went down to the casinos, and the next day . . . he disappeared from Las Vegas, never to be seen again."

"Wow. Mrs. Fuller had connections." Firebird mulled that over. "I'll bet she raised a few kids who ran the casinos."

"Good possibility." He brooded over his coffee. "I lived with her for four years."

"Four years? Why only four years?" Firebird stared at him over her cup.

"I had to leave." The memory still hurt.

"Leave? But you must have been . . . what? Twelve? *Why'd* you leave?"

Should he tell her? She would understand in a way most women never could. But Firebird was smart, too damned smart. When he told her, she'd realize that their first meeting had been no coincidence. She'd know that he'd stalked her, and she'd figure out why.

He was pretty sure he didn't want to engage in that conversation in public, because he was pretty sure she was going to get mad. While he signaled for the waiter, he told her, "It turned out I couldn't tell her everything. Some things Mrs. Fuller was not ready to hear."

"Like what?"

"It's not a subject for a public place," Doug said. "I'll tell you . . . later."

Chapter Sixteen

Later.

Firebird considered Douglas, starting with the top of his tousled blond head, moving across his broad shoulders and muscled arms, and settling on his expressionless face.

Expressionless. When had the man acquired the art of betraying no emotion? He hadn't been that way before. He used to smile more than once every blue moon, and move more like a man and less like a punched-out cardboard figure.

He also gave the impression of complete and total certainty. Like right now, he acted as if he knew, without a doubt, that she would return with him to his house.

If she did, what would happen? She needed to think very carefully before she agreed, because he had one bed, and she didn't think he intended to sleep in a chair. In fact, she didn't think he intended to sleep at all.

Then he said it. The one thing guaranteed to divert her from her worries about her virtue. "Now it's my turn to ask the questions."

"Okay." She put down her cup, and her hand trembled. "Go ahead."

"You never asked me about myself before. You weren't curious about my background. Why do you care now?"

"Because of Aleksandr."

"You want to know what kind of a person his father really is."

"Right."

"Why, after so long, did you decide to tell me about him *now*?"

Trust Douglas to see right to the heart of the matter. "You want the truth?"

"That would be a novel change."

"Okay, I'll tell you." She smiled, but with a tight edge. "But I'll tell you . . . later."

Almost without flickering an eyelash, he managed to look amused. "*Later* is going to be one long, amazing experience."

She retorted, "Later is going to involve a lot of talking and not a lot of—"

Mario appeared beside the table. "You enjoyed your dinner?"

"It was wonderful. Everything was wonderful, but your crust!" Firebird kissed her fingers, tossed them in an extravagant gesture, and realized, in a sensible corner of her mind, that she'd had a little too much wine. "Such a tangy flavor. The perfect sourdough. My mother would kill for your recipe."

Mario beamed and waggled his hand. "No, no. It is a family secret from my dear old grandmother in Sicily. But you bring your mother, and we'll talk."

"I would love to. We've got a few things to finish up, but after that she'll deserve a vacation." Firebird still smiled, but with a wry edge.

In that deadpan voice that made her want to wallop him, Douglas said, "I need the check."

"Tonight, it is on me." When Douglas would have protested, Mario adamantly shook his head. "You come-a in every week with your trooper friends or by yourself, and I let-a you pay. But tonight, you have a beau-tee-ful young lady, and I would-a be remiss if I didn't buy her dinner."

Before Douglas could curtly refuse, Firebird thanked him. "Mario. You are a dear!"

"I know. And if-a this big galoot did not carry a gun, I would-a take you away from him. But alas." Mario put both hands on his heart. "I must suffer, or die."

"Yeah, because your wife would kill you," Douglas said.

"She is a jealous woman. But who-a can blame her? Now." Mario signaled Quentin, who arrived carrying a to-go box and a long paper bag. "I give-a you two tiramisus and a bottle of wine." Leaning over Douglas, he spoke into his ear, all pretense at an accent gone, and loudly enough for Firebird to hear: "To enjoy after." He clapped him on the shoulder, then held Firebird's coat as she slipped into it.

As they walked across the restaurant, Firebird was very aware of Mario babbling romantic compliments in that extravagantly phony accent, of the two construction workers glancing at her and talking to each other, and most of all, of Douglas stalking after her . . . no, herding her toward the door.

When Douglas opened the door, the wind whipped in.

Mario backed away fast enough. "The storm's coming."

Firebird pulled on her gloves and wrapped her scarf tightly around her head. She took the to-go box.

"There's a wind advisory on the bay. With the windchill, the temperature is like twenty-five degrees." Doug didn't want her to freeze up before he got her into bed.

She nodded, and he remembered—he'd insisted it was time for her to 'fess up.

She intended to talk. *Crap.* When had he become such a stickler for the truth?

"We'll hurry," he told Mario, and gathered the wine bottle and stashed it in his capacious coat pocket.

They stepped outside.

He heard Firebird gasp as the wind snatched her breath away. Automatically he reached out and tucked her under his arm. She followed him as automatically, her head against his shoulder.

He put her in the car and walked around to the other side.

The restaurant door opened and closed.

He glanced over, but it was dark. Whoever it was had disappeared into the night, probably walking back toward one of the other houses on the hill, or into town toward one of the hotels.

He needed to get Firebird to his house. There they would be safe, wired, protected from intrusion. Once they got there, no one could touch them.

And they could *talk*.

He grimaced. Yeah, he'd made her promise to tell the truth. But he'd promised to tell the truth, too, and he didn't look forward to that.

They drove toward his house, the house he had bought . . . for her. He parked in his lousy excuse of a garage—that was next on his list to get fixed—and he went around to get her out. He turned her toward the front door.

She resisted, dragged him toward the oceanfront, staggering as the wind blasted them. She wanted to stand and face the raging storm, and he knew why. She loved the mad tempest, the raging waves, the wild blast of glory from across the seas. It fed her soul, as it fed his.

They had that in common. They'd always had their wild natures in common.

They reached the edge of the cliff and stood looking out toward the horizon, black with the night, yet infinite . . . waiting.

The wind was shredding the clouds, opening patches to the stars, allowing the moonlight to ripple across the ground, across the sea, then disappear once more.

The wind blasted. The waves roared. Yet he heard her clearly when she turned to him. "That thing that changed you, that made you leave Mrs. Fuller. I understand. I know. And I have to tell you—" She stopped. Stiffened.

Another sound, one infinitely more sinister, came to his ears.

Low, pleased chuckles, the sound of men who had stalked and trapped their prey.

Doug turned.

His eyesight, always good in the night, picked them out. In the lead, the beasts from the restaurant, the two who had insulted Firebird this morning. Beyond them, four more, gathering like vultures to the feast.

Varinskis.

Varinskis.

"What a pretty girl," one of them said. He spoke with a heavy Russian accent, and he lisped. No, not lisped. *Hissed.* "Ssshe's ssstupid, like all women, but how sssweet of her to bring you here where it's easy to dispose of the bodies."

Doug should have realized they had been followed. If he hadn't been distracted by Firebird's scent, by the possibility of her love, he would have.

No excuse. He had no excuse.

But he did have his service pistol.

Pulling his nine-millimeter, he slid the safety free. Behind him, he heard Firebird heft the to-go box.

He had only a moment to frown, to wonder what in the hell she was doing, when the box flew past his ear and exploded on the Varinski in the lead.

This soft, pretty young woman had been taught to

use every resource, no matter how flimsy, as a defense.

The moon chose that moment to blast out from behind a cloud, lighting the pale cream and mascarpone cheese that smeared the guy's mean, pissed-off face. He roared with fury and wiped ladyfingers out of his eyes.

The other Varinskis laughed.

Doug laughed. He couldn't help it. This was a Charlie Chaplin fight—a Charlie Chaplin fight ending in real death, in blood and despair.

He'd brought this on himself. It was his fault Firebird was in jeopardy.

So without a qualm, he shot the son of a bitch right through the heart.

The Varinski dropped like a rock. That would have almost evened the odds, if the remaining Varinskis were normal size, instead of hulking monsters, dark blots in the moonlight, and if Firebird were a man instead of a soft, pretty young woman—a young woman who pulled a switchblade out of her coat pocket and flipped the two-inch blade out. She held it, point up, and braced her feet like a street fighter.

Soft? Pretty? It was true. Firebird was both of those things. But she would fight, and fight well, until the end.

And the end was near. They faced certain slaughter.

The Varinski who wore the tiramisu pulled his pistol and aimed at Doug.

Firebird threw her knife, piercing his throat.

The Varinski jerked the blade free and tried to

speak, but he could do no more than squeak. She had pierced his voice box. As his blood spurted down his front, a dark stain in the perilous night, he lifted his pistol again.

Twisting swiftly, Doug lifted Firebird over and behind one of the boulders that lined the edge of the cliff. They crouched low on the ground, barely protected by a rock two feet in diameter.

The shot whistled over their heads.

Hands on the boulder, he leapfrogged up and into the Varinski's belly. He lifted him over his head— and over the cliff.

The Varinski screamed in satisfying terror until he hit the rocks . . . with a dull crunch audible even over the sounds of wind and waves.

The remaining Varinskis circled them, and as they did, they changed . . . into predatory beasts. They were a wolf pack, deadly killers, intent on their prey. A deep growl broke from the great wolf throats.

This was not how Doug had envisioned the night ending.

The one with the hiss in his voice stood back, still human, watching, warning. . . . "Don't hurt the pretty girl too much. Ssshe ssshould sssuffer, and we all want a turn, don't we?"

That one was in charge. He was the one to kill.

Doug groped for his pistol.

It was gone. In the charge, he'd lost it.

"We've got only one chance," Firebird said. She rose off the ground to stand beside him. "We've got to jump."

"We can't. That water is forty-five degrees." He

knew this stuff. In his job, he'd seen more than one person go into the drink and come out dead. "We'd have maybe thirty minutes before hypothermia sets in. Then we'd drown."

"We'll survive." Pulling the wine bottle out of Doug's pocket, she broke it across the lead wolf's snout, driving him down and back.

Wine splashed. Blood spurted. The smells mixed.

Desperation and terror mixed in Doug's mind.

The wolf recovered too quickly, and with a whine and then a snarl, it leaped for her throat.

With the strength of a Russian weightlifter, Doug heaved one of the boulders out of the ground and smashed it into the wolf's side.

The beast turned on him, and as it did, another leaped at her.

Moving with the lightness and skill of a matador, she stepped aside and dragged the sharp, jagged remains of the glass bottle across the wolf's face, ripping into its eye.

What a woman.

The wolves slunk back, snarling, regrouping, preparing for the final assault.

She moved close to Doug. "I'd rather chance the ocean than them."

"Can you swim?" he asked.

She glanced at him incredulously. "What difference does that make? We'll be lucky to live through the jump."

"Yeah." They'd be lucky to hit the water instead of the rocks, and if they did hit the water, they'd be lucky to survive the impact.

But the wolves were advancing again, growling, and the one she'd slashed had his remaining eye fixed on her. It glowed red, and foam speckled its lips and dripped off its teeth.

Behind them, the hissing one repeated over and over, "Be sssweet with the pretty girl. Ssshe's our dessert."

Doug and Firebird had no choice.

Grabbing her hand, he said, "Run and jump as hard as you can."

"Right." She kissed him right on the lips.

Together, they turned.

Together, they took a breath.

Together, they raced for the edge of the cliff—and jumped into the darkness.

Chapter Seventeen

The wind whistled in Doug's ears. The ocean thrashed below them, the waves rolling in the moonlight. Doug and Firebird hurtled through the air, toward the sea, toward the rocks that protruded from the water like strong, giant black teeth.

He wanted to hit squarely, not glance off and live for another ten agonizing minutes. But . . .

Please, God, let her live.

Right before they hit, Firebird squeezed his hand. Salt water blasted through his nostrils. Cold scoured his skin like sandpaper. The pressure ripped her hand away from his.

Please, God, let her live.

And he was under, plunging so far down he didn't know which direction was up. Desperately he reached out, wanting, *needing* to help Firebird to the surface.

She was gone. Vanished in the black sea.

Please, God, let her live.

He groped, flailed, trying to catch a hand, a foot, a tendril of hair . . . and he had her! He kicked strongly toward the surface, dragging her after him. He broke into air that felt warm after the frigid sea and gasped in a huge lungful of oxygen. He turned to face her.

He held a handful of seaweed.

The waves lifted him on their swells. The moon shone on the black water.

Firebird was nowhere in sight.

Taking a huge breath, he dove and swam in ever-increasing circles, desperate, searching. . . . He'd had her hand until the water blasted them apart. She couldn't be too far away.

He ran out of breath. Necessity sent him to the surface. Once again, he treaded water, gasping, looking around for a blond head, a bright smile.

Nothing. She wasn't here.

Something stung his shoulder above the collarbone.

A swell lifted him, and he glanced down. Somehow he'd wounded himself, ripped his skin open.

Something plunked in the water beside him, lifting a small geyser, and distantly he realized . . . No, those Varinski bastards up above were shooting at him.

He dove again, swam in circles again—and this time, he saw a glow. Something white and bright in the water, like a light shining in the distance. He swam toward it, reached out his hand, and something brushed it.

A forest of kelp, tangled, alive. In its midst, the thing glowed, a beacon about three inches square.

What was it? Where had it come from? Was it some strange sea creature?

He plunged his hand through the gelatinous stems and gritty blades and grabbed for the light.

The flat, hard iridescent tile fit in his hand—and seared his skin.

But his fingers brushed flesh beneath the light, so he held on, groped, found Firebird's body floating only a few feet below the surface. He grabbed her waist and tried to drag her upward.

She barely twitched; the spark of life was almost gone, vanquished by the bone-biting cold and her lack of air.

Working blind, he ran his hands up her until he came to her head. Seaweed. Giant kelp wrapped itself around her, holding her prisoner, stealing her life. A sticky blade had insinuated itself in her hair. A rubbery strand grasped her around the neck. There by her throat, the strange glow pulsed, then faded, like some indicator of her life force.

No. He wouldn't allow her to go.

Frantically, he ripped at the seaweed, fighting the currents, the blistering iciness.

A huge swell lifted him out of the water.

The kelp held her without mercy, uncaring.

He held the seaweed, caught his breath, and dove down again, fumbling with the knife he carried at his belt. His fingers were clumsy, his skin burning, his nerves frozen.

He wouldn't go up again without her. If he couldn't free her, they would die together.

Desperately, he hacked at her hair, at the seaweed that carelessly tangled the seaborne beacon and Firebird's throat in its cruel, inhuman grasp.

Another wave caught him. He held tightly to her—and with the strength of that mighty current, she was free.

Hanging her over his shoulder, he shot to the surface.

Gasping, he held her against his body and pressed on her chest.

Nothing.

He did it again. *Come on, princess. Come on!*

She spasmed. Coughed. Threw up half the ocean.

A bullet plunked into the water near them.

For a brief second, a surge of anger warmed him. Then he glanced up. The Varinskis were still shooting, but the bullets were falling short—because a riptide was sweeping them out to sea.

They were doomed.

Chapter Eighteen

The Varinski home
In the Ukraine

"Get out of the house. Get out now." Vadim Varinski spoke softly, but with an intensity that should have reached every one of his cousins and brothers. "It's time."

Of course, some of them didn't pay attention, didn't hear, didn't understand.

He didn't care. The ones who were too drunk or too stupid were of no use to him anyway. "Get out," he repeated, but his voice grew softer.

"Let me help you." Georgly stood beside him, taller than Vadim, broader than Vadim, intelligent, resourceful, and, most important, completely and blindly loyal to Vadim. "You can finish in half the time if I help."

Vadim thought for only a moment, then nodded. "You take the back. Make sure you cover the exits,

and be out in"—Vadim consulted his watch—
"three minutes."

"Right." Georgly shoved at Mikhail. "Get in the bus."

Mikhail was a big, shambling Russian bear of a
man, not bright, not handsome, not even completely
human—he grew a pelt of black hair down his neck,
onto his shoulders, down his arms, and onto the
backs of his hands. He shrugged off Georgly's man-
handling, a big grin plastered on his moon face. "I've
never ridden on an airplane before. I can't wait."

"I can't wait, either," Vadim said. The faster he
could get the job done, the better.

Over the last few weeks, he'd been slowly moving
his men out of the house, out of the country, and
placing them in position for the assault on the Wilders. Today, the last plane he'd chartered waited at
the airstrip. None of these Varinskis realized it, but
when they boarded and flew away, they would never
return to the mother country. Vadim had decided it
was time to move forward. He'd eliminated the old
uncles—only one Varinski over forty remained alive.
He'd transferred their assets to a Swiss bank, taking
care that he and he alone should know the account
codes. And he'd arranged to buy a huge old house
in Wyoming that the Varinskis would now call home.

He himself had a condo in New York City.

Only one detail was left to clear up.

Picking up the gas cans, he started into the house.

The Varinski homestead was entirely made of
wood. It was old. It was sagging. It was rotting.

Gas fumes rose to his nose as he liberally doused
the floorboards.

It was going to go up like a torch.

He hurried; this job needed to be done quickly, and it needed to be done right. Because right now, Uncle Ivan lay facedown on the floor in the den, snoring loudly, and only one thing could wake him up—if someone tried to remove the bottle of vodka from his fist.

Vadim had no intention of doing that.

Only to himself did Vadim admit how much Uncle Ivan, with his gnarled joints and staring white eyes, made his skin crawl. Of course, it wasn't really Uncle Ivan who disturbed him. It was the thing that dwelled inside Uncle Ivan, watching the Varinski operations through those blind eyes. Only once since Vadim had taken over as leader had the beast taken possession of Uncle Ivan's body. Only once had Vadim seen Uncle Ivan's white eyes glow blue, and heard the deep, menacing tones of a devil displeased.

Because it *was* the devil. The devil who felt that, because he had granted the pact to the first Konstantine, he had the right to disapprove of Vadim's plans.

Vadim didn't give a shit about that feeble old pact. The pact was disintegrating right before his eyes. Varinski boys grew up to be predators, all right: weasels, snakes, rats. . . . Who was going to hire a fearsome badger as an assassin?

No one.

Worse, half the boys were drooling idiots, incapable of scratching their own asses.

Those were the ones he left in the house to burn and never bother him again.

If the Evil One imagined that by granting old Konstantine the pact, he could exact he'd given Vadim a great gift and claim great loyalty, he had another think coming. Vadim had studied American society, studied the organized crime that thrived there, and he was dragging the family into legitimate corruption.

He didn't need Lucifer anymore.

As he made his way back toward the front door, he glanced into the den.

A square of sunlight from the east-facing window illuminated Uncle Ivan, still unconscious, unaware of the fate that awaited him. Vadim supposed it was a shame, really—the old guy was going to suffer, while the devil would be in his element.

Vadim gave the threshold an extra-large splash of gasoline.

Uncle Ivan snuffled. He lifted his head. "Who's there?" he snapped.

Vadim froze.

The old guy looked around the room as if he could see, and for a moment, Vadim thought his gaze lingered on him, and on the gas can. But when no one answered, Uncle Ivan took a long swallow of vodka, his skinny old Adam's apple bobbing. He belched, dropped his head back down, and was still.

Slowly, carefully, Vadim backed away from the den. When he reached the porch, he dumped the last dribble of gasoline around the outside of the den, beneath the windows, and down on the rickety steps. Uncle Ivan would not escape this conflagration.

Stepping away, Vadim flung a lighted match on the damp wood.

The house ignited with a whoosh. Greedily, the flames ate the boards. Fire danced under the windows, into the open front door, down the corridor.

Vadim heard the first shout, and Georgly ran around the corner, his face blackened with soot, his eyebrows burned off. "You said three minutes." He shook his watch in Vadim's face. "Not two minutes and forty seconds. What the hell's the matter with you? You almost killed me!"

"Oops." Vadim shrugged with patently false innocence. "My mistake."

Georgly growled, the guttural growl of an angry tiger.

Vadim turned his head and looked at Georgly. Just looked.

But Georgly slunk backward.

Vadim never changed into the predator the pact allowed him to become. He wouldn't permit the devil to control him, yet he had a gift. He made people afraid. He always had. And that was power.

"If you're going with me, get on the bus," Vadim said.

"Of course I'm going with you. I'm your right-hand man. As if I would stay without you!" Georgly protested.

"I thought you would feel that way." Vadim waved a hand toward the Varinski homestead, engulfed in flames. "Because what's going to be left?"

Yells and shrieks wafted from inside the house. The Varinski idiots were burning.

The windows on the bus were all down. His men watched, and even from here, Vadim could hear them muttering, could sense their confusion. Right now, the fear of him hadn't yet settled in, and some of them wondered if they should mutiny against the man who would burn their home and their brothers.

"Get on the bus," Vadim told Georgly. "Keep the men under control."

Georgly hurried to do as Vadim instructed, then paused. "When are you coming?"

"I'll come when I know everything's been taken care of." Vadim smiled at the smell of burning wool and electrical wire, laughing when the flames reached one of the gas cans he'd stashed and the explosion rocked the ground. As the heat grew more intense, he backed away.

At last he saw what he'd been looking for. In the window of the den, a blazing male form pranced and whirled, screaming, trying to escape the flames.

Uncle Ivan.

Uncle Ivan tried to open the window. The glass exploded, and he screamed again.

The bus driver, a manservant whom Vadim had hired to drive them to the airstrip, leaped down the steps to puke.

The blaze climbed to new heights, licking under the porch roof, bursting through the wood shingles, igniting the huge dead tree in the side yard. Cars that were parked around the house developed blisters in their paint, and the Volvo began to smoke ominously.

From behind the house, a wild shriek sounded, and a human flame ran toward the creek, igniting the grass as he fled.

Still in the den, Uncle Ivan careened from one window to another, screaming wordlessly. He wasn't a man anymore, merely fuel for the fire.

Satisfied he had handled the matter, Vadim turned away and walked toward the bus. Stepping on board, he looked around at the faces, some sharp with intelligence, some dull with stupidity, some barely human, some in control of their gifts . . . all watching him with terror and awe.

Good. He'd accomplished two deeds—he'd rid himself of Uncle Ivan and his devil, and tightened his grip on Varinski power.

He gestured Georgly out of the front seat.

Georgly gladly went.

To the bus driver, Vadim said, "Stop puking and drive, or I'll toss you on top of the pyre."

The ashen-faced man did as he was told, and as they drove away, Vadim glanced one last time at the old homestead.

Uncle Ivan's flaming figure had somehow clambered out of the house. Now he stood swaying on the porch as the roof collapsed around him. Nothing about him was recognizable. Nothing at all—except, even from this distance, Vadim could see the freakish blue glow deep in his eyes.

"Take that," he muttered, and saluted ironically. Then, pulling his briefcase from beneath the seat, he donned his headphones, plugged in his iPod, closed his eyes, and listened to the Reverend Dean Dowling read his audiobook, *Success Through a Better You.*

Vadim failed to notice, far in the back of the bus, the freakish blue glow that flashed in two brown eyes.

Chapter Nineteen

———✦———

They were going to die. Firebird knew it. The cliffs were dwindling in the distance. The current moved more and more swiftly. The wind ripped at them, and the surface waves tossed them like driftwood.

But she laughed anyway.

She was suffering from hypothermia. She knew that, too. Because otherwise she wouldn't be giggling like the understudy for a Broadway star who'd fallen ill.

She wrapped her arms around Douglas's neck and kicked her feet to help keep them afloat. "Did you know that people suffering from hypothermia are frequently . . . are frequently . . ." She shuddered with the cold and tried to remember what she was saying. "Did you know that people suffering from hypothermia are frequently irrational and uncoordinated?"

The waves rose and fell, huge swells that lifted them into the air, then plunged them underwater.

Douglas tried to keep her head in the air, but she

sputtered and laughed when the icy water struck her in the face. "I know."

"You know what?"

"That people suffering from hypothermia are irrational." He was *not* laughing. In the white moonlight, his face looked as bleak and stony as the cliffs themselves.

"Cheer up, darling. We'll be in China soon." She shuddered again, her teeth chattering so hard they clanked in her mouth. As the spasm eased, she kissed him and sang, " 'I'm gonna get you on a slow boat to China. . . .' "

Another wave rolled beneath them, lifting them high, then plunging them into the depths.

She wiped her face, blew salt water out of her nose, and sang louder: " '. . . Get you, um, in my arms evermore. Leave, um, others waitin'. . .' " She broke off. "I can't remember the words. Do you know the words?"

"No." He leaned his forehead on hers. "Firebird, I'm sorry."

"For what?" She grinned at him.

"It's my fault you're going to die."

"No. Believe me, I know where to place the blame. It's the Varinskis' fault." She rode the rising swell, and at the very tip-top, she lifted her fist and shouted, "You ruthless pricks, I hope you all eat shit!"

The sea sucked her down into the depths. Her muscles were cramping, her bones cracking under the influence of the constant, shocking cold. She was an anchor attached to Douglas, one he clutched with all his might.

This time it took longer to come to the surface, and when she did, she had only one thought in her mind. "Do you think *eat shit* is too crude?"

"No. *Eat shit* is just right."

She felt drunk. She felt silly. But she didn't feel cold now. In fact, she was feeling warmer.

Stupid to feel warmer, but she didn't care. "You need to let me go, but before you do, I have something very serious to tell you." She wrapped her arms around his neck and frowned at him. "It's about who you are. Because if I don't tell you, and I die, you'll never know."

"I'll never let you go. We're going to die together."

"No." She had to concentrate, because she was losing the fight for consciousness. "Listen. About your family. Listen . . ."

A light slipped across the water.

"Hey!" He jumped in her arms, then shouted again, "Hey!"

She watched the light skitter toward them in a detached sort of amazement. "I guess that's it. The light of heaven. But . . . maybe not. Do I qualify for heaven?"

He wasn't paying any attention. He just kept shouting, "Hey!" and waving an arm.

"I'm not really a Wilder, so I do. Except I haven't lived an exemplary life, so maybe not. It depends on how strict the angel Gabriel is about the rules. . . ."

Another light joined the first. The two lights got brighter.

Angels started shouting.

She looked up as they grabbed her under the arms and dragged her onto the boat, and she sang, " 'I dreamed last night I was on the boat to heaven, and a great big wave came and washed me overboard. . . .' "

The light shone right in her face.

Douglas was speaking, wrapping her in a blanket. She couldn't feel it—she was too cold—and when he tried to talk to her, she sang louder, then broke off to say, "I'll bet you didn't know I played the lead in *Guys and Dolls* in high school."

"I didn't," he admitted.

"I can't sing." Her head flopped to one side.

"I do know that."

She felt a vague indignation, but then the shivering started, racking her bones.

She deserved the pain. "I should have told you. . . . Listen to me, Douglas. I should have told you. I almost didn't get the chance. We almost died, and you would have never known. . . ."

He wasn't paying attention. He was listening to the angels, listening with an attitude of concern, then anger.

The angels were talking among themselves in low tones, and she shouted, "A little louder, boys, I can't understand you."

Douglas stood with his hands on his hips. He still wore his uniform, he was dripping and shivering— "Handsome as sin," she said—and he talked back to the angels. He was loud enough, but it still sounded like gibberish to her.

Or—she tilted her head—was it Russian? Her parents spoke Russian. She spoke a little. *"Zdravstvuite,"* she said.

The angels fell silent. The angels stared at her. Stared with their eyes bugging out of their heads.

The boat rocked.

The wind whistled.

One angel reached down toward her throat.

Douglas caught his hand and spoke sharply.

Suddenly, the angels scurried to tend their sails. The captain's strong voice lifted. He shouted orders.

Then the boat took on a life of its own, catching the wind, the waves, the tides, and moved toward a destination she couldn't imagine.

For one moment, her judgment returned. She was alive. Not on a boat to heaven. She knew how close she'd come to death, how close she still was—and she realized that Douglas must be in the same shape she was, yet he stood over her, protecting her.

"Douglas, please." She lifted the edge of the blanket. "Come to bed with me. You know you want to."

Nervous male laughter swept the boat.

She'd been too loud. She had no control.

Tears filled her eyes.

Douglas knelt beside her. "Don't worry. I've got a bigger body mass, I had less wine, and the cold affected me less." He pressed his hand on her forehead. "Go to sleep. I'll take care of you."

"But who will take care of you?" She lifted her violently shaking hand and touched his face. "I promise . . . promise to live so I can take you . . . to your mother."

Chapter Twenty

Firebird woke.

It was morning.

Or something.

She could see light behind her closed lids. But her eyeballs hurt, so she didn't open them.

Her bad ankle hurt, too. *Everything* hurt, but her ankle especially. It was cocked sideways. And she couldn't move it. Because when she tried, that *really* hurt. Finally, in profound irritation, she reached down to pick up her leg and found something in the way. Blankets.

Irritation turned to rage. Viciously she ripped the covers aside. Which made her twisted ankle straighten. Which caused so much pain she shouted, "Goddamn son of a bitch." And at last, she opened her eyes.

She was in Douglas's bedroom. He stood over her. For a moment, memories merged; dinner at Mario's had never happened, and she was facing Douglas again for the first time after the passionate interlude on this very bed.

Then she saw the way he looked, like a man who

had been to hell and back, and the evening at Mario's and in the ocean, with all its confessions and its horrors, tumbled into place.

"You're better." He pulled the covers all the way to the foot of the bed.

She wore an old-fashioned flannel nightgown, long-sleeved and buttoned all the way up to her throat.

Where had that come from?

"How do you figure?" Her voice had an odd rasp, as if it had been rubbed with sandpaper.

"You're swearing." His blond hair hung in insolent curls on his forehead. "It's good to hear that."

"You're weird."

He leaned over, gathered her in his arms, and gently scooted her up onto a cluster of pillows.

She groaned. Her bad knee. Her bad ankle. Every joint in her body ached. Her skin felt raw. Her head pounded.

He offered her an open bottle of water with a straw stuck inside, and two white pills resting in his palm. "Pain reliever," he said. "Ibuprofen. For that headache."

How did he know?

Obvious answer—she must look like hell. She took the pills and washed them down with a drink that didn't stop until the bottle was half-empty. Relaxing back on the bed, she reached up and ran her fingers through her hair—and sat straight up. "What happened to my hair?"

"I had to cut it with my knife." He braced himself as if he expected an attack.

He was a smart man.

"Give me a mirror."

"I don't have one."

She wanted to call him a liar. But he was barefoot. He stood there in jeans slung low on his hips and an old, thin T-shirt that stretched tightly across his shoulders and lovingly molded the ripples of his taut belly. He had a long scratch on one cheek, and a bandage padded one shoulder above his collarbone. Gauze wrapped his right hand, and new wrinkles tightened his mouth.

Her gaze wandered around his bedroom. He'd dragged one of his comfortable chairs over by the bed and placed it so he could watch her. A tray with a half-eaten meal sat near the chair that faced the muted television. There the Weather Channel showed yet another winter storm wound up and ready to hit the Washington coast.

On the bedside table, a single yellow rosebud floated in a clean cereal bowl.

The whole scene had the appearance of a death-watch.

Which brought her to the thing she'd been avoiding: her fragmented memories. "The last thing I remember was jumping. Hitting that freaking cold ocean and being glad because it was the water and not a rock. Getting caught on something." She broke into a sweat. "And struggling until I passed out."

He picked a washcloth off the end table and wiped her forehead and the palms of her hands. The washcloth was cool and damp. His voice was calm and soothing. "You were caught in the kelp. I almost didn't find you in time. Luckily, cold water lowers metabolism, allowing the brain to withstand a much longer period of oxygen deprivation. Mostly it happens with children, but . . . well, you were singing."

"Singing? That's stupid. Why would I have been . . ." Recollection swept through her. "The riptide was carrying us out to sea."

He tossed the washcloth aside and leaned forward, his palms flat on the mattress. "Tell me what you remember."

"I had a flash of waves heaving up and down, so rough, and you trying to keep my head above water."

"You'd swallowed enough of the ocean already."

"We were headed for China."

"You kept saying not to worry, we were fine."

"I figured we'd die of hypothermia before we got there," she said. *Hm.* She was still a little snappish. "How did we get back *here*?"

"There was a boat from up near the Canadian border, filled with Russian immigrants."

I'm going to get you on a slow boat to China . . . Oh, no. She *had* been singing.

"They hauled us on board, and weren't so happy when they saw the state trooper uniform, since they sure as hell *shouldn't* have been out in that weather, and they probably didn't have fishing licenses." The lines around his mouth deepened. "Dumb shits."

"I'm surprised they didn't throw us back overboard."

"They thought about it."

"They talked about it right in front of you?"

"In Russian. They believed I couldn't understand their language."

"You speak Russian?" *Really?* "Why?"

"I speak Spanish, too, and a little Japanese. Remember, I lived in Las Vegas, and I'm a police officer, and a few different languages go a long way."

She wasn't satisfied. Not by a long shot.

He continued, "Then *you* spoke Russian to them, and they saw . . ."

"Saw what?"

"How pretty you are." He glanced to the left, uncomfortable and embarrassed, and he looked just like Aleksandr when he was lying. "Once they saw how pretty you were, they decided they would save us."

"I was *pretty*? Suffering from hypothermia and covered with kelp, and I was *pretty*?" He needed to work on his lies a little more.

"I guess they'd been out there for a while." He seemed to realize how tactless that had been, especially to a woman with her hair hacked half-off, and added hastily, "You're always pretty."

"It sounds like I was almost a really pretty corpse." Something bothered her about this story. Something important. If he would be quiet for merely a moment, she'd be able to concentrate. . . .

But he seemed oblivious, speaking quickly, filling her in with the details. "I told them to take us to the cove where Mrs. Burchett lives."

"Mrs. Burchett?" If he'd been trying to distract her, he'd done a good job. Firebird imagined a sweet-faced widow who welcomed the new state policeman in for a cup of coffee and a warm snuggle on a cold day. "Mrs. Burchett?" she asked frostily.

"We have a thing," he said, as stone-faced as ever.

"I'll bet." Firebird crossed her arms over her chest.

Douglas looked her over, and something in his air lightened. "Mrs. Burchett is ninety-four years old. She lives alone in the next cove over, in the same house where she's lived since she got married seventy-five years ago. Occasionally she falls down. She calls me and I go over there and get her on her feet."

"Oh." Firebird felt foolish, suspicious . . . and surprised. Somehow, she'd never pictured Douglas as the kindly officer who helped old ladies up off the floor. "How did we get there?"

"The fishermen got us into the cove, put us out in their dinghy, and the waves slammed us into the beach." Douglas slithered into the chair as if standing were too much effort. "You were unconscious. I was . . . My energy was giving out. I got us off the beach and to the bottom of the cliff, where I collapsed."

"How far was it to Mrs. Burchett's?"

"Only about thirty steps—straight up the cliff."

No matter how Firebird searched her mind, she couldn't find a wisp of memory that tied her to that moment. "How did we get there?"

"Mostly you bossed me until I got up and carried you up the slope."

"I was still conscious?"

"In and out. Nagging while you were in. Shivering

in the fetal position when you were out. But brave. Always brave, always a fighter." His praise warmed her. "Once you tried to drag me."

Her eyes narrowed as, in her mind, she saw his prone body, and realized that if she didn't do something he would die. She remembered grabbing his arms to move him, but he was a foot taller than she and fully a hundred pounds heavier, and hypothermia had drained her strength. He was wet, he was limp, and she couldn't budge him.

So she nagged.

Apparently, he had responded.

"I only remember . . . bits and pieces, like a DVD with a scratch." She hated that. She wanted to know what had happened, know from her point of view, not through some gauzy filter he used to comfort and divert her.

"We made it, but it was one hell of a climb." He went from stone-faced to grim. "Mrs. Burchett was in bed. I scared her half to death beating on her door, but once she let us inside, she was wonderful. She saved our lives."

"God bless Mrs. Burchett." Firebird looked around the room, at the glimmer of light coming through the west-facing windows. "How long have I been out?"

"We got to Mrs. Burchett's before midnight. We came home after it got dark last night, around eight. It's about five in the morning now."

So about thirty hours. Thirty hours since she'd left the restaurant and hit the water. Thirty hours that she didn't remember. Thirty hours of not communicating with her family . . . She never meant to ignore them for so long. Not now. Not in these dangerous times. "Who knows we're alive?"

"Mrs. Burchett knows you're alive. My boss knows I'm alive. Most of the town probably thinks we've gone off to have an affair. The only people who know we're missing are the Varinskis, and as far as I can tell, they've left town."

"How do you know that?"

"I went out and looked."

"Okay. That's good. So essentially, we're alive because the Varinskis believe that we're dead."

"That's right." He struggled, as if deciding how much to say. "According to my alarm system, while we were gone, the Varinskis visited the house."

Anxious for him, for that part of the house he had so lovingly remodeled, she lifted herself onto one elbow. "What did those pigs do?"

"Nothing."

"Nothing? They did nothing? The Varinskis?" Her disbelief climbed with each question.

"Things were moved, especially in my office."

"What were they looking for?" The question had to be asked, although she feared the answer. If they'd come here for the icon, then they had expanded their search to include every place a Wilder had been or would be.

He picked up the remote and switched off the television. "I don't know."

No, of course he didn't. Yet he knew a lot, more than he'd let on. It was time for a talk, because in this case, what he didn't know *could* hurt him.

She removed the remote from his tightly clenched fist, then tugged at him. "Come and sit with me."

He did, lowering himself onto the mattress with such care, it seemed he was afraid he would break her.

"We need to talk about the Varinskis," she said.

The man had fine-tuned the art of hiding his emotions, but now she saw the sheen of moisture on his brow. "I already know a lot about Varinskis."

"I realize that, and I know why."

"You do." It wasn't a question. More like a statement of disbelief.

"You know, because you're a Varinski, too."

Chapter Twenty-one

Doug's heart thumped hard, once, then settled into a steady, rapid rhythm. "Why do you say I'm a Varinski?"

"Because I saw you. When you followed me. At the university."

Everything he knew, everything he thought about the last two and a half years, changed in that instant. "You saw me."

"I knew I was followed. I knew it was a Varinski. I saw the cougar. The golden cougar." Firebird's words were jerky, pried from her by sheer force of will. "I simply didn't realize it was you. I figured the Varinskis were after me, coming to abduct me, so I did what my father taught me to do."

"Which was . . . ?"

"I got to safety, and I watched. I saw you change back to . . ." She waved her hand up and down his body. "I realized you were one of them. I realized it wasn't a coincidence that I'd met you. I realized you'd romanced me not because you'd fallen in love at first sight, but because you wanted something from me."

She knew who he was. What he was. And that he had, from the first moment, lied to her.

No wonder she had run. "What did you think I wanted?" he asked carefully.

"My parents' location. The Varinskis have a thing about killing them, and everyone in my family. I figured you were the one Varinski who'd finally tracked us—or, rather, me. I thought you seduced me, made me fall in love with you, for a joke." Her voice rose, then wobbled. "I thought you were laughing at me."

"So you left." And had crushed his last hope.

"But now I realize you weren't a Varinski, or even working for the Varinskis. You were looking for your family."

He felt as if he were balanced on the sharp edge of a razor blade, and the wrong word would slice him in half. "What brought you to that realization?"

"I understood about the change you went through. I really did. None better. I'm one of the only women who actually could understand, you know." She smiled at him, but her fingers gathered a handful of Mrs. Burchett's flannel nightgown into a crumpled ball. "You haven't asked why I know about the Varinskis, or why they're after my family."

"Tell me."

"Because my father is—or rather, was—a Varinski. He changed his name."

That, Doug had figured out on his own.

"He was the Varinski leader until he met my mother, fell in love, and got married. For that, Papa had to go into exile. They had three sons one after another." She smiled caustically, as if she'd bitten into a peppercorn. "Then, ten years later, they had a daughter."

"You."

She paused as if gathering her strength. "All my life, that's what I've thought. But it seems I was wrong. In fact, Varinskis produce only sons, and the child my mother bore wasn't me. It was a boy."

Doug's ears hummed. Red spots swam before his eyes. Lack of oxygen, he realized. He was holding his breath.

"The woman who assisted in the birth substituted me for that baby. Then Miss Joyce—that Judas, that bitch—took him into the Nevada desert and abandoned the baby boy to die."

At last Doug could breathe. He could breathe because . . . all his childhood wishes had just been fulfilled.

He had a mother. He had a father. He had brothers. He had a son, and the mother of his son sat there, her wide blue eyes fixed on him, waiting for him to say something that expressed his feelings.

And his predominant feeling was . . . horror.

He had been stupid beyond belief and, for a man who prided himself on his clear thinking and decisive action, pitifully immature.

He had been a weasel, a snake, the Judas she'd accused Miss Joyce of being.

He leaped to his feet. He walked away.

But he didn't have to admit to anything. If he was crafty, and if he moved swiftly to erase his mistake, his new family would never know.

Firebird would never know.

He could fix what he had done. He had to.

He came back and sat down.

"Do you understand what I'm saying?" She took his hand and squeezed his fingers a little too hard. "You're the baby boy."

"I understand." One question had to be answered before he knew what to do. "Are they good to you?"

"Who?"

"Your . . . the family. The Wilders. Are they good to you?"

"You mean, were they angry at me because I wasn't really their daughter?" She was getting huffy. "Because they weren't. I know you don't know them, but that's not the kind of people they are."

Huffy or not, he needed to know. "Your whole life. Have they been good parents and taken care of you?"

"Are you worried about what you're getting into? They're really good people. The whole family. I promise. I love them dearly, and they love me, and I just wish—" She stopped.

"What do you wish?"

"I wish I were still their child. You don't know—" She stopped again.

"What don't I know?"

"Look. If you don't want them, I do." She bounced up on her knees. "I know you've had a rough life. I can't imagine how difficult it's been for you, going through your first transformation and not knowing what was happening, having to grow up in an orphanage and on the streets, and getting a job at the police force when you were so young, so you could find your parents. It must have been awful. I'm not discounting that."

"It was okay." He didn't know what else to say, how to ease her increasing agitation. He didn't even understand what she was agitated about.

"But here you are at last. Your dream is coming true. You've found your family. Papa and Mama, Jasha, Rurik, and Adrik."

"And Aleksandr," he reminded her.

"And Aleksandr. How could I forget Aleksandr?" Her hands were shaking. Her voice was rising. "You're stepping into this spot ready-made for you, and you know what? For you to do that, I have to step out. All my life, I've been the miraculous girl child. I've been the baby. I've been spoiled. Now it's you. And like I said, I know you've had it tougher than me, I know I'm being selfish, but this is what I feel, and I have the right to my feelings."

"Wow. No wonder you were so angry at me for being mad about Aleksandr."

"You have the right to your feelings, too." But she spoke quickly and without an ounce of sincerity. "Just don't act like it's a job offer and you're not sure you want the position. You take it and be grateful, and I'll stand on the outside and try to be gracious."

He thought hard, trying to say the right thing. Instead he said, "So that's what the DNA test was really for."

"Yes, but the test isn't necessary now. Once you told me about being found in Nevada, I knew you were that baby." A tear slipped down her cheek, and angrily she dashed it away. "Once I discovered my parents weren't my biological parents, it was easy to make the connection between the golden cougar who stalked me and the child my parents had lost. You are my parents' son."

He had to get away, get a hold of himself, before he blurted out what he'd done. Gathering up his half-eaten meal, he said, "You're hungry. I'll fix soup."

Firebird watched him stride out of the room, and her stomach sank.

She would have been happier if he'd yelled at her. Instead he had looked exactly as he had fifteen minutes ago—emotionless and still, like a pond waiting for a stone to be dropped into its depths.

When she'd met him at Brown, he hadn't been like that at all. He'd been intense, filled with emotions that bubbled just below the surface, hidden fire that dared her to touch the heart of the flame. In those days, the idea of playing with fire held its own attractions, and she'd taken the dare.

What a child she had been.

With a sigh, she slipped out of bed and made her shaky way to the bathroom. It had been remodeled in cool shades of blue and warm shades of gold, and contained a large glass shower, two copper sinks, and a toilet hidden in its own cubbyhole. As she used the toilet, she grinned at the magazine rack in there. Typical guy, to think of that.

As she washed her hands, she kept her attention

on the faucet, which looked like an old-fashioned pump. Very cool, not at all the kind of thing she would have suspected Douglas would pick out—and as long as she stared at the faucet, she didn't have to look in the bronze-framed mirror over the sink.

She didn't yet have the strength to view her reflection and her poor, half-shorn head.

She heard him in the bedroom, and met him at the bathroom door.

"Are you all right?" His gaze swept her from head to foot, and while his concern warmed her, there wasn't a scrap of passion in his eyes.

Couldn't he see beyond the flannel nightgown?

Apparently not.

"I'm fine." She went back to the bed. She was moving more easily. Her ankle no longer felt as if it would crack. The pain in her joints was easing.

"No bleeding? No injuries that I—"

"I'm fine." She lay down, pulled the covers up, and glared.

He offered a capped and insulated plastic cup. "Tomato basil. I hope you like it."

"I like it a lot." She peeled back the top and took a sip. The heat, texture, and flavors struck the perfect chord, and she sighed with delight. "Wonderful."

"Good." He sat in his chair, rested his elbows on his thighs, cupped his hands, and stared at her.

"Are you okay?" She slurped a little. Embarrassing, but he was right: She really had been hungry.

"Yes."

"Are you angry at me for not telling you about my parents . . . your parents sooner?"

"No."

She took a long drink of the chunky soup, chewed, and swallowed, then tentatively asked, "Then what are you thinking?"

"That I almost got you killed."

"You said that before, I think." She tried to remember the moment, and got the vague impression of sloshing waves. "In the ocean."

"It's truer than ever."

"No, it's not. The Varinskis are after me. They don't know about you. They can't."

He stirred. Stood. Walked toward the window and braced his arms against the frame. The morning light bathed him, tangling in his blond hair, etching his tanned skin with pale gold. His chiseled jaw was thrust forward, his brows drawn. . . .

"You *are* angry."

"Not at you." He turned to face her. "I was—mad that you'd left me without a word. For almost three years, I've been furious that you'd abandoned me, as my parents had. I never suspected you saw me as a cougar. When you came here and told me about Aleksandr, I was livid that you'd had my son and not told me. But now I understand, I understand everything, and you must never feel guilty for not telling me about my . . . about Konstantine and Zorana." He came to the bed, sat, and leaned toward her. "Three years ago, I hurt you by not confiding in you and asking for your help, but don't for a minute believe that I told you I loved you and lied. I meant every word."

"You loved me?" Was he telling the truth, or telling her what she wanted to hear?

"Before I ever met you, I searched your private records—and found scrambled information. It could have been a computer glitch, or operator error, but I didn't think so."

One side of her mouth tilted up in satisfaction. "My brother's wife, Ann . . . she's good with computers, and getting better all the time. She's the one who scrambled the information. It's tough to find any details about the Wilders."

"I went through high school knowing what I wanted to do—become a police officer. Because a man who can change into a cougar, who can track any criminal, can get a job anywhere in the US, and cops have an in when it comes to digging around for information." He continued to watch her, *scrutinize* her. "And because, as you said, I wanted to find my roots."

"If you looked at all, you found the Varinskis." She put the empty cup aside. "They're on the Internet, both as a legend and as a corporate entity."

"I did find them. I found them by the time I was thirteen. I e-mailed them. I told them that I was like them." Douglas looked back at his adolescent self with a derisive smile. "They never replied. Looking back, I realized they must get a hundred e-mails a day from kids who think it would be cool to turn into animals."

"From kids who read too much *Harry Potter*." When she thought about the Varinskis receiving e-mails from innocent children, when she thought about them hearing from Douglas, she wanted to shudder with fear. When she realized that Aleksandr would do things equally stupid, equally dangerous, she wanted to wrap herself around him and protect him from the demons who saw humans as prey—and from the humans who saw children as targets.

"Even before I graduated from high school, I went into law enforcement. I made my reputation right away." He didn't change expressions, but something about the way he held himself made her think he was proud of what he did in his work. "I used that reputation to search for clues about my background. My best theory was that my father was a Varinski, maybe just traveling through, who had found a woman and raped her—I figured that was the most likely explanation, considering that I had been abandoned by my mother."

Firebird nodded. That was logical; Varinskis never mated, never married. Their sons were born from quick, brutal assaults. In fact, the Varinskis' initial indignation about her father stemmed from the seeming insanity of his love and marriage. Later they had another reason for swearing revenge: When they chased after the newlyweds, to protect his wife, Konstantine had killed his brother.

Douglas continued, "Then I found a blog written by one of the young Varinskis. He claimed that since their old leader, Konstantine, had abandoned them to live in America with his wife, the clan had weakened and needed a change of leadership."

Firebird laughed derisively. "I can't believe he was dumb enough to put that out on the Internet."

"Have you seen the stuff people put out there? The first thing an officer does when faced with a crime is go to Facebook and see if someone has bragged or confessed. It saves a lot of trouble."

They shook their heads in unison, two people united by their dedication to maintaining their privacy.

"I thought the Konstantine story was worth following up on," Douglas said, "but in the United States, there were no Varinskis I could find. So I looked for Russian immigrants, specifically Russian immigrants in Nevada and the western United States."

"There are a bunch in northern Washington."

"I talked to them. They all knew stories about Varinskis, stories they would tell their kids to scare them into behaving. They'd even heard about the Konstantine who left the family to marry a Gypsy, and how the clan had sworn vengeance. But they didn't know where he was, or even if it was true."

"Because Konstantine and Zorana had been careful to stay away." She sat up and wrapped her arms around her knees. "Too many Russians would recognize a Varinski when they saw one."

"Yes. You're filling in the gaps." Gratification eased the tautness of his face. "Keeping the tale of Konstantine in mind, I explored the immigration records and found a Russian immigrant couple who had arrived at about the right time, and who had a very unusual last name—Wilder."

"That is *not* an unusual last name," she said tartly.

"It is for a Russian immigrant. So I looked for the

Wilders' current location, and couldn't find it. But I did find Wilder Winery in Napa Valley, and Jasha Wilder, born in the US with a very Russian first name, who had bragged to his employees about his sister, who got a full-ride scholarship to Brown University in Providence, Rhode Island."

Douglas made her uneasy; he was too clever.

"So I found you, and you thought you were so wise, so canny about not giving out information about your family."

"I was!"

"You were a baby." Amusement flickered across his cool face. "I could have cajoled information out of you, but seducing you was my mistake. I spent so much time talking to you, finding out that you spoke some Russian, that you knew your way around glass art because your best friend was an artist, that you painted for fun but took software programming and Japanese so you could work for the winery, that you liked yellow roses and red carnations. . . ."

Her gaze fell again on the yellow rose floating in the cereal bowl beside the bed.

"I found out a thousand details about you, and missed the one I'd sought you out to discover—who your father was, and where your family lived—all because I was fascinated by this so-charming face." His fingertips hovered just above her cheek. "When you smiled at me, your whole face lit up, and I fell . . . so hard."

Maybe she did believe he had loved her. After all, why would he lie? "When I left, you took it badly?"

"Yes."

"Good." She felt as if a weight had been lifted off her chest, and she took her first free breath since she'd seen him change from a cougar into a man. "Because I was devastated."

"Yes, but you didn't . . ."

"Didn't what?"

His fingertips finally touched her face, and with that single touch, he held her in place for his kiss. He opened her lips with his, slid his tongue in her mouth, swirled, and feinted.

Her eyes slid closed. She gave herself up to the sensation, glad now that she'd told him about his newfound family. Glad that he'd explained, and so eloquently, why he had sought her out at Brown, and why he had seduced her.

He had loved her. Did he love her now?

No, he hadn't said that, but perhaps he could once again learn.

And if he didn't . . . well. She'd been alone for a long time. For now, she would enjoy this.

Chapter Twenty-two

Lifting her arms, Firebird wrapped them around Doug's shoulders and pulled him close, and when his chest rested against hers and his heart beat with the same rhythm, he relaxed for the first time in his life.

"Are you hungry?" He strove to sound casual.

She shook her head.

"Thirsty? Tired? Do you need to use the facilities?"

She continued to shake her head.

"Then I would very much like to make love to you." He held his breath, waiting for the most important confirmation of his life.

She smiled that grand and glorious smile, the one that spread to her eyes into the depths of her soul . . . the one that had first seduced him. "I'd very much like that, myself."

Blood left his brain and rushed straight for his dick, and he suspected—he feared—he had enough to run only one of them at a time.

Reaching over, he touched the switches on the bedside table.

The fireplace sprang to life. Low, sexy, jazzy music began to play.

"Is that supposed to impress me?" she asked.

"Did it?"

Taking his outstretched hand, she brought it back to her face and kissed the fingers while saying, "Clever planning. Hand steady as a rock. Smooth move. Suave. All in all, a good job."

Did she know that with each kiss, he grew less suave and more savage?

He stroked her face, spread her hair across her pillow, touched the shorn side, murmured, "I'm sorry."

She smiled at him. "We'll fix it."

Every night since she'd fled, he'd dreamed of holding her beneath him, and every night he had subjected her to wild debaucheries of the kind he would never have tried with the sweet, shy virgin Firebird had been. Every time he had imagined finding her, she was alone and just happened to be clothed in a lace teddy with a garter belt, or a leather bustier, or, best of all, a simple housedress with nothing underneath. But no matter what he did to her—and in his dreams he had been violently, gloriously sexual—she always cried out and climaxed and held him afterward and wept, and begged his forgiveness and gone down on him. . . .

"*Shit.*" Desire slammed him like a million volts of electricity.

She lifted her head off the pillow. "What's wrong?"

"Nothing," he croaked.

He couldn't do any of the things he'd dreamed

and imagined, because it was his fault she'd run away. Yet those scenarios crowded his mind, challenging his control, making him want to take her swiftly, take her again, taste her between the legs, and take her again. No matter that she was innocent of wrongdoing; the demon of desire whispered in his mind to keep her prisoner and sate himself.

Even dressed in Mrs. Burchett's flannel nightgown, she tried his control.

"Are you shy?" She pushed him over onto his back and sprawled across his chest, a warm, squirming armful of fantasy. "Has it been so long that you've forgotten the basics? Here, let me start things off." She unfastened the first four buttons of her nightgown.

He didn't move, transfixed by the hollow of her throat, by the smooth skin of her chest.

She laughed at him and accused, "You want me to do all the work!"

"No. That's not it." He was afraid that if he caught a glimpse of her breast, he would unzip and— *Shit*. He shouldn't have even thought about her breast. Now his dick tried to claw its way out of his jeans.

"Here. Let me show you the basics. First you take off your shirt." She urged him to sit up, and stripped it away.

His tattoo glowed like a fifties Technicolor movie. The reds were true, the blues were cold, the yellows were hot, and all arranged from his shoulder to his belt like the claw marks of a cougar.

He didn't care about that.

What made him cringe was the small black burn

at the base of his throat. The burn that was shaped like a cross.

She saw it all. She didn't seem to care, or even particularly notice. "Then I take off my nightgown." She got up on her knees and stripped *it* away.

She had on panties. *Thank God.*

But the very breasts he had feared were there, small and perfect, with nipples that pointed at his mouth and begged to be suckled. He shut his eyes and blindly reached for her, tugging her forward, and without ever looking, he wrapped his mouth around her breast.

She tasted like whipped cream and cinnamon and sex, and he was starving to death. That nipple poked at his tongue, and as he sucked, it grew more rigid. Inspired, he cupped her other breast, caught that nipple between his thumb and forefinger, and tugged softly.

She shuddered. She wrapped her fingers in his hair and held him in place, and shuddered again.

He lifted his knee between her legs and rubbed, once, twice, and when she sought that pressure, he gave up her breast and flipped her onto her back. He knelt over her, and once again he slid his knee between her legs. But this time he applied a steady pressure and kissed her mouth. Her mouth, her cheeks, her eyes, her ears . . . She was trying to meet his kiss, moving her head to follow him, but he didn't let her catch up.

Because right now, his discipline was holding.

Yet if he kissed her as he wished to, if he thrust his tongue into her mouth, he'd remember his dream of kissing and fucking her at the same time, the fantasy of his hard-driving, thrusting motion that would imprint him on her—

He had to think of something else.

He nuzzled her neck, skimming the soft skin at her throat, then moving across her collarbone, first one side, then the other.

And all the time, the beast in him urged, *Take her. Take her now. Take her hard. Make her yours.*

"You're trembling." She stroked his forehead. "I forgot—you were in the water, too. You had hypothermia. Are you able to—"

He brought his head up so fast, his neck cracked. "I can't stop."

She couldn't ask that of him.

"But will you be hurt if you . . ."

Lowering his head almost to her breastbone right over her heart, he breathed on her like a man clearing a frozen window. He put all the heat of his soul in that breath, pushing oxygen, lust, and desperation through her skin, her tissues, and into her beating heart.

She stilled. Her eyes half closed. She seemed to be listening, absorbing his essence and his desires.

Then, without realizing what she was doing, she fulfilled one of his wicked dreams.

Stretching her arms above her head, she grasped the corners of her pillow. "If I remain very still and let you do whatever you want, do you promise to care for yourself?"

He heard the words, but he couldn't understand through the roaring in his ears. His gaze swept her body, laid out like a bacchanalian feast. He smelled the scent of arousal that rose like an aphrodisiac from her skin. He heard the rush of air through her lungs, the hurried sound that made him realize that she anticipated pleasure.

His tongue flicked out and sampled the unique flavor of Firebird, and then he tasted an edge of fear, too.

Their previous relationship had been brief and intense. They had never shared the easiness of long-time lovers.

And now . . . she didn't know him well, but she did know he had been angry with her. She worried he was still angry with her.

That took the edge off, calmed the desperation.

"Douglas?"

He met her troubled gaze. "I promise nothing, except that when I am done with you, you're going to be very"—he kissed her belly—"very"—he spread her legs and kissed her there—"happy."

Chapter Twenty-three

Firebird finished her last relentless, fabulous orgasm, and relaxed back against the bed.

She could hardly move. Every bone and muscle had been exercised, kissed, massaged, pleasured. Douglas had fed her satisfaction—satisfaction tailored especially to her and her fantasies. Now, exhausted, she rolled her head on the pillow and looked at Douglas.

He looked . . . pleased.

She felt . . . incredible.

And he looked . . . pleased.

When they'd made love before, it had been the clash of two fiercely alive beings who felt and saw and smelled and touched with all the glorious emotions of their souls. She'd burned for him, and she had known he burned for her.

Now, sex with her *pleased* him.

She narrowed her eyes until she was looking at him through nothing more than a slit, trying to X-ray him, to see under his skin, into his thoughts.

No. *Controlling* sex with her *pleased* him.

His voice startled her out of her fury. In that calm, exceptionally civilized manner of his, he said, "I need to tell you why I didn't stay with Mrs. Fuller."

"Sure." Those were the words every woman wanted to hear from her lover after great sex.

"Most guys get to be around twelve, and they have this erection pop up, and they're amazed and horrified and proud." He still sounded calm and civilized, but he rubbed his forehead as if the mere act of talking hurt him. "And so was I, except . . . I knew it wasn't the usual thing to turn into a cougar, too. Even at twelve I had a little bit of logic."

Firebird began to stop thinking about herself. Began to see why Douglas was discussing his puberty when she was still enjoying afterglow. "How did she find out?"

"In addition to everything else—the erection, the pubic hair, the wildcat thing—I developed this tattoo across my chest."

"It's one of those things that identifies you as a Varinski." Firebird knew this stuff for sure.

"So I gathered. But at the time, all I knew was that my body was betraying me in every way possible. My dick was whipping around like a needle on a compass. When I looked in the mirror, sometimes I looked like . . ." He shook his head. "Like a cougar. A golden cougar. And overnight, I had this tattoo branded across my chest. It was big, it was bold, it was colorful. I kept myself covered, but Mrs. Fuller had only two bathrooms, and the one we boys used wasn't exactly the most private of places. The lock was broken; we were always playing tricks on each other with ice water. . . . The little shit who slept in the bunk bed above me saw the tattoo and told Mrs. Fuller.''

"She didn't believe in tattoos.''

"She called me into her parlor and gave me hell.'' He looked into the past, and everything about him told her he was in the grip of painful memories. "She didn't know where I got the money for a tattoo like that, but she feared I was stealing again. She didn't approve of me joining a gang, which she was afraid was the reason for the tattoo. And . . . she wanted to impress on me that no matter what, she still loved me and I could tell her anything.''

"So you told her?''

"I did. But she didn't believe me.''

"So you showed her?''

"I did.'' He fell into a silence that broke her heart. "She saw me change. She saw the cougar.''

"Oh, God.'' The Wilders operated under the cover of secrecy, because Konstantine had taught them—taught every one of them—that no one would understand. No one would believe.

"Like I told you, Mrs. Fuller was a Christian woman with a good heart. And she *did* love me. For a long time, I doubted that, but now I know she did, because she took her own cross from around her neck, the one she always wore, and put it around my neck.''

"That's why you have this cross burned into your skin at the base of your throat.'' Firebird had seen it. She'd wondered. Now she knew.

"That's why.'' His chest rose and fell with his huge

gasps. "The pain was excruciating, but not as excruciating as seeing the expression on Mrs. Fuller's face as
she realized that heaven rejected me so completely."

"What did she do?" With her fingertip, Firebird
traced the scar over and over.

"She cried. She cried."

At that moment, Firebird hated the kind and Christian Mrs. Fuller. "What did you do?"

"I ran away. For the last time, I ran away." He
rubbed at his heart with the flat of his hand. "But
Mrs. Fuller had convinced me I was too smart to let
anyone else control my destiny. So I got myself to
Colorado and finished high school there. Finished
early."

"And went into law enforcement."

"Yes."

"And used your powers whenever you needed to
keep yourself ahead of the game."

"Yes."

Okay. Now she understood—a lot of things. Her
father . . . Konstantine . . . he always told his sons
to be careful, not to change unless it was necessary.
He said that every time they indulged their joy in
flying and running, they slid closer to evil. Closer to
the creator of the pact. Closer to hell, to the devil.

Douglas had indulged his gift in the pursuit of
power and truth.

He was very, very close to losing his soul. And
deep inside, he knew it.

Firebird understood now. They had made love,
and he was *pleased*. Of course he was *pleased*.

He had managed to give her pleasure without releasing the wild part of him. In all his life, passion had proved to be a mistake. Always a mistake. When it came to her, he didn't dare allow himself passion, because he didn't want passion to sweep him away.

He didn't want to hurt her.

Very well. That was fine. It was good that he'd learned such restraint. The men in her family were all awesome in their restraint. Never in her life had she worried that they would turn on her in a rage and crush her.

More important, she trusted them with her child's life.

But they were awesome in their passions, too. Each man loved his woman with his heart, his soul, every fiber of his being—and all the passion of his body. That was the kind of love she wanted. That was the kind of love she would have.

She slipped out of bed, out of Douglas's reach.

At once, his head turned to her.

She stretched, a slow, catlike stretch, one side at a time, with her hands over her head. Then, slowly, she skimmed her palms down the sides of her breasts, down her ribs, and over her hips. "Mmmm." She sighed. "I'm going to take a shower." She strolled toward the bathroom. She paused in the doorway and looked back at him from beneath her lashes. "Are you going to *come*?"

Chapter Twenty-four

Douglas's feet hit the floor hard.

Silently Firebird laughed. She strolled toward the vanity.

She stopped laughing when she saw her reflection. She had bruises around her neck; she looked as if she'd been strangled.

The kelp, she supposed. More bruises on her arms, the kind made by a man's hand.

More supposition—Douglas had caused them in his frantic struggles to get her free.

And her hair . . . Growing up in a family of brunettes and raven-haired people, she had always been vain about her blond sunniness, and she loved this cut. Loved it. Thought it made her look sophisticated, cheeky, and bold, not like *just* Aleksandr's mother, but like the sexual, desirable young woman she was.

It was a harmless fantasy, one that hadn't changed the facts . . . and now one side of her coiffure had been slashed almost to her scalp.

Something had to be done. She opened drawers

until she found scissors about three inches long, the kind used to trim a mustache.

He stood watching her from the doorway, arms folded across his chest, body long, lean, and muscled. His face was still stern, impassive, but she suspected that was a facade.

No. She *knew* it was a facade. Because no matter how much he might wish to have complete control, one body part told the truth, and the truth was—he was horny.

He had the horn to prove it.

With a slight smile, she leaned over the sink, toward the mirror. Taking a longer strand of hair in her fist, she chopped it off.

"Don't." He still leaned against the door frame, arms crossed across his chest, but now his fists were clenched. "Wait until morning. We'll go to a salon."

"Or a barber." She cut another strand. She didn't want to even it up. That would leave her almost bald. But an all-over cut, deliberately jagged and asymmetrical . . . that would work, and keep her until she could get to a beautician. "I can fix it, and I've been wanting a new hairstyle." She was lying.

But he looked so *guilty.* He flinched with every *snick* of the scissors, and best of all, for all his rapt attention to her coiffure, he couldn't keep his gaze on her head. It kept flicking down . . . down to the place he could see when she bent forward.

Poor guy. It must be tough to be so distracted.

"Douglas, could I get you to do the back?" She turned and held out the scissors. "Of my hair? I can't see to do it myself."

"We really should wait." He looked at her breasts, at her belly, at the strip of blond hair between her legs, and wet his lips. "I don't know anything about cutting hair."

"Neither do I, but I know I'm not walking around looking like *this*." She lounged against the counter, her eyes deliberately wide and appealing. "Come on, darling; you have to do me or I'll do myself."

"What?" Dark red stained his cheeks.

"Do me," she repeated. "Cut my hair."

"Oh, all right." He strode forward like a man in total control.

Too bad for him he had that barometer that indicated a storm brewing.

She handed him the scissors, then turned her back and leaned over, legs braced and slightly apart. She looked at him in the mirror.

He was staring, not at the back of her head, but at the crack of her butt.

When he finally tore his gaze away and met her eyes in the mirror, she said, "Just let the hair drop into the sink."

He looked at the scissors in his hand as if he couldn't remember how to work them. She thought for a moment that she'd already broken him—*good work, Firebird*—then he visibly imposed discipline on himself and went to work.

He proved how closely he'd been paying attention. First he cut handfuls; then he took the ends between his fingers and cut again. Every time he ran his fingers across her scalp, she purred and shifted, "accidentally" grazing him with her hip, moving her bottom into the cradle of his thighs. "I love to get my hair cut. I love the sensation of scissors clipping away, and when someone strokes my head, I just melt. Don't you?"

"No." He kept his gaze strictly on his work.

"Men. You're so tough and strict, you don't take the time to enjoy life's little pleasures. When we shower, I'll wash you, and we'll see how you like that."

"I'm not going to shower with you."

He'd done enough clipping.

The new cut made her look thinner, younger— tougher and in need of an eyebrow piercing—but it didn't look like a mistake.

Carefully she pushed his hands away from her head. She turned and faced him. Placing her fingers on his chest, she looked up into his face. "Why else did you come in here?"

"To piss."

Deliberately crude. He was trying to chase her away.

Too bad she'd had brothers.

She allowed her gaze to feather down his body to his straining erection. "All right. But you're going to pee on the ceiling."

She slid sideways along the counter, then sauntered past him and toward the shower enclosure, which was warm with natural gold stone and a decorative ring of bold blue glass tiles. She swung the glass door open, turned on the faucet, and, while she waited for the water to warm, she glanced back at him.

He still had his back to her, but he watched her in the mirror, scissors clutched in his hand, his gaze hot and hungry.

"Come on, honey," she coaxed. "You can sit on the seat and I'll wash you . . . all . . . over."

She saw the flash of supernatural red in his eyes.

He swiveled on his heel and sprang toward her, then stopped and stared at the scissors, forgotten in his hand.

She giggled and slipped into the enclosure.

It was definitely built for two, with a multitude of water jets, an imposing handheld shower massager, a shelf filled with soaps, shampoos, and foaming gels, and a smooth stone seat built onto one end.

A glance toward Douglas proved he still stood immobile in the middle of the floor, held there by the mere force of his will and a pair of tightly clutched scissors.

She sorted through the bottles. "You've got my favorite scents."

As if he couldn't stop himself, he looked up at her, staring through the glass enclosure.

She filled her palm with shampoo, lifted her arms, and scrubbed her poor, shorn head. She ran out of hair too soon. So she rubbed the pale bubbles down her body, inciting him, reminding him of her breasts, her belly, her thighs, and how much she enjoyed her own sensuality. "I love the smell of mint. How did you know?"

"Smelled like sunshine," he mumbled. "Like you."

"What did you say?" She turned her back to hide

her smile, and so he could see her soapy hands slipping over her bottom.

"I said I guess I'll shower with you. There's plenty of room." He paced back to the counter, *so* totally in control of himself, then paced back to the shower.

Hastily she rinsed herself, grabbed the shampoo, and stepped back to let him enter.

It was a big shower.

He was a big man.

But she crowded him into the corner, and when the backs of his knees hit the seat, he sat.

She filled her palm with shampoo, then shoved the bottle into his hand. "Hold this."

"I can wash my own hair."

"Indulge me." She rubbed her fingers on his head, working up a lather, massaging his scalp. She moved slowly, allowing each small circle to ease along the skin just above his forehead, then moving back toward the crown of his head.

But he wasn't relaxing. He was staring, hypnotized . . . at her breasts.

They bobbed in his face as she swayed with the rhythm of her massage.

Who would have guessed he'd be so attracted by the breasts he'd so recently kissed and caressed?

Well . . . she would.

It appeared she'd guessed right.

"Doesn't that feel good?" She rubbed him behind the ears, then scraped her fingernails up the back of his neck.

He stretched as if she'd pulled a thread through

the top of his head. "It's good." He paused, struggling for words. "I like it."

Well. He was never going to be an articulate lover—in fact, right now, he sounded sort of like Tarzan—but she supposed if she wanted eloquence, she could always go watch those stupid butter commercials.

Moving swiftly, not allowing him time to recover, she grabbed a mesh scrubby and the rosemary shower gel, and went to work on his shoulders and chest. The scrubby was new, never used, with enough texture to scrape his nerve endings as she slid it around and around his nipples.

When she did that, his hands lifted toward her— then dropped to grip the edge of the seat.

"You've got a really great body. I love your abs." She stroked his six-pack with first the scrubby, then with her bare hand. "I love this ruff of hair in the middle of your chest, and how it extends down. . . ." She followed her finger with her gaze as it wandered toward his groin and his straining erection. Catching herself, she jerked away.

She had no intention of touching him there. Not until she'd driven him right to the edge of sanity.

But her body had other ideas.

"Stand up," she said, pulling him. When he did, she pushed him around to face the wall. "Put your arms up and lean forward. And spread 'em, mister."

"Are you going to frisk me?" he asked, and his voice sounded an octave deeper than normal.

"Every inch of you." His back, his fine, tight ass, between his cheeks, the backs of his well-structured thighs and calves . . . she even picked up his feet and scrubbed the soles.

He didn't wiggle. He stood as firmly as one of the rock stacks enduring the assault of the ocean waves.

But the ocean always won—eventually.

With her hands on his hips, she turned him again and washed his arms, paying special attention to his palms, then his chest and belly, the fronts of his thighs and calves . . . and now she was on her knees before him, with only one thing that needed to be washed.

She soaped up the scrubby; then carefully, oh, so carefully, she slid the scrubby between his legs, then up the length of his penis to the silken head. "How does that feel?"

"It's . . . rough." He could barely grunt.

"I don't want to be rough." Dropping the scrubby, she used her hands, sliding them around his testicles, exploring, remembering, savoring the sensation of two tight, desperate, ready balls inside his sac.

Yet all the while, she was waiting, anticipating the glide of her hand up and down the length of his penis. And when she touched him, she knew she touched magic.

Each vein rose blue beneath the pale skin, and in contrast to his balls, the texture was smooth, silk beneath her fingers. The head was rosy, and as she lightly rubbed it, the whole organ grew larger, stiffer.

Yes. Magic.

The soap foamed white, then rinsed away, and she bent her head to take him into her mouth.

Finally, he groaned. A long, low, faint groan.

She swirled her tongue, sucked softly, then with growing strength, then softly again. And with each movement, she grew more aware of her nipples tightening in anticipation, of the ache between her legs, the way the water pounded on her back and slid down between her butt cheeks. She was in need, and if he didn't yield soon, she was going to attack.

He held his arms straight out, his hands on the walls, bracing himself as if he would lunge if he didn't.

Belated caution made her catch her breath. For all that this madness was what she had desired, right now, she wondered if she would survive intact.

After all, he was a Varinski.

He rose to his feet. He looked down at her. His eyes glowed red, a constant, furious, menacing glow.

His formidable control had broken at last.

She was, she realized, a woman trapped by her own stratagems.

Without warning, she plunged toward him, intent on knocking him down, dominating him, showing him once and for all she would not be intimidated.

Chapter Twenty-five

Douglas caught Firebird around the waist. Pressed her to the cool floor. Spoke in her ear: "Don't ever try that again. Do you hear me?"

She stared at the gold tile beneath her cheek, watched the water running toward the drain, felt the threat of his erection against her butt.

"Do you hear me?" he repeated.

"I'll never stop." Useless defiance, but true nevertheless.

"Then I will have to wear you out." He ran his hand down her spine, between her legs. He opened her to his exploration, and what he found there made him chuckle. "Almost ready. Almost."

Almost? His fingers had barely brushed her. He'd entered her only slightly. Yet ignominiously, she hovered on the edge of climax.

He reached up, reached down.

She raised up to see what he was doing, but he put the flat of his palm in the middle of her back. "Don't move. You have done plenty."

She was caught in the heat of her mate's loosed

passion, and she was the one who had loosed it. Now she would pay the price.

His fingers found her again, and this time he rubbed with purpose. He opened her, caressed her, entered her . . . and as he did, heat blossomed.

He was using some oil, something that made her buck beneath his hands and claw at the floor.

"What's wrong?" His voice was guttural in her ear.

"It's too much."

He lifted her hips with his arm. "We've barely begun."

His penis slid into her, the whole length, without stopping.

Too full. Too big. Too hot.

He pressed himself inside, holding himself still, waiting for . . . something.

Too much . . . God, why wouldn't he *move*?

Involuntarily her inner muscles rippled along the hard length inside.

And as if she'd given him a signal, he released his passions on her.

He thrust with vigor, with savagery. There was no resisting him, no chance to take charge. She had to move as he directed, accept his domination . . . with each thrust, she came, an explosion of need fulfilled and need aroused.

The water washed down on them. It trickled down her arms and dripped off her chin, singing with its own sweet, warm beat.

She moaned, straining, clenching all her muscles as he drove into her with the rhythm of the sea, the wind, the earth. She rose onto her hands and arched her back, trying to get away, trying to get more. The pleasure was unbearable, and when he slid his hand around her, between her legs, and pressed her clit—she screamed.

Lights exploded beneath her closed eyelids.

Fiercely, he plunged into her, filling her with his sperm—and neither of them cared about the consequences.

Yesterday, they'd faced death.

Today, they faced each other.

She remained on her hands and knees, panting, exhausted, pleasured beyond strength.

And she smiled.

Gradually he withdrew, each ridge and vein dragging across her inner tissues.

She groaned.

He lifted her, turned her, placed her on the seat. He looked like a shark ready to take a bite out of its victim. "Now it's my turn to wash you."

And she realized—he'd just come twice, and he was still hard.

By the time he had finished using the shower massager to rinse her, she was nothing more than a limp rag in his arms.

And that was just the way he wanted her.

Damn her for ripping his control away. She deserved the demon she had unleashed.

He had always planned to find her and drag her away to the lair he had built for her, but he had never imagined he would need so desperately to claim her over and over, in every way possible.

Now, as he dried her, taking care with each part,

wincing at her bruises, sighing about her hair, he wished they had more time. For if they did, he would take her to bed again and show her how many times a starved cougar could satisfy himself . . . and her.

Lifting her, he carried her into the bedroom.

But he couldn't take the time to make love to her again. He had another task, a duty to fix what he had set wrong.

He tucked her in bed, pulled up the covers, kissed her forehead. Her solemn eyes watched him. "Are you okay?"

She knew him too well, recognized the disquiet he took such care to hide.

"That's the question I should ask you," he said. "Are *you* okay?"

A sleepy, sexy smile curled her lips. "I'm wonderful."

"That you are."

Outside, rain licked at the windows, and the wind moaned around the eaves.

The next storm was coming in. Nighttime crept across the land. Exhaustion took control of her mind and her heart.

He placed his hand over her eyes to shut them. "Go to sleep. I've got some stuff to take care of."

Her eyes popped open. She shoved his hand away. "Cop stuff?"

"Cop stuff," he agreed. He wasn't lying, exactly. He did need to check in with his sergeant. He'd ruined his pager in the ocean. Lost a cell phone, too, and his service pistol. Yamashita hadn't been happy about that, but Doug had told him a version of the truth—that he'd plunged into the ocean after a way-ward dog—and Yamashita had been satisfied. He'd given Doug time off, but no more than necessary, for the state police were pretty much always on call. If an accident occurred and everyone else was busy, they'd phone him, and he'd go.

"Don't be gone too long." Firebird looked heart-breakingly young with that punk haircut and that tremulous smile. "I want to take you home. I want to give you to my mother. She will be so pleased."

If Firebird only knew . . .

"We'll go, but first, I've got work to do."

Whether she wished it or not, her eyes closed. "Be careful."

As he watched her sleep, he murmured, "It's a little too late for that."

He tucked the covers around her and headed for his office next door.

There he monitored his state-of-the-art security system. There he kept his computer and all his rec-ords. His chair was leather and adjustable six differ-ent ways. His walnut desk was topped with black marble.

He loved his office. He loved his house. And he feared he wouldn't have them much longer.

Oh, well.

If he had to pay for what he'd done, it was no more than he deserved.

Yet it was up to him to make sure his family didn't pay, Aleksandr didn't pay, Firebird didn't pay.

He searched through the clutter for his Rolodex, found the card he wanted, picked up the phone, and dialed the number. It rang and rang, and no one picked up for one long damned time.

Where was he? Where was that bastard Vadim?

Doug was ready to hang up when at last someone answered.

Music blared in the background. Voices babbled. Women laughed. And some guy with a pronounced Russian accent yelled, "What?"

A party. That little prick was having a party.

"Vadim," Doug said tersely. "Now."

"Who wants him?" the guy shouted.

"The guy he just tried to kill."

The phone thudded to the floor.

Doug waited, unsure whether the kid who answered the phone would actually pass the message on.

But Vadim answered almost at once, and he sounded terse and tense. *"Which* guy I just tried to kill?"

"Doug Black." Doug Black, who would set things right, or die trying.

"Oh." Vadim relaxed, chuckled. "You."

Doug had talked to this guy, told him his history, convinced him he was a rogue Varinski. He had sold himself to Vadim, and yet never had he despised Vadim more. Despised Vadim—and himself. "I got the job done for you. I gave you the coordinates of the Wilders' home."

"I paid you a cool ten mil for that," Vadim reminded him pleasantly.

"And to show your appreciation, you sent your goons after me." Doug allowed every bit of his rage and frustration to show in his voice. Rage at Vadim.

Frustration with himself for being so stupid as to let himself be bought out of loneliness and bitterness.

Vadim wasn't impressed. He laughed. "I didn't send them after you."

"Liar."

"I sent them after the Wilder girl. You got in the way."

Even worse. "I was *about* to get lucky."

"Yeah, sorry. My guys were under orders to get the job done and get it done fast." Vadim's voice grew hushed and thoughtful. "And they told me they had. They said you both went in the ocean and didn't come out."

Doug needed to be careful, very careful, with what he next said to Vadim. "We both *jumped* in the ocean to get away from your assassins. The Wilder girl landed in a kelp bed. One of the stems wrapped around her neck like a noose. On her own, she had no chance to get back to the surface."

"You *saw* the body?"

"I found her." Deliberately, Doug relaxed the hand that held the phone. The needle on his barometer was falling, the wind gusts were rising, and he'd be lucky if the storm didn't knock out the lines before he'd finished his business with Vadim. For sure he shouldn't allow Vadim to piss him off so badly that he broke the phone with his grip.

"Good man." Vadim managed to sound both patronizing and pleased. "Did you drag the Wilder girl to shore?"

"Are you crazy? I was lucky to get out myself.

That is one fucking cold ocean." Doug spoke with his teeth clenched. "I had hypothermia."

"Bummer."

"I'm sure your snake guy is still crying."

"Foka." Vadim chuckled. "Scary guy, isn't he?"

"Is he the one who's going to take care of the Wilder problem?" Doug asked with an elaborate lack of concern.

"I'm actually going to take care of the Wilder problem myself. The situation is too delicate to leave to subordinates."

"What was it you told me you were going to do? Something about letting US immigration know who Konstantine really is and all the crimes he committed, and getting him shipped out of the country with his lovely wife?"

"That was my original plan." Doug could hear the laughter in Vadim's voice. "There've been a few changes."

"What's your plan now?" Doug was feeling sick. "Are you going to wipe them out financially, too?"

"Maybe something a little more than that. I'm just figuring to wipe them out."

Doug wanted to pound on the desk. How could he have been so stupid as to believe Vadim about the Wilders? About anything? How could he have sold himself and his talents to Vadim?

Vadim lowered his voice. "How about the icon? Did you find it?"

"Icon? What icon?"

"You remember. We talked about it."

They had. Vadim had been quite insistent about

wanting it. "I wouldn't know an icon if it bit me on the ass."

A woman's loud shriek punctuated the noise of the party, and pandemonium broke out.

"Hang on," Vadim muttered.

The party sounds grew fainter. Doug heard a door close, and it was quiet.

Still Vadim spoke softly, as if he feared being overheard. "You'd know this one. It's a small white tile, maybe three by three, an antique, with a painting of the Virgin Mary on it."

Doug laughed. "The great Varinski leader is collecting religious art now?"

"Find it, and I'll pay twenty million."

Doug was playing dumb. He had studied the Varinskis, their organization, their history, their legend. He knew which icon Vadim sought. It had to be one of the four family icons the original Konstantine had delivered to the devil to cement the deal.

But those icons had vanished into the mists of time. Why did Vadim seek this one now? Why was this particular icon so important that he would pay such an exorbitant sum for it? How could Doug use this to his advantage? "There has to be more than one Russian icon out there. How would I know if I found the right icon?"

"Pick it up. It'll burn you right to the bone."

Doug flexed his hand. "What's this icon got against me?"

"Not just you. It'll burn any Varinski." Vadim's accent was almost imperceptible. He sounded like a young American, and not a ruthless assassin, but

Doug knew the truth. The guy was relentless in his pursuit of power, and that made his search for the icon all the more interesting.

"So you've got everybody in your organization looking for this stupid icon? I mean . . . everybody who's not at the party with you?"

He could almost hear Vadim deciding how much to say. "My sources inform me that Firebird Wilder might very well have it."

"Shit if I'm going into the water again to search her body," Doug drawled. "I've already searched the stuff she left here. There was nothing like what you're describing."

"Send me everything."

"Are you crazy? I tossed it in the ocean. When it gets out that she's disappeared and I was the last one seen with her, the shit's going to hit the fan. I need an alibi, and I'm saying she was brokenhearted because I wouldn't take her back, and she committed suicide." With disgust in his voice, Doug said, "You really fucked this up for me, you asshole."

"Twenty mil for the icon should soothe your wounded feelings."

"All right. I'll look. But you know, I've been thinking. Last time I sold you information, you paid me, then tried to kill me."

"I told you: You weren't the target. Besides, you're alive now, so stop whining. Twenty million for the icon."

Doug paid no attention. "I know every place Firebird has been. I know where I hid her car. If she had the icon, I'll find it, and when I do, I'd better charge enough so that when your goons come for me, I've got protection. So I'll sell it"—he paused for effect— "for a hundred million."

"A *hundred* . . . You . . . stupid . . . American!" Vadim's youth showed in his stammered astonishment. "I'm not paying that!"

"Then I'll put it up for auction. Someone will pay it."

"You . . . you . . . Whether you find the icon or not, I am going to kill you!" *Now* Doug could hear his accent, loud and clear.

"Ooh. I'm trembling," Doug mocked.

"You dare!"

"I dare one hell of a lot." With a great deal of satisfaction, Doug hung up.

There. He had gotten information, distracted and infuriated Vadim, and convinced him that Firebird was dead.

Now all he had to do was wait for the phone call he knew would come.

Opening the drawer in his desk, he looked down at the coil of seaweed inside the coil that had trapped Firebird beneath the ocean, the coil she had worn like a necklace around her neck.

He grabbed the main stem. With great care, he lifted the kelp. He stared at the small, square white tile tangled in fronds—and the dark-eyed Virgin Mary stared reproachfully back.

Vadim didn't yet realize it, but Doug held all the trumps.

Chapter Twenty-six

Adrik came through the kitchen door as Zorana pulled two loaves of sour bread from the oven.

Her sons always had a way of arriving as the work was done and the eating would begin.

Taking off his coat, he shook off the raindrops, hung it on the hook, then kissed her on the cheek. "Mama, that bread smells great." He kissed his wife next, a longer kiss placed on Karen's mouth, followed by a hum of delight.

"You're damp." She smoothed his dark hair away from his face.

"That's quite a storm." Seating himself at the long wooden table with the other men, he looked seriously at Konstantine, at Karen's father, at Jasha and Rurik. When he spoke, he didn't bother to include the women. "But nothing's been harmed. Everything's still in place, ready to wipe the Varinskis' asses."

"We need more," Konstantine said.

"We'll do as much as we can, Papa. We just don't know how much time we have." Jasha had a list in front of him and a pen in his hand. "As it is right now, we're going to make more than a few of them sorry they ever thought to try to kill a Wilder."

"There are a lot of strangers in the woods these days," Adrik said.

Zorana shook the loaves out of their pans and placed them on the cooling racks.

Jasha leaped up, grabbed one, and seated himself again. "They're not campers, either."

"It's too cold for that." Jackson Sonnet was short and bluff, a sportsman, an outdoorsman, and a hotelier with a sharp sense of what people would and would not do for fun.

According to him, camping in the winter was not a popular activity.

Rurik got up and got the butter out of the refrigerator. "Pass me a piece of bread."

"Hey, Mama made that for me!" Adrik said.

"She's done welcoming you home, you big oaf." Jasha tore the loaf, releasing a burst of steam and revealing the pale, textured interior. "She's as sick of you as the rest of us are."

Adrik smacked him on the back of the head.

Jasha smacked back, and lost the loaf to Rurik's swift sneak attack. "Hey!"

Rurik grimaced as the brown crust burned his hand. He tossed the loaf from side to side as he tore it into smaller pieces. Placing one on a plate, he handed the rest to his father. "So, Papa, the Varinskis have begun to gather for battle. But there are others, too, men who watch us—and them."

"Maybe the Varinskis have servants." Konstantine

sat in his wheelchair, his oxygen tank hooked to the back. Occasionally he put the mask to his face and took a long breath. He might be weak, but he was in his element.

"Or figured you were so helpless they could hire someone to wipe you out," Jackson said.

The Wilder men exchanged incredulous glances, and unanimously declared, "Naw."

"If you say so." Jackson took some bread, slathered it with butter, bit into it, and, with his mouth open, said, "Great, Zorana. Really great."

The women—Zorana, Ann, Tasya, and Karen—leaned against the kitchen wall, watching the men as the loaf disappeared at record speed.

"It's like feeding wild animals," Ann murmured to the other women. "We throw in the food. They snarl at one another, rip it apart, snarf it down, and go back to their plans."

"Not that Rurik's ever really been domesticated, but I've never seen him act so much like a caveman." Tasya made her voice deep and menacing. " 'Fix me some food. Give me some sex. And for God's sake, woman, whatever you do, don't talk.' "

Zorana considered her beloved grandson, seated in his high chair beside Konstantine, gnawing on a crust and chattering away with his uncles and grandfather. "Aleksandr is just like them."

"Firebird left at exactly the right time." Tasya grasped Zorana's arm. "I didn't mean to worry you."

"It's all right. She's a smart girl. I know she's safe." Zorana had to believe that was true. "But you're right. She won't be sorry she missed this. I tell you, it's genetic. They're having the time of their lives. Listen to them."

"There are always bikers and trekkers in the woods," Rurik said. "So land mines are out."

"No good explosions." Adrik shook his head in sorrow.

"The old-fashioned way will work. Traps. Surprises. You'll see. They won't know what hit them." Konstantine grinned like a boy who had been given a present.

"You guys have come up with good ideas. I'm not saying you haven't, and I know the Varinskis can't be killed except by another demon, but what you need is more good weaponry." Jackson leaned forward, his eyes gleaming with excitement and pleasure. Karen's father was not like Konstantine or her sons; Jackson did not seem to hold women in esteem, he did not like Aleksandr or apparently any children, he shied from Zorana's displays of affection, and his greatest loves were hunting, fishing, and camping. Yet he had shown his true mettle when he had fought a team of marauding Varinskis for his daughter's life. He was a man's man, a human Varinski, as it were, useless in family situations, but good to have at your back, and Zorana was grateful to have him. "Enough shots from an M16 rifle will take a leg off, and a one-legged Varinski would find it hard to chase down even you, Konstantine. I've got the money and the contacts to get weapons fast."

"All right. Some firepower would be helpful. But I will not wait for you to return to start the battle," Konstantine said.

"Trust me, Konstantine." Jackson rested his hand on Konstantine's shoulder. "I'll leave later today, and I'll be back before it's over. I wouldn't miss this battle for the world!"

"How can you talk about war with such delight?" Ann was the most engaging of the Wilder daughters-in-law, one of the kindest people Zorana had ever met, and she was frankly concerned about this display of male ferocity.

The men exchanged confused glances.

"We didn't seek this fight, but as long as it's inevitable, we might as well enjoy it," Jackson said.

Tasya grasped Zorana's arm and shook it. "He's not even one of the family, and he thinks like them."

Still Ann struggled to bring the men to their senses. "What about afterward? There's a very real possibility that some of us—some of you—will die, leaving the ones who remain behind to grieve."

"That's what happens in war," Konstantine said simply.

"When it's over, we'll all have to try to pick up the pieces of our lives." The mere idea of violence brought tears to Ann's blue eyes.

"We understand that, darling," Jasha said patiently. "But we didn't seek this fight, and as long as it's inevitable, we might as well enjoy it."

"That is *exactly* what Mr. Sonnet said," Zorana said.

"Well . . . yes. When you're right, you're right." Jasha high-fived Jackson.

The men laughed.

In a flash, Ann's tears dried, and her eyes flashed

with temper. "Jasha Wilder, when this is over, if you're not dead, I'm going to make you wish you were."

Jasha's mouth dropped open, as if he couldn't fathom such a display of ill will from his wife. "Now, honey . . ."

"Come on, girls." Tasya touched Zorana on the shoulder. "Let's take a walk. We're all going crazy with worry."

Jasha shook his head. "You can't go for a walk."

Ann turned on him. "Why not?"

With exaggerated patience, Jasha said, "Because there are strangers in the woods."

Zorana found her open hand raised toward her son.

Ann caught her before she could make contact.

Karen, who up until this moment had been silent, now spoke in a clear, slow, loud voice. "Listen, men. We women need to get out of the house. We need to get out now."

All the men, even Aleksandr, looked up in surprise.

Adrik leaped to his feet. "Of course. I'll take you."

"Pussy-whipped," Rurik stage-whispered.

Adrik ignored his brother. "Where do you women want to go? The mall?"

The women scowled at him, at the other men who sat there nodding as if his suggestion made sense.

"What in the hell are we going to do at the mall? Buy a sweater?" Tasya ripped at her already short dark hair. "You guys are such—"

Karen put her hand on Tasya's arm.

Tasya turned away. "Dorks," she muttered.

Rurik shoved the bench back. "Maybe you'd like to go to a movie? I hear *A Hero's Guide to Enchantment* is playing in town at the old theater."

"Chick flick," Jackson said out of the corner of his mouth.

"That's the idea," Konstantine replied out of the corner of *his* mouth. "They'll come back all soft and weepy, and they'll fix us dinner, then watch one of those home-decorating shows. Afterward—"

"You do realize we can hear you, right?" Tasya asked.

The guys all gestured like, *So?*

"I want to talk. Just us women." Ann's voice rose with each word. "Is there *anyplace* we can go where we can have some privacy?"

"You're probably tired of cooking for us," Jasha said. "Maybe we could all get in the van and drive down and have dinner out?"

"Can we go to Taco Time?" Adrik asked eagerly. "I haven't been to Taco Time since I ran away."

"Right. Four grown men, a little boy, one small house, and an unlimited amount of refried beans." Tasya's voice was dripping with sarcasm. "I don't *think* so."

Zorana didn't think so, either. "We'll make it easy on you. We won't even leave the valley. Instead, we'll go out to the horse barn. We'll take a bottle of wine and some bread and cheese. Aleksandr can play in the straw. We women can talk intelligently without interruption from men who regularly turn into beasts." Dimly, she realized her voice was rising, too.

The guys stared with furrowed brows.

Karen spoke again, slowly and clearly. "We want to go out to the horse barn. Without you men. Is it safe?"

"Of course it is. That's where we're storing all our munitions and—" Rurik brought himself up short. "Before you go out, we'll scope out the barn and the surrounding area."

"Then that . . . is where . . . we will go." Karen turned to the other women. "When you talk to them, if you want them to comprehend, use little words and speak very . . . slowly."

Into the silence that followed, Aleksandr announced clearly, "Humping like bunnies."

Konstantine laughed.

Aleksandr laughed, too, a little boy's crow of delight, and repeated, "Humping like bunnies."

"Where did he learn that?" Ann wondered.

When Zorana glared at Konstantine, he changed his laughter to a cough.

Tasya and Ann packed the picnic basket with the other loaf of bread, good cheese, and a fine Wilder zinfandel. Karen fetched an afghan off the couch and some throws out of the cedar chest in the living room.

Rurik and Jasha headed outside to inspect the horse barn and the perimeter.

As Zorana swept her grandson out of his high chair and wrapped him in a blanket, Konstantine objected. "Don't coddle the boy."

"Don't worry that they're going to turn him into

a sissy, Papa." Adrik gathered up their rain gear. "Aleksandr is already a warrior. Nothing these women do can change that."

Karen lost her temper at last. "Adrik, I only have one nerve left, and you're standing on it."

Adrik brought a jacket and helped her into it, then took her arm. "I love you, sweetheart. Now . . . you're much better, but you're limping still, and I know those ribs are giving you pain. Let me help you to the barn."

She resisted for a moment, then leaned against him.

"Everybody take your cell phone," Adrik called, "so you can call if there's trouble."

"I'm so glad you told me, O wise one. With you around, I never have to worry my pretty little head." Karen pulled her cell from her pocket and showed him.

"Grumpy is her favorite dwarf," Adrik explained to his father.

"I've got the diaper bag." Tasya lifted it off the counter and checked the contents. "Are we ready?"

"Gramma." Aleksandr took Zorana's face and turned it toward him. With that toothy grin that always melted her heart, he asked, "Aleksandr want to play with your treasures."

"What do you say?" Zorana asked.

"Please." He dragged out the word, getting louder and louder, until she agreed.

Ann went to the buffet and brought forth a painted and battered wooden box, large enough to hold the most important memories of Zorana's first life, yet small enough for her to carry.

"I was almost killed stealing that box from your Romany tribe, Zorana." Konstantine lifted the mask to his face and took a long breath of oxygen. "But I did it for you, because you wanted it, and because I love you."

"You're not fooling me with that sick-and-sacrificing-old-man act," she said.

"I don't know what you mean."

"And the innocent act won't work, either."

He was in his element as he plotted their defense. Here in the United States, he might masquerade as a peaceful grape grower, but in the Ukraine, he had been Konstantine, the leader of the Varinskis. His strategies had made them the wealthiest and most feared of the world's crime families, and his ruthless acts had condemned him to hell.

Zorana knew that, battle or no battle, the time of his death was at hand—unless somehow they assembled the four Varinski icons and broke the pact with the devil. Going to her husband, she kissed his cheek, and whispered, "Humping like bunnies, indeed."

"Where do you suppose Aleksandr learned such a phrase?" Konstantine asked innocently.

As she left, Zorana glanced back at her husband.

He winked at her.

The tall barn had been built when Konstantine had caved to Firebird's wistful demands for a horse. The horse was gone, but the barn remained.

The wind buffeted them as they walked to the

barn, and a cold rain fell, but when they stepped inside, a sense of peace and warmth enveloped them. It smelled of hay and leather and a good horse gone to his reward, and Zorana imagined she could hear whispers of love from the hayloft, and remembered the times past when she and Konstantine would sneak out here to get away from the rambunctious boys and their little sister.

By the warm glances her daughters-in-law cast toward the ladder, Zorana suspected they enjoyed similar memories.

"It's safe," Rurik assured them.

"We looked it over," Jasha said.

The bottom floor was taken up with stalls, with logs for the Wilder Fourth of July bonfires, with buckets to douse the Wilder Fourth of July bonfires, and with great piles of things covered by horse blankets.

"I wonder what's under the blankets," Tasya mused.

"I don't know. Whatever can it be?" Ann walked over and started to kick one.

Jasha moved with the speed of light, blocking her foot. "Don't . . . kick . . . the detonators."

"I never intended to," Ann said sweetly. "I just wanted a little payback for all that smelly testosterone you've been spreading around lately."

He wiped at his pale face. "Very funny. Want me to carry the basket up to the hayloft?"

"We can do it. Just"—Ann pushed at him—"get out."

"Adrik will stay out here and patrol the area," Rurik said. "While the *men* plan the battle."

"Only the finest warrior is left to guard the Wilders' greatest treasures." Adrik smiled smugly at Jasha.

Zorana patted her second son's cheek. "A wise man recognizes defeat when he experiences it." She shut the doors in their faces.

Tasya and Ann were already helping Karen up the ladder to the hayloft. When they reached the top, Zorana handed Aleksandr into their outstretched arms and climbed the ladder herself.

The women shed their jackets and unwrapped Aleksandr.

"The men won't be able to hear us up here." Ann spread the tablecloth on the floor and pulled mounds of hay over to act as chairs. "And I have something to say that they're not going to like."

"In that case"—Tasya unloaded the picnic basket—"please tell us. Right now I look forward to making them miserable."

"When Jasha and I first got together . . ." Ann blushed and tucked the afghan around her crossed legs. "I mean, when I first realized he was part of the pact, he was shot with an arrow and I had to pull it out."

"Euw." Karen wrinkled her nose.

"I know." Ann pressed her hand to her stomach. "Worse, while I had my hand inside his shoulder, I sliced my palm open and his blood mixed with mine. It changed me. Ever since, I've felt stronger, tougher."

She leaned forward and shook her finger to make her point. "But more important—when I faced off with a Varinski, I developed claws. Just for a second! But that saved my life."

"Yes!" Karen eased herself down on a seat and set to work slicing off chunks of Brie. "When I tasted Adrik's blood, I was fiercer, and I know I seem weak, but less than a month ago, I suffered a dozen broken bones, and my internal injuries were enough to kill me. The doctors say I have healed at an astonishing rate. I've thought all along it was Adrik's blood that gave me back my health."

Tasya looked at Zorana. "I haven't shared blood with Rurik, but if I could be a better warrior for it, and help with the battle . . . I would."

"I haven't shared blood with Konstantine, either." The tension Zorana had borne since suffering that horrible vision relaxed, and she took her first full breath in almost two years. "But now I intend to. Of course, for me, the benefits outweigh the drawbacks."

"What drawbacks could there be, Mama?" Tasya opened the bottle of wine and filled their glasses.

Ann was the most clear-thinking of the girls, and she answered promptly. "If we share the bond of blood with our husbands, we may share the same fate—if the pact isn't broken and we are killed, we may be condemned to hell as demons."

"Pfft!" Tasya waved that argument away as minor. "I choose hell over an eternity alone."

"Yes." Zorana sat on the floor, settled Aleksandr in her lap, and let her daughters-in-law prepare her plate. "I would rather burn with Konstantine than enjoy all the wonders of heaven."

"Me, too," Karen said.

"And I," Ann agreed.

Zorana offered her hand, palm down, over the tablecloth. Ann's hand covered hers. Tasya was next, and Karen finished it off. The women met one another's eyes and nodded in unison.

"Our own pact," Zorana said. "A good pact, to fight the evil that every night creeps closer."

"Gramma." Aleksandr tugged at her sleeve. "Treasures!"

The women broke their handshake, lifted the wineglasses, toasted one another, and drank.

Then Ann handed Zorana the wooden box, and the girls leaned closer as she opened it.

"What are your treasures?" Karen hadn't been in the family long enough to know.

"Mementos from my former life with my Gypsy tribe, and the only possessions I brought when I emigrated from the Ukraine." First Zorana pulled out a ball of yarn. "Here is the wool I spun as a girl." She gave it to Aleksandr, who first rubbed it on his face, and then, like a basketball player, threw it in the basket.

Tasya applauded. "Two points!"

"Yay!" Aleksandr lifted his little fists.

"This is the spindle I used to spin the yarn." Zorana smiled as a memory sprang to life. "It is also the spindle I used to stab Konstantine when he abducted me."

Karen laughed. "Really? You stabbed him?"

"He deserved it." Zorana handed it to Karen.

"I have no doubt about that," Karen said fervently, and tested the point against her finger.

"Here's my hat, part of the Gypsy outfit." Zorana settled a colorfully embroidered cap on Aleksandr's head. "My grandmother made it for me. She was very wise. They told me that the first time she held me, a squalling newborn, she declared I had the Sight."

Aleksandr took off the cap and stood, then walked across the tablecloth and placed it on Ann's head. "Pretty!" he said.

"Thank you, Aleksandr." Ann posed for him.

"But those are simply tokens of my life." Reverently, Zorana prepared to show her only true inheritance. "Now I will show you the treasure."

"Treasure!" Aleksandr hurried back to Zorana's side and leaned against her shoulder.

Taking an unpretentious brown leather sack from the box, Zorana worked the straps loose and reverently let four stones fall onto the tablecloth before her. One was a chunk of turquoise, worn smooth with handling. One was a shiny, sharp, black slice of obsidian. One was a large, uncut red crystal. Last was a malformed white stone, flat and roughly cut into a small square. "For a thousand years, this collection of stones has been given to the one seer who is born to every generation."

"If I were still a reporter," Tasya told Karen, "I'd do a story about this."

Zorana rubbed the turquoise with her thumb.

"This is a piece of the sky." Next she touched the obsidian. "This is a window into the night."

Karen slid her fingertip across the stone's edge. "Ouch!" She pulled it back and examined her skin. "It cut me!"

"Obsidian is volcanic glass, and the edge can be as sharp as a surgeon's scalpel," Ann told her.

"This is a frozen flame." Zorana handed Karen the crimson stone.

Karen held it to the light, and deep in its heart, the stone gleamed bloodred with hints of blue. She gasped in awe. "Is that a ruby?"

"The biggest I've ever seen," Tasya said.

Zorana cradled the white, malformed sliver of rock in the palm of her hand. "This is the greatest of all. This is purity."

"What is it made of?" Karen asked.

"Of purity," Aleksandr answered with a toddler's impatience. He gathered the four stones—blue sky, black night, red flame, and white purity—and placed them in a row before him. Then, one by one, he named them and placed them in Zorana's cupped palms.

When the fourth stone, the white stone, touched her skin, the earth tilted on its axis, and in her brain, she heard the echoes of her own prophecy. . . .

A child will perform the impossible. And the beloved of the family will be broken by treachery . . . and leap into the fire.

She shuddered.

When she had witnessed the vision, no one understood what it meant, yet one by one, the pieces had fallen into place. Again she heard the voice in her mind . . .

A child will perform the impossible. And the beloved of the family will be broken by treachery . . . and leap into the fire.

She didn't know what it meant—was Aleksandr the child? And who was the beloved? But soon, too soon, she would. She could only pray that no one died before the pact was broken, and if someone must, better her than Konstantine. Better her than any of them. She would gladly sacrifice herself for her children, for their mates, for Aleksandr, and for Konstantine.

"Gramma." Aleksandr shook her. "Aleksandr want the treasures."

Without realizing what she had done, she'd clutched the stones tightly in her fists.

She glanced around.

Her daughters-in-law were laughing, sharing food, and they had noticed nothing. That was fine. They should have one hour not overshadowed by the pact, by war, by worry.

Zorana nibbled on her food and sipped her wine, and observed Aleksandr as he explained to Karen, for the third time, what the stones were and what they meant. She reminisced, "He reminds me of Adrik at that age, very focused and intense."

Her daughters-in-law exchanged glances.

Gently, Tasya said, "Aleksandr is Firebird's son, and we all love him very much. But he's not related to Adrik, or Jasha, or Rurik."

Zorana stared at Tasya. At Aleksandr. At the stones. She listened to his voice, so like her own sons', as he made up a story involving the stones.

And she found herself on her feet. "That's not true. Aleksandr *is* my grandchild."

"Mama?" Ann cast off the afghan and stood also. "Do you mean . . ."

"Aleksandr's father is my son." The realization both broke Zorana's heart and gave her hope. "And Firebird has gone to get him."

Chapter Twenty-seven

About three hours after Doug had spoken with Vadim, the call came in on his cell phone.

"Doug? It's Gloria down at the diner. Listen, I hate to bug you at this hour, but there're some weird guys wandering around downtown tonight. The alarm went off at the restaurant, and the sheriff called and asked me to check on it. He's busy up on One-oh-one—got a three-car pileup. I'm surprised you're not working it." Nosy as always, that was Gloria.

But right now he was grateful. "What's with the alarm?"

"The wind blew a board through the window, and hell, I can't sleep anyway, so I came down to help clean up. These two guys wandered by, right in the middle of the storm, and one of them, when he talked, he sort of hissed."

"Like a snake?"

"Yeah! Do you know him?"

"I thought he'd left town." *Until Vadim called him back in.*

"Like I said, weird. I think they must be on drugs."
Gloria wasn't a simple woman to shake, but now she
sounded profoundly uneasy.

"Did you see which way they went?"

"They got in a car and headed up for the lookout.
I thought they might make trouble up there."

"Thanks, Gloria. I'll go check it out."

"Hey, Doug? You might call for backup. They
really are nasty-looking guys."

"Don't worry. I'll take care of it."

He smiled in satisfaction. Vadim had done exactly
as Doug expected he would: He had set up an
ambush.

Now all Doug had to do was put himself in harm's
way to find out the details of the attack on the Wilders, and hopefully keep Vadim's assassins away
from Firebird long enough for her to return to her
family and warn them.

For they *were* her family. They weren't his—no one
had ever wanted him before, and now they never
would.

Who wanted a guy who had sold his own family
to a pack of vicious murderers?

The light from the bathroom woke Firebird. She
rose onto her elbow and shielded her eyes.

Douglas was a looming silhouette in the doorway.
"I'm sorry to have to wake you."

It was dark outside. The clock said four a.m., but
he was dressed in his state police uniform.

"What's wrong?"

"My boss rang me." He paced toward her. "Someone called in an accident on the highway. I may be a while, so I need to bring you up-to-date."

She'd learned to wake up when she needed to; having a baby had taught her that. Now she roused herself completely, stuck a pillow behind her back, and *focused*.

"The storm knocked out the electricity," he said.

She heard the wind thrashing through the trees.

He continued, "I have a backup generator. The phones are out. I can't do anything about that. But the storm's passing, and because I'm a state cop, the phone company always repairs my lines first, so that should be back up soon."

"If you've got no phones, how did you find out about the accident?"

"I keep a cell phone backup. In my line of work, I can't be caught without one." He pulled it from his shirt pocket and stared at it indecisively. "I should leave it with you."

"No. You need it worse than I do. But I'll tell you what." She took it from him and programmed in the Wilder number. "If you get in any kind of trouble, you can call home and someone will come to rescue you. I programmed them in as autodial number four, for four brothers." She handed it back with a smile.

He did *not* smile back. "Thank you. Good idea. I hope I'm never in that kind of trouble."

"Me, too, but that's what families are for." He didn't yet know that. It would probably take years before he realized how completely he could depend on his brothers, his father and mother . . . and her. But he would learn. She would see to it.

"I went out and scouted around," he said. "I don't smell Varinskis, but in normal mode, the house security system will alert me to any invaders, and in high alert, this room acts as a safe room, and the system will repel invaders. I'll set it for that. You'll be safe while you sleep, but if I'm not back before you get up and want to eat, you *have* to reset the code." He placed a piece of paper with scrawled numbers on the bedside table. "Don't forget."

"I won't."

He placed a Glock beside the paper. "You know how to use this."

She picked it up, checked the safety, hefted it up and down to get the feel of that individual piece. "I can outshoot my brothers."

"I never doubted it." Douglas smiled.

Well, not smiled. But he looked pleased. Well, not pleased . . . but she thought she was beginning to read him better, and *that* pleased *her*.

"The pistol is loaded," he said. "If you go out for any reason—"

"I'll take it."

"I wouldn't leave if I thought there were danger."

"I know."

He reached out, and his fingers hovered an inch from her cheek. "Be careful. Stay here. I'll be back as soon as I can, and then we'll . . . then you can give me to your mother."

"*Your* mother."

His hand fell away. "My mother."

As he turned away, she caught his cuff. "I didn't exactly tell you everything. Not because I was deliberately leaving it out, but because we had so many other things to, um, cover . . ."

He stood as still as a cougar anticipating attack. "What did you leave out?"

There was no way to put this tactfully. "We believe that sooner or later—probably sooner—the Varinskis plan to attack my family and wipe them out."

"Then I guess I'd better finish my business tonight so I can help with the fight." He sounded so prosaic, as if the family's battle were his, no question. Then he kissed her.

He tasted her, he breathed with her, and when he finished, he held her close and inhaled the scent of her hair. It was as if he were saying good-bye . . . forever.

He placed her on the pillows and walked to the door; then, as if he had changed his mind, he walked back. "Tell me—why do the Varinskis want the icon?"

The blood drained from her face. "What . . . icon?"

"They're offering a reward for a Russian icon. I take it by your expression that you know about it."

This the Wilders hadn't anticipated—that the Varinskis would openly hunt for the icon. Didn't they realize that once they indicated interest, every scoundrel in the world would be buying up icons by the dozens, and their chances of finding the one right icon would be diminished?

Of course, perhaps they thought the Wilders' chance of finding them would be diminished, too.

But so far, the discovery of each icon had been miraculous in its own way. She had to have faith that the miracles wouldn't fail them now.

Yet how to efficiently explain the situation to Douglas? "There are four icons. We have possession of three. When we find the fourth one, when we put them together, we will break the pact with the devil."

"So the icon is very valuable."

"It is beyond value. The Varinskis can't allow us to get it, or they're nothing. Listen, Douglas." She took his hand. "My mother had a vision, and in her vision, each of the four Wilder sons will find an icon. The Varinskis don't realize that you're the fourth son, but . . . be careful out there."

"I always am." This time, as she searched his face, she thought he looked troubled. But he leaned down, kissed her with warm lips and cool intention, and she responded.

Then he was gone.

She had misjudged him. He was a good guy. Such a good guy. She'd done the right thing in coming here to get him.

She slid back under the covers and tried to go back to sleep, but she was wide-awake and worried.

The Varinskis were seeking the fourth icon. Offering a reward. Did the Wilder family know?

Firebird had listened to the message from Ann on her cell phone, but she hadn't talked to her mother since she'd left three days ago. She didn't know if they'd tried to call her—her phone was ruined and at the bottom of the ocean.

But surely they'd replied to her e-mail.

She got up, pulled a blanket around her shoulders, and used the code to reset the security system.

Then she headed into the corridor and Douglas's office.

The door was locked.

She stared incredulously at the handle, then tried it again.

Definitely locked.

Her face flushed with hot embarrassment.

He knew she'd gone into his office and used his computer, of course. With a security system like his, he would know every room she'd visited, every faucet she'd turned.

She thumped the door with the flat of her hand.

He didn't trust her?

No. Apparently he didn't.

She had a choking feeling in the back of her throat, a feeling made up of mortification and betrayal.

But he hadn't betrayed her, not really. He just . . . didn't have the same faith in her that she had in him.

Like a bird, a little doubt peeped in her ear: What did he have to hide?

But she ignored that misgiving.

She still needed to communicate with her family.

Okay. No e-mail. The house telephone was out. But Douglas had a new BMW in the garage. He kept at least one extra cell phone. Was another out there?

Grabbing her bag, she headed into the bathroom. When she came out, she wore blue jeans and an earthy brown, close-fitting T-shirt. She had a knife strapped to her wrist and a Luxeon LED five-inch defensive aluminum flashlight in her pocket. She sat down in a chair and laced up her boots. She tucked the pistol in her belt and went looking for a coat to wear—hers had disappeared somewhere in the ocean.

She found a brown leather jacket in the closet, one that must fit Douglas like a glove. The leather was supple, yet strong; the zipper slid up as if it were on ball bearings. She checked the brand name; this thing must have cost a fortune.

And once again the doubt peeped in her ear.

Where did Douglas get the money for this jacket? To remodel this house? For a BMW?

He'd said gambling, but if that were the truth, why had he locked his office?

She found the keys for the BMW right away; they hung on a hook inside the pantry, where Douglas could grab them on the way out.

She set the alarm, turned off the lights, pulled her pistol, and stepped out the back door.

And listened.

The clouds hid the moon's half-light. The night was pitch dark, without a sign of the impending dawn. The wind blew, rattling the loose boards on the porch, vibrating the metal gutters above. The waves rolled into shore.

But she heard no stealthy movement, sensed no predators in wait.

She moved cautiously down the porch and around the house, pausing and listening, but she grew more confident with each step.

If her father was right—and he always was—the Varinskis believed that when she'd gone in the ocean, they'd successfully completed their mission. If they didn't believe that, they would have attacked at Mrs. Burchett's, or here at the house. She was convinced she was alone and safe.

But she didn't put the pistol down.

Douglas's BMW X5 was parked in the gravel parking space.

Her car was gone. Had Douglas put it in the garage? She didn't take the time to find out. Her mortification at Douglas's distrust had changed to uneasiness.

Something was not right.

She unlocked the car and climbed into the driver's seat, locked the door behind her, and placed the pistol in the seat beside her. She stuck the keys in the ignition, in case she had to drive; then, with her flashlight, she went through the console between the seats and the glove compartment. She explored the door pockets, front and back. She felt around under the seats and above the windshield.

No cell phone.

But this car had knobs everywhere. There were knobs on the ceiling, controls for the sunroof, and knobs between the seats on the console. There were knobs on the steering column, on the dash. Douglas's BMW was the polar opposite of her Mercury Milan; it had everything—Night Vision, twenty-way seat adjustment, a lane-departure warning feature. Somewhere there had to be some kind of communication device, or at least real-person assistance.

She poked and prodded, found the park-distance sensors, the heads-up display. . . . Somehow, she stumbled into the history function for the navigation system. She tried to move on to the next utility, and instead moved one level deeper, and brought up the list of everywhere he'd driven his too-expensive car.

She didn't mean to pry.

But two words caught her eye.

Blythe, Washington.

The last time he'd driven this car, he'd driven to her own small town in the Cascade Mountains.

Her mouth was dry, her eyes strained as she examined his route. . . . He had started in Seattle, at the Swedish Hospital, had driven almost to her doorstep, and he'd done it on the same night she returned from Seattle with the proof that she was not the Wilders' daughter.

He had followed her.

He was the one who had watched her that night. He had scouted out the location of the Wilder home.

When she had asked him if he was there, he had lied to her.

Why? Why lie?

The answer was all too evident.

With new understanding, she looked around at the gleaming chrome, the leather seats, the state-of-the-art technology.

And when he had the coordinates, he'd sold the promise of information to the Varinskis. He had assured them he could deliver the Wilders' location, and they'd paid him an advance on delivery. That was how a twenty-three-year-old orphan afforded a BMW, an estate, and a leather jacket.

He'd betrayed his family, his son . . . and his whore.

Because she was nothing more than that to him.

Taking the keys, the flashlight, and the pistol, she eased out of the car. She walked back into the house, skulking through the darkness, listening for trouble. Rage would not make her lose her caution.

She punched in the security code and walked upstairs to his office.

She had given Douglas information about the family and their vulnerabilities. She had let him know that they must have him on their side to win their battle with the Varinskis. She had trusted him when she shouldn't, betraying the family that had raised her and given her everything, condemning her own son to death. Most important, without the fourth icon, the pact with the devil couldn't be broken. Konstantine and the men she considered her brothers, and even her darling Aleksandr, were sentenced to an eternity in hell.

But this locked office door meant Douglas was hiding something. Without thinking twice, she lifted the pistol and shot the lock out of the door.

Let *that* register on his security system.

She stalked to his desk and was almost disappointed to discover it was open. She was more than ready to shoot more locks off.

She rifled through the drawers, and in the third drawer down on the right-hand side, there it was.

The fourth icon, tangled in the seaweed that had tried to choke her, drown her.

Each of my four sons must find one of the Varinski icons. Only their loves can bring the holy pieces home.

That had been Zorana's vision.

But that was crap. Firebird wasn't Douglas Black's love. Because he had screwed her silly. He had told her he loved her. He had bared his heart and soul to her.

And it had all been lies.

Chapter Twenty-eight

Doug slowly drove the steep, dark, winding road toward the lookout, his powerful spotlight sweeping from side to side as he watched for the trap he knew had been set for him.

Yet in a separate part of his mind, he worried. He worried about leaving Firebird alone in his house. He worried about what Vadim Varinski had planned. He worried about his son, Aleksandr. Never before had he had anyone to worry about; now he discovered that having a family came with a price.

Remembering the cell phone in his pocket, and the number Firebird had programmed in, he changed his thoughts. Having a family came with a price—and a refuge. All his life, he'd had no one at his back. Now, how odd to think that if he were in trouble, someone would come to his aid. Or, at least, Firebird thought someone would come to his aid.

His spotlight picked up a debris field. He slammed on his brakes.

Nice fake-out.

He pointed his spotlight toward the edge of the

road. And there it was, a car dangling off the edge of the embankment with its front tires off the pavement.

Maybe not a fake-out, after all. Maybe the Varinskis had been having a little too much fun. If that was the case, Foka would be having a hissy-fit. Or in Foka's case, that would be a hisssssy-fit.

Doug laughed at his own humor, adjusted his spotlight, and examined the car for the driver or passengers. He couldn't see anyone.

Where were they?

He pulled his service pistol and palmed his knife, then eased out of the patrol car. The stench of Varinskis struck him like a blow.

There had to be at least five or six of them out there.

Foka really overestimated Doug's abilities. Or maybe this was a matter of pride. Maybe this time Foka wanted to make sure he killed him.

As Doug stepped away from the car, a massive wolf leaped out of darkness. He turned sideways and sliced with his knife as the beast drove him onto the pavement.

The Varinski's howl of pain vibrated through him. He caught the snout that went for his throat, twisted the neck beneath his arm, and, as hard as he could, bit down on an ear. To his immense satisfaction, blood filled his mouth. He twisted harder, felt the legs kick, the claws scratch . . . the neck snap.

One down.

Out of the corner of his eye, he saw the others gather. Three more wolves and two men, one slight and thin, the other a massive, James Bond bad-guy type.

He used the dead body to block his movement, brought his pistol up, and shot. The big guy went down hard, gurgled, and died.

Then, from behind, someone kicked Doug in the ribs.

His next shot went wild. His breath blasted out of his lungs. He coughed. He shot again, emptying his clip, sending one of the wolves into the forest yipping like a puppy.

The guy behind him clubbed Doug, and as his head wobbled on his neck, kicked the pistol out of his hand. Placing his massive foot on Doug's neck, he turned him facedown on the pavement and held him there.

Six of them. Seven counting the dead wolf. That shit Vadim believed Doug had the icon, and he'd sent seven of his goons to retrieve it.

Doug slanted his eyes up and saw the twin of the guy he'd shot.

Great. Good way to win friends and influence people. Kill his twin.

The thin Varinski spoke quietly to his men. "Wolvesss are of no use here. I need men."

The two remaining wolves looked at each other in doubt.

"Change now," the thin one said. He didn't raise his voice, but Doug saw the wolves take a step back and the transformation begin. "That'sss better." He stepped forward, into Doug's spotlight.

Ugly. Shit, this guy was ugly. Narrow forehead, pointy snout, sharp teeth, wide neck—he looked like a huge, mutated lizard from a bad SF flick. And

Doug recognized the voice. This guy had been in charge of the attack on the cliffs.

"Foka," he said.

"How flattering. You know my name." Foka's tongue flicked out to touch his lips. "You'll scream it soon."

"What do you want?" Doug asked.

"Goga, explain to our American cousin what we want," Foka said.

Goga dug one hand into Doug's hair, wrapped one around his throat, and lifted him to face level. In a blast of garlic, he shouted, "Where's the fourth icon?"

"Where's my hundred million dollars?" Doug asked.

"You are not in the position to negotiate," Foka said. "The fourth icon. Tell us now, and we'll ssslaughter you right away. Hold out, and you will sssuffer."

Doug got his feet under him. He seized the hand that held his throat. Used his other hand to jab Goga's windpipe. As Goga released him and fell backward, gagging, Douglas kicked up and out.

His foot glanced off Goga's shoulder.

Goga wrapped his elbow around Doug's knee and twisted.

Doug felt his knee crack.

Pain. Pain like nothing he'd ever felt before.

The other two Varinskis growled and advanced.

Doug paid them no heed. Instead he did a fast low crawl and punched autodial number four.

Behind him, Goga bellowed with laughter.

Even Foka chuckled as he asked, "What are you going to do? Call for backup?"

No, asshole, I'm passing information to my family about you and what you want. I'm sending them to rescue Fire-bird, and maybe . . . to rescue me. And kill you.

One of the wolf-men kicked the phone out of his hand, and as his fingers broke, he heard a woman answer, "Hello?"

Chapter Twenty-nine

❦

"**H**ello? Hello?" Zorana sat up in bed.

"Wrong number?" But Konstantine didn't believe that for a second. Not now. Now with the stench of Varinski growing strong in his nostrils.

"I don't think so. You have to listen to this." She turned on the light and put the call on speakerphone.

"Sure." What with planning the battle, he hadn't been sleeping well anyway. He might as well have a conversation with—

"Where's the fourth icon?" a deep voice bellowed, but at a distance. "Give us the icon!"

"I sold it to the Wilders." The voice that shouted an answer sounded strange, yet familiar.

So did the sound of breaking bones.

"You had better be lying." The voice was quiet, but the menace carried clearly into their bedroom.

"What do you care?" that almost-familiar voice shouted. "Vadim says you're going to attack them before the month is out. When you do, get it back."

"You ssstupid fool. We attack today, once Vadim arrives. That'sss enough time for them to unite the icons and—" That soft, horrible, sibilant voice broke off. "I must call Vadim. Goga, Dimitri, Grigori, Lyov—make sure our little cousin is not lying to me."

Zorana muted the phone. "What is it? Who is it?"

"Someone's getting the crap beat out of him by a bunch of Varinskis, and I'd guess"—Konstantine looked at his wife, so pale, so brave—"I'd guess it's our son."

Zorana pressed the warning alarm beside the bed.

"What are you doing?" Konstantine asked. As if he didn't know.

"I'm going to send someone to save him."

Adrik arrived first, wide-awake and fully dressed. He advanced into the room slowly, listening to the repeated demands for the fourth icon. "Somebody's getting the stuffing beaten out of him."

"Your brother." At this first sign of her missing son, Zorana pressed a hand to her heart, but her voice was steady.

"I figured." Adrik rubbed his shoulder. "I wonder if I can get a bead on the GPS in that phone."

"I can." Ann stood in the doorway. She wore pajamas and a robe, but her eyes were as alert as Adrik's. "Put it on hold. I'll pick it up on the living room computer."

"Great!" Adrik headed out.

Jasha stood behind her. "What can I do to help, *kasatka*?"

She turned toward her computer setup in the living room. "Put on the coffee."

Jasha followed her out, complaining, " 'Make my coffee. Type my letters. Chase me around my desk.' You treat me like your secretary." But before he stepped out, he grimly looked back at his father, and his message was clear.

He had information to pass along, intelligence he'd learned last night on his foray into the Varinski-filled forest.

Konstantine nodded. They would speak later.

"I'll start breakfast," Tasya said.

"I'll help." Karen followed Tasya toward the kitchen.

Konstantine had been blessed in his children and their wives.

Rurik arrived, yawning. "What did I miss?"

"You, lazy son, you can help me up." Konstantine cursed the weakness that tied him to a wheelchair and slipped like evil through his bloodstream.

But all night, he had been plotting another tactic. . . . He waited until Zorana had gone into the bathroom before asking in a low voice, "How many detonator caps do we have left?"

"A few." Rurik helped him walk from the bed to the wheelchair. "Why?"

"The Varinskis have been gathering out there for what? A day? Yet no move on the house. Why not? We appear virtually defenseless. Four women, three Varinski men in the prime of their lives, but only three, and me, an invalid in a wheelchair."

"And Aleksandr," Rurik said.

"And Aleksandr," Konstantine agreed.

"Papa, shouldn't we send the little one away?" Rurik checked the gauge on the oxygen tank that hung from the back of the chair.

Konstantine patted Rurik's troubled face. "My son, there is no safe place. Not even here, but better he should stay with us, with the people he loves, than go to strangers and there to die. For they will hunt him. They will kill him. Varinskis are very thorough."

"I know, Papa."

"Your brother"—Konstantine gestured toward the phone—"your long-lost brother just passed us information we must utilize. The Varinskis will attack us today." He placed the oxygen mask over his mouth and nose and took a long breath. He was reserving his strength, for when the time came, he *would* beat the Varinskis.

He had no choice.

"They're waiting only for their leader, and perhaps reinforcements."

"You don't think we should wait," Rurik surmised.

"Surprise is always a good element in a battle." Konstantine leaned toward his son and stage-whispered, "If you can get me a detonator, I promise I can surprise them."

He told Rurik his plan, and while his son chuckled, Konstantine preened. Obviously, he hadn't yet lost the old gift for strategy.

Their second line rang.

Rurik and Konstantine exchanged glances. More bad news?

Zorana stepped out of the bathroom, a towel on

her head, her face gleaming and damp. "Who is *that*?"

Rurik looked down at their caller ID. "The When You Are Wicked Diner?" He punched the button to open the line on the speakerphone.

The woman on the phone said, "It's Firebird."

Konstantine flinched. He hadn't heard that anguish in his daughter's voice since he'd last questioned her about Aleksandr's father.

Zorana hurried toward the phone, ready to take command of the conversation.

Konstantine waved her into silence. "What is wrong, little one?"

"Papa." Firebird took a long, wobbly breath. "Papa. There's nothing wrong. Nothing that hasn't been wrong for a long, long time. Aleksandr is well?"

"Very well," Konstantine said.

"My baby . . ." Firebird took another breath. "I suppose you probably figured some of this out, but I left to find Aleksandr's father. I did. His name is Douglas Black, and he is also your missing son. I didn't realize that before, of course, I thought he was a Varinski who had tracked me down and seduced me for information about my family. About the Wilders."

Konstantine cracked his knuckles and considered the first lesson he would teach his newfound son— if he lived through the beating the Varinskis were now inflicting on him.

Firebird continued, "It turns out I was more right then I realized. Douglas . . . Douglas Black sold us out to the Varinskis."

"No!" Zorana took a step toward the phone.

"Before I knew that, I gave him information. About us. I'm sorry, Papa." Firebird's voice broke. "I'm so sorry."

Konstantine was sorry, too. Sorry that one of his own would betray his family. Sorry that she had suffered for it.

"Excuses can be made," Rurik murmured.

"There are no excuses for immorality," Konstantine said coldly.

Before he could tell Firebird the truth—that Douglas was getting the snot kicked out of him by his erstwhile allies—she added, "But listen. This is the important part. I'm coming home."

"No," Konstantine said in alarm. "Stay where you are. I start the battle this morning."

"I have to come home, Papa. I've got the fourth icon."

Konstantine wanted to shout with joy. He wanted to weep with horror.

His daughter, the baby he had dandled on his knee, had in her possession the fourth icon. The fourth icon! The one icon that would unite the others and break the pact with the devil.

"I know it's supposed to come to the one your son loves, but Douglas doesn't love anyone, so I suppose it came to the one your son *screwed*." Firebird spit the word. "So the prophecy is correct in its way."

They had no time for bitterness. Konstantine said, "Firebird, you are right. There is no choice. You do have to come home." For she was now in more danger than any of them.

Rurik stepped close to the phone. "Where are you?"

"In Rocky Cliffs, in the When You Are Wicked Diner." Now that she'd delivered her message, she was sniffling.

When Rurik spoke, he used his Air Force–captain command voice to snap her out of it. "Firebird, is there someplace you can meet me? Someplace flat?"

"Um. Yeah. Yes!" She sounded startled. "I can drive north toward Shoalwater State Park. There's a parking lot there."

"Perfect. I'll be there in less than an hour."

"In less than an hour?" She sounded confused and heartsore. "But—"

"Get out of there *now*, before they track you down," Konstantine added.

They heard the click as she replaced the phone.

Zorana grabbed Rurik's arm. "Bring her home. Somehow, bring her home."

"I will, Mama." Rurik patted her hand, then turned toward the door.

Adrik ran in, smiling savagely. "Ann got it. I know where our long-lost brother is, and I'm going after him."

"Make sure some of the Varinskis follow you," Konstantine said. "And make sure they don't come back!"

"Yes, Papa," the boys chorused.

Rurik hooked his elbow around Adrik's neck. "Come with me."

"Come with you?" Adrik snorted. "I'll drive. I'm faster."

"Yes, you can drive us to the airfield," Rurik answered.

Adrik stopped, narrow-eyed and wary. "What are we going to do at the airfield?"

Rurik said words guaranteed to put pride in a father's heart. "We're going to steal a helicopter."

Chapter Thirty

Doug didn't know how long the Varinskis had been cutting on him. It seemed like days. It was probably no more than an hour, because the sun still hadn't risen above the horizon. But if he had to say one thing they did well, it was torture. They had hefted him up onto the hood of his patrol car, gotten out the pocketknives, and gone to work. They cut off his shirt and one of his nipples. They probed between his ribs. And he didn't even want to think about what they'd done to his hands.

Blood, when it started to dry, got very sticky. And Doug wondered what Yamashita was going to say about the big red stain on the car. Did the enzymes in blood ruin a paint job?

Foka stuck his face close to Doug's and in his heavily accented voice said, "I am bored with you. I am bored with your resistance."

"I'm not resisting. I told you. I sold the icon to the Wilders."

Idly, Doug wondered how many bones they'd broken. Other than his knee, his ribs, and his hand, he was feeling pretty good. Of course, that might be because the loss of blood was shutting down his brain. . . .

"Vadim doesn't believe you. He said you are greedy. He said there are other bidders out there who would have paid more. He sssaid you haven't had time to get your bids." Foka leaned his ugly face close. "There are other body partsss Goga can cut off."

Goga grinned and nodded.

"Onesss that hurt worssse than a little finger. Do you know what they are?" Foka asked.

Doug knew exactly what they were. He lifted his head off the windshield. Smiled insolently at the ugly trio, and especially at Foka. "Are you one of those guys? The ones who love to play with another guy's family jewels?"

"*Koshka*," Foka hissed, and when he did, the pupils in his eyes changed from round to up-and-down slits.

"*I'm* a piece of shit? This from a guy who not only likes to play with another guy's jewels, but really likes it when they're *his* family jewels, too?"

Foka gestured to Goga.

Goga slammed his fist into Doug's gut.

Great. A little soft-tissue damage, too.

When he finished gagging, he thought the roaring in his ears would subside. It didn't. It grew louder and louder. Then a whirlwind struck, filling the air with dirt and cedar, and a light as bright as the sun blinded him.

It wasn't his imagination, either, or the onset of death. The Varinskis were shielding their eyes and shouting in dismay.

God had arrived to exact his vengeance on them all.

Then a voice at the edge of the light spoke, and Doug knew it wasn't God.

It said, "You shits are going to be sorry for picking on my brother."

Doug couldn't believe it. His family had arrived, and in a helicopter, no less.

A panther, black as the night, leaped onto the two wolf-guys, slashing one across the face, snapping the other's neck with a single bite.

Doug rolled off the hood, taking Foka down with him, and as they fell, Doug pulled the pistol from Foka's belt and blasted him right through his cold lizard guts.

He figured he had five shots left, and as he rolled out from behind the car, he emptied every round into his tormentors.

"Come on. C'mon!" Firebird paced beside the car, biting her nails down to the quicks. With every step, she was aware of the icon tucked beneath her bra against her heart.

Once she'd found it, she'd gotten out of that house at top speed. She hadn't hesitated to take the Glock, or Douglas's car, either. She needed power if she was going to get this icon home without interference from Douglas and his Varinskis. The stop in Rocky Cliffs had been brief, long enough to call home, and the drive to Shoalwater State Park had been nerve-racking.

She glanced around again. "C'mon, Rurik."

She hadn't wanted to stop in the empty parking lot filled with mounds of soggy leaves and faded white lines painted on black asphalt. She had wanted to keep driving, to get as far away from Douglas as she could. She didn't want to face him, and not merely because he'd murder her, although that was a pretty good reason. No, she couldn't bear to watch him smirk at having so cleverly fooled her into betraying her family—and giving him a blow job while she did it.

Where was Rurik? What did he think he was doing? She could have driven Doug's Beemer home in four hours, or five if the traffic was bad, and as long as she didn't get stopped too many times by the state patrol, and as long as Doug hadn't reported his car as stolen.

The lousy son of a bitch.

He probably had. Had probably demanded she be arrested for shooting off his lock. If he realized how gleefully she would shoot off his—

The *chop-chop-chop* of helicopter blades interrupted her pleasant musing. It was coming fast, getting louder by the moment. She looked north along the shore, and there it was, black and white, silver and red, coming fast, dusting the treetops, creating a whirlwind of debris. The aircraft hovered over the parking lot, then gently came to rest on the asphalt. The passenger door opened, and she looked across the seat to Rurik gesturing her in. She ran, head down, as the blades chopped the air, blasting her until she settled in the seat. Before she'd even buckled in, he lifted off, straight up into the air, and once she was secure, he set a course east and north, flying fast.

She donned the headset.

He spoke into the microphone, his voice right in her ears. "What the hell happened to your hair? It looks like you backed into a lawn mower."

"No, it got chopped off with a knife."

She could almost hear him groping for the right answer. After a pause of thirty seconds, he said, "Great helicopter, huh?"

"Smooth," she muttered. But it *was* a great helicopter, shining and clean, with complicated gauges and rich leather seats.

"It's a Bell 206B3 JetRanger III, seats five, does two hundred and twenty kilometers per hour. . . ."

She glared witheringly.

"Or, for you landlubbers, one hundred and thirty-six miles per hour. We'll fly straight home and be there in fifty minutes, give or take a minute." His gaze flicked toward her. "Do you have it?"

"The icon?" She pressed her hand against the small, hard square hidden against her body. "It's in a safe place."

"Heaven does not hold me in its favor, but I have been praying that the fourth icon would be found." With typical brotherly bluntness, he said, "You found it? Are you *sure* you're not our brother's true love?"

"Where'd you get the helicopter?" she asked.

"Oh, come on, Firebird. Tell me what he's like."

"He's a sneaking, lying, underhanded weasel."

"Really?" Rurik was clearly horrified. "A weasel?"

In this family, she couldn't even use a metaphor. "No. He's a cougar. But that doesn't change the facts. He *should* be a weasel."

Rurik must have heard the wobble in her voice and feared a bout of tears, for he said, "I borrowed it from a friend."

"What?"

"The helicopter."

A hunch made her say, "Does he know you borrowed it?"

"He won't mind. He's a former Air Force pilot himself, a guy with a flair for making money. He's always got a new toy to play with." Rurik concentrated very hard on the gauges and the horizon.

She plucked the clipboard off the dash and glanced through the flight records. "It's only been out twice."

"Yeah, I'm breaking it in."

"I didn't know you could fly a helicopter."

"Sure. Remember, when I change, I'm a hawk. I can fly anything."

"Really." She turned toward him. "Tell me, how many helicopters have you flown?"

"I've done a lot of work in a helicopter flight simulator."

She'd grown up in this family of daredevils. It took a lot to make her lose her cool. But this time, he'd managed it. "This is your first time at the controls?"

"Don't shriek like that!" He tapped his helmet over

his ear. "It's merely my first time in the air. And I'd like to point out that *you* were driving a nice Beemer."

"I borrowed it from a friend." Firebird bared her teeth in a ferocious smile. "He won't mind."

The radio crackled to life. "Rurik, you bastard, what are you doing with my JetRanger?"

"Just taking it out for a spin, Ethan. Just taking it out for a spin."

"I just traded the old one in on that beauty, and if you get one scratch on its pristine paint job—"

"Oops! Was that a goose hitting at two hundred and twenty kilometers per hour?" Rurik shouted.

"A single scratch," Ethan shouted back, "and I'll have you arrested and locked up in a prison cell so deep, the only way you'll know it's Christmas is if you have an erection to play with!"

For the first time since she'd found the icon, the tension slid out of Firebird's shoulders, and she smiled.

Rurik touched her cheek with his finger. Still with that outrageous innocence in his voice, he said, "Gee, Ethan, you're being awfully strict about this. It's not like I even know how to fly a helicopter."

Firebird settled into her seat and allowed the men's quarreling to distract her from her worries, from her sorrow, from the awful truth she'd left behind, and the formidable responsibility she faced at home.

She held the fourth icon. Now it was up to her, and her alone, to unite it with the other three and end the pact with the devil.

Chapter Thirty-one

※⬦※

Doug woke slumped in the passenger seat of his patrol car as it raced down the highway, the siren screaming. He stared at the mile markers that whipped past at a horrifying speed, and in a voice that was no more than a croak, he asked, "What the hell are you doing?"

"Getting us home in a hurry." A hand appeared before Doug's face. "I'm your brother Adrik."

"For the love of God, put those fingers on the wheel," Doug said.

The hand disappeared. "You worry too much."

"I'm a cop. It's my job to worry." Doug rolled his head toward the driver.

Except for the dark hair and green eyes, this guy looked like the guy Doug saw in the mirror every morning—tall, broad shouldered, exotic, and meaner than shit.

Wow. He really did have a brother.

A brother who could save Firebird. "Someone needs to—"

"—go after Firebird?" Adrik finished. "Someone is."

"Honest?"

"*I* don't lie."

"Thank God," Doug mumbled, and slowly inched up in the seat.

As far as he could tell, every part of his body had been crunched, ripped, broken, and chopped. While they'd tortured him, he'd screamed like a little girl, but he had his revenge—he'd killed a man who looked like a lizard, taken out one more, and watched with satisfaction as Adrik, his panther brother, had cleaned the road with the last of them.

Now Doug should have been a wreck, physically and emotionally, but instead, when he realized that his family had sent someone to save his ass, he felt good. "I'm your brother Douglas," he said.

"I want to congratulate you."

"For living through that torture?"

"No. For having a normal name." Adrik gave a crack of laughter. "We Wilders live to be tortured."

"Glad to carry on the family tradition."

"Here. This is for you." Adrik handed over a bottle of water. "Drink it all. You're a Wilder; we're fast healers, but you're in shit shape, and we'll need you to keep up your end in the battle. There's a sandwich for you on the floor, too." The water quenched a horrible thirst, and the mere mention of a sandwich made Doug's salivary glands work overtime. He dove into the brown bag and brought out a twelve-inch tuna salad on wheat and a big bag of chips.

A *big* bag of chips.

"Open those up and put them in the middle." The tires squealed as Adrik took an exit off I-5.

"In a minute." Doug scarfed down half the sandwich before he could unwrap his fingers from the sub. "Thanks, man, I needed that."

"You're going to make our mother very happy," Adrik said obscurely.

Doug opened the chips and wondered why the mere mention of his mother made his palms sweat. When he thought about what he had to confess . . .

"By the way, sorry about your finger. After we killed the Varinskis, I looked around for it, but no luck."

Doug lifted his right hand and held it before his eyes. Only a bloody stump remained where his little finger had been. "You couldn't find it. They chopped it off a little at a time."

"They did something to your other hand, too."

Doug lifted his left hand and stared at the deep gash in his palm. "Oh, yeah. I remember. They wanted to take my thumb, but they were using a pocketknife and the bone was too tough. So they gave up and went for the little finger."

"That sucks." Adrik sounded as if he knew exactly how much it sucked, and also knew Doug would survive to fight again. Soon.

If they weren't killed by his driving. Adrik dug into the chips with one hand, and used the other to shove his dark hair out of his eyes.

"What are you steering with, your pecker? Really, man," Doug said. "Slow down."

"I was a juvenile delinquent, you know. Driving a patrol car is a lifelong dream." Adrik sounded cheerful. "Besides, we have a war to fight."

"Later." Doug ate another bite of the sandwich and a handful of chips.

"Papa's pushing up the schedule. So Rurik and I led four Varinskis on a wild-goose chase on the way to the airfield, and when we had them trapped, we eliminated them. That'll help, but not enough, because the battle is starting right about"—Adrik glanced at his wrist, not that he wore a watch— "now."

Doug appreciated a brother with a sense of humor. He wasn't as happy as Adrik pressed down on the accelerator. "The speedometer only goes to a hundred and twenty."

"We want to beat Rurik home." Adrik laughed out loud. "We haven't got a chance—the chopper will take fifty minutes. But I do love the speed."

"Why do we want to beat him home?"

"Because he's the one who has Firebird."

"He has her safe?" Doug wanted to collapse in relief. "You know that for sure?"

"I do know that for sure." Adrik's friendly tone disappeared. "I also know she said you betrayed us to the Varinskis."

The torture Doug had suffered was nothing compared to the anguish of having Firebird find out what he'd done. "She knows?"

Adrik's expression was about as friendly as the lizard's when he'd hacked at Doug's finger. "Everyone in the family knows."

"Fuck everyone in the family. I don't care about the family. I don't know the family." Vaguely Doug knew he had alienated the man who had rescued him from certain death. "But I love Firebird, and I screwed up so badly. . . . I love her, and she's got to hate my guts."

"That's pretty much what she said."

If Doug had been thinking, he would have noticed that Adrik sounded friendly again, like he approved of the guy who loved his sister above all else.

"I don't know what I'm going to do to make it up to her."

"Just a suggestion—if I were you, I'd save her life."

"What are you talking about?"

"Firebird's got the fourth icon."

"The hell you say." How had she found the icon? When Doug had left, he'd locked his office door. What had she done to get in? And why?

Adrik continued, "The Varinskis have already surrounded the valley, more are coming all the time, and they'd do anything to kill the bearer of the icon."

Suddenly, all the aches and pains, all the questions and guilt that plagued Doug fell away. "Drive faster," he said.

Chapter Thirty-two

"As you know, the fourth icon is on its way. The other three are upstairs in the safe room waiting for the chance to be united with it." Konstantine sat at the kitchen table, directing operations in that calm, confident manner he had always used on untried troops. "Yet Ann has discovered for us on her computer that the young leader of the Varinskis, Vadim, will in an hour land in Everett on a private jet. He has hired for himself a limousine to bring him here, and another for his private guard. He brings with him a dozen men. These will be the best fighters and strategists the Varinskis have to offer. The troops that surround us . . . are not." He gestured in a circle toward the outside of the house. "We need to provide a distraction so Rurik and Firebird can bring us the icon. We need time for Zorana to put the icons together and break the pact. And, of course, we want to provide young Vadim with such a scene of chaos that when he arrives, he weeps like an infant. So for all these reasons, I have decided to take the initiative and commence the battle. Now, I know we are few."

He understood the meaning of understatement, especially now, when six people sat facing him—four women, one man, and a child.

Yes, the odds *were* against them.

Zorana, Ann, Tasya, and Karen were fierce in their determination and their defense of their loved ones. They were well taught in self-defense. But they were soft, in the way of women. They hated to hurt even a feeling.

His daughters-in-law were dressed like soldiers, in camouflage, and carried sidearms, but they could not dupe a professional warrior. They had breasts and hips. They smelled of flowers and spice. They were women.

Jasha was also dressed in camouflage, and the weapons he carried were many.

Konstantine had instructed Jasha in battle since the day he was born, and probably had been harder on him than on his other sons, for Jasha was his eldest. Yet while Jasha was a great warrior, he was one against many.

And Aleksandr was the diamond of the family, pure, strong, and in need of protection. He stood on the bench beside Karen, putting his puzzle together and looking up occasionally to add a word or two, usually, "No!" or "Humping like bunnies!" and once, "Bad Varinskis!"

Konstantine continued his pep talk. "But we have many advantages over the Varinskis. I have watched as their men gather in the woods surrounding the valley."

Even better, last night, he had sent his sons out

among them as spies. Why not? The beasts outside didn't know every cousin or stepcousin, and in the dark, his sons looked, moved, and sounded like Varinskis.

"Since the days when I was in command of the Varinskis, the organization has grown sloppy. Many of these striplings are untrained. They came without provisions or supplies. They are hungry and they are cold. They cannot move until their leader gets here. Best of all"—he smiled—"they believe us to be weak."

"What are *our* disadvantages, Papa?" Karen sat across the table, her hands folded before her.

One disadvantage, he thought, was that very intelligence that understood how perilous their mission had become.

He answered honestly—what choice had he?—and he answered completely. "The Varinskis are the devil's best troops, and there are at least a hundred men out there. Men with evil flowing in their veins. Men who like to kill, who enjoy torture. They will tear you limb from limb."

Tasya lifted her chin. "I have the same mercy for the Varinskis that they had for me and mine."

"That is wise," Konstantine said. "The biggest disadvantage we have is that they are fighting to be special, to turn into birds of prey and soar on the wings of the storm, or become wolves and run through the forest, or become great cats and leap from tree to tree. I have experienced the joy of those freedoms—they are intoxicating, addictive, and each time I indulged in the pleasures, I grew more vicious and less human." He looked down at his hands, at the big bones and emaciated muscles, and wished fiercely for the chance to revel in those freedoms one last time. Then, with a sigh, he resigned himself to being human, only human, forever, for whatever time God had planned for him.

Looking up, he observed a similar wistfulness on Jasha's face.

Yes, Jasha knew. He and his son were wolves, and the wildness in their souls did not wish to be caged.

Konstantine confessed, "Also, *I* am a disadvantage. To you. To all of you. I take my medicine; I breathe from my tank of oxygen. I fear at the crucial moment, I will fail you."

Jasha laughed long and loud. "Papa, you're no disadvantage. Without you, we would have no battle plan. Most of all, we will beat them all and break the pact so that you might live long! And when you pass into the next world, we want to know that when our turn comes, we'll meet you at heaven's gate."

His son was a good man. A good man. Touched, Konstantine said, "I would like that, too. I will go down fighting. This, at least, I can promise."

Ann offered her hands to Jasha and Karen, and one by one everyone at the table joined hands. "They are the Varinskis," she said. "They are the Darkness. We're fighting them, so that makes us the Light. Let us remember that, and live up to the name."

Aleksandr beamed around the table and swung the hands he held.

Konstantine's chest filled with pride. "For a woman,

Ann, you give a good speech. You would make a very fine general."

To his surprise, Ann sighed.

"You can take a man out of the Old Country, but you can't take the Old Country out of the man," Jasha advised her.

Konstantine didn't understand what he had said wrong, but sometimes, it was nothing more than a woman thing, so he did not care to try. Placing his glasses on his nose, he picked up the paper in front of him. "Jasha, take Ann and her computer. Make it obvious that you're leaving. Some will follow you, as they followed Rurik and Adrik. When you have taken them far, lose them, take Ann to her Internet connection, and let her work. Ann, you know what to do."

"Move the money from all the Varinski accounts, everywhere I've found them, into the accounts of deserving charities." Ann's pale complexion glowed with anticipation. "Give me two hours, and I will wipe them out."

"I know that I'll be here, and I'll fight the good fight," Tasya said. "But I am so proud of you, Ann. I don't know if we're going to be able to destroy the pact—"

Jasha interrupted, "The fourth icon is coming. Rurik and Firebird won't fail us."

Tasya nodded. "Yes, but no matter what, being poor is really going to hurt those Varinskis."

Ann beamed. "I can't wait."

"Jasha, come back as fast as you can." Konstantine

looked at Ann over his glasses. "I do not like to leave you alone, but—"

"Papa." Ann placed her hand over his. "I have defeated a Varinski before. I will again." She looked meaningfully at Jasha. "I have defeated a Varinski, and I have captured and tamed a Wilder."

"As have I." Tasya smiled wickedly.

"And I," Karen said. "How did *you* do it?"

"Extract blood from him? I bit him," Tasya confided. "He liked it."

"So did I. So did he." Ann smiled up at Jasha. "We are one."

Jasha scowled mightily. "I don't want you to share my fate should I die."

"That is my decision, my love," Ann answered.

Konstantine shot Zorana a startled glance.

She smiled serenely.

He, too, had been bitten in the night. He, too, had liked it, or at least liked the activities that accompanied it. "What is the point?"

"Your blood gives us strength," Zorana said.

"And they will perhaps burn in hell with us for sharing that bond," Jasha told his father.

Konstantine stared at his wife: petite, protective, loving, fierce. "Only *I* am assured of suffering in hell if I should die before the pact is broken. But to think that you would voluntarily share that fate . . ."

Zorana rose and came to his side, took his hand, and knelt. "There was never a doubt, my love. Neither time nor distance can ever separate us. You are the best part of me."

Tears rose to his eyes. He slid his hands around

her neck under her hair. Pulling her close, he pressed his lips to her forehead and murmured, "Many years ago, Zorana, you saved me from myself. No matter where my destiny leads me, I will love you into eternity, in this world or the next."

When at last he lifted his head, Ann stood with her face buried in Jasha's chest, and Tasya and Karen were wiping their damp eyes with paper towels.

Konstantine gestured for one of the paper towels and blew his nose like a mighty trumpet. "Now, we must hurry. This Vadim, this leader, will be here within two hours. So, Ann and Jasha, you leave now." When Ann hesitated, he said, "You have already said your good-byes. Now!"

Jasha wrapped her in a coat and bundled her out the door.

Konstantine listened for their car to start, and when it did, he waved Tasya toward the window. She had been a reporter; he trusted her account.

"Ann's driving. She's backing up. Going forward. Backing up, going forward. That's not a three-point turn, it's a thirty-point turn. Now they're turned around and are leaving. And there's one of the Varinski vehicles on their tail." Tasya turned back into the room and almost smiled, but not quite. "They pulled at least five Varinskis after them. I only hope Ann can drive well enough to shake them when it's time."

"Ann is very accomplished. If she decides she should learn something, she is like a librarian. She does research, and she takes classes." Konstantine picked up his paper again. "Since the time she first became Jasha's woman, she has taken driving classes.

Not the kind so the insurance vandals charge you less. No. She learns how to foil a kidnapper, how to drive too fast, how to skid and turn. My daughter Ann—she is neither as sweet nor as helpless as she looks."

"She does hide her light under a bushel," Tasya said in wonder.

"What is this bushel?" Konstantine asked.

Karen shrugged. "I don't know what it means, either."

Konstantine rattled the paper. "Then we will finish. Tasya, you will take Rurik's place in the planning. Karen, you will take Adrik's place. You all know what to do?"

Everyone nodded.

"Then we will begin in nineteen minutes, at precisely ten a.m." He smiled broadly. He had been anticipating this moment for a very long time. "Zorana? If you will assist me in my preparations?"

Chapter Thirty-three

❧

Zorana pushed Konstantine onto the front porch. "I don't like this," she muttered. "There has to be another way."

"There are a hundred ways, but this is the best way to start." He kept his attention on the crowd of Varinskis who stood outside the picket fence around his lawn. They watched him, two dozen strong and growing as more and more disobeyed Vadim's command to remain hidden and wandered out of the woods to watch the show. Dressed in his pajamas and bathrobe, he slumped in his wheelchair, tubes in his arm and up his nose, the ever-present tank of oxygen hooked on behind.

"Go play your part," he told Zorana. "And try to look feeble."

She walked to the railing and waved at the Varinskis.

They didn't wave back.

"My husband, the great Konstantine, knows who you are and that you've been watching us," she called.

Konstantine called her back. "Louder."

"You said to look feeble, so I didn't want to bellow. It's not as if I don't know how," she snapped nervously. "After all, I have been married to you for thirty-seven years."

"You are a great comedian." But he didn't say it loudly; she was under stress, and it would do him no good if she tried to throttle him in front of the whole contingent of Varinskis.

"My husband, the great Konstantine, knows who you are and that you've been watching us." Zorana did indeed know how to bellow. She proved it now. "Because of your great skills of observation, you know our sons left us. So my husband wishes to offer you a deal."

No one made a move toward the porch. No one pulled a pistol and aimed.

Konstantine's theory was right—they were waiting for instruction from their leader.

"My husband, the great Konstantine, wishes to offer himself as a sacrifice for his family." Zorana was getting into her role, gesturing largely, using a stage voice. "You will take him and do as you wish with him, and in return, you'll allow us to leave here in peace!"

Amusement rippled through the crowd.

Then someone hushed them, and a voice rose from the back. "We agree to the deal."

"You'll take him in our place, and let us go?" Zorana's voice rose above the quarrels that broke out by the speaker.

The same voice said, "What harm could there be?" Then, more loudly, "We do agree."

Zorana paced back to Konstantine. As she covered him with a blanket and tucked it around the cushion beneath him, all her despair, pain, and love shone in her eyes.

"Don't worry, *liubov maya*," he said. "Have faith. In this, I am the expert."

She kissed him lingeringly. "I would be happier if you weren't enjoying yourself so much."

"I'm not enjoying myself," he protested.

"Liar."

He hid his smile with his oxygen mask. He slumped in his chair, moved to the top of the handicapped ramp his sons had built him, and, with careful control, rolled down and onto the front path. When he reached the gate, he lifted his oxygen mask away and gestured toward one young man with feathers sprouting from his head. "Open it, sonny. Show some respect for the great Konstantine."

The kid walked forward, unhooked the gate, and held it wide while, with trembling hands, Konstantine replaced the mask, put his veined hands on the wheels, and rolled through. Konstantine heard him mutter, "*That's* the great Konstantine?"

Konstantine moved forward into the crowd, letting them surround him, and the incredulous murmurs grew into taunts.

"You're the Konstantine who led our family to its golden age?"

"You made us great and glorious and feared?"

"You're old."

"You're sick."

"You're nothing. Nothing!"

They were a pack of salivating dogs with no thought beyond the obvious.

They were fools.

He looked toward the porch.

Zorana had not gone inside, as instructed. She stood on the porch and watched, and when she saw him glare at her, she lifted her chin.

He was thirty feet from the gate. The crowd of Varinskis had grown to thirty, then forty as they filtered out of the hills and came to watch the show. They pressed in, groped him, tore at his clothes. One ripped at his face with a claw.

In a flash, Konstantine ripped back. He could not allow his mask to be dislodged.

The youth snatched his bleeding hand away.

The mob leaned back, surprised at his display of fury.

As he slumped once more, they pressed forward, angry at themselves for their brief fear.

The voice from the back moved forward, calling, "Let me at him. I made the deal; let me have my piece of him."

A quieter voice said, "Yes, let Afonos through. Let him see what he has done that Vadim will kill him for."

"Shut up, Kolya. Vadim will not kill me. Not when he has just killed so many others. He cannot afford the loss of another man."

Interesting, Konstantine thought. This Vadim was killing his own?

On the other hand—Konstantine looked thoughtfully at the Varinskis—some of these things weren't men and weren't beasts. They were weird and horrible combinations of both, like the guy with the feathers coming out of his head, like that one with snakelike scales on his skin and the pupils that contracted into narrow slits. The pact with the devil was breaking apart, and the things that failure had created made Konstantine's flesh crawl.

A brawny thirty-year-old stepped in front of the wheelchair. Placing his hands on his hips, Afonos stared contemptuously down his nose at the wrinkled bathrobe, the ragged slippers, the oxygen mask, and at Konstantine, who trembled and drew the woolen blanket up to his neck. "The great Konstantine, indeed. Do you not remember who we are? We are Varinskis. We are the Darkness. We do not honor deals made with a foolish old man who offers himself as a sacrifice."

"You won't?" He groped under the blanket, found his weapons, and armed himself.

Afonos continued, "We're going to take your family. We're going to rape your wife and your daughters. We're going to——"

"Shut up." Konstantine pushed himself out of the wheelchair. He held the blanket over one hand, and with the other he ripped off his mask. Clutching it in his fist, he jerked the plastic tubing free of the oxygen tanks, triggering the timer on the detonator. *One.* He stood toe-to-toe with Afonos. *"Poshyol ty."*

While Afonos gaped at the insult, Konstantine pulled the pistol from the pocket of his robe and shot Afonos through the heart. Then he shot the man behind Afonos, and the man behind him. *Two. Three.*

Dropping the blanket, he pulled the machete from its sheath against his leg and slashed left and right. He ran through the path he'd cleared, kicking off his slippers, revealing his running shoes, and all the while in his head he counted, *Four. Five. Six. Seven. Eight.*

He dove for the ground.

The bomb strapped to the wheelchair detonated. His oxygen tank exploded. Shrapnel blasted in every direction.

Varinskis screamed, some in pain, some in fury. Some never made another sound.

Konstantine looked around, calculating the damage at about twenty dead and wounded. But just as many and more had escaped damage. They stood dazed, incredulous, then in mounting rage. And all the while, more Varinskis were coming out of the trees.

Trembling from exertion, Konstantine got to his feet. He sheathed his machete and put his pistol in the holster at his waist.

The growl that rippled through the Varinskis was a single sound, a unified beast.

When Konstantine had planned this, he had feared he would collapse at the wrong moment.

Seeing those faces change from human to animal, from savage fury to rabid madness, gave him the incentive he needed to stay on his feet. Dropping the machete, he sprinted toward the steep ravine, toward the dam he'd built to irrigate his grapes. He needed to time this right—it was even trickier than the bomb on the wheelchair—but if Tasya performed, he might live long enough to see the sunset.

Tasya was a brilliant young lady, for the ground rumbled beneath his feet.

On the hill above him, chunks of concrete flew into the air.

Tasya had blown the dam.

Looking up the deep V of the ravine, he saw a green wall hurtling down, destroying trees, rolling boulders as water thundered toward him—and toward the Varinskis who followed close on his tail.

Just in time, he swerved straight up the side of the gorge, leaped and grabbed a tree root. He kicked at the Varinski that followed, knocking him back and into the others. They fell like dominoes into the torrent. Then he clambered clear as the icy water thundered beneath his feet, sweeping his pursuers back into the valley, drowning them, crushing them with debris and burying them in mud.

But at last his diseased body rebelled at the strain he'd put on it. He gasped. Groped for his medicine.

Another spasm racked him. He held his chest in agony.

The medicine. It was close. So close. In his pocket . . .

With trembling fingers, he got out the bottle, tried to open it . . . dropped it.

Blackness closed in, stealing consciousness. He fought; he had too much left to do to fail now.

Yet fighting accomplished nothing.

What the Varinskis could not do, this wretched disease had.

He was done.

He would die here in the dirt.

Chapter Thirty-four

H is daughter-in-law had other ideas.
A woman's voice: determined, energetic. "Papa, get up now. I'm taking you back to the house. Papa. Now!"

Konstantine opened his eyes.

Tasya looked down at him, her dark, curly hair framed by green trees and blue sky, her blue eyes sparkling with resolve.

"Run," he said faintly. "Leave me."

She knelt beside him. She picked up the bottle and frowned, stuck a pill in his mouth and said, "Swallow. Now! Now!"

He swallowed. "No chance for me," he whispered. "Save yourself."

"Save myself?" She wrapped her arms around him and tried to lift him. "So that Mama will kill me when I come back without you? Do you think I'm *crazy*?"

Stupid girl. He was too heavy for her. She would hurt her back.

So he got to his knees.

Pain shot up his neck and down his arms.

He gritted his teeth, waiting until the agony subsided.

He stood.

"Better to die on your feet and fighting, right, Papa?" Tasya slid her arm under his shoulders and helped him, one step at a time, down the slope.

He stopped and gasped for breath. Haltingly, he asked, "Where do you think you're going to take me? Do you think the Varinskis are going to let us walk back to the house like a couple of girlfriends out for a stroll?"

"No." Tasya glanced at her watch. "But if we get down there in time, I'm betting that Karen will provide us some cover."

"Ahhh." Konstantine remembered, and maybe it was the medication, but probably it was the pleasure of imagining what next would thunder down on the Varinskis' unsuspecting heads.

They reached a spot with an unimpeded view of his valley.

The wall of water had blasted out of the ravine, flushing Varinskis like so many turds down a sewer pipe. It spread out across the lower end of the valley, the end planted with vines. It ripped up his grapes and spread sludge, tree trunks, and chunks of concrete across the well-tended acres. The water reached its limit just short of the house, and the picket fence looked like a dam against the flood. Everywhere he looked dead Varinskis were sprawled facedown or faceup. The ones who still lived struggled to stand in the cold, slippery mud. They examined their ruined firearms, cursing at the top of their lungs.

The Wilders hadn't taken out all the Varinskis—there were more coming down into the valley—but they'd knocked down their numbers and infuriated them.

A dozen still dry, still unhurt, still human, prepared to blast the house with a rocket launcher.

Zorana and Aleksandr were in there.

The remaining Varinskis prowled across the valley in their animal form, roaring and growling, seeking their prey. Seeking the Wilders.

His daughters-in-law were that prey.

"No." Konstantine took an unwary step. "No!"

Tasya caught him and held him in place. "Wait, Papa. Wait! Listen!"

From high above the other side of the valley, they heard a detonation. Then a growl. Then the rapidly rising rumble of thunder.

The Varinski warriors stopped. They looked up and around.

Logs, huge logs weighing tons, roared down from the mountain, rolling and bouncing, gaining speed as they spun downhill, headed for the area in front of the house, toward the men who would destroy Konstantine's home, his wife, and his grandson.

He exalted in the power of the logs and their stampede. He watched closely, fearing a miscalculation, that one might flip end over end and rip open the walls of the house.

But no. The rocket launcher went flying. The men who would have shot it disappeared into the mud or were tossed like puppets on a stick. The logs spread a swath of death and destruction across the battlefield, killing and mutilating dozens of Varinskis, leaving a few, only a few, untouched.

Satisfaction settled into Konstantine's bones and pumped through his wounded heart. "I watch the Disney Channel with Aleksandr, I see the *Swiss Family Robinson*, and I learn how to fight. See? There is no modern bomb that could cover so much ground and wreak such destruction, and yet leave my land pristine. In the spring it will bloom again."

Tasya watched in awe. "That log trick is *so* Washington State. An environmentally friendly weapon."

Konstantine held up his palm.

She high-fived him. "Victory. Now we can wipe them out. We've won!"

"Not quite." Konstantine's sharp eyes picked out the shape of a limousine as it cruised up the winding drive, heard the purr of its motor.

No, not just one limousine. Two. When the lead car came around the last corner, the driver slammed on the brakes. The other screeched to a halt behind it.

"What the hell?" Vadim sat up straight and stared at the destruction before him—destruction brought upon his troops by a family of grape farmers. He stared at his men facedown in the mud, at the still-shuddering logs, at Varinski bodies tossed among them like so many cords of wood . . . at the old-fashioned, American-style house, still pristine in the middle of destruction, a symbol of the Wilders and their success.

His men, his bodyguards, sat in awe.

Konstantine had done this. With inferior weapons wielded by his sons and their women, the great Konstantine had reinforced his legend—and made a fool of Vadim.

"Wow." The weak and ignorant American driver craned his neck to see, then picked up his phone. "I have to call this in. Someone really kicked ass here."

Cold fury coiled in Vadim's belly. Pulling his pistol, he shot the driver.

His head exploded. The windshield shattered. Blood splattered the glass, the wheel, the ceiling.

Vadim turned to his men.

Now he had their attention.

In the soft tone he employed like a velvet whip, he said, "Kill them all. Raze the valley. Burn the house. Burn the forest. Don't leave a single creature alive."

Four men, tall, well built, dressed in dark suits, leaped out of the blood-spattered limousine in the lead. Another six piled out of the second limo.

One man, younger than the others, stepped out in front. His rage was palpable—and even from across the valley, it was intimidating.

This youth had power. Konstantine could feel it.

"Vadim!" The call went up from the human Varinskis still on their feet. They hurried toward him, leaping logs and slipping in the mud. The wolves growled, and the great birds of prey swooped and screamed.

Vadim held up his hand.

They stopped.

He spoke, a single word, inaudible at such a distance.

The Varinskis shrank back.

He spoke again, and they cheered.

Konstantine knew what was coming.

The men of Vadim's bodyguard shimmered in the sunlight; then, one by one, they changed. Six became tigers, large, tawny, ruthless, led by cruel instinct and a cat's love of the hunt.

They prowled forward, heads down, heading across the field of battle and toward the Wilder house.

There his wife and grandson waited with the three icons.

Vadim, the Varinskis, and the devil himself intended to finish them.

Two of Vadim's men took to the air as eagles, black and white, with wings that spanned seven feet. They soared high, their black eyes searching for their prey—for him, for Tasya, for Karen, alone on the other side of the valley.

"Come." Konstantine tugged at Tasya. "Let us get into position."

Yet no matter how strong his will, he had no *hurry* left in him. As he stumbled along the tree line, he had to keep his gaze on his feet, for every step was a challenge, made greater by the pine needles that slipped out from under his feet, the brush, the stones, the patches of old, dirty snow.

Tasya helped him, encouraged him, but their progress was painfully slow.

"You must go on without me. You must continue fighting." He pulled his arm from hers.

"Promise me you'll keep walking." Her tenacity reminded him of an English bulldog, yet here in the forest, with the tall trees surrounding them and danger all around, she looked so fragile, so young.

"I promise." He pushed her away from him.

High above, he heard the telling scream of an eagle.

He glanced at the two men by the limo.

One reached inside the open door and brought out one rifle, then another.

Vadim lifted the rifle and pointed it toward Konstantine.

"Down!" He flung himself toward Tasya.

He heard the shot.

Tasya screamed, twisted, and hit the ground. She held her thigh and rolled in agony. Blood pumped from between her fingers, turning them crimson.

"No!" They were supposed to kill *him*. He crawled toward her. "No, daughter. No!" He ripped the tie out of his bathrobe and tied it above the wound, tried to pick her up and head toward the house.

No. *No!* It couldn't end this way, with his failure to save Tasya's life.

As if that were the signal they'd been waiting for, seven men moved out of the woods, camouflage paint on their faces, and surrounded Tasya and Konstantine. They held their rifles with expert ease, and considered Konstantine and Tasya with cool, dark eyes.

Varinskis. More Varinskis. *Damn them.*

They would finish Tasya. They would kill him. He closed his eyes, prepared for the bullet that would end his life. He took his final breath . . . and identified the subtle scent of their bodies.

His eyes popped open. "You are Rom. Gypsies!"

The leader was young, strong, dark-haired, a male version of Zorana in her youth, with eyes of black steel. "Very good, Konstantine." Taking Konstantine's hand, he helped him to his feet and, with notable insouciance, said, "I'm Prokhor."

"What are you doing here?" Konstantine asked.

Turning to one of his soldiers, Prokhor said, "Stop Tasya's bleeding; then let's get them to the house."

"How do you know her name?" Konstantine asked.

"We've watched you for a long time. We know everyone in your family," Prokhor said.

The medic dropped to his knees beside Tasya. He gave her morphine, and while he cleaned her wound, Konstantine asked Prokhor, "*Why* do you know us?"

"Until the icons are united, we protect you."

"Why?" When Konstantine had stolen Zorana, her tribe had sworn vengeance. What had changed?

Prokhor bared his strong, white teeth. "We will have no luck, enjoy no prosperity, until we fulfill our destiny. And that destiny is to protect you and yours so you can unite those icons!"

"How did you *know* your destiny?"

"We had a convocation of the Rom and asked for knowledge. It was given." Prokhor shuddered.

Konstantine shuddered, too. He'd seen the devil at work in the world. He'd seen his beloved wife seized by a vision. He'd learned to dread the evidence of the otherworld. He supposed it was a sign of age, but . . . he wanted peace. He wanted to tend his crops, love his wife, bounce his grandchildren on his knee, advise his sons, annoy his daughters.

He stroked Tasya's sweaty forehead. She was quiet now; the morphine had done its work, and the medic had almost completed the field dressing.

Prokhor placed his rifle on his shoulder, pointed it across the valley, and squeezed off a shot.

It was a distance of more than half a mile, yet Vadim spun and fell. Like a roach, he crawled and scurried toward the protection of the limo, his bodyguard on his heels.

"Missed," the leader said laconically.

But Konstantine recognized a good sniper at work. "You hurt him."

Another shot slammed Vadim's bodyguard against the car—that shot hadn't come from this side of the valley.

"We've got three men on the other side." Prokhor lifted his walkie-talkie and listened to the report. "They've got Karen safe."

Konstantine sighed in relief.

"Hurry," one of the other men said to the medic. "Vadim's bodyguards are on their way."

The tigers sprang into a run, loping across the valley. Above them, the eagles circled and screamed encouragement. Other Varinskis joined in the hunt, changing to wolves, to hawks, to beasts more dreadful than any nightmare on earth.

One Rom lifted Tasya in his arms. Another broad-shouldered youth hefted Konstantine over his shoulder. The whole group sprinted forward.

Branches slapped at them. They swerved and

dodged, jumped a trickling creek, slid in an icy patch deep in the shade.

As Konstantine bounced against the hard shoulder, he struggled to catch his breath, to view the action below.

The tigers were running at an angle, intending to cut them off before they reached the house.

"Go down into the valley. It's our only chance. We'll hold them," Prokhor shouted, and he and two of his men dropped to one knee and lifted their rifles to their shoulders.

The others ran on, cutting a path toward the valley floor and an easier course.

Behind them, Prokhor pulled the trigger, and a tiger roared with pain.

Return fire blasted through the trees.

Konstantine heard the grunt of a man fatally wounded. Lifting his head, he looked back and caught a glimpse of the Romany scrambling around their fallen.

The runners broke out of the trees.

The tigers were close enough for Konstantine to see their whiskers and their smiling, sharp teeth. An eagle dove out of the air, talons out, beak open. "Put me down," Konstantine said. "We've got to fight!"

The Rom skidded to a halt and let Konstantine slide off his shoulder.

"Go on," Konstantine shouted at the man who held Tasya. "Take her in."

Her bearer dashed toward the house, two Rom at his heels.

Two of the tigers peeled off after them.

Two more furious, muddy, still-human Varinskis joined in the chase. One lifted his weapon and shot.

A tiger turned on him and snarled.

"What happened?" one of the Rom asked as he settled their rifles on their shoulders.

"Varinskis enjoy the close-in kill." Konstantine pulled his pistol and pointed at the tigers racing toward them. "Especially now, when they face defeat. They want to rend her limb from limb, eat her while she still lives, use the horror to immobilize us."

The three Rom edged away from Konstantine. They had remembered who—and what—he was.

One Rom squeezed off a shot, blowing a hole between the tiger's ears.

The tiger stopped, shook its head, then fixed its yellow eyes on them and snarled.

"Keep shooting," Konstantine commanded. "Don't stop."

These Rom would die. He would die. But perhaps Tasya would live. Perhaps.

Then, across the valley, an explosion rocked the ground.

The battle stopped.

Konstantine looked in time to see debris flying from the remains of the first limousine, then to see the second rise like a living being and burst into a million pieces.

Behind, on the road, Jackson Sonnet sat on a motorcycle, waving his fist in victory.

Three wolves who were running to join the assault on Tasya turned and sprinted toward him.

He shot one with his 30-06 hunting rifle. The wolf

struggled to get up, but its leg was shattered. Jackson holstered the rifle, revved his motorcycle, and raced back down the road.

The tigers returned to their attack on Konstantine and the Rom, and their eyes glowed red with fury.

Then, like a flying miracle, a black-and-white, silver-and-red helicopter swooped over the mountain, down the slope, and into the valley.

The cavalry had arrived.

Chapter Thirty-five

"Watch this." Rurik turned the helicopter sideways and ripped across the valley, moving like a giant scythe, skimming low, sending tigers and Varinskis skidding onto their faces.

"Oh, yeah?" Firebird spotted the eagles diving and swirling in the sky. "Get us close to one of those birds." They reached the other end of the valley, and Rurik pulled sharply up, slowing their airspeed to zero. He dropped the nose and executed an immediate hard rudder turn to place the eagles outside the cockpit. Firebird had removed the clipboard from the dash; she opened the door and sailed it like a Frisbee.

It whipped through the air, rotating like a buzz saw. The metal clip sliced into the eagle's wing, the impact of the board knocking the bird sideways, then into an uncontrolled dive.

Rurik clapped her on the shoulder. "You always were the best at moving targets."

A shot from below whistled past her ear and buried itself in the ceiling.

"You son of a bitch, I'll teach you to shoot at my

sister." Rurik turned so sharply her door slammed shut. He dumped the nose toward the shooter. The sensation was like going down the first hill on a roller coaster. She had no breath; her heart raced. The Varinski's cruel face grew closer and closer, his eyes narrowed as he aimed at Rurik. Just in time, Rurik jerked the helicopter level and rudder-turned so quickly, the landing skid hit the Varinski in the chest, knocking him facedown and sending the rifle into the mud.

Rurik circled the helicopter in a spiraling climb as he surveyed the battle scene. "There's Papa. Varinskis have got him pinned down."

"He's got guys with him. Protecting him." She watched the camouflage-clad warriors, saw how fearlessly they fought. "Who are they?"

"I don't know, but watch this." Rurik swept down on the attackers and sent them scattering.

"The soldiers have picked up Papa. They're running for the house." Firebird's heart pounded. She'd never seen Rurik in his true element—flying hard, taking chances, proving once and for all that he was the great pilot he claimed to be.

Closer to the house, she saw another group fighting a desperate battle, while one man stood apart, holding . . . Oh, God, he was holding a woman, and the woman was hurt. Firebird touched Rurik's arm. "Is that Tasya?"

He'd already seen her. "Yes."

Tasya struggled in the guy's arms, trying to stand. "She's alive," Firebird said.

"She's going to stay that way." Rurik performed a

swirling, diving maneuver so fast and so hard that, for the first time, Firebird closed her eyes.

But they didn't crash, and she opened her eyes when Rurik said, "That'll keep the bastards away until we get you inside." He took the helicopter down and around the house, flying fast enough to blow shingles off the roof. "They're scattering. We're going around again, and I'm going to stop at the back porch and tilt your side down. Jump. Move quickly. Stay low. Firebird—keep living."

"You, too." She discarded her helmet, unbuckled her seat belt, and braced herself, one hand on the dash, one hand on the door. "I'm ready."

He headed around the last corner and stopped so suddenly she thought his eyeballs hit his visor. As he tilted the helicopter, she dropped toward the door. Opening it, she slid out like an omelet out of a pan.

She hit the ground hard.

Above her, the helicopter rumbled like thunder and whipped around, pulled pitch, putting her in the tornado of the rotor's downdraft, then headed up and over the house.

She stayed low and ran toward the porch, up the stairs, to the back door. She hit it hard.

It was locked.

Of course. It would be stupid to leave the door unlocked, like an invitation to marauding Varinskis. She fumbled in her pocket for her key.

A bullet slammed into the trim beside the door.

She jumped back.

Another ripped through the wood siding close to her head.

She backed away again and looked for cover.

Nothing. The Wilders had cleared the furniture off the porch.

Another bullet struck close to her feet, and she jumped.

From out by the horse barn, she heard jeering male laughter, and a heavily accented voice shouted, "See, boys? I told you she could dance."

Another shot sounded—but this time not aimed at her.

A Varinski fell out of the hayloft, smashed into the ground, and didn't move.

Jasha stepped out of the forest. He was equipped with a semiautomatic rifle and a deadly expression. "Go on, Firebird; I'll cover you." He shot the lock off the barn door.

She leaped back to the kitchen door. The key slid into the lock. She opened it, stepped into the kitchen, looked back to wave at Jasha—and saw a falcon diving out of the clear sky, talons aimed for his head.

"Jasha," she shrieked. Pulling the Glock from her belt, she shot it out of the air.

With the butt of his rifle, Jasha smashed it to the ground.

From inside the barn, a volley of shots sounded. He staggered back, blood streaming down his face. "Go on," he yelled. "Hurry!"

She slammed the door, locked it behind her, and hit the floor.

Bullets ripped through the door.

She low-crawled across the kitchen, across the living room, while pictures flashed through her mind.

Jasha. Arrogant, know-it-all big brother Jasha, fighting against impossible odds . . . and dying?

Rurik, going back for Tasya. Firebird knew that he would happily die for his wife.

Adrik . . . where was Adrik? What would he do to keep Karen and his family safe?

And Papa . . .

Would they all die?

She wouldn't allow it.

Racing up the stairs, she burst into her bedroom. "Mama!" she hollered. "Mama, it's me!" Grabbing one of Aleksandr's toys, she aimed at the trapdoor in the ceiling. "Mama!"

It slammed open. Zorana looked down, her face white and strained. She tossed a rope ladder into Firebird's hands.

The window shade was down, but Firebird climbed fast. Bullets penetrated siding and Sheetrock easily, the Varinskis kept up a steady barrage, and any random shot might take her out. And she wanted to live.

She might be a changeling, brought to this family by the devil's machinations. She might have slept with Douglas Black, a despicable traitor, and helped by giving him the information that had led to this assault.

But she had the fourth icon in her possession.

She would end this pact. She would end it now. She owed her family for their love and kindness.

She owed the devil, too. She owed him his downfall, for he had ruined her life.

She flung herself onto the floor of the attic.

Zorana shut the trapdoor and locked it.

The attic was stuffy, the ceiling low, the window dormers deep. Konstantine had had the walls reinforced, so bullets could not penetrate. He'd stashed food and water, enough to support a short stay. There was a bed and a crib, a chair and a white-painted table. Zorana's box of treasures was on the floor and open, and Aleksandr sat among the stones, one set at each corner of the compass—south was blue sky, north was black night, west was red flame, and east was white purity.

Perhaps Zorana had set the stones around him in the hope of protecting him from evil. But perhaps . . . he had done it out of instinct.

He was, after all, Zorana's grandson by her youngest boy, Douglas.

Aleksandr's chubby face lit up when he saw Firebird, and he leaped to his feet. "Mama! Mama, Aleksandr missed you!"

"I missed you, too, sweetheart." Firebird sat up and caught him when he ran into her arms. "My baby."

"*My* baby." Zorana sat down and wrapped Firebird and Aleksandr in her embrace.

Never mind that Firebird wasn't Zorana's birth daughter; here with Zorana she was safe, she was loved . . . and Aleksandr extended their magic circle.

Zorana knew . . . somehow she knew what was in Firebird's mind, or maybe it was in her mind, too, for she said, "It's not blood that builds the bonds of love. It's the hours spent in the middle of the night with my sick baby daughter, the time driving her to gymnastics, the pride when she got her scholarship, the joy of watching my first grandchild come into the world, the tears we cried when we watched *It's a Wonderful Life*."

Firebird wept now. "Don't forget *Ghost*."

"And *Titanic*." Zorana wept, too.

"While the guys snickered."

"You have given me so much, and I wish—" Zorana stopped and blinked. "*Dorogoi*, what happened to your hair?"

Firebird's tears became laughter. "It's a long story."

Aleksandr tugged at Firebird's neck and pointed to the window. "Mama, Gramma watches."

Recalled to the now, the two women listened. The helicopter roared overhead, bullets flew, and even worse, beneath the sounds of modern battle, they heard the growl of beasts and the victorious shrieks of hunting birds.

Zorana took Firebird by the shoulders and shook her. "The icon."

"Yes." Firebird pulled it from between her breasts.

"That's my girl. The perfect spot." Zorana gestured to the table in the middle of the room. She had laid a rich red cloth over the top, for red was the holy color of the Russians. On the cloth she had placed the three icons.

Ann had found the first one. In it, the Virgin Mary held the infant Jesus, while Joseph stood at her right hand.

On the icon that Tasya had found, the Madonna's face was pale and still, her dark eyes large and sorrowful, and a tear gathered on her cheek. For in her lap, this Madonna held the crucified Jesus.

On Karen's icon, the painter had portrayed Mary as a young girl, a girl who foresaw her destiny and that of her son. Her sad, dark, knowing eyes gazed at them, reminding them that she had given her son to save the world.

Firebird put the fourth icon in the place left for it, then hoisted Aleksandr up on her hip.

The three of them stared with awe into the dark eyes of the Madonna. The icons were old, the painting stylized, yet the pigment had been fired onto the tile, and the colors glowed as if they were new. This time, the artist had painted her ascending to heaven.

Of course. The fourth icon would be the holiest of all.

There they were, four visions of the Virgin Mary. Once, a thousand years ago, they had each been part of one icon, the icon of the Varinski family. The first Konstantine had murdered his mother for it. The devil himself had slashed it with his flaming sword and cast the Madonnas to the four corners of the earth.

Now the icons waited to be reunited.

"Do it, Mama," Firebird whispered. "Hurry."

Zorana pushed the icons together—and they waited for a miracle to happen.

Chapter Thirty-six

Vadim huddled behind a pile of logs on the edge of the battlefield, nursing one hell of a headache.

The shot that had struck him had sliced through his scalp. If he were anything but a Varinski, he'd be dead. As it was, the wound was rapidly healing, for Varinski blood was strong and full of evil magic.

He could feel that blood bubbling with the rage that heated him.

His men had disobeyed him, taken whatever bait Konstantine had dangled before them, and gone into battle early. Many were dead now, killed by primitive weapons, and Vadim, who had left the Ukraine with a surplus of Varinskis, was now down to a precious few.

Worse, when news of this fiasco got out, he would be a laughingstock among assassins. He'd sent one hundred and fourteen men against a family of three brothers, one old invalid father, five silly women, and a two-year-old, and so far, he'd lost at least seventy men. *So far.* Nothing would keep this quiet . . . unless he managed to kill every single Wilder. And he would. Before this day was done, he would wipe that vermin from the face of the earth.

Not that he had a choice. Those explosions had ruined his beautiful limousines—and left him standing here when he should be on his way to a new name and a new life paved with the gold from a thousand Varinski-executed assassinations.

At least, that had been his plan if anything went wrong today.

He simply had not foreseen that he would be without transportation.

A faint moan nearby caught his attention.

Georgly. Vadim's best lieutenant, his brother and his best friend, had been shot by a sniper, then had his face blown half-off by the explosions that destroyed the limos. He struggled to rise, and as he did, the blackened skin grew and sealed the space where his left eye had been. He staggered to his feet, whimpering and limping.

Worthless. Georgly was worthless.

And all that whimpering got on Vadim's nerves.

Taking the Glock from the holster around his chest, he cocked the pistol.

Georgly's head turned toward the sound. His single eye widened. His hands came up as if that puny defense would deflect the bullet. "No. Please, Vadim, no!"

Vadim shot him in the heart.

A voice spoke so close to his side, he jumped and swung his pistol around.

"Why did you do that?" Mikhail asked. He wasn't the brightest of Vadim's men, but he was alive and capable of fighting—and he'd sneaked up on Vadim, although Vadim did not understand how.

"I hate a whiner." Vadim stood and kept the barrel pointed at Mikhail.

Mikhail looked different, a little sharper than normal, and his voice sounded . . . funny. Maybe the others had sent him to assassinate Vadim. He wouldn't doubt it for a minute.

That was what he himself would have done.

"You need living men. You have lost most of my army."

"Your army?" Vadim smirked. "Who are you? Nobody, that's who."

"You're good at setting fires." Was Mikhail's tone critical? Did this oaf really dare to challenge Vadim? "Yes. Of course you are. You gave Uncle Ivan enough vodka to swim in, turned his blood into an incendiary, then spread gasoline throughout the house and lit a match. What a spectacle that was." Mikhail's voice really did sound funny, sliding down, gaining more and more bass, as if he could suddenly sing baritone opera. "Listen to me closely. Stop sulking on the fringe of the battle. Find gas. Find a match. Burn the house. Now. It is old and dry. It will go up like kindling and kill the women who are inside."

"Good idea. I'll order the men to bomb the place." Vadim wanted to get away from this guy. Something about him was not right.

But when he tried to walk off, Mikhail grabbed him and held him with a grip of cold steel. "No. Not a bomb. I want fire. I am very fond of fire. It is painful, it is long, and it gives a taste of the torments to come. For even as I speak, the women imagine they can unite the icons and destroy the pact. They cannot—nothing can unite the icons—but they deserve to suffer the agonies of hell for trying, and their men deserve to suffer the agonies of love before they die, too."

"You can't tell me what to do." That voice. That voice. Where had Vadim heard that voice?

"Can't I?"

"Who do you think you are?"

"I know who I am. Do you?" Mikhail scrutinized him, a slight smile on his wide lips—and deep in his eyes, a blue flame glowed.

Vadim staggered backward.

He *did* know. He recognized that voice. The timbre was a little different, the tone a little younger, but . . .

"I see you have figured it out. You are a smart boy, Vadim; I always said so."

"But I torched . . . I torched the house. I torched Uncle Ivan," Vadim was screaming. He heard himself, but he couldn't stop. "I saw him burn with my own eyes."

"You destroyed one of my best tools. For that, and for thinking I could be removed, you will pay." The devil laughed, and the cruel sound reverberated throughout Vadim's black and rotted soul. "Did you really think you could ever get rid of me?"

Chapter Thirty-seven

Firebird stared at the icons against the red cloth, stared so hard her eyes hurt.

Nothing happened.

Zorana darted to the window and looked out.

"Did that do it?" Firebird asked. "Somehow, I expected . . ."

Zorana turned back, her eyes as dark and tormented as the Madonna's. "The Varinskis are still out there. Still animals. Still attacking."

"That can't be." Firebird rearranged the icons. "This has to work."

"Mama, Aleksandr do the puzzle."

She placed Aleksandr on the floor. "No, honey, Mama do the puzzle." She rearranged them again, more frantically. But no matter what she did, nothing happened. Because . . . she pointed in horror. "Look at this. It's not all here."

Zorana hastened back to stand beside Firebird. "What are you talking about?"

"There's a piece missing." The edges of each icon were curled, uneven, burned in spots, as if the devil had cut them with a sword of flame. But they fit together everywhere—except in the middle.

There a chunk was missing from each icon. Not a big chunk, one about the size of the tip of Firebird's little finger. It wasn't obvious when the icons were separate. But the lost piece made it impossible to reunite them.

Firebird swallowed. "I can't believe it. The prophecy said, 'Four sons, four loves, four icons.' It didn't say *anything* about an extra piece."

"I didn't see this. In my vision, I didn't see this at all." Zorana leaned over the table and tried to press them together, as if somehow she could mold the ancient, flinty material into a new shape.

Outside, Firebird heard the piercing wail of a police siren. Her head snapped up.

Douglas. In the depths of her mind, she'd been waiting for him.

Douglas had arrived to help his relatives.

The question was—*which* relatives?

She ran to the window.

A Washington State Patrol car swerved around the wrecked limousines and ripped up the driveway with the throaty roar of a police interceptor engine at full throttle. One Varinski in a business suit was running toward the back of the house; they almost creamed him.

The patrol car cut a cookie through a pack of snarling wolves racing to attack the group protecting Tasya.

Wolves flew into the air, then fell to the earth in human form.

Douglas was on *their* side. He had taken his stand with the Wilders.

The car headed toward the mob attacking Konstantine. Varinskis lifted their automatic weapons and shot two bursts into the car.

"No!" Firebird strained forward. "Douglas!"

The windshield blew out. The tires slipped on the mud. The car made a swift turn, skidded—and flipped.

The two groups protecting Tasya and Konstantine had combined, were surrounded. As the women watched, one of the tigers leaped and brought down a fighter, broke his neck, ripped open his abdomen— and began to feast.

Firebird and Zorana turned away, crying in horror, and when they turned back, it was over.

But Zorana gasped, her eyes wide with terror. Brokenly, she said, "Oh, no, my love. No, I beg you. Don't."

For the first time in her life, Firebird saw her father change—change from an enfeebled old man into a huge, ferocious gray wolf with a pointed snout rich with strong teeth, and glowing red eyes. The transformation lifted the curse of his illness, and he attacked the tigers with intelligence and ferocity, proving why he was the fabled leader of the Varinskis.

"He changes because he knows he has no choice," Zorana said softly. "He sees they have no chance, so he'll go to hell fighting . . . for us. He sacrifices his soul . . . for us." She looked at the icons on the table, at their failed hope of freeing Konstantine from the damnation promised him. She purposefully walked toward the trapdoor.

Firebird leaped and grabbed her arm. "Don't."

"If the icons can't break the pact, then I will die beside your father." Zorana yanked herself free. She went to Aleksandr and hugged him fiercely, and determination and anguish gleamed in her eyes. "Save him. If you can, save him."

Opening the trapdoor, she dropped the rope ladder and disappeared through the hole.

So it was up to Firebird. She had to save her father, her family, her son . . . her lover. She could not give up.

At the table, she stacked the icons and placed them once more.

Aleksandr dragged a chair over, climbed up, and shook his head disapprovingly. "No, Mama. Treasures. Gramma treasures."

Outside, a crash rattled the windows and shook the house.

As quickly as she could, Firebird returned to the window.

In what remained of the vineyard, the helicopter lay in ruins, shot out of the sky. The passenger door opened, and a brown hawk—Rurik—flew up and soared toward the escalating battle around Tasya and Konstantine.

Flames started out from under the hood of the patrol car. Soon, the gas tank would explode, and inside, no life stirred. "Douglas . . ."

Zorana sprinted across the yard and jumped the fence.

Four Varinskis ran to intercept her.

Knives flashing, eyes deadly, she turned to face them, a tiny Gypsy woman who would rather die than live without her husband.

From behind the house, a huge wolf ran to help her. *Jasha*. Jasha would fight at his mother's side.

"Mama, *treasures*," Aleksandr insisted.

"Go ahead and play with them, little one," she said. Clutching the windowsill so hard her fingers turned white, Firebird watched the destruction of everything she loved. Five minutes ago, she had been sure the fourth icon would turn the tide. Now . . . the Wilders were losing the battle.

Then . . . Douglas crawled out, half-clothed, covered with blood and bruises, but alive. "Get away from the car," she whispered. "Get away before it blows."

He turned and crawled back in.

He was crazy. *Crazy*.

Firebird wiped tears out of her eyes as quickly as they formed, desperate to view every movement, to figure out what in the hell he was doing.

He backed out, dragging an unconscious Adrik after him.

She clutched her chest in relief. Douglas had saved Adrik. He had saved her brother.

Then the wolves arrived, snarling and brutal.

Douglas shot the first three. They flipped, fell, twitched, and were still.

The others kept coming, swarming around the two men like fire ants consuming a tender morsel.

Firebird couldn't stand to watch.

She turned and faced into the room.

Aleksandr stood on the chair again, rearranging the icons.

She couldn't stand *not* to watch, and turned back to the window.

In Douglas's face, she saw grim fury. He might be defeated, but he would think like a man—and fight like a cougar. He stripped off his pants and boots. His bones melted and reknit into the bones of a great cat. Golden hair covered his skin. His teeth gleamed and his claws slashed.

Behind him, Adrik staggered to his feet, shook his head to clear it, and in a flash, his clothes came off, and he transformed into a great black panther. The two men, her brother and her lover, fought the Varinski onslaught with their primitive, beastly weapons: claws, fangs, pure brute muscle, and furious resolve.

Beneath Firebird's feet, the floor shuddered hard, once, twice.

She braced herself. "What was that?"

The Varinskis must have lobbed a grenade through a window.

But no. The shaking increased, rattling the window frames, the rafters, the furniture.

Outside every fight came to an abrupt halt. The intensity of the shaking increased. The trees swayed violently, as if blown by a great wind. Shingles fell off the roof, and the glass in the window on the other side of the room shattered. Fumaroles opened in the valley, spewing hot water and steam.

"Earthquake." Firebird clutched the wall. "Earthquake!"

Birds fell from the skies. Birds . . . that, as they fell, turned into men, men who screamed in fear and hit the ground with bone-crunching force.

She whirled toward Aleksandr, to snatch him in her arms and protect him.

He stood on the chair beside the red-clothed table, his dark brown eyes wide. "Mama, Aleksandr make the puzzle."

"What? You . . . That's . . ." *Impossible.* She stumbled across the shuddering floor toward the table, and the closer she got to the icons, the less shaking there was. It was as if the earthquake originated with the icons, and the icons protected Aleksandr.

He stood, his wide, little-boy grin beaming. "Look. Aleksandr make the puzzle."

It was true. Aleksandr had united the icons. The four visions of the Madonna looked as glorious and new as the day they were created.

Chapter Thirty-eight

Firebird fell to her knees beside the table and rested her forehead on the red tablecloth. Grateful tears welled in her eyes, and she whispered, "Thank you. Thank you."

"Mama?" Aleksandr patted her downturned head. "See the puzzle?"

She took a long breath and raised her head. She smiled at her wonderful, brilliant, darling boy. "I see. That is so good. Mama is proud!" Gathering him in her arms, she hugged him with all the love and joy in her heart.

He hugged her back and placed a big, sloppy kiss on her cheek.

Standing, she set him back on the chair. "Tell Mama what you did."

"Aleksandr used Gramma's treasure." He coughed and rubbed his eyes.

Firebird looked over at the pieces of her mother's treasure that had been set so carefully at each compass point. Three stones, red, blue, and black, rattled with the shaking of the earth. The white stone, the one that was purity . . . was gone.

At last she understood.

From the day that the pact had been enacted, the devil had feared that someone, somewhere, would put them back together and steal from him his most wicked servants, the Varinski beasts. So before he divided the icons into four, he cut a piece from the center and gave it to a tribe of wanderers—Zorana's Romany tribe.

That was why the seer of the tribe had a stone called purity.

That was why the tribe had a seer at all. For even the tiniest piece of the four icons brought a great gift—the ability to see the future. A future without the devil's pact.

Firebird wrapped her son in her arms and held him. Just held him. And remembered her mother's prediction.

A child will perform the impossible.

Aleksandr had saved them all.

The shaking slowed and stopped. Keeping Aleksandr in her arms, she went to the window.

The tigers, the wolves, the wild dogs, the birds of prey were gone. Men, naked men, stood in their places. Humans with nothing special about them.

Douglas was a man again. Adrik, Rurik, Jasha were men again.

Konstantine was a man again.

And they were smiling.

The Varinskis had prospered only because of the

power given them by Satan. Now they were nothing, for they didn't know how to be mere mortals.

Now they were Wilder prey.

"Come on, little boy. It's time to go." She walked toward the trapdoor, her son in her arms, free from the horror that had held them in thrall for all their lives.

Smoke oozed out of the opening as if it were a chimney.

Aleksandr coughed again. "Mama, I can't breathe."

She looked down into her bedroom. Fire crawled along the floor and spread up the walls.

Her heart thumped, began to race.

She slammed the trapdoor shut and ran to the front window. Flames leaped past the glass, and the heat drove her back.

"Mama?" Tears filled Aleksandr's eyes. He coughed and buried his head in her shirt.

She ran to the back window. The horse barn burned with all the vigor of dry wood and hay. The giant tree that grew outside her bedroom blazed feverishly.

This was no normal fire. The inferno consumed the house too quickly, and from all sides. Someone— some Varinski—had set the blaze.

Her family would live and prosper.

"Mama?" Her child was heavy in her arms.

She and Aleksandr were going to die.

"It's okay." She went to the crib and got his blanket and Bernie, the soft yellow duck with the bright orange bill. She opened a bottle of water, thoroughly wet the blanket, and threw it over Aleksandr's head.

Ignited by the heat, the red cloth beneath the icons caught on fire, and the paint on the table crackled and bubbled. Fire ate at the edges of the trapdoor, and the hinges glowed red. The floor grew hot under her feet. The boards smoked and warped. Flame ignited along one long crack, then another, chasing her from place to place.

It's all right. I can still breathe. Aleksandr is still alive. We have a chance.

They had no chance. She knew it.

But she opened another bottle of water and splashed it on the floor. It steamed, then boiled.

The trapdoor fell into the blaze below. With a roar, the wall behind her went up in flame. The floorboards cracked and tilted toward the open hole in the floor. The angle grew greater and greater, until she could no longer stand, and with a scream, she slid right into the heart of the inferno.

She landed on the floor of her bedroom. All around her, flames ripped through the house, but somehow, she'd landed on the one spot where the fire had winked out.

Lucky, she thought. And, *I can still breathe.*

"Mama!" Aleksandr peeked out from under the blanket. "Let's go."

"Yes." She wasn't going to sit here and wait for the house to collapse around her. She didn't know how to give up. She had to try to escape. She had to try. "Let's get out of here."

Chapter Thirty-nine

❧

Douglas stood back-to-back with his brother Adrik and laughed aloud. He was battered, bruised, broken, in pain. Yet he laughed because he had a family, a brother who fought for him, and he was free from the devil's control.

And because somehow, he would make Firebird his.

It wouldn't be easy. He knew that. He knew she wouldn't easily forgive him. He might not deserve to be forgiven. But if they'd managed to come this far, to live through the plunge into the ocean, to unite the icons and break the pact, to fight against insurmountable odds and win—he could find some way to make her love him again.

Adrik laughed, too. He had a huge bump on his head, he bled from a myriad of tiny cuts caused by the shattered windshield, and still he laughed.

Here and there, across the field of battle, Doug heard other laughter.

His family, his *family*, was laughing. Laughing with joy, with pride, with relief. They stood on their own soil in their own valley, amid destruction and death, and knew they had won the greatest battle of all.

The Varinskis were *not* laughing.

They stood stunned, lax, released from the devil's pact . . . human. All human. They had all changed into beasts. They had abandoned their clothes, their rifles, their knives, their pistols, to effect the transformation. Now every Varinski and Wilder on the field was naked, their only weapons their fists and their fighting skills.

"This is going to be one good brawl," Adrik said.

"You're right." Doug leaped into the fray, smashing skulls, breaking arms and legs and ribs.

The Varinskis fought back with slowed reactions at first, then with increasing desperation. One whimpered. One wept.

Did they never think this moment might come? Did they not imagine someday they'd have to fight fair?

Well, if fair was fighting with overwhelming odds still in your favor. Thirty Varinskis—or was it forty?—fought on the battlefield against a contingent of Wilders and their allies.

Doug attacked, feinted, dodged. Varinskis surrounded him and Adrik, teaming up on them, but the two brothers were protecting their home and family, and they attacked with an enthusiasm the Varinskis struggled to effectively meet. Doug punched at one behemoth of a Varinski, hitting him over and over in the hardest head Doug had ever had the privilege of meeting, when the guy stopped. Just stopped.

And stared over Doug's shoulder, his eyes getting wider and wider.

Doug smashed him in the face.

He staggered away, and still stared.

At his back, Doug felt Adrik jolt as if he'd been given a fatal wound. "Fire." His voice rose. "Fire!"

"*Pojzar!*" the Varinski said.

Fire? Doug heard the crackle of dry wood. He flung himself around.

The Wilder house was in flames.

Across the battlefield, Zorana screamed, "My babies!"

Her babies? Who was in there?

She had been using her knives, slashing her way through a crowd of Varinskis that surrounded Konstantine and Tasya.

Now, Doug didn't see what she did, but Varinskis were on their backs, dead or dying, and she tore toward the house.

"Mama, no!" Adrik knocked their attackers aside to intercept his mother—*their* mother—before she ran into the inferno.

In Adrik's moment of distraction, a Varinski went for his back.

Doug scavenged a knife off the ground and threw it squarely between the guy's shoulder blades, dropping him where he stood.

Then Doug ran, too, dread coiled like a snake in his gut.

Adrik trapped her before Zorana reached the fence. "You can't go in!" he shouted.

She struggled, fighting like a wildcat. "Firebird! Aleksandr!"

No.

Doug couldn't breathe.

No, it isn't possible.

He couldn't see for the red that washed across his vision.

Firebird and Aleksandr . . . were in there? In the fire?

He felt a stabbing pain in his shoulder, looked down, and saw a knife protruding from his biceps. He looked up. One Varinski had collected the knife and thrown it. Now he and another Varinski charged.

Afterward, Doug didn't know how he'd done it, but one Varinski was on the ground with his throat slashed; the other was fleeing toward the forest. Then Doug sprinted past Adrik and Zorana toward the house.

The heat was so intense, the picket fence around the yard was smoking. He jumped it without pause. The air was so hot he couldn't breathe. The flames licked at him, shriveling his skin. He felt his eyebrows melt, his hair frizz and die. But he couldn't let his love die in there. He couldn't let his son die before he had lived.

A huge weight hit him from the side, knocking him down, rolling him away. Someone, some man, pounded on his head, shouting, "You're on fire."

Doug tried to catch his breath. Instead he coughed. He struggled, but someone else grabbed him under the armpits and dragged him. Men were talking, shouting at him, while he fought. At last he heard Adrik's voice, recognized Adrik's voice.

"Douglas, listen to me. You can't go in there. Listen to me. The fire's too hot. The house is going to fall. Douglas, they're already dead." Adrik's voice broke. "Firebird and Aleksandr are already dead."

Dimly, Doug heard women screaming. But maybe not. Maybe that was the fire that roared in his ears.

He looked up into the dirty, scratched, bruised, strong faces.

Jasha. Rurik. Adrik. Zorana. Konstantine. The two daughters-in-law . . . he couldn't remember their names now.

Everyone had fought bravely.

Everyone was crying now.

He pushed them away.

One by one, they stepped back.

He stood. He looked at the house, at the flames reaching for the sky. He tried to comprehend, to feel sorrow. He knew the agony was there, waiting to pounce, but right now, he felt nothing.

Then, in his madness, he heard laughter.

He looked and saw a group of six Varinskis gathered around one man. They slapped him on the back, pummeled him affectionately.

"Vadim," they said. "Vadim did this. He is our hero!"

Doug took a step toward the group. Then another. Then another. Then he was running toward them. He plowed into them, tossing them aside like toothpicks, to get to the man in the middle.

Vadim. Dapper in a designer suit. Smirking at him.

Taunting him. "What's wrong, Douglas?" Vadim said in his perfect English. "Are you unhappy that your woman is finally, really dead?"

Doug slapped him across the face, an openhanded, insulting slap that snapped Vadim's head sideways.

Astonished, Vadim turned his head and looked at Doug. "You dare—"

Doug slapped him across the other cheek. The sound echoed like a gunshot across the battlefield.

Vadim grabbed Doug's wrist and twisted.

The pain was instant and irresistible. Doug flipped and went down on his knees.

"I'm going to kill you," Vadim said. "I'm going to kill your whole family. Your bitch is just the beginning."

The valley fell silent.

Doug's wrath started slowly, rising from his fingertips and toes, climbing his arms and legs, filling his abdomen, his chest, his brain. A killing frenzy built, flashing colors inside his skull. Red and yellow, purple and scarlet. He clenched his shaking fists until his nails dug into his palms.

All around him, Doug heard the growl of infuriated men, the snarl of vengeful women.

The battle was joined once more.

The Wilders were killing Varinskis. The berserker rage had fallen on them all.

Doug slammed his foot backward into Vadim's knee.

Vadim screeched and fell forward.

Doug was free.

Mad with rage, he plucked the knife from Vadim's

belt and slashed, opening a thin line across Vadim's throat.

Vadim pulled a pistol and aimed.

But no. Knives and pistols were too impersonal. Doug wanted to feel Vadim's face break under his fists, feel Vadim's blood splash warm against his skin.

He wanted revenge.

He wanted justice.

Vadim fired as Doug kicked the gun out of his hands.

The bullet buried itself in Doug's hip.

He didn't care.

Vadim chopped at his throat, and dimly, Doug realized how much damage Vadim's trick had done. But rage vanquished the pain, and he moved in close, his knuckles breaking Vadim's nose and jaw, his fists cracking Vadim's ribs.

Vadim got his arms beneath Doug's thighs and flipped him over.

Doug came up and rammed his head up and into Vadim's breastbone.

Vadim flew through the air, his arms flopping like a rag doll's. With a clatter, he landed on a battered old metal five-gallon gas can, and Doug realized . . . that was how he'd done it.

Vadim used gasoline stolen from the Wilders to ignite the fire that burned their house, that killed their daughter and grandson.

Firebird and Aleksandr never had a chance.

"You are going to die." Doug stalked forward.

Vadim took one look at Doug, at the insanity that

promised revenge. He clambered to his feet and tried to run.

He tripped on the gas can. Gasoline splashed him.

Doug picked him up by his collar and his belt, lifted him above his head, and carried him toward the burning house. "Bring that can," he said to nobody in particular.

Vadim screamed and screamed, struggling against Doug's hold, but his arms and legs flailed in the air, and all Doug had to do was twist his collar one way and his belt another, and Vadim shrieked in pain.

"Broken ribs are a bitch, aren't they?" Doug said. He knew. Eventually, he was going to feel his own broken ribs, the bullet in his hip, the place where his finger had been.

But now, all he could feel was a need for vengeance.

The blaze was at its height.

The south wall collapsed with a roar. The roof ridge was sagging. Soon, the fuel that fed the flames would be gone, and all that would be left were ashes.

But Doug had one more thing to feed the fire.

With a mighty shout, he tossed Vadim in like a log, through the missing wall and into a room ablaze with pieces of furniture, with electronics that exploded and wiring that sizzled.

Vadim leaped up, screaming, and tried to run.

Doug took the gas can Adrik handed him, and with deadly accuracy he threw it. The battered red metal knocked Vadim's feet out from under him, then exploded in a fireball that made Doug and the man beside him duck.

Vadim still screamed, but Doug didn't care anymore.

Turning his back, he walked away. Looked up. Saw people watching him.

His family and, mixed among them, guys in military clothing.

And Varinskis. Still more Varinskis to kill.

One huge, shambling, bearlike man with glowing blue eyes and a deep, deep voice, said, "I truly am very fond of fire. It is painful, it is long, and it gives a taste of the torments to come."

Doug started toward him.

The big man saw Doug's expression. The blue glow faded. He backed up—and ran. The others followed, scattering across the field, scurrying into the woods, glancing behind, falling, picking themselves up, and running again.

The leader of the military unit placed his hand on Doug's shoulder. "We'll take care of them." He spoke to the other Wilders. "We'll clean up the stragglers. We'll send you an ambulance and transportation. Don't worry. We'll handle it all."

Doug took a few more steps—and stopped.

Behind him, he heard another crash.

The front wall of the house had fallen away, and inside, the flames roared and danced.

They danced with Firebird's ghost.

Doug withered and died inside. Across the valley a woman limped toward them, escorted by two of the military men.

Adrik gave a glad cry. "Karen!" He ran to her,

picked her up, kissed her as if she were his very life. . . .

Every punch, every stab wound, every broken bone Doug had suffered flared into agony.

Or was it simply that he now could feel his broken heart?

His legs failed him. He sank to the ground. He wanted to cry, to curse heaven, to beg that *he* be the sacrifice. Not Firebird. Not Aleksandr. Not the innocents. He was the one who had betrayed the family. He was the one who deserved to die.

All around him, Wilders collapsed with him. They cried. They cried as a family.

Adrik helped Karen walk, and as she got closer, Doug could hear her sobs. "From up on the hill, I saw the fire start. But I was hurt by one of the logs, and my guards wouldn't let me come down. They tried to call, but you were fighting for your life and . . . Oh, Adrik!"

For the first time since he was a boy sitting in Mrs. Fuller's parlor, tears filled Doug's eyes. He gave a hard sob, one that ripped at his dry throat and made him bleed inside. Another sob followed, and another.

Zorana put her arm around him. "Douglas. Douglas, don't. It's not your fault."

He looked into his mother's face, and she looked back.

"It *is* my fault. This is my fault. All of it. You should spit on me." He looked around at Adrik, at his other brothers, at Tasya, pale with pain . . . at his father, now tall and strong, but with grief etched on his features. "I brought this battle on you. I sold you to the Varinskis. You should *all* spit on me. You should throw me on the fire to die like Vadim."

Konstantine still stood, but now he knelt beside his wife and rubbed her back. "We all had a part to play to bring the prophecy to fulfillment." He sighed heavily. "Your part was the hardest to bear."

"It's my fault for not insisting, on that day twenty-three years ago, that I *had* borne a son." Tears swam in Zorana's eyes and spilled down her cheeks. "If we hadn't lost you, you wouldn't have been . . . lost."

"There's plenty of blame to go around," one of the brothers said. "But what good does that do us? For now, we need to clean up."

"For God's sake, Jasha!" Adrik said.

"We will take the time to grieve." Jasha's voice choked, then grew strong. "But it's winter. It's cold. We're hurt." He gestured around at the men. "We're naked. Tasya needs medical care. We all do. We need to leave this place now, find somewhere to sleep tonight."

"Jasha is right." Rurik spoke now. "Freezing to death will not bring Firebird back. Our suffering will not give Aleksandr life once more. We've got to go."

"No." Zorana dug her fingers into Doug's arm. "No."

Konstantine embraced her, helped her stand. "Yes, *ruyshka*. Our sons are right. First we must live. Then we will grieve."

"The house is going to collapse, and when it does . . . it's not safe here." Tasya swayed.

Rurik picked her up and walked away.

One by one, the family stood.

Doug didn't move. He stared at the burning house, his eyes dry. It would take more than a minute to deal with his grief. It would take a lifetime.

Some sorrow was too deep for tears.

And sometimes, a man wanted something so badly, he saw what he knew could not be true.

In a hoarse voice, Doug said, "Someone is walking out of the house."

Chapter Forty

A t the urgency in Doug's voice, every head turned.

A woman. A woman carried a boy-sized lump on her shoulder and walked through the fire.

No, that wasn't right—the fire embraced her.

The flames parted as she walked, then closed in behind her. The walls crumpled behind her, yet she strode steadily toward the place where the front door had been, disappearing when the inferno flared high, appearing again when it died back.

"Is it Firebird?" Zorana asked in a trembling voice.

"Impossible," Rurik said.

"Not impossible. We all see her." Doug started toward the house, toward her.

Adrik grabbed him. "It's a trick of the devil."

Doug turned his head and looked into Adrik's eyes. "If it were your love, wouldn't you go to her?"

Adrik's grip loosened.

Doug walked forward, pacing toward the illusion—if she was an illusion—as she walked out of one fire-storm in the house and into another on the porch.

Zorana tried to follow, but Konstantine held her back. "Leave him. It's right that he take the chance, and if it is . . . if it is our Firebird, it's right that he be there first."

Zorana curled her fingers into the lapel of Konstantine's robe. "Yes. You're right." But she trembled with the need to go to her daughter, to her grandson, and in a quiet voice, she recited the end of the vision. " 'The beloved of the family will be broken by treachery . . . and leap into the fire.' " She looked up at Konstantine. "It is Douglas's treachery of which the prophecy speaks."

"Then it's up to him to make it right," Konstantine said.

The heat from the fire had blackened the winter-blighted lawn. Doug felt the crunch as the blades fractured beneath his feet. He heard the fire as it greedily licked the wooden structure. He advanced on the figure in the flames, moving on the fire as if it weren't hot, weren't cruel, weren't deadly.

The figure held up her hand to halt him.

He stopped, held in place by her wishes.

And Firebird stepped off the porch and into the world.

Flames still engulfed her.

He rushed toward her, ready to put them out.

Again she gestured, and it was as if he'd slammed into a wall.

Moving with extreme deliberation, she flicked the flames off one hand. Then the other.

They fell into the grass, sizzled, and vanished.

She brushed the flames off one shoulder; then,

with great care, she lifted the blanket and shook the fire away. She wiped her face, her hair. . . . Gradually, Firebird emerged from the flames, whole and clean, glorious and beautiful. She walked toward him.

The bundle on her shoulder stirred, tossed aside the blanket, lifted his head. . . .

Doug couldn't stand still anymore. He ran forward, grabbed them in his arms, held them as hard as he could. They didn't vanish, and he shook as he hugged them. "Are you real? Because if you're not, I don't care. I thought you were dead, and I can't stand to live in a world without you."

She pushed away and frowned at him. "Of course I'm real." She looked him over. "You look a little worse for wear. What did they do to you?"

He brushed off her concern. "Are you really real?"

"Did you get hit on the head? Because you're being weird."

Okay. She *sounded* real. She *sounded* exasperated.

He took a deep, relieved breath and felt the heavy, horrible burden of fear and anguish lift from his soul.

Firebird was alive. She had walked through a fire so intense and hungry no mere human could survive. Yes, it was impossible, but even now, he could feel the power humming through Firebird, exerting a force field that kept them safe.

The little boy had had enough of being ignored. "Are you my daddy?" he demanded.

"Yes. I am your daddy." Doug picked them both up, held them in his arms. "And I'm taking you away."

"Daddy." Aleksandr pointed at the Wilders, still standing clustered together. "Aleksandr go there!"

"Right." Doug walked toward them. Toward the women, wiping tears off their cheeks, toward the men, straining as if they could barely bear to stand and wait.

He reached the fence, walked through the gate—and it was as if the essence that had been holding the house together dissolved. The structure disintegrated with a roar, a mighty conflagration making its last report.

Doug didn't worry, didn't run.

But the house's collapse broke the family's will. They rushed forward to surround Douglas, Firebird, and Aleksandr.

"Hurry!" Jasha herded them away from the danger.

"You're safe." Zorana took Firebird's hand, stroked Aleksandr's head, and cried happily, "You're safe."

"H-how?" Adrik stammered. "Little sister, how did you do that?"

Adrik didn't seem the kind of guy who stammered.

"I don't know how I did it." Firebird kissed her son's head.

Konstantine held Zorana's other hand and led her, led them all, down the road.

"You have to tell us more than that." Zorana's voice was ragged with emotion and hoarse with smoke.

"I was panicked." Firebird shrugged. "Of course. I was sure Aleksandr and I were going to die. I thought about jumping out the window—I thought we might survive, and if not, it would be a better way to go."

Doug tightened his arms around her, his chest tight with delayed fear and anguish.

For a moment, only a moment, Firebird leaned her head against his chest. Then she straightened. "I was holding Aleksandr when I fell through the floor. Actually, the boards sort of tilted me like a teeter-totter, and I landed very softly right in the middle of the fire. The flames were burning everything except around *me*. So I told Aleksandr we were going to get out of there. I thought we were dead, that we didn't have a chance, but as we moved, a cocoon of fire moved with us. It was warm, but it didn't burn. Aleksandr kept talking to me from under the blanket, so I knew he was all right. And I kept walking." She fell silent as if, even now, she wasn't quite of this world.

Doug couldn't help himself. He shook her a little, as if reminding her that he was there.

She glanced up, focused on his face, and smiled as if the sight of him brought her back to earth.

"Go on," Konstantine encouraged.

"Yes, Papa. I wouldn't want to leave my brothers frustrated because they didn't know the whole story." She drolly looked from brother to brother.

"Then hurry up," Jasha said.

She took a few quick breaths, as if still surprised that she could. "The fire seemed to be doing what I wanted, holding the house together until I could leave. I kept walking. Out of my bedroom, into the hall, down the stairs . . . I wasn't afraid. The flames caressed me. The fire was . . . is . . . my friend. It would never hurt me."

"The fire protected you from something worse," Doug said abruptly.

"That's right," she said in surprise. "How did you know?'

"It kept you alive and out of the hands of the devil." Doug stared uneasily toward the woods. He remembered that man with the blue-glowing eyes, and hoped the guy ran far away, because . . . because Doug wanted never to see him again. He didn't even want to know for sure who he was.

As they rounded the curve that would hide the valley from their eyes, she tried to turn and look. "No, *ruyshka*. Let us not watch the end. Let us look to the future, instead."

She put her head against his chest and let him lead her.

The old man was wise. No one looked back. No one wanted to stay and watch the house turn to cinders, look out over the ruined vines, see the bodies of the dead Varinskis and the remains of the Romany soldiers killed in battle.

When they had rounded the corner and the valley was out of sight, they stopped.

Rurik put Tasya down on a log and seated himself beside her, holding her as she leaned on him. "The Rom are sending an ambulance," he told her.

She nodded, her mouth tightening with pain.

"Is Ann all right?" Karen asked.

Jasha pulled the phone away from his ear, and the grim-faced warrior became a fond husband. "She's fine. No problems, no Varinskis, and she did it! She transferred the funds out of their accounts and into a charitable trust to be administered by . . . her."

Firebird told Douglas, "When you meet her, you'll never believe Ann is our resident computer hacker."

Doug didn't want to let Firebird go, but the pain of his ribs was growing, his hip was throbbing and bleeding, and for all that he had lost only his little finger, the pain was big. So he let her slide to her feet, and embraced her until he was sure she was steady. "Are you tired? Do you want me to hold Aleksandr?" he asked.

She looked him over, her gaze lingering not on his nakedness, as he would have wished, but on the gunshot wound to his hip. "I think I'd better keep him."

Konstantine said, "I've got clothes for all of us hidden in the woods. Jasha! Adrik! Before the help arrives and questions are asked that we cannot answer."

Startled, Doug looked at Firebird.

"It's true," she said. "Papa has always preached that we should be prepared for any eventuality. There are more than clothes hidden in those woods."

It was less than five minutes later when Konstantine and the two brothers returned, dressed and carrying clothes for Rurik and Doug—clothes Doug discovered fit him very well.

"He is built like a Wilder," Konstantine said with satisfaction.

Karen examined the wounds on Adrik's face, then made him sit at her feet while she removed splinters of glass. He complained mightily.

Doug looked meaningfully at Konstantine. *Give me a moment with Firebird,* he meant. *Let me propose.*

"Come here, lad." Konstantine collected Aleksandr out of Firebird's arms.

Aleksandr beamed. "Grampa is strong."

Konstantine beamed back at the little boy cuddled against his chest. "Yes, my boy, I can finally hold you as God intended."

Firebird looked her father over, at his stern face, his broad shoulders, his barrel chest. "Oh, Papa." She clasped her hands together. "You're cured."

It was true. The sick man Douglas had spied on through the window had vanished, and in his place stood a mighty warrior.

"The pact is broken. I will live to the fullness of my years, long enough to see this little one grow and prosper, and maybe enjoy more grandchildren"— Konstantine looked his children over with a glint in his eye—"and when I die, I pray I have pleased heaven enough to go there to wait for your mother."

Firebird, Tasya, and Karen burst into tears.

Zorana covered her mouth to contain her sobs.

Jasha muttered, "Silly women."

"They're so sentimental," Rurik said.

Adrik coughed. "Yeah, it's embarrassing."

The brothers turned away and rubbed at their eyes.

For this family, it was as if this miracle among all the others was the greatest.

Doug envied them that—this closeness to their father, this affection with one another. He didn't have that yet. But in time, he would.

Yet mostly he was frustrated, needing to settle things with Firebird *now*.

In the distance, a siren sounded. The ambulance? The police? Who knew?

Without a doubt, someone had heard the gunfire.

Doug looked back at Firebird and saw Zorana hugging her. He didn't have much time before the authorities arrived, yet he didn't know how to separate a mother and her daughter.

Konstantine looked meaningfully at Doug and wiggled his fingers toward the two women. *Go on!*

Doug shrugged helplessly. When it came to this sentimental family stuff, he didn't know what to say or how to act.

"Zorana, come here," Konstantine said in a voice of command.

"Of course, husband." Zorana wrapped her arm around Firebird's waist and brought her to Konstantine. Holding out her arm to Doug, she invited him into her embrace. "I am so happy. So happy! The children all have met their perfect mates. We are all alive, although we bear our wounds." She touched the bloody stump of Doug's finger, and cast a worried glance at Tasya. "We have broken the pact with the devil, fulfilled the prophecies, and my relatives no longer oppose our marriage."

"That was indeed a concern for me." Konstantine rolled his eyes.

Zorana smiled at him, a charming, winsome grin. "When I am content, you are content. Yes?"

His stern, broad face softened. "Most certainly, yes." He looked at his wife, tremulously happy, at Doug, unsure how to proceed, at Firebird, alive. . . .

The sirens got closer and closer.

Doug could almost see Konstantine making an executive decision.

Konstantine lifted his chest, squared his shoulders, and used the voice radio deejays used to announce a new, improved deodorant. "We are a family united by pain and sorrow, victory and joy."

"Papa really is better." Jasha slid down a tree trunk and onto the ground. "He's making a speech."

Rurik and Adrik grinned and groaned.

Konstantine rolled on without paying his disrespectful children heed. "We have endured pain, separation, and despair. But now . . . now we celebrate! Our sons are all returned, and our daughters are fertile. We will rebuild our home in these wonderful United States of America, and we will live in prosperity!"

"Fertile?" Karen blinked in amazement. *"Fertile?"*

Tasya started giggling and didn't stop.

Doug suspected the morphine might still be working on her.

"Now Zorana and I are pleased to announce that our daughter, Firebird, will marry our son Douglas—"

Tasya giggled louder. "He left off two words— *or else.*"

"—and they will live happily ever after." He looked from Doug, horrified and immobile, to Firebird, quiet and enigmatic. "I speak the truth, do I not?"

Firebird considered Doug for a long moment. Then she nodded. "Of course, Papa. It shall be as you wish. Douglas and I will marry and give Aleksandr the mama and papa that he deserves."

Chapter Forty-one

"**D**id you see that the only newspaper that got the story right was the *National Enquirer*?" Adrik rooted through the pile of newspapers on the table in the kitchen in the house Konstantine had rented.

"I thought they said we were attacked by aliens." Karen looked up from the *Seattle Examiner*.

"No, that was the *Star*," Rurik corrected. "The *National Enquirer* said we were attacked by Varinskis, a well-known and ancient assassination cult that wanted to kill us because we attempted to destroy the devil's hold over their leader."

Adrik smirked. "They also said the thing that made us fight back was when the Varinskis hired aliens to impregnate Jasha."

Slowly, Jasha turned away from the counter and the pastrami sandwich he was assembling.

"Like we would care if aliens impregnated Jasha," Adrik finished.

The laughter in the kitchen started slowly and grew.

Jasha flexed his hands and leaped at Adrik.

The two of them hit the floor, wrestling like two idiots.

Aleksandr sat in a high chair and banged the tray with delight.

"It's been a long time since Adrik disappeared, and when he came back, everything turned grim pretty quickly." Today was Douglas's first day out of the hospital, and Firebird was trying to bring him up-to-date with his new family—give him brief rundowns on their characters, tell him a bit about what they'd been like growing up, point out their foibles and their strengths. "They're fighting, but it's not serious. They're merely blowing off steam."

Douglas nodded.

Konstantine scooted his chair away from his wrestling sons, ignoring them as if they were two exuberant puppies. "The news station said we'd been attacked by a right-wing group because we were successful Russian immigrants."

Jackson Sonnet puffed out his chest. "I gave them that angle."

"Good one, Dad." Karen gave him the thumbs-up. "As disinformation goes, that's the most believable."

"Oh, yeah? Wait until Jasha has that baby." Rurik ducked when Jasha threw a butter knife and knocked his coffee cup over.

"All right!" Zorana threw a kitchen towel to Rurik. "Mop that up! Jasha, Adrik, that is enough!"

Rurik mopped. Jasha and Adrik sat up.

"Our neighbors donated or loaned us everything in this house, and I do not want you boys breaking things." She pointed. "Adrik and Jasha, sit up and stop behaving like hoodlums. Douglas"—she came over and kissed him on the forehead—"you sit here and be a good example for your brothers." She returned to assembling the ingredients for *shchi*.

"Suckup," Jasha said out of the corner of his mouth.

"Screwup," Douglas answered.

This house was twice as big as their family home in the valley, but the kitchen had the same crowded, convivial atmosphere.

So it wasn't the house that created the ambience. It was the people, and Firebird wanted Douglas to love them as much as she did.

But since they'd brought him home from the hospital, Douglas had been quiet. He'd been quiet in the hospital, too, but she'd put that down to pain, healing, and dealing with his really pissed supervisor about the wrecked patrol car. Now she realized that Douglas had been uncommunicative ever since her father had announced their wedding.

Perhaps marriage wasn't what Douglas had intended.

Adrik sighed mightily. "I confess, I'm bummed. Even if I swore off turning into a panther, it was so cool to know I *could*."

"You're married," Karen said pertly. "You don't need to be out catting around, anyway."

The guys groaned.

"And Rurik shouldn't be flying the coop." Tasya smirked at her husband, the former hawk.

"Jasha had better not be running with the wolves." Ann started giggling and couldn't stop.

Everyone turned to look at Firebird. She sighed heavily. "All right. I'll say it. Now that he has me, Douglas has no business going out and chasing pussy." She glanced to see if she'd made Douglas laugh.

She hadn't.

If he had a sense of humor, he hid it well.

"What? Does everyone think I am so old and unappealing I am unable to turn into a wolf and chase women?" Konstantine looked reproachfully at Zorana.

"No, Konstantine." She patted him fondly. "But everyone knows I keep you on a tight leash."

"Come here, woman." He caught her waist and reeled her in. "For that pun, you shall pay the price." He pulled her across his lap and kissed her while she struggled . . . but not too hard.

"Would you two stop with the kissing? At least in front of us?" Rurik covered his eyes.

"Haven't you ever seen your papa kiss your mama before?" Konstantine sat Zorana up.

"Yes, but not all the time," Jasha said. "You're scarring us for life!"

"Humping like bunnies," Aleksandr said helpfully.

The family dissolved into laughter.

"Where did he *learn* that?" Firebird asked.

"I don't know." Konstantine shrugged. "Children. They pick up the oddest phrases."

"You are bad, Konstantine." Zorana returned to the stove.

"That is not what you said last night," he answered.

"No, Papa, no!" Adrik covered his ears. "I beg you, stop!"

"Even after Papa got sick, he would chase Mama

around the kitchen, dragging his oxygen tank and IV tubes," Firebird told Douglas softly. "He adores her."

Douglas nodded.

"What I want to know is how the *Star* knew that Firebird was in the house when it caught on fire." Tasya sat with her leg bandaged and straight out on the bench. "Who saw that? Who sold them the story?"

"One of the Varinskis wasn't as dead as we wanted to believe. Or someone from the town heard the noise and was watching." Ann looked from one to the other. "We vanquished one battalion of the devil's army. Let us not believe we vanquished the devil himself."

The cheery kitchen grew quiet and bleak.

Then Jasha said, "When she's right, she's right. And she tells me she's right all the time." He cowered when she punched his shoulder, then stole a kiss.

"What I like is the sidebar about Miss Joyce." Rurik snapped one of the papers back and placed it on the table. "According to the *National Enquirer*, she is the first provable case of a human being spontaneously combusting."

"They say she did make it back to the house, so technically I didn't kill her by leaving her in the sun. Too bad." Zorana slammed through the kitchen drawers. "I know Sharon brought me a slotted spoon. Where do you suppose I put it?"

Karen got up to help her look. "Apparently it wasn't the sun that was frying Miss Joyce. It was the devil's own frying pan."

"Served her right," Ann said.

Everyone looked at Ann in bewilderment.

"She's usually the nice one," Firebird explained to Douglas. "But she does have a thing about justice."

"When I think that she stole an infant and abandoned him to die . . ." Ann clenched her fists.

"Ann was an orphan, too, abandoned at birth," Firebird told Douglas. "I think you two have a lot in common."

"You, also," he said.

"Yes. You're right." Firebird didn't want to think about it, but somewhere out there, she had parents. Now she would have to decide—search for her biological family, or let them go. She looked around the kitchen at the family she had here, and remembered that her parents had abandoned her. She suspected she would not bother to search.

"Miss Joyce could have used our Firebird's way with the flames." Zorana forgot the spoon and faced Firebird. "Still I don't understand how you did, but I am so grateful that you did."

In the five days since the battle, the family had faced many challenges: reporters, police investigators, doctors, hospitals, stitches, and bullet extractions . . . and even now, Firebird felt odd about her miraculous escape from the fire.

All her life, she'd been breathtakingly normal in a family of extraordinary people. Now she had walked through the fire, and they all stared as if she were the miracle.

"Miss Joyce called you one of the abandoned ones." The frying pan drooped in Zorana's hand. "I thought she meant an abandoned infant. I wonder if there's more to it than that?"

"There is with Ann," Jasha said. "No one knows how, but she has a mark on her back, and in the right circumstances, she has powers."

"Not any I can control." Ann shook her head at Jasha.

Firebird rubbed the spot on her back that *had* burned, still burned, when she caught sight of Douglas. He watched with an intensity and an emotion that she couldn't read. Hastily she took her hand away and stared at him, wanting to know what he thought, what he intended.

"I have to go lie down." Douglas stood and walked out of the kitchen.

Firebird excused herself and followed.

Jackson sighed mightily. "I hate to say it. I've had more fun in the last couple of weeks with you folks than in my whole life put together. But I got a business to run. After breakfast, I gotta go."

"We hate to lose you." Konstantine reached over and shook Jackson's hand. "But we understand."

"You'll come back and visit," Zorana said. "Every year we celebrate the Fourth of July, and Firebird's birthday, and now Douglas's, with a picnic and many friends. You are always invited."

"Wouldn't miss it for the world." Jackson smiled genially.

Jasha's sigh matched Jackson's. "Ann and I are like Jackson. Now that the crisis is over, Ann and I need to get back to the winery."

"Tasya and I have got an archeological site that made us an offer." Rurik rubbed his hands in delight. "They want us to make one of those docudramas about the dig, and now . . . well, we're going to take it."

"It'll be good to get back to a dig," Tasya said.

"When you're better," Zorana said warningly.

"I am better." Tasya's smile tilted a little off center. "I think we were given one gift for winning the battle. The Wilder blood still heals."

"I thought that, too. I've been popping stitches all day!" Adrik turned to his parents. "I've got a video game to market, and I think Karen is itchy to get back to her spa and see how much damage the Varinskis did. So . . ."

Konstantine turned to Zorana. "What do you think, my love? Will we be able to live alone?"

"Let me think." She put a finger to her cheek and smiled. "Yes!"

Jasha looked toward the bedrooms. "What do you suppose is happening with Doug and Firebird?"

"She followed him so they could communicate," Ann answered.

"That poor son of a bitch." Aleksandr shook his head sadly.

Everyone stared at the little boy in the high chair.

"That's it." Zorana glowered around the kitchen at her children, all hiding their faces and muffling their snorts. "There will be no more swearing in this house. And you!" She slapped her hand down on Konstantine's shoulder. "You—you may not speak at all!"

Chapter Forty-two

Firebird followed Douglas to his bedroom.

He was straightening up, making the bed . . . getting ready to go.

She leaned against the door frame, hoping she looked casual rather than lost. "Douglas, what's wrong?"

"I need to go back on duty. My boss doesn't like people who fake sickness so they can take leave." He went into the bathroom and got his toothbrush.

"You got out of the hospital today. Not even your boss would say you're faking it."

He opened the drawers and got the clothes she'd bought him and flung them into the duffel bag she'd also bought in the superstore in Burlington.

"You're packing." She took a breath and said what needed to be said. "So I guess this means you don't really want to marry me."

"I didn't say that."

"No, you didn't. In fact, you never said you *did* want to marry me. My father said it. You simply stood there, and I assumed Papa was speaking for you, and I agreed." She was so hurt her lip was quivering, so embarrassed she wanted to run away. But this had to be finished now. "By the way you're behaving, I would guess I was wrong."

"I do want to marry you." Douglas stood looking down at his duffel bag as if it held the map for pirate's treasure. "But not for . . . not because you want to make your father happy."

"Make my father happy?" Embarrassment turned to outrage, and she straightened up off the door frame. "What the hell do you mean, make my father happy? You think I'd get married because he wanted it?"

"And for Aleksandr's sake."

"Because I'm weak-minded? Is *that* what you think?" The flames were blazing again inside her, and this time, someone was going to get burned.

"I don't think you're weak-minded, but I don't know why else you'd marry me." He looked up at her, his gaze steady and unflinching. "I am the guy who sold your family to the Varinskis."

"*Your* family. They're *your* family, not—" She took a breath and tried not to shriek at him. Or rather, not to shriek at him more. "I swear, if you tell me that you think that's one of the reasons I agreed to marry you—so I could stay in the family—I will make you wish the Varinskis had finished you off."

He didn't say anything. But he didn't have to. He wore that expression, the look that said he did believe it, or at least he had thought it.

"Do you really believe that I need *you* to be part of this family? They love me. They love me no matter what. And you know what?" She paced forward and got into his face. "They love Aleksandr. They'd love Aleksandr even if his father wrote diet books and hosted a talk radio show! So don't think you're doing me any favors by marrying me, because I don't need your help. I mean, my family raised me from the day I was born. What kind of people do you think they are?"

"Actually, you seemed a little worried that they wouldn't love you."

She took a breath to retort, and remembered—she *had* been worried. "I was wrong." She rubbed her head. "Mama is right. Every one of you Wilder men is terminally stupid. I don't know how you have functioned in life without me."

"I haven't. I've been miserable." He sat on the edge of the bed. "When you disappeared from Brown and I couldn't find you, do you know what I imagined? I thought you were a prisoner somewhere."

"How dumb is that?"

"Did you see any of those Varinskis on the battlefield? They *are* my relatives."

"Oh." She subsided. "Them."

"Once I figured out you were somewhere in Blythe, I watched for you." Doug was sober, intense. "I'll never forget the first time I caught a glimpse of you after so long. You were working at the Szarvas Art Studio. You were still blond, still smiling, as cheerful as you'd ever been, but you looked less like a girl and more like a woman. I saw you'd suffered grief and pain, and I knew you'd been alone, without me to care for you. That pissed me off big-time. I'd been so mad at you for leaving, but when I saw you, I became worried you'd been taken against your will."

"By who— Wait. You thought my family had kidnapped me?"

"As far as I could see, you were healthy, but you had no life. You only went to work and then home, and when I tried to follow you, I couldn't. Every time, I lost you on the road."

"Lost me?"

"A fog would close in and I couldn't follow your taillights."

"Really." She thought hard about that. "I always thought Mama had a way with the weather, fending off the storms. . . . I'll bet she fixed it so no enemy could find us without an invitation."

"You really have a spooky family."

"No. *You* really have a spooky family. And I know that when I was in college, I told you I loved my family."

"Yes. You did. But let's face it—abused wives love their husbands. In college, I fell in love with you because you were the brightest, wittiest, most friendly, outgoing girl."

"I thought you fell in love with me because you were horny." She sat beside him on the bed.

"It would have been easy to find other girls willing to take care of *that*." He had a quirk in his cheek. "You weren't easy, and you complicated my plans."

Remembering how intensely he'd courted her, and how strongly she had resisted, she said, "Remember that when you want to take me for granted."

"I could never do that."

They sat silent, two people uncomfortably perched on the edge of the mattress and at the brink of painful revelations.

Yet when she glanced sideways at him, he looked the same as he always had: stolid, steady, muscled, impassive . . . and alone. He was the loneliest man she'd ever seen.

He looked at his hands as if staring into a memory. "Right before you . . . broke into my house, I was called to the scene of a single-car rollover involving a mother and her two kids. She'd been escaping her abusive husband. Turned out she didn't have a driver's license. He wouldn't let her have one. She missed the curve by Shoalwater State Park and died in the crash."

Firebird hurt for the family, but more than that, she hurt for Douglas. "The children? Are they okay?"

"They were fine. A few cuts and bruises. The bad part was the scars their father had already put on them. Their mother's aunt is taking them in, and I'm told she and her husband are good people." He looked into her eyes. "I see shit like that all the time. I know what cruelty men are capable of, so I thought that you . . . I didn't think you'd seen me change, and I couldn't figure out why else you would leave me like that.'

Gently, she said, "I didn't go out into the world because I was afraid that if I did, you'd discover the truth about Aleksandr and take him."

"I know that now, but at the time, I figured your family—who were, after all, originally Varinskis—had you virtually imprisoned, probably terrified to leave. I didn't know what to do to free you. I was actually planning a kidnapping of my own."

"Cool!" *Too revealing.* "I mean . . . so how did you get ahold of the Varinskis?"

"Eight months ago, the Varinskis got hold of me. They were skulking around looking for the Wilders. I was skulking around looking for you. They discovered I was like them."

"A predator?"

"Exactly. Vadim did a little research and discovered the letter I'd written so long ago telling them I was a Varinski. He contacted me with an offer of a nice check—half in advance—if I discovered exactly where the Wilders lived. It took me a lot of tries before I followed you all the way in, and your brothers—"

"Your brothers," she reminded him.

"And Jasha and Rurik almost caught me." Douglas looked down at his hands. "I was stupid. Vadim said he wanted revenge; he wanted to hit your father . . . my father where it hurt. He was going to expose him as a criminal and get him sent back to the Ukraine, and ruin the fortune your family had acquired. I figured I would swoop in, rescue you from the prison in which they kept you, and take you to my house, the house I bought with the money the Varinskis paid me, and you'd be grateful and love me forever." As he told her his dreams, he was squirming with discomfort. "Stupid, huh?"

She put her hands over his. "It's sweet, in an apocalyptic, end-of-the-world sort of way."

"Believe me, I never dreamed they'd try to unloose

all-out war. I mean, come on! This isn't some dictatorship, or a third-world country. There are laws!"

"As Vadim found out, to his misfortune."

"I've made so many mistakes. I should have trusted you the first time I met you, and told you who and what I was. I should have trusted you when you came to me again, and told you what I'd done. Most of all, I should never have given in to the evil of my soul and joined with the Varinskis." Manlike, he added, "You can't ever forgive me."

Womanlike, she said, "Do not, I beg you, tell me what I can and cannot do. It's a bad start for our married life."

"Seriously. I don't want you to marry me for your father's peace of mind or our son. I want you to marry me for the same reason I want to marry you."

The way he spoke, the way he looked . . . she was starting to get hopeful. "And what's your reason for wanting to marry me?"

"I love you with all that I am."

She slid her arms around his neck and kissed him. Kissed his cheeks, kissed his eyes, kissed his chin, kissed his lips. "That's exactly the reason I want to marry you."

He looked at her, searching her face as if he had to see the proof. Then he stood up and rummaged through his duffel.

She watched, feeling a little stupid, a little used, the woman who had just given her whole soul into this man's keeping—which apparently reminded him that he needed to pack his clean underwear.

But he pulled out a small black velvet box—a ring box—and slid to his knees beside the bed. "Firebird Wilder, you are my only chance for happiness. Will you marry me?" He popped the lid.

The ring inside was platinum, the stone a diamond. Or, at least, she thought it was a diamond. It was a little hard to see.

"I bought this when I met you the first time. I was going to give it to you that night you finished your finals, and tell you who I was—the cougar was my subtle little hint—and ask you to marry me." His complexion flushed as he spoke. "I bought the ring on a policeman's salary, so it's smaller than I'd like, but I've carried it with me ever since, and I thought we could get you a bigger one later, but—"

"Never!"

He blinked in surprise.

"We are never going to get me a bigger one." Firebird was laughing and crying. She let him slide it on her finger. She looked at it from all sides. "This is exactly the ring I want. It's perfect." She cupped his face and kissed him, then kissed him again. "This is absolutely perfect."

Konstantine and Zorana waved Douglas and Firebird off to Las Vegas for their first wedding—before Zorana would let them go, she made them promise to celebrate a second wedding with the family, and for all Konstantine's grousing, he was glad of that— then stood on the porch of their rented home. "Listen to the silence," Konstantine said. "Have we ever not had a child living at home?"

"Briefly." Zorana nodded. "I seem to remember it. Do you think Jasha and Ann will know what to do with Aleksandr?"

"If not, they'd better learn." Taking Zorana's hand, he said, "Let's go for a walk."

"Now? I wanted to order some good cookware off the Internet. Those pans I'm using are worthless." But she clasped his fingers and followed him down the steps.

The street in Blythe was narrow and lined with trees, but it was a street, with neighbors and car noises and a loud radio next door. Konstantine missed his home. He missed the quiet, the pines, the grapes, his recliner, his toilet, and his own bed.

"Where are we going?" she asked.

But he knew she knew.

It took an hour to walk to their valley.

When they rounded the corner, they stopped and looked, and Zorana cried to see the ruin of the past thirty-five years, and Konstantine sighed again.

Then they both straightened their shoulders.

"It's not so bad," Konstantine said. "The vineyards and orchards are flooded and burned, but the Rom have done as they promised—the bodies are hauled off and the logs stacked up. Your relatives—when we rebuild, they should come and visit."

"I'll tell them."

She surprised him. "You know how to reach them?"

The little witch looked sideways at him. "I have my ways."

They walked toward the house. In the end, even the fence had caught fire and burned.

"Gutted," he said. "A total loss."

"Yes, but look!" She hurried through the scorched grass, into the blackened square where their house had stood. Lightly, she stepped over the charcoaled beams.

"Be careful." He watched her anxiously as she bent and he lost sight of her. "What is so important that you must go in there now?" he rumbled in a low voice.

She heard him, of course. Her head popped up. "Nothing much." She started back toward him. "Only your heritage." She arrived at his side. She held a flat, square tile covered with ash. She blew it clean, so that the white and gold and cherry red shone like new, and offered it to him with her blackened hands.

His family's revered icon.

He braced himself for the pain and slowly reached out to take possession. He wrapped his fingers around the edges. . . . It did not burn him. He brushed his palm across the surface, over the four Madonnas. Each visage showed the Virgin Mary in a different aspect: joy, sorrow, pain and glory.

His ancestor, Konstantine, had killed for these icons.

Konstantine's mother had died for these icons.

The devil had been defeated by these icons. Not forever. Not on all fronts. But when the icons were reunited, he had lost his dearest servants, and for that, Konstantine gave thanks.

He looked around at his land, still here, still rich, still fertile. He looked at the forest that surrounded it, where the wild creatures mated, flew, ran, lived. He looked at the sky, blue and warm with spring, breathed the air of freedom, and knew the joy of life reborn. "We have to plant again."

"And rebuild the house, bigger this time."

He turned on Zorana. "Woman, the planting will cost a fortune. We don't have the money for a bigger house."

"We have insurance, and we will borrow from our sons."

"We should *not* borrow from our sons."

"Very well, *I* will borrow from their wives."

"You . . . you dare! Woman!" He towered over her.

She stood up to him. As always, she stood up to him. "Konstantine, the troubles are over. By this time next year, we will have four new grandchildren. When they visit, where are you going to put them? We need a bigger house!"

Almost he smiled to hear her making her plans. Almost, but he kept his face stern. "You foresee grandchildren? Not one, not two, not three, but four?" He showed her four fingers and lifted his eyebrows. "Are you having a vision?"

"A great vision, Konstantine." She placed her hand on the icon. "Of you and me in a home with the Madonnas glowing in the corner, placed on a red tablecloth. Here on our land, we will live to be very old, surrounded by grapes and babies and happiness."

"Humph." He lowered his fingers. "Then I must be a seer, too, for I see the same vision."

And they were both right.

Don't miss any of Christina Dodd's *New York Times* bestselling *Darkness Chosen* series. . . .

In *Scent of Darkness*, we met Jasha Wilder, the first brother to attempt salvation for his cursed family. A shape-shifting wolf, Jasha introduced us to this compelling world.

In *Touch of Darkness*, we met Rurik Wilder, who shape-shifts into a hawk. Rurik, a learned archeologist, traveled Asia searching for clues that would allow his family some peace.

In *Into the Flame*, we met the shape-shifting cougar Doug Black, an angry young cop searching for the answers about his past. His one true love may hold the key to more than just his heart.

And now read on for an excerpt of *Into the Shadow*, where we meet Adrik Wilder, a sexy shape-shifting panther, who continues his brothers' journey to break the evil pact that has held his family in thrall for centuries—until a woman comes along who changes the course of destiny. . . .

The dream started as it always did, with a gust of cold Himalayan air striking Karen Sonnet's face.

She woke with a start. Her eyes popped open.

The darkness in her tent pressed on her eyeballs.

Impossible. Tonight she'd left a tiny LED burning.

Yet it *was* dark.

Somehow he'd obliterated the light.

No. No, it was a dream. Just like all those other nights.

But she could have sworn she was awake. She heard the constant wind that blew through this narrow mountain valley, whistling through the granite stones outside and buffeting the ripstop nylon canopy that protected her—barely—from annihilation. She smelled the stale scent of tobacco, spices, and body odor her cook had left behind. She felt the menacing cold slipping its fingers into the tent. . . .

She strained to hear his footfalls.

Nothing.

Still, she knew he was here. She could sense him

moving across the floor toward her, and as she waited each nerve tightened, stretching. . . .

His cool hand touched her cheek, making her gasp and jump.

He chuckled, a low, deep sound of amusement. "You knew I would come."

"Yes," she whispered.

Kneeling beside her cot, he kissed her, his cool lips firm, his breath warm in her mouth.

She hung suspended in time, in place . . . in a dream. Yet he kissed as if he were real, not a shadow in the night, and as he lingered, her body stirred, her breasts swelling, the familiar longing growing deep inside.

How many nights had it been? Two months? More? Sometimes he didn't come for one night, two, three, and on those nights she slept deeply, worn out by the hard work and the thin air at this high altitude. Then he'd return, his need greater, and he touched her, loved her, with an edge of violence sharp as a knife. Yet always she sensed his desperation and welcomed him into her mind . . . and her body.

This time, it had been almost a week.

He slid the zipper down on her sleeping bag, each tooth making a rasping noise, each noise making Karen's heartbeat escalate another notch. He started at her throat, cupping it, pressing on the pulse that raced there. He pushed the bag aside, exposing her to the cold night air. "You wait for me . . . naked." He pressed his palm between her breasts, feeling her heart beat. "You're so alive. You make me remember. . . ."

"Remember what?" He sounded American, without a hint of an accent, and at the times of madness, when she thought he must be real, she wondered where he was from and what he was doing here.

But he didn't want her to think. Not now. Greedily, he caressed her slight breasts, one in each palm. His hands were long, rough, callused, and he used them to massage her while with his thumbs he circled her nipples.

She made a raw sound in her throat.

"You're in need." His voice deepened. "It's been a long time. . . ."

"I've been here."

"And that was my torment."

It was the first time he'd ever suggested he needed this as much as she did. She smiled, and somehow, in this pitch dark, he must have seen her.

"You like that. But if you've tormented me, I must torment you in return." His head dipped. He took one pebbled nipple in his mouth and suckled, softly at first, then, as she whimpered, with strength and skill.

He made her go crazy.

But, then—any woman who dreamed a shadow lover was already halfway to insane.

She grabbed a handful of his hair, and discovered how very long it was . . . and soft, and silky. She tugged at him, pulling his head back.

"What do you want?" His voice was a husky whisper.

"Hurry." She was chilled. She was desperate. "I want you to hurry."

"But if I hurry, I won't get to do this." He pushed the sheet down farther, caressed her belly and thighs. Lifting her knees, he spread her legs, exposing her to the cold, shocking her, making her suck in a startled breath.

"Let me see." He tilted her hips up. "Are you ready?"

His fingers glided from her knees along the tender skin on her inner thighs to the dampness there. With a delicate touch, he opened the lips and dabbed a touch on her clitoris. "I love your scent, so rich and female. The first time, it was your scent that called me to you."

Horrified, she tried to draw her legs together. "I bathe every night."

"I didn't say you smelled. I said you have a scent that calls to me." His nails skated up and down her thighs, pushing them apart again . . . and they were sharp, almost like claws. Almost a threat. "Not to any other man. Only to me."

"*Are* you a man?" The question slipped out, and she regretted it. Regretted injecting reality into the dream.

"I thought I had conclusively proved my manhood to you. Shall I do it again?" The hint of warning was gone; he sounded warmly amused, and the finger he pushed inside her was long, strong . . . and clawless.

The impact made her fling her head back, and when he pushed a second finger inside, her hips moved convulsively. "Please. Lover. I need you."

"Do you?" Slowly he pulled his fingers back, pressed them in, pulled them out . . . and as he pressed them in, he pinched her clit between his thumb and forefinger.

She screamed. She came. Orgasm blasted her away from this cold, bleak mountainside and into a fire pit. Her thighs clamped around his hand. Red swam beneath her closed eyelids. Heat radiated from her skin.

He laughed, one compelling stroke following another, feeding her madness until she collapsed, shivering and gasping, too weak to move.

He covered her with himself.

"I can't," she whispered, and her voice shook. "Not again."

"Yes, you will."

"No. Please." She tried to struggle, but he stretched out on top of her. Her head was buried in his shoulder; obviously, he was tall. His body, heavy with muscle, pressed her into the cot. His flesh was cool and firm. His shoulders, chest and stomach rippled with vigor, and his heart thrummed in his chest.

Power hummed through him, and he easily held her as he probed again . . . but not with his fingers.

She was swollen with need, and his organ was big, bigger than both his fingers. As he worked himself inside her, she whimpered, her body gradually adjusting to the width, the breadth, and all the while the aftermath of climax made her inner muscles spasm.

He held her wrapped in his arms, clutching her as if she was his salvation.

And she embraced him, her arms gripping him against her chest, her legs clasped around his hips, giving him herself, absorbing . . . absorbing all his ardor, all his need, knowing this was a dream and wanting nothing more.

When the tip of his penis touched the innermost core of her, they both froze.

Darkness held them in a cocoon of heat and sex and emotions stretched too tight for comfort.

Then their passion flashed bright enough to light the night.

He pulled out and pushed back in, thrusting fast and hard, dragging her with him on his quest for satisfaction.

She held on, rapture flowing through her with the heat and intensity of lava.

The tempo built and built until above her his breathing stopped. He gathered himself, rising high above her, holding her knees behind him . . . then plunged one last time.

Ecstasy exploded her into tiny fragments of being. She came, convulsing with pleasure, until she was no longer an austere, lonely workaholic, but a creature of joy and light.

Unhurriedly, he dropped back on top of her, bringing the silk sheets and sleeping bag up to cover them. Reaching down to the floor, he pulled a large blanket over them . . . but no. She touched it with her hand and discovered fur, thick and soft. A skin of some kind, then.

Had he taken her on a trip back in time, back to a century where a man brought the woman he desired proof of his hunting prowess? Wasn't that a better explanation than madness?

As the perspiration cooled on their bodies, as their breath and heartbeats returned to normal, she realized—nothing had changed. She reclined on her narrow cot in her tent at the foot of Mount Anaya. The darkness still pressed down on her; the sense of wrong in this place still oppressed her. Tomorrow she would rise. He would be gone. And she would go to work, another day spent in hell. And she wept.

Penguin Group (USA) Inc.
is proud to present

GREAT READS—GUARANTEED

We are so confident you will love
this book that we are offering a
100% money-back guarantee!

If you are not 100% satisfied with
this publication, Penguin Group (USA) Inc.
will refund your money!
Simply return the book before
October 5, 2008 for a full refund.

ALSO AVAILABLE

INTO THE SHADOW
Christina Dodd

The third book in the exciting new series about an ancient evil that lives in the modern world.

Blessed—or cursed—with the ability to change into a sleek panther, and driven by a dark soul he's accepted as his fate, Adrik Wilder abandons his family and his honor to pursue a life of wickedness. He excels at every vice, including kidnapping Karen Sonnet to use for his selfish purposes.

But Karen's spirit and passion make him question the force of his family's curse. And when a new evil emerges, Adrik must choose whether to enact revenge on his enemies and redeem his soul, or save Karen from a fate worse than death...

Available wherever books are sold or at penguin.com